Praise for THE WENDY HOUSE

'A funny and insightf[...] for a girl to have it all'
Cosmopolitan

'Edwards-Jones is sha[...] on you'll want to buy this book. It's totally irreverent, reliably sexy, and razor-sharp on modern life and manners too'
Jessica Adams

'A funny, feisty, feel-good read'
Company

'Jones is spot on with the social nuances of London life and the relationship between the sisters . . . a comic masterpiece'
Marie Claire

'Anyone who's been travelling will recognise the feelings you experience on return . . . Edwards-Jones takes up the debate of single and successful versus domestic goddesshood and asks just who and what the modern woman is supposed to be'
Glamour

'As you'd expect from the author of the fantastic *My Canapé Hell* and *Shagpile*, *The Wendy House* is a feisty mix . . . told with Imogen Edwards-Jones's usual dry wit and spot-on observations'
Heat

'Replete with the kind of cutting satirical humour that made *Shagpile* a triumph over formulaic chick-lit stories'
Scotsman

'Edwards-Jones satires her characters with wit that is commendably restrained and slick . . . a credible social satire'
Sydney Morning Herald

Praise for SHAGPILE

'If you've watched *The Ice Storm* and read *The Rotters' Club*, consider yourself well-primed . . . Tank-top-tastic'
Heat

'A poignant love story against the backdrop of swinging Solihull, it's hysterical and heartfelt – great stuff'
She

'A master of biting contemporary satire . . . *Shagpile* is stuffed full of fantastically cringe-making set-pieces and pin-sharp period observations. Edwards-Jones has an appallingly wicked sense of humour but she can also do heartbreak, and is more than capable of exploring the darker side of human relationships'
Mirror

'*Shagpile* is as entertaining as a Mike Leigh film tangled with *The Likely Lads*'
Scotsman

'Sharp, acutely funny and wickedly well-observed'
The Big Issue

'Funny, satirical read [that] takes us through the seamy world of swinging in 70s Solihull . . . good holiday material'
Hello

'Utterly gripping and very, very funny. Pure genius'
Daisy Waugh, author of *The New You Survival Kit*

Praise for MY CANAPÉ HELL

'A spirited satire on celebrity culture . . . A dark, insider's view of fashionable stars and happening bars, the book crackles with acute observation and hilarious one-liners'
Wendy Holden, *Mail on Sunday*

'A bitingly funny satire . . . sharp, witty and vastly entertaining . . . a stylish debut'
Heat

'One of the funniest books of the year'
Shebah Ronay, *Mirror*

'A wickedly incisive wit dissects the highs and lows of the cocaine and champers set'
Cosmopolitan

'Relentlessly of-the-minute . . . a modern morality tale with a happy ending'
Daily Mail

'Absolutely hysterical, I could not put it down'
Candace Bushnell, author of *Sex and the City* and *Four Blondes*

Also by Imogen Edwards-Jones

MY CANAPÉ HELL
SHAGPILE

About the author

Imogen Edwards-Jones is an award-winning journalist, columnist and broadcaster who writes for many national newspapers and magazines. She is the author of two previous novels, the highly acclaimed *My Canapé Hell* and *Shagpile*, available from Flame. She was born in Birmingham and lives in London.

IMOGEN EDWARDS-JONES

The Wendy House

FLAME
Hodder & Stoughton

Copyright © 2003 by Imogen Edwards-Jones

First published in Great Britain in 2003 by Hodder and Stoughton
A division of Hodder Headline
First published in paperback in 2003 by Hodder and Stoughton

The right of Imogen Edwards-Jones to be identified as the Author
of the Work has been asserted by her in accordance with the
Copyright, Designs and Patents Act 1988.

A Flame Book

1 3 5 7 9 10 8 6 4 2

A CIP catalogue record for this title is
available from the British Library

ISBN 0 340 82309 7

Typeset in Plantin Light by Palimpsest Book Production Limited,
Polmont, Stirlingshire
Printed and bound in Great Britain by
Mackays of Chatham plc, Chatham, Kent

Hodder and Stoughton
A division of Hodder Headline
338 Euston Road
London NW1 3BH

For Leonie
The very best of sisters

ACKNOWLEDGEMENTS

I'd like to thank Kenton for being my support, my sounding board, my husband and my friend while doing this book. I would also like to thank my mother and stepfather for putting up with me while writing it, and my brother and father for their support while talking about it. Plus Daisy, Candace, Ant, Sean, Alek, Claudia, Kris, Peter, Sebastian, Sarah, Tom, Katya, Gay, Adam, Xander, Mike, Michele, Laurie and Cathie, who have allowed me to moan, brought me vodkas and looked very much as though they were listening. Also there's the wonderful Jessica Adams who has been a true trooper, guiding me through this and down the long and winding War Child road – while we edited *Big Night Out* along with Maggie Alderson and Nick Earls. So thank you all, I could never have done it without you. Finally I'd also like to thank Simon Trewin for his splendid agenting, Phil for her marvellous editing, and all at Hodder for their great publishing.

I

Never has the smell of wet concrete been so appealing. Nor has the flaring glare of neon strip lighting been so welcoming. Even the nylon uniform of the surly girl selling cold, curling sandwiches appears charming. In fact, Charlotte Adams is so relieved to be home that everything looks wonderful.

Striding through Heathrow airport, she finds it hard to stop staring and smiling at anyone who catches her eye. With scrappy bleached hair and bright green eyes, she is sporting one of those deep, hard, weathered, leathered tans that comes from nearly five years roaming Africa. Strong for her slight frame, Charlotte carries her rucksack high on her back, a heavy silver hard case in one hand and a small leather bag in the other, as she makes her way towards arrivals, and the nearby taxi queue.

Excited and animated, she unconsciously stamps her heavy boots on the pavement and sighs loudly, desperate for the queue to get moving. Don't they know she is in a hurry? It's cold, the knee-length khaki shorts she is wearing are totally inappropriate and she urgently needs a shower. Puffed and stuffed with in-flight food, Charlotte can't wait to kick back at Kate's house for a couple of weeks of pure R & R. As the end of the line approaches, her stamps and sighs get louder. Eventually she finds herself almost at the front. She smiles sweetly at the two French suits who offer up their taxi, if only to rid themselves of this slim yet rather intimidating female standing right behind them. She gets in and whips the door shut. Sliding around on the chilly leather seat, she asks for 'Shepherd's Bush' and immediately turns on the heater. It blasts out enough cold air to freeze-dry fruit.

'I'd wait 'til we get going a bit if I was you,' announces the driver, as he flicks his fag butt across a lane of traffic. 'Needs servicing.'

'Right,' smiles Charlotte, gripping the door handle as they corner a roundabout, not wanting to leave the patch of seat that she has just managed to warm.

'Been away?' asks the driver as he turns down the radio and flicks his eyes up towards the rear-view mirror, taking in her burnt, freckled nose and white eyebrows.

'Um, yes,' she replies, thinking it the more polite of her two responses.

'Anywhere nice?' he continues.

'It wasn't really a holiday,' smiles Charlotte, wondering why she is going down this conversational cul-de-sac.

'Right,' he replies.

They rattle out of Heathrow, under the tunnel and out towards another large roundabout and the M4 intersection. The driver says nothing. He continues to say nothing. But most annoyingly of all, he asks nothing either. The glamour, the romance and the danger of Charlotte's five years away hang in the air like a tempting peach and he doesn't seem interested. She leans forward in her seat, irritated by his lack of curiosity.

'It was work,' she announces, after a five-minute break of total silence.

'Right you are,' he replies, nonchalantly flooring the accelerator as he reaches the open road, tapping away at his on-board computer as he moves into the bus/taxi lane.

They continue in silence, save for the painful moan of the straining engine and the rushing sound of undertaking cars.

'I've been away for nearly five years,' says Charlotte,

leaning in closer to the sliding window partition so the driver can hear above the noise of the engine. 'All over Africa,' she continues. 'But mainly East Africa plus the occasional trip west and south. But mainly east. I'm a photographer, a photo-journalist . . . I take photographs for magazines and newspapers, as well as books. But mostly magazines.' She pauses, an expectant smile on her plump lips. She leans even closer to the window partition, awaiting some sort of feedback. He continues to drive, his interest decidedly unpiqued. 'They're mainly war photos,' she continues, undeterred. 'I spent a lot of time in Rwanda, some time in Angola and Zaire. I obviously did the floods in Mozambique, you know, a while ago, as well as a lot of the other stories you'll have heard of. Like the white farmers in Zimbabwe? Losing their farms? You know, Mugabe?' The man's face looks blank. 'Zimbabwe,' she repeats, '. . . was Rhodesia?'

'I nearly went there once,' replies the driver, inhaling heavily on his short butt.

'What, Zimbabwe?' asks Charlotte, cheered that the bloke is finally engaged by her and the exotic nature of her travels.

'No,' he mutters. 'Africa.'

'Oh?'

'Yeah, one of those packages.' He exhales.

'Right,' she says.

'Decided against it,' he says, and then adds, 'Went to Marbella instead.'

'Oh good,' says Charlotte, her smile not reaching her eyes.

'Yeah,' he nods. 'I need a proper English in the morning, you know, none of that foreign muck.'

She collapses back into the seat of the cab, sliding the window shut. The short grey strip of hair that circles the driver's head like a tennis band no longer looks endearingly middle-aged. And his thick steel-framed specs that initially made him appear erudite now make him look like a grubby paedophile. She is more annoyed with herself than anything. For opening her mouth and showing off like a child in the first place. It's pathetic. Why would the man be interested? Why isn't she more like those taciturn, laid-back types who she hangs around with between stories in Kenya? The international group of journalists, artists and well-travelled Bohemians with long-vowelled drawling voices who are too cool to care what anyone thinks of them? Maybe it's just because she is excited. Maybe it's because she hasn't seen her younger sister in nearly five years that she feels slightly anxious, over-enthusiastic and garrulous.

God, Kate, she thinks, resting her chin on her rough, parched hand as she stares out of the window at the drizzled countryside. Her little sister Kate must have changed beyond all recognition in the past five years. She was naughty, single and a pot-smoker when Charlotte left, but she has married and had two babies in the time that Charlotte has been away. And Charlotte has not been party to any one of those events. All due to circumstances beyond her control, mind you. But still unavailable all the same. She did make her sister's wedding, but not the crucial build-up, or the denouement. She arrived very much as a guest and left before the bride and groom. It had all kicked off again on the Rwandan border and she had been given a choice between the hen night and bridesmaid duties and a five-page *Newsweek* commission. Her career, as always, had taken precedence. And as for the birth of Kate's two sons, Charlotte was, unfortunately, needed in Mozambique and Zaire respectively.

There had initially been some tension, anger and indeed bitterness, mainly stirred up by their mother. But they have since talked it out. They have bonded and come to some sort of understanding, over the course of lengthy telephone calls and conciliatory emails, in which they have concluded that sisters are perhaps the cruellest, yet the most forgiving, of siblings. For not only do they really know how to hurt each other, but they are also capable of an understanding beyond the realms of duty. Being the same flesh and blood – as well as the same sex – they both agreed, was bound to make things a little complicated.

Charlotte smiles as she passes the reassuringly pulsating Lucozade bottle that still pours bubbles and flashes the time (18:35) and temperature (8 degrees). She suddenly notices a huge Russian blue and gold onion dome that certainly wasn't there when she left. But then lots of things appear different and changed. The cars on the road look clean and flash. The advertising hoardings are distractingly bright. They scream about alien products and offer to satisfy needs she doesn't know she has. And the noise and the traffic are disorientating. In comparison with the dark red earth of Africa, everything in the cold light of this September late afternoon seems a little grey. Even the white-skinned pedestrians around Hammersmith roundabout look drab and recently exhumed, their clothes dark and dull. Yet the sharp, tailored fashion looks decidedly affluent. All Charlotte can do is stare.

'Where exactly in Shepherd's Bush do you want?' asks the driver, suddenly sliding back his window.

'Oh, right, hang on a sec . . .' Charlotte panics and riffles around in her leather handbag for her directions. 'Um, um,' she says, scanning the paper print-out for something resembling sense. 'Oh . . . halfway along the Uxbridge Road and on the left,' she announces. 'Number fifty-eight.'

As they approach the green, with its confusing lanes of traffic converging from every angle, Charlotte nods her head, confirming remembered territory and haunts once well-visited. The bakery where she and Kate would shell out on prawn sandwiches and the occasional doughnut. The charity clothes shop where Kate had once found an old Chanel skirt. The small newsagent where they used to leave a set of keys in case either or both of them got locked out. But this was all long ago when she and Kate were flatmates living on lentils, rice and garage-bought meat pies. They pass the Empire building and Barclays Bank where they spent many a damp, drenched hour waiting for buses or resorting to minicabs.

Sitting forward in her seat, with her eye on the meter, Charlotte searches through her small beaded purse for two twenty-pound notes. What sort of tip does one give these days? she wonders, as they turn into Kate's street. Something exorbitant, she supposes, as she gets out of the cab and hands over both the notes, before bracing herself slightly for the walk up the short flagstone path.

Dumping her heavy bag and hard, silver camera case on the doorstep, she rubs her clammy palms down her khaki shorts and with a determined slap of her thigh rings the bell. An elegant trill elicits random shuffling from the hall.

Her sister flings back the door and stands on the step with her arms outstretched, her fingers splayed. She looks very different. Her dark hair is short, smooth and swingy, her face is covered in overtly discreet make-up, her eyebrows have most certainly been plucked, and someone else has buffed her nails. Dressed in a dark, knee-length skirt, with knee-length black suede boots and a short tight black V-neck jumper, Kate looks slim, soignée and even slightly sophisticated.

'Charlie!' she squeals with obvious delight as she tightly embraces her sister on the threshold. 'You look great!' she adds, standing back and rapidly checking her up and down, taking in the unfashionable boots and the brown muscled legs in need of some serious depilation. 'Wow,' she grins. 'It's so-o-o great to see you . . . Come in, come in . . . you must be knackered.'

'Works so much better with a lime, don't you think?'

'Oh . . . um, absolutely.'

'I can't remember exactly where I picked it up. A fabulous cocktail book I was given, I think. But I now can't do the boring old lemon thing any more. Weird, isn't it?'

'Very.'

'So . . . ?' says Kate.

'So . . .' repeats Charlie.

'So tell me, then,' says Kate, settling back into the sofa. 'What's happened to you in the past, what is it . . . four, nearly five years?'

'Oh God, yeah, must be,' smiles Charlie. 'So much, it's actually very hard to know where to begin . . .'

'Yes, I can imagine,' says Kate.

'Mmm,' says Charlie.

'Well, you've heard most of my news,' breezes Kate, running her hands through her hair before flopping fashionably down on the fat sofa again. 'Mum's kept you more or less up to date and with all the emails and phone calls, there is not that much more to add . . . the wedding was obviously amazing. I know you came, but you know, you didn't really . . .'

'Well,' says Charlie, about to justify herself for the one hundred and second time.

'Anyway,' continues Kate. 'Everyone said I looked absolutely beautiful, which is nice. Do you remember how thin I was? God,' she laughs at herself, patting her bosom. 'God, it was a great party. Every single one of the one hundred and fifty guests had a good time, which is so-o-o unusual . . .' She smiles, evidently very satisfied. 'And now I have Alfie and Ben, who have lit-er-ally changed my life. Alfie is, of course, a genius. The teacher says that he is the cleverest child in his year. And Ben, well, Ben may well be g-a-y.' She hoots with laughter, throwing herself back into the sofa, raising both her expensive boots off the ground. 'Not really, obviously, but he is terribly good at potato printing and that sort of thing, and seems to be very fussy about what he wears.'

'But he's only two, isn't he?'

'Two and a bit. I know, isn't it hilarious? I have no idea where he gets it from.'

'So how old's Alfie exactly then?'

'Four going on forty. He's very funny. The things he comes out with . . . I should write them down, really, because they're so-o-o amusing. I have a friend who does, but these things are only really entertaining for the parents.' She picks some fluff off her skirt, and smiles. 'Oh God! The other day he came back from a friend's after refusing to eat a burger, where apparently he'd shouted at the top of his voice: "I'm not eating that. Everyone knows fast food kills you!" Isn't that brilliant? The things children pick up. Amazing.'

'Amazing,' repeats Charlie. 'So is it all going well with Alex and everything?' She smiles.

'Oh . . . really well,' nods Kate enthusiastically, draining her glass with a rattle of ice. 'The only real problem is that I don't get to see him enough. He's off so early in the morning to the City that he never really sees me, or the children, and what with squash and various business dinners and stuff he often doesn't get home till quite late. It's mad really, and when he does come back, all he wants to do is sleep. The weekends he's flat out most of the time. But, you know, it's hard keeping a beautiful house like this going with two children . . .'

'No, it must be,' says Charlie.

'I know,' nods Kate. 'I don't know how I do it some of the time.'

'Yes . . .'

'So, how about you?' asks Kate. 'I mean, I do know most of it. I'm sorry about . . .'

'Oh, don't be,' interrupts Charlie quickly. 'That was a long time ago.'

'Anyway . . .' Kate inhales through her teeth, filling the conversational void almost immediately. 'All that traipsing around? It must be . . .' She searches for the correct word. 'Well,' she smiles, clapping her hands. 'So where was the worst place?'

'The worst?'

'Yeah, the worst.' Kate smiles, leans in and tries to look encouraging. 'You know, where you were at your most miserable.'

'There were a lot of places that weren't much fun,' replies Charlie.

'Oh right,' nods Kate, leaning back again.

'But I suppose Rwanda, Angola and Zaire were bad. The things that I saw there I had no idea human beings were capable of. It was horrific.'

'Mmm,' nods Kate. 'Awful.'

'Oh God . . . mutilated bodies, charred bodies, headless, limbless, mass burials . . . we used to come across bodies of looters left in the street as a warning to others.'

'Oh, awful.'

'It wasn't very nice,' says Charlie rather quietly.

'Mmm, no, awful.'

'People say you get used to seeing these things, like water off a duck's back.'

'Mmm.'

'But you don't, and if you do then there is something seriously wrong with you. Some of the guys I was with can no longer live in the real world.' Charlie takes a swig of her drink and sighs.

'Right, no, awful.'

'They have pockets full of pills, can't sleep and are obsessed with where the next disaster, the next crisis, the next killing fields are going to be. They move around the world from zone to zone meeting up in Kosovo, Kashmir or Kabul, like a pack of adrenaline junkies.'

'They sound a bit frightening,' suggests Kate, swirling the ice around in her empty glass.

'Don't get me wrong, most of them are fabulous guys, but they have just lost the plot a bit, which I suppose is to be expected.'

'Yeah, right, yeah awful.' replies Kate, picking more fluff off her skirt. 'So where was the best place, then?' She smiles cheerily.

'Oh, that's difficult . . .' Charlie rolls her eyes and starts searching around in her small leather handbag at her feet for some cigarettes. 'There are so many beautiful places . . .'

'Good.'

'There's a place, Lamu . . .'

'I think you wrote to me from there.'

'. . . In the north of Kenya. It's amazing, the parties I went to, the dancing I have done on that beach, the dawns I have seen . . .'

'Right, good . . .' Kate smiles.

'Or perhaps diving off Pemba, off Tanzania, but there are so many places . . .' She looks at her sister, who is swinging one of her boots and looking at it admiringly. 'But you know, we have plenty of time for this.'

Charlie finally lights a cigarette. Kate gets up and opens a window, then hands over a stolen Pont de La Tour ashtray that has been through the dishwasher a few too many times.

'The house does look fantastic,' says Charlie, standing up with her drink in hand, pre-empting the inevitable tour. 'How long did it take to do?'

'Oh, about eight months, properly, but it's still not finished yet,' says Kate, half drawing the thick, lined and interlined, curtain. 'It's what's known as a work in progress, really,' she smiles. 'Do you fancy a tour?'

'Great,' says Charlie, only managing to sound half surprised. 'And you could show me where I'm sleeping at the same time.'

'Absolutely,' she nods. 'You'll have to put that out,' she adds, indicating the cigarette. 'We don't allow them upstairs. It'll give the children breathing problems.'

'Of course,' smiles Charlie, shrugging her shoulders like a fool. 'Hang on one sec then.'

Following her younger sister up the stairs past the row of framed Matisse-u-like prints and on to the heavily carpeted landing, Charlie can't help thinking how much her younger sister has changed. A firm follower of hennaed principles and hessian rights as a student, she was always the first to initiate a sit-in, start an argument or mount some sort of petition. In her early to mid-twenties she sported the post-feminist push-up bra with all the confidence of a succulent cleavage and swanned her way around the account managing third floor of the advertising company Bedford Kennedy and Partners. She was feisty, funny, clever and naughty. She drank too much, swore a lot, slept with far too many men and had the best collection of racy underwear Charlie had ever seen. She drove a clapped-out car full of empty sandwich cartons which she could never remember where she had parked, or dumped, for days, sometimes weeks, at a time. She reported it stolen once, only to have the police point out to her that it was, in fact, in the next-door street. She smoked dope. She could roll a nice, straight, neat spliff and occasionally carried cocaine. Unlike most of the other gurning bores who worked in advertising, it was a birthdays and Christmas thing that never got out of control. In short, Kate was great, and this new incarnation is disconcerting, to say the least.

Where on earth had she come from? Charlie is the first to admit that she has missed the most recent most defining moments in Kate's life. Married life and the birth of two children are most certainly events that most people would describe as significant. But how can someone change that much, that quickly? She appears so different that Charlie doesn't really know where to start, how to get to grips with her younger sister at all. So on reaching the landing, she decides against her natural inclination towards confrontation and interrogation, and tries a gentle mollifying technique instead.

'You have done so well with the house,' says Charlie, eyeing a large framed expanse of navy blue canvas desperately emulating some sort of fecund ethnic backside. 'With all the art and everything.'

'Oh, all the art is Alex's,' replies Kate, leading her way towards the master bedroom. 'OK, OK,' she continues. 'This isn't quite finished in here but ... that's the sleigh bed that we spent just *ages* trying to find ... plus these really special lamps that I fell in love with from the Conran shop. They're sort of Philippe Starck but not quite as modernist ... We're going to have a walk-in wardrobe through here,' she explains, her arms funnelling forward like an air hostess on emergency exit demonstration, 'for all my stuff and Alex's, so we're almost there. In here,' she adds, walking into a large limestone bathroom, 'in here, we have a huge walk-through shower with chrome everywhere there, and there ... and here we have my favourite thing, a really modern free-standing bath in the far corner. When I saw they had one made entirely of glass I just couldn't resist. Alex was having none of it, but I worked and worked on him,' she giggles. 'But you know, I was right – it really has made the room. And that's what really sells houses – kitchens and bathrooms.'

'It all looks and sounds really great,' smiles Charlie, her arms folded across her stomach.

'But it's a long-term project,' nods Kate, smiling gently at the children's loud bathtime laughter that drifts down the stairs. 'You know, softly, softly etc. There are some people who get their houses done all at once. You know, all architects and interior designers, which I think is a bit vulgar. It's all done to someone else's taste. I mean, really. What do you think?'

'Tell you the truth, I don't really know. I haven't actually thought about it that much,' says Charlie.

'Take it from me, it's a no-no. You'll have to pick up on all these things now that you're back from the sticks,' laughs Kate, running her hands through her hair. 'Now,' she adds, clearing her throat, 'let me show you round the other rooms.'

Kate's tour of her lovely home takes about twenty minutes. She takes her sister slowly, surely, step by step through the whole deconstruction and reconstruction business, inviting her to imagine just how horrible the place was before she and Alex got hold of it.

'It was home to three whole families,' she says, as she closes the door behind the nanny's flatlet which takes up the whole of the top floor. 'I mean, can you imagine that,' she shivers, climbing down the stairs. 'All those people, in such a small space.'

'No,' smiles Charlie, thinking of a lot more people in even smaller spaces.

'A lot of people are impressed with our imagination, you know, being able to see beyond the squalor. But when I came round it the first time all I could see was potential. We had to fight off a developer for it, but we've done so well. Doubled the price in two years.'

'That's good.'

'I know . . . really good. Property has gone up a lot round

17

here, of course. It's the overflow from Notting Hill and Holland Park. Ever since they made that film.'

'What film?'

'Oh come on, Charlie, don't be thick. That film . . . *Notting Hill*? With Hugh Grant? And that actress . . . ?' She clicks her fingers. 'Julia Roberts.'

'Oh right . . . vaguely. I didn't actually see it. It was on a plane I was on, once . . . but I ended up falling asleep before the end.'

'Did you? Really?' asks Kate sounding surprised. 'Oh, it went down very well over here. Anyway, the point I'm making is . . . because of that film loads of rich Americans have come over and want flats in the area because they think they might run into Hugh Grant or something like that, and as a result everywhere else is much more expensive . . . if you see what I mean?'

Charlie does see exactly what she means, but her sister sounds uncomfortably like an estate agent. She stands at the top of the stairs and stares at the faux Matisse, craving another vodka and tonic. Having been so excited, tight to the pit of her stomach with the thrill and anticipation of seeing her sister for the first time in nearly five years, she is now sad, deflated, a little disorientated and at a loss to find some sort of common ground.

'Shall we go downstairs and have another drink?' she suggests. 'I would also love another fag.'

'Okay,' replies her sister, deflated at her sibling's lack of enthusiasm for interior design. 'But I can't go mad,' she warns. 'It's a school day tomorrow . . .'

'Is it?'

'It's Tuesday today, silly,' laughs Kate. 'I have to be so careful with hangovers and things, it's a nightmare. I mean, have you ever tried to look after a two-year-old when you've overdone it the night before?'

'Um, no,' replies Charlie. 'But friends of mine do have children in Africa and they don't seem to mind . . .'

'Really?' replies Kate, wrinkling her nose slightly as she pulls down the sleeves of her black sweater. 'I don't think that's very responsible.'

'I don't think they really think about it,' says Charlie, sparking up a cigarette as soon as she crosses the threshold to the kitchen. 'They just get on with things.'

'Well . . . I know I just couldn't do it.'

'Right,' says Charlie. 'It's just different over there.'

'You can say that again,' laughs Kate, efficiently opening one of the french windows into the walled garden to waft out Charlie's single curl of cigarette smoke. Turning round briskly she then struggles to open the enormous shiny fridge. Such is its industrial-strength suction that when it finally gives way, she tumbles backwards towards the kitchen table. 'Always pisses me off, this bloody thing,' she exhales, regaining her composure. 'And to think it was nearly a couple of grand.'

'What, for a fridge?' asks Charlie.

'Oh yeah,' replies her sister, squatting down to take a closer look at the mixers compartment. 'Oh God . . . We've only got organic lemonade for the vodkas,' she continues.

'That sounds fine,' replies Charlie, balancing a baton of cigarette ash, scanning the surfaces for something resembling an ashtray.

'I can't believe Peta has done that.'

'What?'

'Forgotten the tonic.'

'Never mind,' smiles Charlie, flicking her fag ash quickly on to the floor and kicking the evidence under the free-standing, distressed-pine Conran dresser.

'No . . . but really, it's very irritating.'

'I'm sure we'll cope.'

'Well, yes, it's not really a matter of that . . .' says Kate, huffing back up off her haunches and turning round. 'Um, do you want an ashtray for that?'

'Oh . . . Please.'

'Right,' smiles Kate, wafting around her expensive kitchen. 'Ashtray . . . ashtray . . .' she mutters, a bottle of organic lemonade swinging at her side. 'Ahhh, there we are,' she smiles, picking up a metal Q-shaped object that smacks of another restaurant steal. 'Shall we go into the other room?'

Back through into the sitting room and Charlie busies herself smoking while Kate pours the drinks in the kitchen and comes through with a tray and a small hand-thrown ethnic bowl of olives and salted almonds.

'So do you like the house?' she asks, flopping back on to some cushions that simultaneously exhale.

'Oh, I think it's great,' smiles Charlie.

'Really?'

'No, really.'

'Because I've always wanted to show it to you, you know, being the big sister sort of thing. To see what you think.'

'You don't want *my* approval?' asks Charlie, clasping her chest.

'No,' dismisses Kate, swatting away the idea with her hand. 'I just wanted to know . . . you know, what you thought.'

'Well, I think it's marvellous,' lies Charlie convincingly, leaning forward and grinning, preparing to chink her glass.

'Thanks,' smiles Kate. 'To my marvellous house!' she raises her glass.

'To your marvellous house,' chinks Charlie. 'And your children.'

'Oh God, yes,' giggles Kate, tucking her hair behind her ears. 'Them too.'

They chink again.

'And your husband!'

'Of course!' She laughs. 'How could we forget him?'

They chink again.

'Talking of which, where is he?' asks Charlie. 'It's eight thirty. He must be back home soon?'

'He could be playing squash,' shrugs Kate, popping a single almond into her mouth. 'I'm not altogether that sure. Either way, he should be back soon.'

'Oh,' shrugs Charlie. 'I hope he's not too late. I have no idea how long the alcohol will stave off the onset of jet lag and culture shock.'

'Yes, right,' replies Kate vacantly, sitting back into her sofa and crossing her neat black-booted ankles on the low cherry-wood coffee table.

The two sisters sit opposite each other, both with their boots on the table, both nursing a vodka, organic lemonade and slice of lime on their laps. Charlie sits and smokes, checking out her sister's sitting room, while Kate stares at her hands, finding fault with her French-polish manicure. A stiff silence settles upon the room. The dark sky outside succumbs to light rain. Charlie flicks her ash into the stolen ashtray, glancing at the pile of style magazines neatly stacked in a rack to the left of the gas-fired fireplace. There is an almost complete collection of *Wallpaper**, plus a hefty number of *Elle Interiors*, interspersed with a random selection of *House & Garden*, and *Living Etc*. Kate is nothing if not thorough when it comes to finding out what other people think. Some of the older copies have yellow post-it notes sticking out – no doubt marking the pages of objets and interior decor tips that she found particularly enlightening. Charlie takes a swig of her drink and pulls her shorts out of her crotch before shifting back into the sofa. Tired of the imperfections of her manicure, Kate drains her glass with old-fashioned gusto and stands up quickly.

'You don't have a sister come back from the dead that often,' she laughs, slightly too loudly. 'So I think we should celebrate.' She waves her glass back and forth by way of a serving suggestion. 'Do you fancy another?'

'Mmm,' says Charlie, downing hers with the well-practised movement of a woman who has spent a lot of her time in male company. 'Absolutely,' she smiles.

'I don't know if I can take another lemonade, though,' announces her sister, spinning back round. 'It's bloody disgusting, isn't it?'

'Tell me where the nearest shop is and I'll go and get some more.'

'Oh, no,' says Kate, her eyes starting to shine as the second vodka kicks in. 'Fuck it,' she announces. 'I'll get Alex to get some on his way home.'

'Really?' quizzes Charlie, her pretty blonde brows furrowing.

'Oh, yeah,' insists Kate, running her hands through her swingy hair. 'I'll call him on his mobile. In the meantime we can have . . .' She presses her index finger against her pleasantly plump lips as she walks into the hall.

'Shots?' suggests Charlie nonchalantly.

'Oh my God,' says Kate. 'I haven't done those for years.'

Kate stands in the hall, feet mid-stride, atrophied through indecision. Her balance seesaws from left to right as the machinations of her brain manifest themselves in some sort of bizarre swinging pendulum. The weighing-up of guilt versus pleasure takes a whole fifteen seconds before she turns to her elder sister and smiles.

'Well, why not?' she announces to herself. 'I am just going to say goodnight to my children – they should be in bed by now – and I'll be down in about ten minutes for shots.' She claps her hands for extra assertiveness. 'Right,' she announces halfway up the stairs. 'Shit, I better remember to phone Alex first.'

As Kate disappears on parental duty, Charlie helps herself to a cold shot of vodka and readies herself for a quick snoop around her sister's sitting room. The set-up is conventional enough, with two large sofas opposite each other and a low wooden table in between. Apart from the marvelling at her own marvellousness snaps all over the place, the only other decoration in the room is some piles of casually scattered drift-wood and a couple of what can only be described as 'white' paintings. Both the large canvases, one over a fireplace and the other over a low-slung retro thirties dresser, are covered in daubs of textured white paint and gobs of non-textured white paint. The stained wooden floors and lack of rugs make the room echo and feel cold.

This is an unwelcoming and uncomfortable room, thinks Charlie as she lies back on one of the cream sofas, her long brown legs swinging over the arm, and stares at the modern white plastic lamp-fitting suspended from the ceiling. She is overtired and depressed and all she really wants to do is slip into something indecently comfortable and get rather drunk with her younger sister. Instead she has this smart house to contend with, a difficult sister, plus a couple of unfriendly children who already seem to be able to sense her lack of street credibility from across the kitchen table. Not to mention Kate's husband, a man who has featured so little in Charlie's life she could count on the fingers of her left hand alone the number of times they have met. She leans over and picks up the 'Q' ashtray and balances it on her stomach.

'Hurry up!' she shouts from the sofa, in a voice that she hopes is loud enough to travel all the way up the flights of stairs. 'I'm bored here all on my own and we need to get rip-roaringly pissed before your dull husband comes home!' she jokes. 'Do you hear me!' she shouts some more, her body stiff with exertion. She flicks ash into her navel as she lies back down.

'I'm afraid her dull husband is already here,' comes a clipped, moist voice from the other side of the sofa.

'Oh dear . . . shit . . . Alex,' says Charlotte, laughing and pinking with total embarrassment as she whips her legs off the sofa and stands up rigid. Cigarette in one hand, ashtray in the other, she doesn't quite know what to do by way of a meet and greet scenario, so encircles him with one giant hug, still holding each object. 'How lovely to see you after all this time,' she breezes, hoping that enthusiasm will see her through the gaucheness of their reintroduction. 'How long has it been?'

'Nearly five years,' comes the stiff reply from the equally stiff body that Charlie is hugging.

'As long as that?' she replies.

'Yes.'

'Anyway, how have you been? I love your house . . . and your children . . . what a lot you have done and achieved in all that time. Still working at the same bank . . . what's its name?' Charlie knows that she is rambling, but mortification has given her verbal diarrhoea and she doesn't know how to relieve herself.

'Yes, yes, yes, I'm still working at the same bank,' replies Alex uncomfortably, both smiling and pushing her away at the same time. 'And I am glad that you like my house and my family, they cost me enough.' He laughs in dry little short bursts like a machine gun. 'Anyway, if you will excuse me a minute I must go and get out of these clothes.'

Charlie stands back to find Alex dressed in a pair of neat white shorts and a slightly damp white tennis shirt that clings to his narrow chest. His legs are white and long and thin. Almost entirely devoid of hair, they end in a pair of white terry socks and an expensive pair of trainers with non-stain soles especially designed for squash.

'Oh right, of course,' insists Charlie. 'I didn't notice.'

'Indeed,' says Alex, running his hands through his thick mop of sweaty dark hair.

'Good game?' asks Charlie rather too keenly.

'Indeed,' says Alex.

'Did you win?'

'Of course.' He smiles and turns to leave the room.

'Darling? Is that you?' comes Kate's voice, as she bounces down the stairs like an overexcited Labrador. 'I didn't hear you come in.'

'Indeed,' replies Alex. 'Neither did your sister.'

'Look at you!' exclaims Kate.

'I didn't have time for a shower at the club.' He smiles. 'I thought we were having dinner with your sister.'

'We are, we are,' smiles Kate. 'I was just putting the children to bed.'

'This late?' asks Alex, looking at his watch. 'It's gone quarter to nine. Isn't that bad for their routine?'

'I'm sure it won't matter just this once,' says Kate. 'Anyway, how often do I get to welcome my sister back after all this time?'

'Indeed,' replies Alex. 'I'm going to have a shower.'

He turns and leaves the room, popping his squash racquet into a designer hatstand before he goes upstairs. For a conventionally attractive man, Alex looks conventionally rather unattractive when undressed or out of his suit. He has a good crop of dark hair and pleasant, if slightly myopically pale, blue eyes plus a strong straight nose. But he is about as physically potent as a peperoni. Too slim and too effete, his hands look more suited to pushing pens than any form of hunting or gathering.

Charlie remembers when she first met him propping up some hard-arsed stiff stool in a wine bar off the King's Road. Kate had introduced him as some bloke she'd scored and she recalls being quite impressed. He looked urban and angular and really quite handsome, but it wasn't until a couple of weeks later, after they'd all gone ice skating, that she'd ceased to find him attractive in the slightest. All skin and bone, there was something about the way his thin backside hit the ice that made him lose all his charm.

'Is he OK?' asks Charlie after Alex walks up the stairs.

'I think so,' breezes Kate, standing smiling by the door. 'Why?'

'Oh, I don't know,' replies Charlie. 'Maybe it was something that I said.'

'I shouldn't think so for a minute. He's probably had a difficult day at work.' Her sister smiles some more. 'Anyway, let's have one of those shots.'

'Do you think so?'

'Oh, I know so.' She grins, whipping her tangle-free bob behind one ear. 'And then we'll have a think about dinner.'

Two shots later and it is obvious that, despite her vodka-fuelled efficiency, Kate has done nothing but think about dinner all day. By the time Alex comes down the stairs, dressed in a blue and white striped open-necked shirt and a pair of pale beige chinos, she has already served up salmon and coriander balls with their own sweet chilli sauce which she must have spent the majority of the afternoon preparing.

'These are just . . . well, to keep us going before supper,' smiles Kate, popping a rustic bowl of balls on the steel-topped kitchen table.

'God, these are delicious,' says Charlie with her mouth full as she leans over to pick and dip another ball with her left hand. 'They must have taken ages to make.'

'No, not really,' lies Kate with a flick of her hair. 'It's just a question of organisation.'

'Well, they're great,' says Charlie, chewing away.

'They're not as good as they were the other day,' declares Alex, sitting down at the table, eating two at the same time.

'Different fish,' shrugs Kate. 'Last week's came from that very expensive fishmonger up the road and this was supermarket stuff.'

'What . . . supermarket?' says Alex, about to empty his mouth of balls in disgust.

'Oh, no, no, it's still unstained, undyed, unfarmed, organic and from Scotland,' insists Kate, looking concerned.

'Did it have friends and a social life?' jokes Charlie, helping herself to another.

'What?' asks Kate.

'Nothing,' replies her elder sister, biting the inside of her cheek.

'It's just that I refuse to eat the non-organic stuff these days,' explains Alex, pursing his lips slightly as he picks up another ball and dips it delicately into the sauce with his thumb and forefinger. 'You know,' he continues, 'it was after I read a piece in *The Sunday Times* magazine about farmed salmon and how dyed and covered in lice they all are. I just thought I must do my bit for the environment. You know, help out so to speak.'

'Oh, absolutely,' says Charlie, nodding vigorously.

Alex smiles, very satisfied with himself, and pops another ball into his mouth. Her sarcasm is lost on him. It is lost on her sister as well, for Kate is not even listening. Caught up in a whirlwind of wok-frying and pan-griddling, she is trying to make sure the charred lines on her chicken breasts are straight so as not to detract from their sizzling sumptuousness, while at the same time checking that her pok choi is not burning but merely softening to an al dente texture.

'Ginger and garlic chicken with a soy sauce marinade plus some stir-fried Chinese veg all right for everyone?' she asks, turning round briefly from her industrial-sized gas cooker.

'Fine,' says Alex.

'Sounds amazing,' replies Charlie at the same time, her green eyes smiling.

'Do you want me to lay up?' offers Alex after a pause, as he gets up from his seat and saunters over towards the wine rack.

'God, if you could,' smiles Kate, all pink and pressured with a wooden spoon in each hand. 'That would be a great help.'

'Can I do anything?' asks Charlie.

'No, no,' insists Alex. 'You just rest there.' He smiles. 'Darling,' he asks, 'where do we keep the knives and forks?'

It takes Alex a full five minutes to find all the ingredients necessary for laying a table. Quizzing his wife on each and every journey he makes around his evidently unfamiliar kitchen, he finally puts it all together with uncoordinated abandon on the table, and awaits murmurs of appreciation from the two women.

'*A tavolà*,' he announces, as Kate dishes up the chicken breasts on their bed of Chinese vegetables, taking care to wipe around the edge of each plate with a damp cloth.

'Yes, well done, darling,' says Kate, putting down the plates before searching through the drawers for some napkins.

'This looks delicious,' enthuses Charlie. 'I haven't eaten like such a king in years.'

'No, really, it's nothing,' says Kate, exhaling back into her chair.

'We eat like this all the time,' says Alex.

'Gosh,' smiles Charlie.

'Oh yes,' continues Alex. 'We'll have no truck with processed food. Will we darling?'

'No,' says Kate.

'Gosh,' repeats Charlie.

'So much better for you,' says Alex, with his mouth full. 'No chemicals.'

'I'll drink to that,' says Kate, taking a large swig from a rather large glass of red wine.

'Nice red this,' says Alex, doing the same. 'I've gone off all those thick New World Chardonnays – they are so last year.'

'Don't you mean last millennium?' laughs Kate.

'Are they?' asks Charlie. 'I wouldn't really know.'

'Well, the wine trade has got very interesting recently . . .' says Alex.

While his wife and her sister sit and slowly eat their supper in silence, Alex holds forth, giving a lecture on New World wines versus Continental wines and how they compare with those from places like South America and indeed the Lebanon. For a man who has just turned thirty-five years old, Alex thinks he knows an awful lot about wine. Some of it he has gleaned from a Channel 4 series he watched last year, some of it he read in a *Wines of the World* book that Kate bought him for Christmas last year, but the majority of it comes from the garrulous chap who runs Oddbins round the corner.

'All very fascinating, don't you agree?' says Alex.

'Mmm,' says Charlie, not really listening to her brother-in-law, but rather enjoying her chicken.

'So,' says Alex, with a large sniff. 'Got a boyfriend?'

'Who, me?' asks Charlie, slightly taken aback.

'Well I'm certainly not asking my wife the same question, am I?' chortles Alex.

'Alex, you can't ask questions like that,' says Kate, her eyes rounding with faux indignation.

'Why not? She's not a lesbian,' chortles Alex some more. 'Or are you?' he adds, firing off a few rounds of laughter.

'Um, no,' replies Charlie. 'To both of your questions. No . . . I'm not a lesbian and, um, no, I don't have a boyfriend.'

'Oh, poor you,' says Kate, her head flopping to one side in sympathy.

'Yes, poor you,' agrees Alex. 'I mean, it's not as if you're ugly or anything.'

'No,' laughs Kate, flapping both her hands at their shared mutual joke. 'There isn't anything wrong with you at all.'

'Maybe she's a bit too, you know . . . careerist,' suggests Alex to Kate as if Charlie has just left the room.

'Now, Alex and I have discussed this . . .' confides Kate.

'You have?' asks Charlie, looking horrified.

'Oh yeah,' she continues. 'And anyway, we think that it's because you've been abroad for so long that you can't find a man, and maybe you are too interested . . .' She clears her throat. 'Um, how can I put this . . . you are too interested in your work . . . I mean, I've found this with friends of mine who have failed to find men. They always profess to be married to their job, which is only a way of compensating for being on their own. But if they do find a man, all that happens is their lives are so organised and busy there is no room for the man to fit in. It's a vicious circle.'

'But I love my work,' protests Charlie. 'And I'm good at it. I've been nominated for an award . . .'

'We all know you're nominated for an award. All Mum talks about is you being nominated for a bloody award. Well, well done you,' smiles Kate, drinking some more red wine and warming to her subject. 'But you know, there is a point when being so careerist is quite frankly a bit sad . . .'

'Sad?' repeats Charlie, slumping back into her chair.

'Yup, sad,' repeats her sister, burping slightly through her back teeth. 'People begin to start thinking that you're denying your femininity and that, you know, you'll be left on the shelf, with your ovaries drying up like walnuts. And then you'll end up with baby hunger . . .'

'Baby what?'

'Baby hunger,' she repeats. 'And take it from me, I've met some women who are simply starving . . . and it's not very attractive.'

'It isn't?'

'Oh no,' nods Kate, looking like a woman who has diligently read and digested her glossy magazines and Sunday supplements.

'No,' agrees her husband, looking equally confident.

Charlie doesn't know what to say. Her sister and her husband have obviously had too much to drink and are taking their angst out on her. There is some back-story to this conversation that she is not in a position to argue with. She would dearly love to have a stand-up row with the two of them, but she is tired and quite drunk herself, and bearing in mind that she has not seen her sister for nearly five years, the first night around her dinner table is not the appropriate time for a pissed and protracted feminist argument. But she is hurt all the same. How dare they sit around discussing her lack of partner? They have no idea exactly what she has been through during the past four to five years. They have a vague idea about the loves she has had and lost in the most unbearable of circumstances. But they don't really understand. And they shouldn't pretend to. However, it is pointless, she concludes, to have all this out with them as they sit around their good-taste kitchen table, in their good-taste house, with their good-taste children asleep upstairs.

'No,' says Charlie with a controlled smile. 'Maybe you're right.'

'You see!' trills Kate, immediately leaping out of her seat. 'I was right, I was right.' She points triumphantly at her husband. 'She's my sister and I knew it. Who's Mr Wrong now?'

'I'm Mr Wrong now,' agrees Alex with a resigned smile. 'And you're Miss Right.'

'Sorry, what's going on?' asks Charlie, putting her elbows on the table and shaking her head, looking extremely confused.

'Oh God.' Kate flops back down into her chair with a

wide smile. 'It was just a bet we had about this dinner I've organised . . .'

'It's not a dinner,' argues Alex. 'You've set her up.'

'I haven't!'

'You have!'

'Well, maybe just a bit,' giggles Kate. 'We've got people over tomorrow for dinner in your honour.'

'Normally it would just be a seven, what with you being on your own and everything,' explains Alex. 'But Kate's made a special effort and trawled through her address book . . .'

'And rung loads of people . . .' she adds.

'To find you a man!' grins Alex. 'I said you wouldn't be interested. Especially after everything that's happened, but . . .'

'I said you would!' Kate clasps her hands with delight.

'Great,' says Charlie, her head falling into her right hand.

'I knew you would see it our way,' insists Kate, wagging her finger and getting up from the table. 'It's all going to be such . . . good . . . fun!' She claps her hands together in her excitement. 'Pudding anyone? Baked peaches with Amaretto zabaglione?' She smiles. 'Just a little something I made earlier.'

2

The next morning Charlie wakes up before anyone else and lies in bed staring at the sky-blue ceiling covered with a constellation of gold-stencilled stars. Dawn is just breaking over Shepherd's Bush and she can hear the gentle, unfamiliar moan of traffic, peppered by the occasional high-pitched squeak from a taxi as it brakes, and the thunderous progress of a bus.

She hasn't slept well. Quite apart from the mattress being overly soft and yielding and too many frilly cushions and pillows on the bed, her brain just would not stop working. Totally disorientated by her return to London, she spent the whole night questioning her reasons for coming back, weighing up in her mind whether she fitted in here any more. She kept on asking herself what she was hoping to achieve here. Why had she come back after all this time away? What was she expecting? She was only supposed to be here on some sort of extended holiday. A break from her hectic life for the first time in nearly five years. A career hiatus. Was she hoping for some grand reunion with her friends? A home-coming party with all her family together? Long, deep, rebonding conversations with her sister? In fact, what had happened to her sister? What had happened to the feisty Kate she left behind over four years ago? Was it she, Charlie, who was out of line, gone off on some weird tangent? Or were there a lot of other women, apart from Kate, who thought that marriage and children coupled with a sort of Stepford Wife domesticity were the main reasons why women burnt their bras and threw themselves under passing royal nags?

It was all so confusing. She lay there tossing and turning and hearing over and over the various little terse phrases that tumbled from her sister's neat, pursed lips while they sat around her neat, pursed dinner table. 'Poor, poor you . . .', 'All alone . . .', 'On your tod . . .' 'We rang around everywhere . . .', 'Went through my whole address book', 'We really searched . . .', 'trawled through . . .', 'Trying to find you someone . . .' The embarrassment. The humiliation. When did people stop being impressed or even pleasantly satisfied that you had a job that you loved, and start feeling sorry for you because you weren't married? Or that you didn't have a relationship to speak of? At what time precisely did the pity set in? When did the whispers start circulating? When did people start telephoning up their exes? Or apologising that they were only five, or seven, or nine for dinner? When did the rest of the world start to worry? When did the rest of the world start thinking that it was their duty to get involved?

It was confusing last night, and it is still confusing for Charlie this morning as she lies in bed, her neck stiff through lack of sleep, her eyes puffy with jet lag, listening to the rest of the house as it begins to stir.

Outside the sky is still a dark, dull purple when she hears either Alfie or Ben start to whine, low and grizzly, at around six-thirty. Next, dead on six forty-five, Charlie hears the loud bleeping of Alex's alarm clock fire through the sanded and stained floorboards beneath her bed. The bleeping is followed by the loud baritone banter of the *Today* programme on Radio 4. It distorts as it echoes around the tiled bathroom at a volume loud enough to be heard above the power shower.

The last to wake is Kate, for there is no other movement from the master bedroom until the children are released from the floor above, all bathed and dressed by the extremely efficient au pair. Like a pack of wild dogs they hound down the stairs and hammer at the bedroom door, only to launch themselves on to the bed when they finally gain access. Charlie hears Kate make great play about being winded by her offspring, moaning and groaning in abject, yet obviously false, pain.

'You've killed me,' she moans and groans through the floor.

'No, we haven't, no, we haven't,' the shrill young voices repeat over and over.

'You have, you have, listen to me, I'm dying,' insists Kate, making gross dying noises while her children squeal with delight.

'Daddy! Mummy's dead,' they shout to their father, who, oblivious, continues to rinse his hair. 'Wake up, Mummy! Wake up. We love you. We love you, Mummy! Wake up!' They proclaim their adoration at the top of their voices until their mother is heard eventually to get out of bed.

Charlie yawns and stretches in her bed above, smiling as she listens to this domestic scene which must be repeated every morning. Her sister does sound happy, she thinks. After all, what does Charlie know? She sits up in bed and, swinging her slim, tanned legs over the edge of the blue-white sheets, resolves to get up, get dressed and face them.

'Sleep well?' asks Kate, looking smooth and manicured in her cream silk pyjamas and matching dressing gown as she stands at the other side of the kitchen table, a wooden spoon already in her hand. The two boys are both sitting, their legs swinging expectantly at the table. Both with big, round, blue eyes, sporting identical red-checked shirts and matching cord trousers, they look the picture of innocence and anticipation.

'Mmm, I slept very well indeed,' lies Charlie, already dressed in a pair of old-fashioned dark jeans that hang off her and an old, creased navy blue jumper that smells of damp, suitcases and mothballs.

'I'm making porridge,' smiles Kate. 'Do you want some?'

'Um,' says Charlotte. 'I haven't had that stuff in years.'

'Alfie loves it,' continues Kate, stirring a pan. 'Ben is a bit more dubious . . . but it's so good for them that I insist.'

'Right,' says Charlie, flicking on the kettle and running her hands through her wet, bleached-blonde hair which hangs stiff and straight to her shoulders. 'I don't normally eat breakfast . . . don't have enough time,' she mutters. 'It's usually a cup of black coffee, a fag and then off.'

'Oh,' says Kate, sounding both disapproving and disappointed. 'You've missed Alex,' she continues, recovering slightly. 'He left about ten minutes ago, when you were in the shower.' She adds, 'Anyway, he sends his love and says he'll see you tonight . . . he can't wait.'

'Can't wait for what?' says Charlie, staring at the kettle, willing it to boil.

'He can't wait for the dinner tonight,' replies Kate, turning round from the cooker, an encouraging smile playing on her mouth. Her lips shine with their daily lubrication by Elizabeth Arden Visible Difference Eight Hour Cream for extra suppleness.

'The dinner?' replies Charlie, pretending that she has forgotten about last night's conversation, in the vain hope that tonight's situation might disappear.

'The dinner that I'm cooking tonight in your honour,' grins her sister again.

'Yeah, right,' says Charlie, suddenly sounding extremely teenage.

'Oh, don't be like that,' insists Kate. 'You might like Adrian.'

'Adrian . . .' repeats Charlie. 'I don't think I have ever liked an Adrian in my life.'

'Now you're being babyish,' scolds Kate, in a manner that makes Charlie bristle with irritation.

'I'm not.'

'You are,' replies her sister, before adding feebly, 'and anyway, he doesn't look like an Adrian.'

'What is an Adrian supposed to look like these days?' asks Charlie.

'Oh, I don't know,' exhales Kate, stirring her porridge with unnecessary vigour. 'You know, nerdy.'

'Well, maybe I like nerdy.'

'You do?'

'Well, no . . .'

'You see . . .'

'You see . . . what?' asks Charlie, sounding a bit more irritated than she intends.

'Oh, nothing,' replies Kate, just as the toaster pops loudly. 'Toast?'

'Please,' says Charlie, sitting down next to her elder, snot-sniffing nephew. 'Do you have any Marmite?'

'My God, you don't still like that disgusting stuff, do you?' asks Kate with a relieved smile.

'I'm afraid so,' laughs Charlie, picking up a knife and beginning to butter her toast. 'It's considered a luxury where I've come from.'

'I'm sure,' smiles Kate.

'Anyway, who else is coming to this wretched dinner?'

Kate sits down and, picking up Charlie's first piece of buttered toast, she begins animatedly to discuss her friends. First is Claire who, from what Charlie can gather, is really quite a celebrity. She has her own column in a Sunday newspaper supplement where she tests beauty products to the delight and delectation of the nation. She is quite a girl-about-town and occasionally appears in the gossip columns at a lipstick launch or a PR party for some new hair-care range. She doesn't even, and Charlie doesn't quite understand the importance of this, have to make a reservation at The Bush Bar and Grill. She just swans in, apparently, and nearly always gets the right table right away. With a background in *Cosmopolitan* and *She* magazines, she and Kate met at a beauty convention in Birmingham, years ago, when they were launching a new, revolutionary depilating product. Kate was pregnant with Alfie and working on the advertising account, and Claire had come along to write about the event. She was apparently 'glamorous even then'. They had bonded over coffees and shared a mutual love of massage and Harvey Nichols, they had been firm friends ever since.

'You'll really love her,' insists Kate. 'Everyone does,' she adds, her shoulders raised in her enthusiasm. 'I mean, we're really good friends. I suppose I call her every day.'

Claire's boyfriend, or live-in partner, Tim, is another story. His father is a famous historian and academic who writes well-received tomes on Hitler and 'lots of other dictators', occasionally appearing on *Question Time* and *Any Questions* on Radio 4. Tim is also extremely clever and wants to be a writer. But, unlike his father, he thinks academia is 'so over', so he is putting all his energies into becoming a novelist. A firm follower of the zeitgeist, he had several rave pieces printed in various hip magazines in the nineties, and is now concentrating his efforts on writing for men's monthlies like *Esquire* and *GQ*. 'He thinks there are far too many books written by women,' explains Kate, while wiping Alfie's nose with some kitchen roll, 'and that the moment for proper men's stuff, or New Lad-Lit as he calls it, is literally just around the corner.'

As well as the achingly hip Claire and Tim, Kate has invited a couple called Sam and Emma who are, as she explains, really old, old friends of Alex's. Sam was at school with Alex and they also went to Durham University together.

Emma and Sam are both lawyers working for the same chambers. They specialise in criminal law, or is it tax? She can't quite remember. But they got married last year in a very glamorous ceremony just outside Oxford, with a marquee and two hundred guests, and since then Emma has given up her job. And they have just had a baby.

'So it should all be great fun,' says Kate, getting up from the table to clear the plates. 'Even if you don't like Adrian, you'll have lots of other people to talk to.'

'Yeah,' agrees Charlie, stiffly drinking her thick, rather cold coffee. 'It all sounds, um, marvellous.'

'I knew you'd come round,' says Kate, bending over to fill the stainless steel-fronted incorporated dishwasher.

'What does Adrian do?' asks Charlie.

'Oh,' says Kate, picking a reluctant and worming Ben out of a seat that is attached to the far end of the table. 'He works in advertising. He has the office opposite me – or had, I should say.' She laughs hollowly. 'Seeing as I no longer work there.'

'Oh,' says Charlie, inhaling at the thought of such a fun evening. 'Sounds great.'

Having given their mother a full ten minutes' worth of talk time, accompanied only by the occasional juice spill plus hurling of porridge and/or toast, both Alfie and Ben are bored by the lack of attention and decide to show it. While Ben has resolved simply to scream at the idea of having to put his feet on the floor, Aflie is standing behind his chair hitting the metal-topped table with his metal spoon. The hammering noise is worthy of an overly efficient blacksmith with a stable of ponies waiting to be shod. Kate, having looked so calm and sophisticated and glamorous in her cream silk ensemble, is now obviously out of control. While Ben clings to her, pulling her dressing gown off her shoulders and using her pyjama bottoms like a stepladder with his feet, she tries to extricate the spoon from Aflie's dexterously moving hand.

'Stop it, stop it, stop it,' she shouts. 'Bad boy, bad, bad boy, give it to me.'

'No-o-o,' yells Aflie as he runs around the kitchen, hitting anything that gets in his way.

Charlie joins in. Unaccustomed to dealing with small children, she approaches Aflie, crouching nervously with her arms out as if trying to catch a truculent chicken.

'Come here,' she says, smiling widely, edging forwards. 'Come on, and stop that banging.'

'No,' comes his confident reply, as he runs, spoon held up high in front him, ducking underneath her outstretched arms.

'Come on,' she says again.

'No,' he replies.

'Come on, you little . . .' says Charlie, gritting her teeth and managing to swallow the last distinctly grown-up part of the sentence.

'Jesus Christ,' shouts Kate from beside the cooker, as with one final twist Ben falls to the floor, taking with him a clump of her hair, which sprouts out of his fat fist like a sheaf of dark brown corn. 'Peta-a-a-ah,' she shouts loudly. 'Peta-a-a-h. Peta-a-a-ah.' The desperation in her voice carries her cry all the way up the stairs.

'Coming!' comes the muffled reply from the top of the house.

'Now look what you've done,' says Kate severely. 'Peta's coming to take you to nursery.'

The mere mention of Peta causes the two boys suddenly to behave. Like the threat of 'The Parents' on older children or 'The Headmaster' on a rowdy class, by the time Peta arrives, her huge breasts and thin hair still swinging as she enters the room at speed, the two boys look as if Lurpak wouldn't melt in their tiny little mouths. 'Thank God for that,' sighs Kate, immediately handing Ben over to the hirsute Dutch girl. 'What took you so long?'

'I was just brushing my teeth before I take them to school,' Peta explains quickly. A speck of minty white saliva in the corner of her mouth is testament to her telling the truth.

'Right, yes, of course,' says Kate, obviously slightly embarrassed at such an evident loss of control in front of her sister. 'Yes, yes, indeed. Right, so off you lot go then?' She continues as efficiently as she can. 'Off to playgroup and all those things . . .' She smiles and turns to look at her sister. Puffing out her cheeks, she adds, 'It's always such chaos in the mornings. Come along now, everyone, coats! Follow Peta and get your coats on.'

The two children obediently follow Peta out of the kitchen and into the hall. Kate kneels down on the limestone floor and helps Ben into his navy puffa coat, while Peta does the same with Alfie. Meanwhile, Charlie, feeling slightly useless, remains in the kitchen and, flicking the kettle back on for another cup of coffee, sits back down at the table and, rather exhausted by the last five minutes, lights up a cigarette.

'Oh God, thank God for that,' announces Kate as she comes back into the kitchen having kissed and hugged and waved and kissed and hugged and waved her children goodbye. 'I have no idea how people manage without help,' she announces as she sits down. 'I mean, if I didn't have Peta I would never be able to do anything for myself at all.'

'I know,' agrees Charlie. 'They are sweet, but they are bloody noisy. I can't quite get the appeal, myself. A little older, perhaps, when they start asking fabulous questions, then I find them a whole lot more interesting.'

'Alfie's at that stage already. But then he is a genius,' says Kate. 'Just you wait till you have one of your own,' she smiles, wagging her finger. 'Then you'll understand quite how rewarding they can be. Honestly, I don't know how people think their lives are fulfilled unless they have children.'

'I don't think that's very fair,' says Charlie, smiling. 'You have no idea about other people's lives. They might be very fulfilled without children.'

'They might think they are,' says Kate, raising a finger, 'but they just don't know until they have them.' She finishes with a small, neat smile.

Charlie is stunned. But she elects to inhale deeply on her cigarette and blow the smoke in a long, large, grey cloud towards the ceiling.

'Anyway,' continues Kate, rubbing her hands together like she has won the argument and is simply moving on out of superior tact. 'Let's change the subject.'

'Mm,' agrees Charlie.

'What do you want to do today?' she asks, getting up to open the french windows. 'You've got me all morning, now that the children are out. And I've asked Peta to give them lunch, which is something I normally do. So we could shop, have a girls' lunch. Or we could shop. Have pedicures . . . they're always great. Or we could shop, and you could have a haircut and a blow-dry or something like that. You could do with a bit of maintenance, couldn't you?' she laughs. 'Or we could shop and go the whole hog, pedicures, manicures, massage and miss lunch altogether. What do you think?'

Charlie stubs out her cigarette in her barely drunk cup of coffee and, sounding rather sheepish, says, 'Um, I wasn't banking on you being around this morning at all. What with all your domestic commitments and everything. I had rather thought that I might go to my photographic agency and say hello to a few mates. Sort through some contact sheets and maybe see if I can repair one of my lenses that has a hairline crack after I dropped it at Nairobi airport.'

'Oh,' replies Kate, raising a shoulder, looking put out.

'Can't you take a day off from working, just for once, and spend it with your sister?'

To refuse would be pointless and Charlie knows it, although the idea of a whole morning filled with retail therapy and general pampering gives her narcolepsy. She concludes that if she is ever going to get on with her younger sister, she is not only going to have to make an effort, she is also going to have to meet her halfway.

Not that Kate should be surprised by her sister's reticence, for Charlie can't have changed when it comes to traipsing around department stores. Even before she left London nearly five years ago, she wasn't much of a retail groupie. Clothes, fashions and floaty ensembles did not really appeal. She was a big boots, jeans and jumper type of girl, occasionally resorting to the old short skirt, plunge top and underwired breasts routine, but only if the situation really required it – like at her last agency's Christmas party just before she announced her resignation. Or when trying to infiltrate a gang of South London pimps who preyed on Eastern European immigrant women, who she eventually photographed for the *Observer* magazine.

Anyway, it isn't so much that Charlie is not keen to spend the whole of her first morning back in the capital undergoing a makeover of Richard and Judy proportions, it is the fact that Kate has become so very interested that Charlie finds disturbing. They used to laugh about those sorts of women, Charlie remembers as she wanders around upstairs in her white bedroom with its sky-blue ceiling. They used to lie back on the sticky, stained, spliff-burnt carpet in the flat they shared together and laugh for hours about these unreconstructed females who were pleasing men rather than themselves. They used to take pride in the length of their armpit growth, and the fact that the hairs on their legs poked through their thick woollen tights. Kate had, it was true, smartened up her act when she got promoted in her advertising job, but on the whole she was just as hippy and hairy as the rest of them. She would play sassy successful vixen during the week, and then eco-warrior at the weekend. They both knew their Dolcis from their Dolce e Gabanna, but neither of them was particularly interested in labels or could afford couture.

'Claire says they've got this great new totally organic skincare range just as you come in on the left at Harvey Nichols,' announces Kate as she corkscrews her behind into the back of a cab.

'Really?' replies Charlie, resting her chin on the window as they pass by the £1-buys-all bargain shop on the Shepherd's Bush roundabout.

It's raining outside. Not the sort of warm, delicious deluge that Charlotte is used to, the sort that announces itself with a hot, humid build-up like you've been in a sauna all afternoon, only to climax in a torrential downpour that sends everyone running for cover and their waterproofs, or in more hedonistic times a shampoo bottle and some conditioner. This rain is feeble and damp and only serves to paint the pavements a darker grey and dull the morning light to the colour of pencil lead.

'Terrible weather,' says Kate. 'Whatever happened to the Indian summer we were promised?'

'It's probably still in India if it knows what's good for it,' mumbles Charlie through the hand pressed against her brown freckled cheek.

'Don't be like that,' insists Kate. 'I'm sure it will brighten up later.'

Eventually the taxi drops them at the corner of Knightsbridge and Sloane Street and Kate positively skips into Harvey Nichols. Bright and shiny like a shrine to the Gold Card, everywhere she turns Charlie's senses are stimulated. New products, new smells, new colours, new packaging, it is a visual and sensual feast. Excited and yet repelled by this Aladdin's cave of retail opportunity, she follows her sister around like small child in a supermarket, randomly picking up totally inappropriate goods, only for her younger sister to replace them with a well-practised sigh. They cover each floor methodically, in a well-organised, well-executed plan of attack. Kate spends almost a whole hour amongst the new Whistles collection trying on everything from the cream trousers with the sequin flowers on the buttocks to the silk chiffon cardigans that Charlie, sitting on the floor shrugging her shoulders at each and every item, can see no practical use for whatsoever. Eventually, having travelled via hair, beauty, fashion and make-up, they arrive on the top floor to have a sushi lunch that gyrates and rotates in front of them on a conveyor belt, teasing them with options, possibilities, choice.

When they finally make it home, Charlie looks, as Kate put it so tactfully in the taxi, 'a whole lot more presentable'. She has been de-hoofed and de-scaled, depilated and coiffed. She accepted a blow-dry, at her sister's insistence, and gritted her teeth as more and more 'product' was applied to her sun-bleached hair, making it a lot less 'dry and fly away'. She even bought a dress, an article of clothing that Charlie hasn't worn in years. Kate said it looked 'great', and in the absence of any helpful dissenting opinion, Charlie dug deep and bought it.

Sitting somewhat uncomfortably in her new skin, Charlie perches at the steel-topped table, smoking heavily, watching her sister whirl around the kitchen like a domestic dervish, creating a 'relaxed and easy' supper for her 'relaxed and easy' friends. The blender is on maximum, the cooker is on high, the rings are all on full steam and the pestle and mortar are grinding the crap out of each other. Kate drizzles and griddles and throws together all afternoon. Quite why, after a morning full of pedicures, manicures, massages and retail, she doesn't just buy something boil-in-the-bag from the top floor of Harvey Nichols and pass it off as her own is quite beyond Charlie. It has something to do with wanting to try out this new 'Nigella' pudding, with some 'Jamie Oliver' starter, combined with a 'Wozzer' main, that has her juicing and slicing and splicing when she could be drinking, smoking and talking.

By the time Alex turns up at seven o'clock with a box of wines under his arm, selected for their elegance by his friend at Oddbins, Charlie has helped herself to more than a couple of glasses of last night's leftover red and smoked nearly an entire packet of Marlboro Lights.

'Busy day?' he asks, as he walks in and dumps the box in the middle of the table.

'Oh, very,' replies Kate, sweating so much over the hob that her smooth blow-dry is beginning to curl and kink at the ends.

'It was exhausting,' says Charlie. 'Simultaneously filing photos for five different newspapers on deadline has nothing on a shopping trip to Harvey Nichols. You may think I'm joking,' she smiles, 'but I'm not.'

'Jesus,' says Alex, licking his soft pink lips as he looks Charlie up and down. 'You look totally different. It's amazing what a wash and brush-up can do.'

'And a haircut and manicures and all that stuff,' grins Kate from the other side of the kitchen.

'Don't tell me I look half decent,' says Charlie, with a quick smile that doesn't reach her eyes.

'But you do,' he chortles, his Adam's apple flying up and down his throat like a yo-yo. 'It is a vast improvement.'

Having delivered his verdict on Charlie's makeover, Alex goes upstairs to bond with his sons who, under strict Dutch supervision, are armpit deep in allergy-free soapsuds and plastic ducks. After a couple of minutes of informal chat, he moves on to the master bedroom to change into his dinner party host outfit, which consists of a pair of black Diesel jeans and a black, loose-fitting Nicole Farhi cotton-linen mix V-neck jumper that he teams with a pair of dark desert boots. The boots are so clean, smart and box-fresh, the only drought they could have experienced was when they ran out of San Peligrino in the Europa on the King's Road. Clearly feeling smooth, smart and soigné without being too obvious, Alex comes back downstairs and immediately offers to mix up martinis. Pottering about in the alcohol-allotted area of the kitchen with its wine racks, corkscrew and lemon-slicing board, he pulls out his cocktail book and a set of silver shots measures.

'Right,' he announces, running his forefinger down the list of ingredients. 'This is just to get us going a bit before everyone arrives.'

'Sounds great,' says Charlie, lighting another cigarette, picking up the Q-shaped ashtray and making as if to move through into the sitting room. She has already worked out that the only way she is going to get through this evening is to drink enough to make advertising executives appear deeply interesting.

'Sounds fine,' says Kate, intimating that there is a proviso. 'Except not for me,' she smiles. 'You know the children and, honestly, I don't want to be drunk before everyone arrives. And I don't want you to start ruining your supper.'

'Oh, come on, Kate,' says Charlie. 'You used to be able to drink like a fish.'

'That was a long time ago,' she replies.

'Jesus, not that long ago.'

'You may well be a war-trodden hack who survives on nothing but cigarettes, whisky and that foul, air-dried biltong stuff, but I'm not,' she says with a flick of her increasingly less coiffed bob.

'Anyway, how old are you now?' asks Charlie, choosing to ignore her sister's lame attempt at sarcasm.

'Nearly thirty-three,' she replies.

'God, do you know you're the only person I've ever met who ages themselves up,' says Charlie, exhaling on her cigarette. 'You're not thirty-three for another six months.' Kate shrugs. 'Anyway,' continues Charlie, 'I'm thirty-five, but I still claim the right to get drunk and behave badly whenever I want.'

'Well,' says Kate, 'that's fine . . .' She adds, 'will you please stop smoking so much in my kitchen? You have had almost an entire packet this afternoon. My children have to have breakfast in here.'

'Calm down,' says Alex, finally intervening. 'Charlie, go into the sitting room and I'll bring you a cocktail in a minute, and Kate, you try and relax. You always get like this before you entertain,' he says, putting a designer arm around her designer shoulders. 'I'm sure it will be a triumph . . . as always.'

'I need to go and watch the news, anyway,' says Charlie as breezily as she can. 'See how many possible commissions I'm missing out on.'

Charlie takes her offensive cigarettes with her. Sitting back into the fat cream sofa, she turns on the television and fails to find anything other than a gardening show, a home decorating show and something to do with how-to-cook-fish-on-a-beach-without-a-pan show. She switches it off and stares at a large black and white pregnancy shot of Kate that stares defiantly back. Eventually Alex arrives with a vodka martini in a proper martini glass, complete with a twist of lemon expertly curled and floating on the top.

'I hope it's OK,' he says, his hot hands leaving frosted

fingertip marks on the glass as he hands it over. 'I haven't made one of these in a while.'

'It's delicious,' replies Charlie honestly, after taking a sip.

'Splendid,' he replies. 'I followed the recipe to the letter.'

There is a loud but tasteful ring, which resounds around the house.

'Doorbell!' shouts Kate from the kitchen, just in case Alex hasn't heard.

'On my way,' he replies. Taking up a remote control from the collection that is lined up on the arm of the sofa, he slips Sting (unplugged) on the stereo before leaving the room to answer the door.

First through the sitting room door is an ashen-faced young man with blond electrocuted-looking hair. He has dark pink bags under his eyes and looks as though he has spent the last six months of his life living entirely on a diet of cocaine.

'Hi, hi, hi, hi,' he says as he hunches into the room loaded down with armfuls of white plastic padded things and pale pink bags. 'Do you know where I can put all this stuff?' he asks.

'Um, what is it?' asks Charlie, putting down her drink and making vague motions towards looking helpful.

'Baby stuff,' he says, sounding exhausted and out of breath.

'What sort of baby stuff?' says Charlie.

'Oh God, I don't know,' he replies, sounding rather desperate as he drops it all at his feet. 'Feeding shit, changing shit, pumping shit, you know . . . baby shit.' He smiles.

'I haven't got one,' replies Charlie. 'I wouldn't know.'

'God,' he replies, puffing out his cheeks. 'Don't. They're a bloody nightmare.'

'Darling?' comes a clipped female voice through the door.

'Yeah,' he replies.

'Darling,' she repeats, popping her head round the door. 'Oh, hello,' she says, acknowledging Charlie. 'Darling,' she continues, 'you can't put all that there. I need it upstairs. Take it upstairs. Go on, hurry up. Upstairs. After me.'

They both leave the room, bickering their way upstairs. When they come back down again, the woman is holding a pink plastic walkie-talkie thing in her right hand.

She strides round the room trying to find an appropriate flat surface. 'Darling,' she says in her crisp, nasal voice. 'Darling. Where do you think. Here? Or here?'

'Um, there looks okay?' He points to the photograph of a naked Kate clutching her maternal bosom.

'Here . . . really? Do you think so?' says the girl, putting down the pink plastic box and propping it up against the photo frame.

'It's as good a place as any,' replies the man.

'Well, it's your responsibility,' she says. 'I'm turning the volume up to maximum just in case.'

'Sam, Emma, have you met Charlie? Kate's elder sister?' announces Alex as he wafts through the sitting room door, two martini cocktails in his hands.

'No,' says Emma with a smile, flicking her shoulder-length brown hair off her rather long, narrow face. 'Hello.'

'Hello again,' says Sam, gauchely shrugging his shoulders. 'Sorry about all the mayhem. It's only the second time we've gone out to dinner with the baby.'

'Right,' says Charlie.

'Got any of your own?' asks Emma as she sits down opposite Charlie, pulling her black A-line skirt over her knees.

'Um, no,' smiles Charlie, flicking her ash into the Q in front of her.

'Oh,' giggles Emma. 'But I thought Alex said that you were Kate's elder sister.'

'I am.'

'Right,' smiles Emma, tugging at her skirt again.

'What's your baby, then?' asks Charlie, trying to be polite.

'It's a girl,' replies Emma, sitting back in the sofa and beaming with pride. 'Called Eve.'

'That's nice,' says Charlie, for want of something positive to say.

'Isn't it?' gushes Emma. 'God, Sam and I spent ages trying to work out what to call her, and went through, you know, all the usual, Lily, Chloe, Matilda, Poppy . . . and then, suddenly, I came up with Eve, you know, the beginning of creation, our beginning of creation, as it were. The first girl . . . our first girl. She's six weeks old. Do you want to see the photos?'

'Maybe a little later,' interrupts Sam, with wide blue and slightly apologetic eyes.

'Christ, I'm sorry,' says Emma, flapping her hands around her face. 'I've become one of those nightmare women who thinks the world revolves around them and baby,' she laughs. 'But you must come and see her later. She's upstairs, in your room, I think.'

'Indeed,' says Alex with a soft pink smile as he walks into the room and stands between the two sofas, frosted glass in each hand. 'Cocktail anyone?'

'Not for me,' smiles Emma, patting her life jacket of a cleavage. 'I'm still breast feeding.'

'Yes please,' says Sam, flopping down next to Charlie before accepting his glass. 'Those your fags?' he asks, propping himself up on his elbow.

''Fraid so,' smiles Charlie.

'Oh God, could I have one?' he asks, looking desperate.

'Only if you close the door,' says his wife, shaking her horsy head in disappointment. 'Anyway, you were meant to have given up.'

'Of course,' smiles Charlie, offering up her packet with one cigarette pulled out by way of a serving suggestion. 'Steal as many as you want.'

Alex paces around the room in his smart desert boots, offering up nuts and crisps as well as some warm cheese straws that arrive fresh from the kitchen. He serves Emma some elderflower cordial with a gentle non-alcoholic fizz and turns Sting down slightly so that she can hear her baby breathing through the pink plastic intercom that she has relocated to the arm of the sofa. Sam consumes his cocktail and smokes his cigarette with the zeal of someone who hasn't seen either in rather a long while. His conversation is eclectic as he moves from topic to topic with the concentration of an insomniac. He covers work, photography, Rwanda, Zimbabwe, last week's Manchester United game and maternity bras in the space of about ten minutes. His mind wanders, his replies are sometimes illogical, he laughs at odd moments and, due to his sudden intake of alcohol, his cheeks blush the deep dark pink of an embarrassed adolescent. By the time Kate comes in with the same salmon and coriander balls she made the night before, Sam looks as though he's in need of some comfort food and an early night rather than the few *amuse bouches* that he is supposed to share with friends.

'Sorry, sorry, sorry,' smiles Kate as she arrives with her ethnic bowl of balls.

'Such a nightmare, cooking,' she sighs, 'when all you really want to do is talk to your guests.'

Wearing a dark purple V-neck jumper and the same long boots as yesterday, she has opted for a black silk chiffon skirt that flares like rose petals and stops at just above the knee. She has an extensive collection of beads and bangles and little pale purple crystals wrapped around her wrists as well as a rather hefty Mexican silver pendant that hangs low between her breasts and swings around her ribcage. And as she floats past, offering round her tasty morsels, she smells strongly of peaches.

'So,' she says finally, sitting down next to Emma. 'How are you feeling?'

'Fine,' says Emma, flicking her dark hair behind her ears. 'We've had a few problems with wind and puking and that sort of thing, but she really is terribly good. I think girls are, aren't they? Much better than boys.'

'Um, no, actually,' says Kate, with a slightly over-generous smile. 'I actually meant you.'

'Oh God,' she laughs, bouncing up and down in situ on the sofa. 'Me? Oh right! Oh, I'm fine . . . aren't I, Sam?'

'What?' says Sam, looking pink and puzzled, halfway through his second cocktail and third cigarette. 'Oh what, you? You're fine.'

'That's great then,' breezes Kate, getting up off the sofa to go and be more useful elsewhere. Still holding her balls, she walks over to the stereo on the other side of the room and starts flicking through the CD rack for something other than Sting (unplugged). Finally finding Dido, she pops it on and turns back towards her guests rather satisfied. 'Alex,' she asks, scratching her neck in irritation, 'where do you think Claire and Tim are? They're over half an hour late.'

'They're always late,' says Alex, his mouth full of organic nacho cheese-flavoured crisps.

'I know,' replies Kate. 'But Adrian's not here either,' she says loudly, out of the corner of her mouth, moving her head and indicating towards Charlie, who is sitting smoking quietly on the sofa.

'Well?' mouths Alex, shrugging his shoulders in a manner that obviously absolves him of all responsibility.

Just as Kate is beginning to think that all her planning and organising and culinary timing might be turned on its head by the selfishness of her friends, the doorbell goes and she visibly relaxes.

'Hi, everyone, sorry we're late,' sighs Claire with a flick of her highlights and a long, loud, showy sigh. 'It couldn't be helped. I had to go to the launch of this new perfume at Selfridges on the way.' She sighs again. 'You know, pressures of work, pressures of work. But . . .' she pauses for dramatic effect, 'look at the goody bag!'

She squeals with delight as she walks across the room towards Kate, opening the bag and proffering up her cheek to be kissed at the same time. Dressed in a tight pair of black trousers with a sequin stripe down the outside of each leg, plus a transparent black shirt complete with black underwired bra, Claire is most certainly glamorous. Her heels are high and silver, her hair is blonde and glossy, her nails are dark and shiny, her lips are pale and matt. Following on behind her as she enters the room is a tall, lean, long-haired man in a pair of brown beatnik glasses, wearing jeans and a tight blue shirt with long lapels that is half undone so that he can show off both his smattering of chest hair and the leather thong tied nonchalantly around his neck. They are a striking-looking couple.

'Oh, Claire, look at all this stuff,' exclaims Kate, her head down, her hands scrummaging around in the goody bag.

'It's all a present,' replies Claire, dismissing her own generosity with a flick of the hand. 'Hopefully to make up for the fact that we're late and that we haven't brought you any wine.'

'You're not late,' insists Kate, sniffing a free sample of scent. 'Come along, Alex,' she chivvies. 'Hurry up and get everyone some drinks.'

'Yeah, cheers,' says Tim as he shuffles Sam along the sofa. 'I'm bloody thirsty,' he announces, his fist already in the crisps.

'So am I,' agrees Claire. 'In fact, I would go so far as to say I'm parched. There is nothing that dries the throat out more than a lot of free champagne.'

'Yes,' agrees Kate. 'I've always found that as well.'

Kate flicks her hair and flops down next to Emma. She sits back with an exuberant sigh and pats the cushion to the left of her, indicating that Claire should come and join them.

'Well, this all looks great,' says Claire as she slips in between the coffee table and the sofa, looking at herself in the large mirror opposite the fireplace as she does so. 'I really like what you've done to your sitting room. New Labour green is the colour to have,' she says before sitting down.

'New Labour green?' repeats Kate.

'Oh yeah, certainly,' shrugs Claire in a manner that suggests everyone knows what she is talking about. 'You know, pistachio is to the post-millennium what Thatcher yellow was to the eighties.' She smiles and pops a cashew into her matt mouth. Kate still looks confused. 'In the eighties,' Claire sighs, slightly bored that she's started this conversational tack, 'everyone painted their houses and flats that bland, inoffensive ochre yellow. It was the thing, all the rage, particularly if they wanted to sell it at an inflated profit. Anyway, now everyone's using pistachio.'

'Oh,' says Kate, smiling weakly. 'That's good,' she adds, flicking her hair again. 'I love your shoes,' she continues, overtly complimenting her guest in an effort to keep her evening smooth and free-flowing.

'Aren't they great?' Claire agrees, giving a little nod to Alex as he arrives with her drink. 'Gina,' she announces, lifting her silver-shod foot off the floor for all to admire.

'God, I would never dare go to that shop,' says Kate, leaning forwards to covet more closely. 'It's so-o-o expensive.'

'But I get a discount,' announces Claire. 'Forty per cent,' she lies, doubling her reduction and her importance at the same time. 'You should come with me.'

'I'd love to,' grins Kate at this tempting offer that has been dangled in front of her about a dozen times.

'Claire, Tim, you know Emma and Sam, don't you?' interrupts Alex, using his right hand to span the sofa divide.

'Oh yes,' says Emma, leaning across Kate to tap Claire's knee. 'We've met before.'

'Have we?' asks Claire, trying to furrow her brow that was recently Botoxed for an article in *ES* magazine.

'Yes,' continues Emma undeterred. 'It was at Alex's birthday party in the garden last year. You'd just had a bath in caviar for some newspaper thing and you were asking everyone if they could smell fish.'

'Was I?' says Claire, shaking her head. 'How hilarious . . .'

'God, Claire, you are funny, I remember that,' says Kate.

'I remember that treatment,' continues Claire. 'The most expensive bath in Europe or something like that. Amazing stuff, like sitting in jam, really, but so good for you. My skin was amazing afterwards. Do you remember, Kate?'

'Absolutely,' confirms Kate. 'Your skin was wonderful.'

'Anyway, hello again,' smiles Claire, giving Emma a little wave across Kate's thighs.

'Good. Now that we've cleared that up,' says Alex, 'I don't believe either of you has met Kate's elder sister Charlie.'

'So you're Kate's sister,' mumbles Claire through her mouthful of martini, pointing with her short, dark, square fingernails. 'The intrepid Lara Croft photographer. I've heard so much about you,' she adds with a swallow and an expansively generous smile.

'Really?' asks Charlie. 'All of it suitably offensive, I hope,' she says with a half smile, exhaling smoke and stubbing out in the ashtray in front of her. 'Um, no,' laughs Claire. 'I've heard you're very interesting and have done lots of fascinating and dangerous things. Lovely dress, by the way,' she adds, checking out Charlie's new outfit that, with her brown legs, she has teamed with a pair of sequin flip-flops. 'Um, very black . . .'

'So you're Charlie, are you?' asks Tim, making short shrift of a cheese straw.

'Yes,' she smiles.

'The one who lives in Kenya?'

'Yeah, I rent a house in Nairobi with some friends, but I've been living all over,' she replies, shifting in her seat, leaning forwards to talk across the flushed Sam who is relaxing back into the sofa cushions listening to Dido.

'I think I might have seen some of your stuff,' sniffs Tim.

'Really?' asks Kate, sounding rather surprised. 'Have you? How amazing!' She laughs.

'Really?' says Charlie, leaning further forward. 'It's mainly East African stuff. But I travel all over . . . where I'm sent, really. I work sometimes for Reuters, AFP, whoever pays me to go to whereever they want me to go.' She laughs.

'Oh,' he says, taking one of her cigarettes out of the packet on the coffee table. 'I thought you did books.'

'I have,' she nods. 'I illustrated a book on Angola and I've contributed to a couple of others "from our own correspondent" books that have been written about various wars I've covered.'

'I write books,' says Tim, sitting up and twisting his knees towards her.

'Really?' replies Charlie.

'Yeah,' he says, exhaling his cigarette smoke out of the corner of his mouth and letting a couple of strands of his dark hair fall across his face for poetic effect. 'They're, you know, very profound novels on the state of masculinity. The one I am doing at the moment is a bit like, um, have you seen the film *Fight Club*?'

'No.'

'Oh, well, a bit like that.'

'Right.'

'Sort of angry-young-man stuff.'

'Sounds very interesting,' says Charlie.

'Oh, it is,' replies Tim, confidently. 'It is very interesting.' While Tim nods profoundly on the sofa, talking at Charlie about emasculation and male inner anger, Alex sits laughing with Claire. They are sharing a huge joke that no one else has heard the punchline to, and are rather ostentatiously enjoying themselves. Kate and Emma are perched at the other end of the sofa, closer to the fire, discussing an ecologically-sound nappy service that picks up your non-disposable, dirty nappies on a daily basis, launders them and returns them all neat and ironed the following morning. They smile in mutual agreement, and occasionally, between sips of elderflower cordial, Emma picks up the pink plastic intercom and shakes it to check it's still working.

'I have simply no idea where Adrian can be,' announces Kate suddenly, getting up from the sofa and clapping her hands to get everyone's attention. 'But it really is time we went through to eat.'

As the assembled company stand and gather together to move through to the kitchen where Kate has laid up her 'relaxed' supper, the doorbell rings

'At last,' she says with a wide and terribly relaxed smile. 'Adrian.' She walks to the door with her cocktail in her right hand, opening it with her left. The whole party gathers behind, waiting for Adrian. 'Hi,' says Kate as she pulls open the door.

'Bring me the spinster – I want her alive!' declares Adrian, laughing, grinning and inordinately proud of his bastardised

Star Wars quotation as he pours through the doorway, bottle of champagne in one hand. 'Oh fuck,' he smiles as he pulls himself up straight and falls back a step. 'I wasn't expecting a welcoming committee. How bloody late am I?'

'Very,' says Kate, her mouth tight. 'But seeing as you are finally here, you'd better go through.'

'Shit, Christ, sorry,' says Adrian as he straightens himself and tries to pull himself together. 'I had a few drinks with some mates after work,' he whispers rather loudly, spitting into Kate's ear. 'I slightly forgot the time.'

Kate is furious but hides her anger in sing-song efficiency, placing her guests and talking them through the first course – a fig and mozzarella salad with roquette and Parma ham. Claire is next to Alex, while Charlie has Tim on one side and the overly-refreshed Adrian to her right. Everyone talks politely and tucks into their food, except for Adrian, who, plump, and smelling heavily of cigarettes, possibly cigars, but most certainly some sort of drinking establishment, sways in his seat and views his salad with a deep suspicion.

'What are these?' he slurs eventually, leaning over towards Charlie, jabbing a fig with a fork.

'Figs,' says Charlie.

'Oh,' replies Adrian, nodding expansively enough for his whole head and shoulders to move with him. He sits quietly and digests the information. 'Figs?' he repeats, leaning back towards Charlie.

'Yes,' she confirms.

'I thought you only had those if, you know . . .' he winks, contracting the whole of one side of his not unattractive, if slightly shiny face. 'If you couldn't um, well . . . shit.'

'Some people consider them a bit of a luxury,' explains Charlie, rather amused by the ineptitude of her so-called date.

'Interesting,' he replies, cutting off the smallest of small segments and putting it gingerly into his mouth. He chews and ponders, nodding quietly to himself. 'They're quite nice,' he announces suddenly in Charlie's ear. 'Not bad at all. Good figs!' he confirms loudly across the table, raising a glass to Kate, who only just responds. 'Right,' he adds all of a sudden, as if he has just remembered the purpose of the evening. 'Who is the spinster I've been told to entertain?'

'Er, here,' says Charlie, helpfully putting her hand up as the rest of the table falls silent.

'You!' says Adrian leaning back in his chair to take a better look. 'But you're rather attractive . . . not the moose I expected at all.'

'Thank you,' smiles Charlie. 'You're more amusing than I had anticipated, as well.'

After about five minutes, Kate gets up to clear the plates. Adrian's pathetic attempt at eating is obviously all he can manage, and instead of leaving his salad in front of him, Kate elects to tidy up quickly, sweeping the evidence of his drunkenness away. Next up is some organic lamb with couscous and chickpea and mint salsa. While Kate serves and collects her compliments, Alex fills up Claire's glass and asks her again about where she was earlier that evening. Sam fills his own glass to the brim and starts to drain it with a steely determination, while his wife rushes upstairs for the third time to check on the baby. Tim starts to engage Charlie again about the marvellousness of his novel when Adrian leans over.

'Little boys' room,' he announces with a wink before walking out of the kitchen, hitting his shoulder on the door frame as he goes.

Kate's lamb is a triumph, and everyone agrees, although Claire and Adrian hardly touch theirs. Claire because she is too busy drinking, smoking, laughing and resting her breasts on Kate's dining table, and Adrian because he never returns from the little boys' room.

After about half an hour, just before Kate's chocolate and almond tart with crème fraiche is served, a search party is sent out around the house. Claire and Alex disappear off to search the top floor together, while Kate does the front garden, Tim mans the kitchen, and Sam and Emma cover the master bedroom suite. But it's Charlie who finds him. Fast asleep, flat on his back, snoring and looking snug on one of the fat cream sofas in the sitting room.

The dinner carries valiantly on. The tart goes down a storm and Emma has seconds, which apparently is fine seeing as she's still breastfeeding. There is a move to sit soft, eat chocolate, drink coffee and liqueurs and get down to the nitty-gritty chats of the evening, but Adrian's snoring is relentless, and with Sting (unplugged) back on nearly full volume (and the plastic intercom right next to Emma's ear just in case) no one can really concentrate on what the other person is saying.

Emma and Sam are the first to leave, baby being used as a convenient and plausible excuse. Then Tim suggests that Claire and he leave. Exhausted by talking about himself all night, he is finding his partner's exclusive conversations with Alex mildly irritating. Kate and Alex see them off at the front door, one arm round each other as they wave. But as soon as the door is shut, she bursts into tears.

'Well that was a bloody unmitigated disaster,' she cries. The fat tears of the failed hostess fall down her hot flushed cheeks. 'All that effort.'

'No it wasn't,' says Charlie, rushing to her sister's side. 'It was great fun. I loved it.'

'Honestly, darling,' insists Alex from the sofa. 'You pulled it off very well.'

'No I didn't,' she sobs. 'No I didn't. I mean, look at him.' She throws her arm towards the snoring Adrian, still passed out like a plaice on her sofa. 'I mean *look*!' she says. 'That wasn't supposed to happen.'

'It couldn't matter less,' laughs Charlie, giving her sister a comforting kiss on the forehead.

'But you don't understand,' wails Kate.

'It's fine,' smiles Charlie, running hands through her pale blonde hair.

'But you don't understand,' repeats her sister.

'Understand what?'

'It's a nightmare,' she announces, her arms out by her sides, her face fuchsia with frustration and alcohol. 'I know you've been through your tragedy, Charlie, but that was over two years ago now.'

Charlie says nothing, but she takes a step back from her sister and looks at the floor.

'You have to get back into the saddle,' continues Kate without missing a beat. 'Otherwise, quite frankly, there will be no saddles available. And I should know because I have looked everywhere for you, and I mean *everywhere*. I have phoned everyone, asked everyone, gone through everyone's address books and phone books and email directories for you, and he –' She points at the bloater on the sofa – 'he was just about the only half-decent man I know left. There really is *no one else*!' She shrugs dramatically. 'It's all compromise from now on.'

'And Adrian wasn't?'

'Not for someone of your age,' she replies, standing at the foot of the stairs. 'You can't pick and choose like you used to, Charlie. Don't you realise? You really aren't a very attractive prospect any more.'

3

The next day Kate and Charlie agree to disagree. Her sister's hysterical and obviously drunken accusation that there was no man left alive who would have Charlie had shocked her to the core. It was not so much the ridiculousness of the statement that annoyed her, because Charlie knew men did like her and want her, but it was the fact that Kate, in her thoughtless pursuit of her sister's grand happy ending, had involved all her wretched little friends. The terrible sadness of her case had been discussed all over West London in concerned, worried and delighted tones. The hours they must have spent sifting through her personal life. The secrets Kate must have shared, the intimate stories she must have told, in order to keep them all interested. It was the mileage they had all obviously got out of her so-called tragically single situation while sitting around their dinner tables in corners of smart destination restaurants that really incensed her. Who were they to take pity on her? Who were they to feel sorry for her with their torpid office-bound lives? Their tedious pension schemes? And their terrible interior decorating problems?

But instead of really talking about it, instead of sitting down and having it out with each other, Charlie and Kate do what many families do: they are polite to each other, courteous in the extreme, and never mention exactly what is bothering them, brushing it tactfully under the increasingly lumpy carpet. Sensing that something might be in the air, Alex leaves early for work. He has an important Thursday morning meeting with a client, or so he announces, before running out of the house and down the street a full half-hour before Charlie even thinks about getting out of bed.

For the first half of the day the sisters hardly speak. They breakfast in near to complete silence, passing milk and butter like an old-fashioned couple who have lived together in embittered contentment for over fifty years. They avoid each other as much as they can. They each have long, languid showers at different times. And Charlie does a tour of the small, dank garden, taking a vital interest in some dying plants, while smoking three unnecessary cigarettes by way of a statement. Before either of them is left alone in the house with little to do except sigh a lot, or confront each other and smooth out their differences, Kate disappears off with her children, accompanying them with Peta to nursery. She mutters something about having a few appointments in town, and says she won't be back until around three o'clock.

The relief in the house is palpable; the building positively relaxes as Kate and her entourage march down the street. Left on her own, Charlie takes the time to unpack her things. Her trusted rucksack has been propped up in the corner for a couple of days now and really needs emptying and sorting out. Unpacking from the top, out come some of the most inappropriate African things – shorts, suncream, arnica, mosquito repellent, small T-shirt tops, kakois, or sarongs she'd bought and bartered for in various outposts on her travels. Normally quite adept at organising herself, preparing for long journeys in hostile environments, Charlie smiles as she lays these articles on her bed, remembering how she'd packed in such a hurried and horridly hungover state.

She had drained the last drop of vodka just as dawn was breaking over the Karen suburb of Nairobi. Failing even to make it to her rather poky bedroom, she'd passed out on a huge cream divan in the sitting room and woken up, flat on her stomach, dribbling into the upholstery with her fingertips dragging along the red cement floor. Opposite her, across the smouldering cigarette butts and gently spinning bottles, snoring like a right porker, was the beautiful Art. Known as Arthur to his mother, but Art to his mates, the handsome Adonis is six foot two inches of pure bronzed muscle and dark, lush, curly hair. Half South African, half English and pure bushman, Art is able to survive the most extreme and unpleasant of environments and is Charlie's best friend.

The only son of a plant pathologist, he grew up with his best mate, Jack, trawling around the wild plains, savannas and deserts of South Africa. Raised by parents in the same nomadic business, they imbibed a love and in-depth knowledge of their surroundings. They spent their childhoods on camping holidays in the Transvaal and the Kruger, eventually working as teenage tour guides in the Karoo. They were so close growing up together with almost no one else around to distract them from each other, people often mistook them for brothers. It was inevitable that they would decide to work together as adults. They teamed up as a devilishly handsome journalistic duo – Jack doing the writing, and Art supplying the photographs.

Charlie met them both when she was covering the evacuation of UN staff from Southern Baidoa, after some warlord high on quat had gone on a bloodletting spree. They strode into the aid workers' camp she was staying in and asked for accommodation. She remembers being struck dumb by their gorgeousness. Tall, tanned hunks with wide, kind smiles, dark, curly hair and thighs of steel are a rarity anywhere, but especially out in the journalist field, where the normal fodder is overweight hacks with alcohol problems and ex-wives drained dry of adrenalin. As luck would have it, the camp was full, so Charlie, on a whim, decided to offer them to share her storeroom. They accepted, paid her in whisky, and the three of them became the best of friends.

They travelled from hot spot to hot spot together, from Somalia to the Southern Sudan, from Rwanda to Zaire, Mozambique to Zimbabwe, but never in competition, always as allies. They helped each other, nursed each other through malaria, dysentery and the most evil hangovers. They carried each other's equipment, shared facts and jokes and dodgy bug-ridden bunk beds. They reported on gun battles and got high on marijuana. They downed bottles of cheap whisky and shared packets of Sportsmen cigarettes.

They all went to spend Christmas together in Lamu in the north of Kenya and that's when the love affair began. They'd been to a party at Peponi, the glamorous beachfront hotel famed for its fun and decadence and alcoholic Old Pal cocktails. Jack and Charlie, after a few tumblers too many, decided to take a midnight walk along the never-ending beach. They kissed under the moon, made love in the surf and then, of course, everything changed. They talked of living together and eventually of marriage. They talked of conquering the world together as a wonderful, unassailable team. They talked of travelling forever. They talked of being different and special and fated always to be together. Amazingly, Art didn't mind. In fact, Art was pleased. His two best friends together. What could be more perfect?

But then he and Jack went to Angola to photograph 'The Mutilados' in a small southern armpit of a town for a worthy American magazine. Jack trod on a landmine and came back in a black plastic bag. It was ironic really, because he'd been shouting at his mate all day to look where he was going, to be careful where he stood when he took his photographs of legless and armless children. 'This is one of the most mined countries in the world,' he'd kept on saying. They'd been laughing and joking one minute, and then Jack had walked

66

round a tree to take a leak. The mine took both his legs off instantly. His death was quick. That was the only consolation they could find as the two of them sat in the dark drinking litres of bourbon to dull the pain. That was two and half years ago and Charlie is much more positive now. She and Art still remain the best of friends. They live around the corner from each other in Karen, in Nairobi. His house, a web of cables and computers and sweet-smelling dark room chemicals, is the drop-off point for passing photographer pals. Despite its aroma of dank socks, it's always more organised and together than hers.

Charlie's house is empty-fridge chaos, with plenty of vodka but not a slice of toast in sight. She half-heartedly rents a room from an aristo-heiress, Sophia, who has houses in London and Italy and can't really work out where to be at any one time. But Sophia gives great parties. And when she entertains, half of Nairobi turns up. The night before Charlie left on her extended holiday, Art came round with half of Kenyan society to see her off. How long would she be away? She couldn't say. But she had been saying she needed a break for a while and she had a good excuse to go home. She was still paying rent to Sophia – everyone knew she would be back. So Art and Charlie and the group of hippies and hacks, junkies, liggers, artists, artisans and the beautifully connected, drank and joked and laughed all night and Art, in a fit of alcohol-induced generosity, promised to drive his 'best friend in the whole wide world' to the airport the next day. That was just before he too passed out, dressed only in his white linen karate trousers. Horizontal in the old wood and wicker colonial chair with its two long plank arms supporting his legs, he had looked desperately uncomfortable. But Art is like an animal, he can sleep absolutely anywhere.

She'd packed, chatting and distracted, feeling dreadful with a fat furry tongue and room spin, and now she is paying the price. For as Charlie lays out all the items randomly shoved into her rucksack, she realises she really has nothing to wear at all.

'Art, Art, Art,' she mutters as she hauls out another bikini with a gusset full of golden sand. 'I blame you for all this.' She smiles, thinking of the mad dash to the airport, the hurried goodbye at Customs and the rash promise to send anything on that she might need. 'At least Kate will be pleased,' she says to no one in particular. 'This means a whole new retail opportunity.'

With her meagre possessions unpacked and folded into an old-fashioned pine chest of drawers with turned handles that must have mistakenly slipped through the modernist net, Charlie is at a loss what to do. Sitting on her bed she unclicks her silver case and checks to see if her cameras are still there. Her Leica M6, Nikon F3, and Nikon Dl plus her Contax T2 with her 50ml, 28ml and 110ml lenses are all encased in their grey protective foam. She slowly runs her fingers over the steel frames and long, cold lenses, feeling kind of naked without them round her neck. They have swung between her bosom almost every day for nearly half a decade and it feels uncomfortable, too light, not having them there. She thinks about ringing up a couple of picture-desk editors and photographic agencies she works for to tell them she's in town. They might give her a job? Something to do? But she hasn't got the energy or enthusiasm to face them. She needs to be feeling strong and on form for such upbeat boyish banter, and her sister has annoyed her and wrong-footed her and made her doubt herself. She closes the box and, running her fingers through her hair, walks slowly downstairs.

Instead of being constructive, organising meetings or anything at all useful, Charlie takes the opportunity to wander around. Half nosily interested in her sister's things, half self-conscious in these unfamiliar surroundings, Charlie sorts and pokes through the kitchen cupboards for anything that might prove mildly diverting.

After ten half-hearted minutes of opening and shutting, the only secrets that Kate's stainless steel-covered doors reveal is that not all her provisions are organic. Behind all the tins of happy vegetables, pots of well-adjusted jams and bottles of virgin oils she finds a couple of tins of deviant-looking sweetcorn and a dusty, cancerous-looking flat package of ready-made, heat-in-the-tin, steak and kidney pie. Tickled by her discovery, Charlie sets about a quick riffle through the unit drawers that are either side of the six-hobbed cooker. They prove initially to be a whole lot less entertaining, containing lacklustre items such as balls of string, Sellotape, rubber bottle stoppers and a couple of packets of photographs.

Sitting down at the table in her white T-shirt and red and black kakois, Charlie helps herself to a cup of coffee and flicks through the snaps. The first set is of Kate and the children. Kate on a tropical beach in big, black bathing suit, holding up a very small Ben by the arms as if trying to teach him to walk. Kate and Ben sitting together on a large white fluffy hotel towel, looking rather sweet. There's Kate again, in the sea this time, plus one small naked white child in virulent orange armbands, bawling its head off as it runs out of the water. There's another of Alex, looking thin, hairless and luminous white, in yellow Bermuda shorts with bright pink shoulders and a turquoise pork-pie hat, standing in the surf, a son in either hand. Classic family photos, thinks Charlie, as she flicks and sips her coffee at the same time. Smiling at the scenes, she is mildly amused at their amateur framing, the lack of focus, the glare, flare, over-exposure and general burning of the film, and the possible use of old processing chemicals in the lab.

She hopes the second packet proves to be more interesting. The setting is a party, a black-tie event, and everyone looks really rather drunk. Including the person who is taking the photographs: plenty of heads are missing, there are some feet shots, and red-eye abounds. There's Kate looking slim and pretty in a sleek red dress. Wearing a heavy layer of make-up, she looks older and very sophisticated indeed. Alex is dolled up in his black tie and appears a lot more presentable than he was on the beach. His hair is a touch too long, but he looks rakish and really quite handsome. Best friend Claire is there, her smooth blonde hair looking a bit more flicked and wild. She is in a skintight black dress split so high at the front that in some shots you can see her knickers. There are a few shots of Tim with a ponytail in a black shirt and black tie with his arm possessively around Claire as they pose by a table, sitting down at dinner and then, later, hamming it up on the dance floor.

But it is one particular headless shot that catches Charlie's eye. It is of Claire and Tim and Alex – she can tell that by the clothes they are wearing – and in it Claire and Alex are holding hands. Not that there is anything wrong with holding hands, but there is something in the way that they are holding hands, tightly, together, two at a time that makes Charlie look again. They look intimate; they look as if they wish Tim wasn't there. She flicks back through the party packet and takes another look. In the threesome shots, obviously taken by Kate, Claire and Alex are standing together, sometimes cheek to cheek, but always with his arm tight around her waist, while Tim stands stiff, on the other side of her, his arm across her shoulders like a brother, father or benevolent uncle rather than the lover he is supposed to be. Maybe she is reading too much into this, thinks Charlie as she looks again. Maybe they are all just great friends. But there is something about the holding hands shot that makes her feel sick.

She puts the photographs away. Alex and Claire were very friendly last night, she remembers, lighting up a cigarette. In cahoots, giggling and laughing together, they had, if she thinks about it, actually been quite irritating. But someone as glamorous as Claire would never look at someone like Alex. For as long as Charlie has known him, Alex has been an uptight, tight-lipped, tight-buttocked, City boy who rarely lets his hair down. Even when drunk, his conversational banter only extends as far as cricket and geography. Although certainly bright, he has one of those well-sprung, analytical brains that is brilliant with figures but unamused by fiction. However, as Charlie knows, having twice lost Trivial Pursuit against him, he is as competitive as hell and his poker face belies what is really going on behind those myopically pale blue eyes of his. A proficient father, easily capable of bathtime ducks and chats after work, he doesn't seem to have wholeheartedly embraced the New You-New Dad thing that Charlie has read endlessly about. But then what does she know? She has only met him a few times. Kate has always said that Charlie doesn't know him at all. She even once intimated, when drunk and slurring on the sofa, that half of Alex's talent lay in his underpants. 'Donkeys don't even come close!' she boasted. Much to Charlie's surprise.

But a City boy and father of two wouldn't exactly blend in with Claire's well-honed image of a girl-about-town with friends in high places and a freebie goodie-bag permanently dangling off her shoulder. Gifted or not in the manhood department, what could this man's appeal be for a girl like that? Nothing. Trophy shag Tim is much more her style. Known enough in those tricky, intellectual circles, Tim also travels well in the lighter, triter satellites due to his rave and New Lad-Lit credentials. Anyway, she and Kate are best friends. It is ridiculous. If there is any notion of sisterhood left, the idea is preposterous and damned well destructive. Is she looking for holes in her younger sister's relationship because she is jealous of it? Jealous of the stability she has created for herself and jealous of the family she has? Charlie snorts out loud at such an idea.

Sitting smoking at the kitchen table, listening to the ticking of the huge wall clock, she suddenly decides to pick her big leather handbag up off the floor and, rattling through it, hauls out her address book. It is a large, red, mock-crock Filofax affair, stuffed with wads of visiting cards and curling Post-its that bulk it out to the size of a bonk-buster bestseller. Rusting fastener unpopped, it bursts open on the table, spilling some beige cards boasting ornately of self-important officialdom across the table. Leafing through coloured pages covered in bleached, crossed-out and almost indecipherable scrawl, she runs her fingers down the telephone numbers of long-forgotten friends. Some have a whole collection of numbers by their names, indicating their progress through life from flat to house, from job to job, from lover to lover. Charlie hardly knows which are the correct numbers to call any more. There are some that are more reliable, or whose life is no longer in a state of flux. Her godmother, for example, is still in the same place after all these years. Other numbers are well and truly dead. Or at least their owners are.

Halfway down a relatively clear pink page, she comes across her old friend Alice. Alice. She smiles. Hard-working, naughty, cynical, chain-smoking Alice. She is exactly the sort of person who Charlie would dearly love to see. A photographer's agent who runs her own small firm in Soho, she was the first person to take Charlie on straight after Southampton University, where she'd studied English and Philosophy and nothing to do with photography at all. Alice had generously looked through Charlie's amateur snaps – a couple of black and white shots of old women in Greece, a lucky close-up of a luminous student's face poking through graffitied cement when the Berlin Wall came down. Alice liked what she had done enough to offer to get her work photographing models, a couple of actors and a clown convention in East London. She also liked her enough to fire her 'for her own good' and tell her to 'piss off to Africa or Russia or somewhere like that and do something interesting'. So she did, and they had sporadically kept in touch. Charlie had emailed a couple of shots that she had been particularly proud of, and they'd exchanged Christmas cards and the odd drunken late-night phone call. Yes, she smiles, picking up the telephone, Alice is exactly the person I would like to see.

'Hello, Alice Fraser Associates?' comes the efficient and brusque reply after one ring.

'Alice? Hi, it's Charlie,' she says, grinning broadly on her own in the kitchen.

'Charlie?'

'Yeah, Charlie Adams.'

'Oh my God, Charlie!' replies Alice. Her enthusiasm is such that she degenerates into a hacking mass of phlegm at the other end of the line.

'Christ, are you OK?' asks Charlie, buoyed up by her response but rather concerned just the same.

'What? Oh, don't be silly,' continues Alice, totally under-whelmed and undeterred. 'Just a by-product of some rather nasty flu and a heavy night out last night.'

'Glad to hear you haven't changed,' laughs Charlie.

'What me?' hacks Alice again. 'Don't be silly. Anyway,' she adds, inhaling heavily down the line, 'don't tell me you're in London, because, if I'm not mistaken, I certainly can't hear one of those shitty echoes down a crap inter-national line.'

'I am in London,' announces Charlie triumphantly. 'And I was wondering if you were free for lunch.'

'Free for lunch? Of course I'm free for lunch. I am always free for lunch if I want to be, I own the company, I can do what I like!' she laughs, and then adds, 'Hang on one sec.'

Charlie can hear her thin hand cupping the receiver, trying to muffle her end. 'Gavin, Gavin,' her voice mumbles through. 'Do I have a lunch today?' Charlie can't hear his response. 'Cancel it,' she says before returning to full volume. 'Got rid of whoever it was,' she says. 'Boring little twat anyway. So, where do you want to go?'

'Don't ask me questions like that,' laughs Charlie. 'I haven't set foot in this town in five years. All the places I know have probably closed down, or are now embarrassing to be seen in. Not that I ever knew where to go when I was here before.'

'All right, all right,' dismisses Alice. 'I'll bloody choose. Come to my office for one and we'll go somewhere round the corner from here. See you later,' she coughs. 'I can't wait.'

'Neither can I,' says Charlie, pressing the button on the walkabout phone and extinguishing her cigarette in her cold cup of coffee.

Speaking to Alice has put her in a much better mood. She was beginning to feel quite alone in this cold, wet and unfriendly town where everyone talks about designers she has never heard of, children she hasn't got, and recipes she can't be bothered to cook. The idea of having a long lunch with Alice is a deliciously wicked alternative.

Back upstairs in the white room, she goes through her drawers in the vain hope that her fashion options might have altered since she unpacked, but it's still the same old tat. Putting on the old dark-blue jeans and mothball jumper she wore yesterday, she sets off out of the house and up the street, looking for the tube. By the time she reaches the Uxbridge Road, laziness and drizzle get the better of her and she collapses into the back of a cab and asks for Soho.

Arriving at Shaftesbury Avenue a little too early for lunch, she asks the cab to stop so she can wander up Wardour Street towards Alice's office. She gets out by the Queen's Theatre.

It's nearing lunchtime on a Thursday and the place is busy. Charlie walks slowly, taking it all in with a wide smile.

The traffic is at a standstill, filling the road with its stagnant exhaust. Thin girls in black suits look for a place to light-lunch. Pushy blokes on mobiles shout instructions down the phone. Tense young men wearing long leather coats weave up and down in their walking boots, clutching jiffy bags of video tapes close to their chests. On the corner of Old Compton Street, the atmosphere is more languid. Men with close-cropped hair and multiple piercings chat or sit in neat rows in steamed-up café windows, checking out the talent as it parades past.

It takes Charlie a full ten minutes of excited and engaged strolling before she arrives at Alice's office in a cul-de-sac off Wardour Street. Alice is standing in the window, backlit by a standard lamp on her desk, smoking and gesticulating down the telephone. She waves as Charlie approaches and points with a sharp long finger towards a shiny black front door. Gavin presses the buzzer to let her in. Slim, sexy and young as Alice likes her men, he is dressed in a black polo neck and jeans, with a surprisingly plump backside as last seen on Michelangelo's David. He presses one finger to his lips, points her in the direction of a red office sofa and makes a coffee-drinking gesture.

'No thanks,' Charlie mouths back, before perching on the corner of the sofa and smiling at her friend.

'Yup . . . yup . . . yup . . . mmm . . . yes, well . . . no,' says Alice down the telephone, mouthing 'sorry' with her scarlet lips before sucking on her cigarette again.

Matt black and chrome and in need of some refurbishment, Alice's office is covered in huge black and white framed photographs, either given to her by her clients or reproduced at her request. Some of the images are automatically familiar, having graced the covers of numerous magazines. Others are striking images of beautiful women in obscure poses, phallic cars from various ad campaigns, and a close-up of a perfume bottle between a cleavage – shot in the name of art. And just in case the work of the agency isn't obvious enough to all who enter, there are row upon row of framed magazine covers and spreads in a wall of tribute behind Gavin's desk.

'Now, look,' says Alice suddenly in a sharp voice that Charlie has never heard before. 'This really won't do. I mean, Jesus Christ, how much work do we have to do before you pay us on time? I've had enough of your inefficiency. I've had enough of your empty promises and, quite frankly, I've had enough of your shitty little magazine. I want a cheque biked over here this afternoon, for the full amount, otherwise I shall start charging you interest and I am never doing business with you again. Is that understood?' She pauses. 'Well, good. Good day to you too.' She slams the phone down and jabs her cigarette into an ashtray so full that butts tumble and spill on to the surrounding desk. Alice doesn't seem to notice. 'Cunt,' she exclaims with both hands splayed dramatically in the air. 'Don't you just hate wankers who don't pay on time? Anyway . . . bloody hell, don't you look good?' She grins and walks over, puckering up her lips and planting two red circles either side of Charlie's face. 'You look fabulous,' she continues, rubbing the two red circles off Charlie's cheeks as if she were a small child. 'Brown, blonde, slim and sexy – living abroad obviously suits you. Don't you think, Gavin? Don't you think? Don't you think my friend is sexy? Poor Gavin,' she whispers loud enough for him to hear. 'Poor Gavin – hasn't been laid in weeks. I'm introducing him to all my sexually frustrated girlfriends for a bit of Mrs Robinson action, but he's having none of it. *Gavin*,' she says loudly.

'What?'

'Are you sure you're not gay?'

'No,' comes his jaded reply. Gavin has obviously been

asked this question so many times that he has ceased to pretend to find it amusing.

'He's lying,' smiles Alice as she turns round and picks a black floor-length cashmere coat off the hatstand behind the door. 'He's far too handsome to be straight.'

Alice Fraser is of the school of thought that if, by any chance, you find a 'look' that suits you, you should stick to it no matter the fashion. It is just unfortunate that Alice found her 'look' *circa* 1988. Combining black with black on black, plus golden accessories and a virulent red lipstick, she was once nicknamed the Magenta de Vine of photography and hasn't changed her image since. With sharp, shiny, bobbed hair the colour of mahogany and pale skin that does not respond well to natural light, she has delicate, pretty features that look slightly oriental. Her dark eyes turn up at the corners, as does her perma-red mouth, and there is a feline essence to her movement that a lot of men find momentarily irresistible.

''Bye,' she says, giving Gavin a little wave from behind the door. 'Be good.' Gavin rolls his eyes. 'Any problems, I'm on the mobile.'

'Yes, yes, yes,' he says. 'Have a nice lunch. See you later,' he smiles. 'Or maybe not.'

Alice links arms with Charlie as they walk out into the rain.

'Yuk,' says Alice as she hunches her shoulders. 'Don't you just hate the bloody rain in England? It's so damned boring. Now,' she continues, not waiting for Charlie to reply, 'are you hungry?'

'Quite,' says Charlie.

'Marvellous,' replies Alice. 'So am I. Let's go to this new place that has just opened up on Shaftesbury Avenue. If that's okay?'

'Sounds perfect.'

A few briskly walked minutes later they are installed either side of a white linen tablecloth, divided by a urine sample bottle containing a lonely white orchid, and staring at menus over a yard long. The destination place is light and airy, with plenty of green plants and an unwaxed wooden floor. All the tables are occupied by young, affluent-looking people, half of whom look as though they should be famous. The noise level is high and the pitch distinctly baritone. The air smells of truffles, garlic, and all things Mediterranean.

Alice has obviously been here a few times and is developing the reputation of a regular. The head waiter comes over and is obsequious and subservient as she orders a bottle of fizzy water and, after a second's hesitation, a bottle of 'something nice and dry and white'.

'I tend to have the pumpkin soup with a drizzle of truffle oil and the risotto of the day,' says Alice by way of serving suggestion.

'There's a hell of choice,' exhales Charlie, looking at her yard of dishes. She gives up and picks through her leather bag, searching for cigarettes.

'Must be a bit daunting, actually,' suggests Alice, flicking her inch-long ash on to the tablecloth next to the ashtray. 'I had a photographer once who spent a lot of time in Russia. It sent him really quite mad. It was a long time ago, mind you, when they had nothing over there expect for borscht and vodka and the odd bit of salted fish. But when he got back, he couldn't cope with the bright lights, big city aspect of London. You know, all the greed and retail. He left the country immediately and had to sit on a beach in Thailand for a month to recuperate. Poor bloke. But it worked out in the end, you know, because once he got back he was clubbing and taking drugs like the rest of them.'

'It is a bit of a culture shock if I'm honest,' admits Charlie, taking a large slug of chilled wine. 'So many things have changed. Especially my friends. Well, actually I haven't seen many of them yet. But my sister has changed an awful lot.'

'What, older, wiser and a lot more boring?'

'Yeah.'

'Tell me about it,' laughs Alice. 'No one wants to go out on the razzle any more. They can't cope with the hangover. They've got too much work to do. Too many deals to make. Honestly. There was a time when Thursday night was the new Friday, and now staying in is the new going out.'

'Yeah,' nods Charlie, inhaling on her cigarette not following exactly what her friend is saying but agreeing entirely with the sentiment.

'Cookery is the new pornography.'

'Yes!' says Charlie pointing her finger in agreement.

'Domesticity is the new rebellion.'

'Yes!'

'Interior design is the new pop art.'

'Yes?' says Charlie, slightly less convinced by this idea.

'Talking of which,' says Alice, leaning over to have a look in her very expensive black Prada handbag with a thick shiny metal handle, 'which do you prefer?' she asks, taking out a piece of paper and handing it over to Charlie.

'What, art?' says Charlie without looking down.

'No, beds,' says Alice, blowing a cloud of smoke through her red ring of a mouth.

'Oh,' smiles Charlie, her heart sinking. 'How interesting.'

Alice, or so she explains, is doing up her flat. It's quite a modest place on Regents Park Road in Primrose Hill, or so she says. Charlie has never been there. Theirs is the sort of friendship that takes place in bars, restaurants and at other people's parties. Alice has never given a party in her life, yet she is a regular at everyone else's and always the last to leave. Anyway, her business is doing better, she has signed an extremely hot new photographer who they can't seem to get enough of at *Vanity Fair*, and she has decided that a bit of a flat revamp was the least she owed herself for all her hard work.

So all her weekends are spent in Heals, Conran, Habitat, and a shop called Purvis Purvis on the Tottenham Court Road. However, unlike Kate with her Post-it reminders of other people's good-taste decisions, if Alice does anything, she does it well. She will investigate the ramifications of every choice she makes before actually doing it. She will also manage to find *the* person who everyone wants, and become their friend. Either that or she will discover someone, give them a little helping hand and create a star. She has done it time and time again with photographers: pushed someone in a direction that they had never thought of, helped them discover a talent they never knew they had. As a result, Alice now has an in-depth knowledge of paint finishes and the mobile number of a decorator called Penelope, who apparently is the woman to know.

'God, when I told my friend at *Wallpaper** magazine about Penelope, she said they'd be interested in doing an At Home piece when it was all finished. Wouldn't that be fab?' she smiles, taking a sip of Sicilian white. 'I have always rather fancied myself doing an At Home.'

'I thought you thought they were ghastly,' says Charlie, a little perplexed by this statement.

'No-o-o,' says Alice, taking the smallest spoonful of her pumpkin and truffle soup. 'At least, not in such a fab mag as *Wallpaper**.'

'You can't win this one,' smiles Charlie. 'You forbade me to do an At Home shoot a long time ago, saying, and I quote, "They are the reason why third-rate celebrities exist, and why would you want to propagate their uselessness".'

'Ah,' replies Alice. 'Did I really say that?'

'Yes.'

'Oh, um, well, maybe, from a photographic point of view, they are certainly a bad thing. Not very good for the career. Particularly if you're planning to make a living out of war and reportage, you should try and avoid Pasty Palmer and Darren Day at home. But for me, they're fine and marvellous. Anyway, Elaine at the Out There Agency, will be so jealous.' She shrugs and lights another Benson and Hedges.

'So you're doing all this to make Elaine at the Out There Agency jealous?'

'No, not really,' smiles Alice. 'But it would be nice if I pissed her off in the process. And got a nice house and some snaps for the album into the bargain.'

'You're terrible.'

'I know,' smiles Alice, wrinkling her nose. 'But isn't it fun?'

Alice and Charlie sit and move their porcini risottos around their white bowls. Their conversation flows along with their wine. They gossip about who is doing what, and where. They chat about the best places to work, the best payers and the peaks and troughs of other people's careers. A bloke called Nick Worth who won loads of awards last year is now on his uppers. He became arrogant, he showed off and everyone got bored of him and his fabulousness and now he can't get any work. Andrew Edwards, one of Charlie's greatest rivals, is unfortunately doing exceptionally well, having just had the cover of *Time* and *Newsweek* simultaneously. Alice is thinking of trying to poach him from the agency he has been with for years, and Charlie is trying to be diplomatic.

'But you don't do reportage,' she says. 'You do advatorial, commercials, album covers, glossy magazine shoots, that sort of thing. You wouldn't know a hard news story if it blew up in your own stationery cupboard.'

'I could learn,' Alice whines. 'I could expand my horizons.'

'But you never wanted to do that with me when I suggested it what, five or six years ago.'

'Well, that was different.'

'Why?'

'Because . . .'

'Why?'

'Just because.'

'Because, I'm female?'

'Well, yes.' Alice smiles, looking rather sheepish.

'*Oh no*,' says Charlie loudly before leaning back into her pale tan leather-backed chair in mock shock. 'Don't tell me you fancy him?'

'Only a little bit,' admits Alice, putting her two index fingers together in front of her nose about a centimetre apart.

'Liar!'

'OK, a lot,' confesses Alice, her forehead flopping on to the table as she resigns herself to her defeat. Her shiny dark hair swings across her face like a luxurious pair of stage curtains.

'Alice Fraser,' says Charlie, sounding like she is about to scold a child. 'You naughty thing.'

'Oh God, I met him at this newspaper do the other day at the Grosvenor House and I thought he was drop-dead gorgeous.'

'He is certainly that,' says Charlie. 'But he is a total tosser. He has broken more hearts than I have had cold suppers in the Bush.'

'I know, so everyone tells me,' she says, her mouth curling into a sad smile. 'But I rather thought that if I poached him, and impressed him, and was slightly like his boss, I might get him that way. Lure him into bed with my business brains and acumen.'

'That is one of the saddest things I have ever heard,' laughs Charlie.

'I know, isn't it?' says Alice. 'I don't know . . . it's just

a fantasy that keeps me going on a wet Thursday afternoon.'

'But of all the people to choose.'

'I know.'

'And anyway, might I say . . . I don't think getting him into
bed is a problem. I think keeping him out of everyone else's
while he's supposedly being faithful to you is the really tricky
thing. I mean, quite apart from all the women's hearts he has
broken in this country, and I can vouch for a whole load more
because I personally have had them crying on my shoulder in
various bars all over East Africa, I think he has something like
four illegitimate children around the world.'

'It's only two.'

'Two what?'

'Children.'

'Well two illegitimate children, then. Who he never sees,
of course.'

'One's in the Lebanon and the other's in Haiti. It must be
quite hard.'

'Don't tell me you know their names as well, because I will
have to leave the table right now,' laughs Charlie as she stubs
out a cigarette.

'I'm not that bad,' smiles Alice. 'But I know they're both
boys.'

'Oh God, I don't know, *really*,' laughs Charlie again.

'I'm just sad.'

'Yup,' agrees Charlie. 'You are very, very sad.'

'Talking of which, how are you after all that Jack stuff?'
asks Alice, leaning in, looking serious.

Charlie, sits back sharply, not expecting the question. She
runs her hands through her bleached blonde hair and lets out
an enormous, long sigh that appears to make her shrink in
size. 'It's just one of those things, isn't it?' she says stoically,
breathing heavily through her nose, digging her fingernails

into the palms of both her hands. Her eyes sting with a thousand hot needles as she holds back the tears. She is not normally this emotional, but the alcohol and the directness of the question have wrong-footed her. 'Life is very cheap out there,' she smiles, buying some time. 'There isn't really that much to say. He died doing what he loved, with someone he loved. There aren't many people you can say that about.' She repeats the line she has used over and over again when asked such private and probing questions out of the blue.

'Yeah, but it must have hit you hard,' nods Alice. 'You were going to marry him, weren't you?'

'We'd talked about it,' replies Charlie in a quiet voice, looking down at her brown hands. 'But Jack was very impulsive, he was always changing his mind. He wanted a wedding on the beach in Lamu. He wanted one in the Bush, then in South Africa with loads of friends. He once suggested we ran away and did it somewhere totally stupid, underwater, off Tanzania. I never had a ring and we never set a date, so I suppose in the eyes of someone like my mother, we were never really engaged.' She smiles again and takes a sip of wine.

'Mm,' says Alice. 'Well I think he sounds wonderful – sorry, sounded wonderful,' she corrects herself, somewhat embarrassed.

'Don't worry, Art and I are always talking about Jack in the present tense,' says Charlie. 'It's sometimes very hard to think that someone who was that full of life is dead. I don't really think he is. Art and I always think that he is all around us. I often find myself asking him questions, asking him his advice and straining to hear the response . . .'

'His mate's quite dishy, isn't he?' smiles Alice, trying to lighten the tone.

'Very.' Charlie smiles back, shifting in her seat with relief, understanding exactly what her friend is doing. 'In fact, he would do for you,' she nods, batting the suggestion over like a tennis ball.

'No-o-o,' replies Alice, sending it back.

'Why not? He's a photographer,' says Charlie, laying her hands out, palms up, as if offering Art up as a tasty platter.

'He lives in Kenya, what's the use in that?' moans Alice.

'Ah, I'm afraid you have a point there,' confirms Charlie, emptying the bottle of wine into her friend's glass.

'Shall we get another one of those?' suggests Alice, raising her rather finely plucked eyebrows.

'I'm not sure . . .'

'Why not?'

'OK. Why not indeed?' shrugs Charlie, slouching into her leather-backed seat.

She isn't in a rush to get back to Shepherd's Bush. Awaiting her is a judgemental sister, two mewing and spewing kids and a scrawny and unfaithful husband. Not that she knows for sure that he is unfaithful. She doesn't have any evidence to bandy around when she is casting her aspersions, just some photographs of a good night out had by all. But there is something in the way they related to each other last night, the giggles and whispers. She didn't even say thank you when he gave her a drink. Isn't that's a sure sign that they know each other very well? They even went upstairs together on their own. There was no reason whatsoever for that. And anyway, the camera never lies, they say. Well, she knows that's not entirely true, she is a bloody photographer after all. But there is something about the way the two of them acted together at that party that sends shivers down her spine.

'What do you do when you suspect someone is having an affair?' asks Charlie, not really meaning to ask the question out loud.

'Oh Lord,' shrugs Alice. 'Like I'm really the one to ask,' she says sarcastically. 'I'm rubbish at relationships. I go for people like Andrew Edwards, the sort of man who should have a Government health warning tattooed on his forehead. "This man is seriously dangerous to your health." It would surely save us all the trouble of falling in love with them and then finding out. I think my longest relationship was a confidence-inspiring six months, and that's because the bloke lived in Paris and didn't see me that much.'

'Yeah, maybe you have a point,' smiles Charlie, pouring herself more wine and taking rather a large slug.

'You're serious, aren't you?' says Alice, leaning forward.

'I'm afraid so.'

'Anyone we know?' asks Alice, rubbing her hands together unconsciously, keen on finding out some new gossip.

'Well, not exactly.'

'Oh, go on,' she goads.

'I don't know,' says Charlie, suddenly feeling some loyalty towards her sister.

'I promise I won't say a word,' says Alice, dramatically crossing her pert breasts and zipping up her scarlet mouth.

'It's not so much that,' says Charlie shifting uncomfortably in her seat. 'It's just that I don't really have very much evidence.'

'Okay, okay,' says Alice, flapping her hands dismissively. 'What evidence have you got?'

'Photographs.'

'Aha,' she says, sounding slightly the worse for her bottle-and-a-bit of wine. 'The camera never lies.'

'Well, both you and I know that that's not true. Look at all the model photos on the walls of your office. Airbrushing, lighting, angles – you can change anything.'

'Yes, yes,' nods Alice. 'But what have you got. Full coitus?'

'No.'

'Fondling breasts?'

'No.'

4

Alice and Charlie finish their lunch at about four o'clock and Alice suggests in a jovial and distinctly drunk fashion that she might take the rest of the day off. She declares that a shopping trip, rather than returning to the office to sexually harass poor Gavin, is certainly the more dignified of her two options. So under the influence of alcohol and her friend, Charlie's American Express card, which she normally saves to get her out of tight spots in foreign climes, goes on to take the sort of battering last seen on New Year's Eve three years ago in a South African nightclub with Jack and Art.

She and Alice teeter and trip their way around Liberty, randomly pulling out black outfits and forcing each other to try them on. Alice wafts up and down the dark wood and carpeted area outside the changing rooms in a couple of floaty numbers that, she announces, make her feel like Cathy in *Wuthering Heights* – all dramatic and vulnerable and overemotional at the same time. Charlie finds a couple of pairs of smart trousers, some useful shirts, one lovely snug cashmere jumper and a sharp tailored couture frock that makes her feel like a Hollywood movie star *circa* 1955. She tries it on in purple, but Alice makes such a face that she is eventually forced to buy it in black instead. So much more useful, her drunken friend insists, lolling on the counter, a turquoise silk Chanel headscarf pulled tightly around her cheeks.

'You can wear it at the awards,' says Alice as she plants

another red circle on Charlie's cheek, slamming the cab door. 'See you next week,' she waves, before bending down unsteadily to pick up her own, rather heavier, shopping bags.

By the time Charlie finally makes it home, it is dark and the two boys are already in the bath.

'Hi,' she says breezily, swinging her purple and gold bags as she walks in trying to assess the tension.

'Hi,' replies an equally breezy voice from the confines of the kitchen.

'Have you had a good day?' asks Charlie as she walks into the kitchen, dumping her spoils on the stainless steel topped table with an exaggerated, exhausted sigh.

'Actually I have,' replies Kate, looked rather flushed. 'Oh wow,' she says, clapping her hands in delight. 'Been shopping?'

'Yup, I'm afraid I have, and I'm really rather pissed,' grins Charlie. 'I've had what's known as a liquid lunch. A two-bottler to be precise.'

'A two bottler?' inhales Kate.

'Yup,' says Charlie breathing in deeply, trying to sound less under the influence.

'I'm afraid I had a flute too,' admits Kate, raising her eyebrows and putting her hand over her mouth at her own terrible naughtiness as she tries to bond with her sister. 'It was something of an emergency.'

'Right,' nods Charlie.

'No, really,' insists Kate. 'Not something I would normally ever do. What with the children.'

'Well,' says Charlie. 'Give or take a bottle, I guess, we are more or less evens,' she shrugs, scraping a chair across the limestone floor before slumping into it heavily.

'Let's have a look at your stuff,' asks Kate, rushing over to rattle through Charlie's bags. 'Wow, you must have spent a fortune.'

'It seems that way,' says Charlie. 'But I can always take them back.'

'Absolutely not,' says Kate, pulling out the snug cashmere jumper. 'This is wonderful . . . Oh, as is this dress,' she adds, pulling out the black evening dress. 'I bet you look fantastic in this, with your lovely brown boobs and great legs.'

'Maybe,' says Charlie. 'I don't think I have ever owned anything so glamorous, or indeed that expensive,' she says.

'Well, you deserve it.'

'Mm,' says Charlie, non-committal. 'So what did you do?'

'Well . . .' says Kate.

'May I?' asks Charlie, pulling out a cigarette.

'Sure,' replies Kate with an expansive shrug. She smiles. 'But only if I am allowed a little tiny puff.'

''Course,' says Charlie. 'You can have a whole fag if you want. I have packets and packets of the things upstairs. So tell me about your day.'

'Well I felt so rotten this morning,' she says, taking a cigarette out of Charlie's hand and sucking the end. 'I had a terrible hangover and I didn't sleep . . . sorry about last night, by the way.'

'Couldn't matter less,' smiles Charlie.

'I don't know what I was thinking . . .'

'You weren't.'

'No, you're right, I wasn't,' nods Kate, sucking the cigarette sodden before handing it back to her sister. 'Anyway,' she continues as Charlie hands the wet butt back, demonstrating that she'd really rather not, 'I went to yoga at the Life Centre after I dropped the children off.'

'Yoga?'

'Yeah, I know,' smiles Kate. 'You may look surprised but I did quite a lot when I was pregnant and never really have the time to do it now, but anyway, I went and met up with a girlfriend of mine, Anna, who is there quite often and who

I had half arranged to meet. We were pregnancy pals. I had dinner at her house once. Alex came and we never went again. Then, when the class finished at about twelve-thirty, we went to Kensington Place, next door. We had a glass of champagne and discussed our marriages . . . you know, that sort of thing.'

'Yeah?'

'Well, actually,' Kate leans in to whisper, wetting her lips. 'I don't think hers is going very well.'

'Right,' replies Charlie. 'In what way?'

'I don't know, to be honest. She wasn't that forthcoming, but I gather they don't really talk very much any more, and she thinks he might have got bored of her.'

'Oh, right.'

'I know, sad, isn't it? They haven't been married that long. Five years I think. She got pregnant on their honeymoon and we all know that's a famously bad thing to do.'

'So did you.'

'Not on the honeymoon itself.'

'But quite soon after.'

'I know, but it's the honeymoon, so they say, that matters.' says Kate, distractedly pulling up the sleeves of her jumper. 'They marry you and you get fat immediately. It's an old wives' tale, isn't it? On the other hand you would have thought that you were confirming their masculinity and being an earth mother. I mean, who the hell knows? Least of all men.' She laughs a dry laugh. 'You're lucky if they think about anything other than themselves and their enormous problems anyway.'

'Yes, well,' says Charlie. 'It all sounds like a load of bollocks to me.'

'You're quite right,' says Kate, running her hands through her hair. 'I'm sure it is.'

'So what else?'

94

'Oh God, we chatted about loads of other stuff, actually, it was excellent fun.'

'Great, so you're feeling much better, then?'

'Yes,' laughs Kate, stubbing her cigarette out on a side plate in the middle of the table.

'Shall we have a drink?' asks Charlie, hauling herself out of her chair and walking in the direction of the industrial-sized fridge.

'Good idea,' says Kate. 'Alex won't be back till quite late.'

'Really? Why not?' asks Charlie.

'A squash game, I think. It's a tournament at his club. He's been talking about it for ages. I just haven't really been listening,' she shrugs. 'So he's not back for dinner or anything.'

'Great,' says Charlie.

'Great?' asks Kate.

'I didn't mean it like that,' says Charlie quickly. 'It's just nice to have you all to myself.'

'That's sweet of you,' says Kate. 'Hurry up and get out the vodka before I get too sentimental.'

Kate and Charlie sit cross-legged on their chairs around the kitchen table drinking their vodka and sharing cigarettes. They order a Chinese take-away, at Charlie's dogmatic insistence, as she explains that she has had positively erotic dreams about the stuff while abroad.

'Oh my God, Peking Duck,' she drools as her sister tries to find the menu in the drawer next to the six-hobbed cooker. 'Prawn crackers, sesame toast, egg fried rice . . .' She slaps her palms on the table in a gastro-frenzy at the mention of each delicious dish. She moans and throws her head back, panting and laughing in mock ecstasy.

'Shut up, shut up,' smiles Kate. 'You're like bloody Meg Ryan in that bloody film.' She carries on looking through the drawers, pulling out a ball of string, a roll of Sellotape and two packets of photographs while searching for the menu. 'God, I can never find anything in here,' she moans. 'The kids are always going through this drawer looking for sweets.'

'Stir-fried veg, spring rolls, cashew nut chicken . . .' Charlie is rambling, overcompensating, trying to assuage her guilt at having nosed through her sister's drawers. 'When was the last time you had any of those fabulous things?' she asks.

'Obviously a bloody long time ago because I can't find the menu,' replies her sister. 'It's all so bad for you . . .'

'Sod that.'

'Aha,' she declares. 'Here's the damned thing.'

They order enough for a family of four, and smoke and drink some more while waiting for their food to arrive. Kate disappears upstairs for about twenty minutes to kiss her children goodnight before coming back down again with renewed enthusiasm for their girls' night in.

'So,' she says, taking a whole cigarette to herself this time and lighting it with the consummate ease of an erstwhile professional. 'Tell me about your day. Who did you see?'

Charlie talks her sister through her lunch with Alice, describing how Alice intends to tempt Andrew Edwards with her feistiness and seduce him with her accounting ability.

'God,' laughs Kate, taking a swig of vodka and tonic with a slice of lime. 'She sounds like some fiscal black widow. What will she do after she's finished with him? Report him to the Inland Revenue for insufficient deposits and dodgy receipts?'

'I know,' agrees Charlie. 'And the guy is such an arsehole. He's been unfaithful to every single woman he has ever slept with.'

'Really?' says Kate, taking a drag on her fag.

'Oh God, yes, every single one.'

'I hate that,' says Kate, shaking her head.

'I know,' agrees Charlie. 'And the terrible thing is that half the women who shack up with him don't know until it's too late.'

'Really?' says Kate, ostentatiously puffing her cheeks out as she exhales her cigarette. 'How awful.'

'Mm,' agrees Charlie.

'I mean, I'd like to know, wouldn't you?'

'Oh Lord, yes.'

'It is sort of one's female duty, you know, to tell someone, don't you think?' says Kate.

'Absolutely,' nods Charlie. She pauses and then asks in the lightest of tones, 'I mean, you'd want to know if Alex was being unfaithful, wouldn't you?'

'*Alex?*' Kate snorts a mouthful of vodka and tonic through her nose. The bubbles fizz up through her sinuses as she breaks down into a hysterical coughing fit. 'Alex?' she hacks and coughs, turning bright pink and snorting again before finally regaining her composure. 'I have no idea why that is so funny!' she laughs, popping a section of her dark hair behind her ear. 'It's just the idea of someone else finding his puny little body attractive. I have a feeling it's an acquired taste and I'm the only one with that affliction.'

'Yeah,' laughs Charlie heartily, shaking her shoulders rather too much.

'I don't think he even likes sex that much, bless him,' continues Kate. 'I think he expends any excess energy he's got on the squash court. But we've been together so long now . . . I don't expect these things matter that much any more.'

'Yeah,' nods Charlie pretending to agree as she stubs her cigarette out. 'Of course it doesn't. But you would like to know, though? If someone knew something?' She inhales deeply, puffing up her chest.

The telephone rings.

'Oh yeah, course I'd like to know,' says Kate, swatting the

question back with her hand as she gets up from the table and walks around the kitchen trying to find the portable telephone. Picking up a copy of the *Evening Standard*, she finally finds it. 'Not that he is, of course, anyway, so . . . Hello?' she says, running two conversations into one. 'Mum,' she adds. 'It's Mum,' she mouths to Charlie across the table. 'Yeah . . . Yeah . . . No . . . She's here . . . Of course . . . I'm sure she is . . . No, tomorrow. No, I did tell her, she's very keen to come down, of course she is . . . Why don't you ask her yourself? I'll hand you over. Wait there.' Kate covers the phone and whispers, 'F-u-c-k,' in a low, quiet voice. 'Charlie, I am so sorry,' she says. 'Mum has got this lunch for you tomorrow and I totally forgot to tell you. Please say that you know about it and you're looking forward to it. Fuck, fuck, fuck,' she repeats. 'I don't know what the hell I was thinking,' she says before handing the phone over.

'Mum!' says Charlie. 'I was just about to call you. How are you?'

'Very well, Charlotte darling, very well indeed,' comes the terse, tense and refinedly nasal Home Counties reply. 'Now, your father and I were wondering, are you gracing us with your presence tomorrow, or have we killed the fatted calf for nothing?'

'Of course I'm coming,' replies Charlie. 'I've been looking forward to it,' she lies. 'What time?'

'Just before lunch,' replies her mother, shouting slightly and speaking very slowly like she is communicating with someone who is hard of hearing.

'Kate is sweetly lending me her car,' says Charlie, smiling at her sister who nods and shrugs in response.

'Is she?' annunciates Mrs Adams. 'Are you sure you're insured for her car?'

'Yes,' lies Charlie, having no idea.

'Really? Are you sure? It's such a waste of money, darling,

coming by car. Why don't you take the train, use public transport, we pay for it after all … and then you can take a cab from the station, or if you're very lucky your father might come and collect you. Jim?' She calls, barely moving her mouth away from the telephone. 'Would you collect Charlotte from the London train?' There is some sort of murmured response that Charlie can't hear. 'Charlotte, darling, did you hear that?'

'Um, no.'

'Oh,' she replies, sounding surprised. 'Your father said that just so long as you come on the early train, he will collect you from the station.'

'Um, thank him for his generous offer,' says Charlie, grinning at her sister. 'But will you tell him not to worry as Kate is very insistent that I borrow the car.'

'Are you sure? Because I know what you young are like,' continues her mother. 'You won't be allowed to drink and drive. Unless of course you're planning to stay the night. Are you planning to stay the night?'

'Well, I haven't seen you in almost five years, so I rather thought that I might,' says Charlie.

'Oh,' replies her mother, sounding slightly wrong-footed. 'Jim?' she says again. 'Charlotte is saying that she might spend the night.' Her father mutters something again. 'Oh, your father says that's fine for you to spend the night.'

'Wonderful,' says Charlie, trying to sound enthusiastic. 'See you tomorrow then.'

'Don't be late, darling,' says her mother. 'I've invited the Scotts over for drinks at twelve-thirty.'

'Great, the Scotts,' replies Charlie loudly, as she glimpses her sister corpse out of the corner of her eye. 'Fine, I promise I won't be late, I'll see you tomorrow.'

'I can't believe you did that,' says Charlie after she puts down the phone.

'I can't believe you've arranged to stay the night,' replies Kate, wide-eyed with shock.

'If you think I can get through lunch sober, you have another think coming,' says Charlie, draining her glass.

The next day, Kate lends Charlie her car. It's a guilt thing, an attempt at currying favour for not passing on the message and giving her sister enough time to think up an excuse not to have to go home.

Not that Kate and Charlie hate their parents. They certainly don't. They love them very much. But going home to the new cottage in Surrey that Jim and Jennifer have bought on the outskirts of Cranford village, where Charlotte and Kate grew up, is just plain boring. For Jim and Jennifer appear to have limited interest in their daughters' progress through life, and rarely if ever ask them any questions. When the two sisters were a little younger – before the wedding, Africa and babies – they used to place bets with each other about how long it would take before either of them was asked a single question. One Christmas, they both got quite hysterical when – after two days of conversation about everyone else in the village, how well the garden was doing, and the enormousness of the parsnips Jim had managed to grow – their father finally asked Kate a question. It wasn't a difficult question. It was something along the lines of, 'So how's advertising?' But Kate spat her cold cut halfway across the polished dining room table and Charlie fired an arrow of snot out of each nostril and had to leave the room thinking she might actually pee. Then Jennifer lost her already diminutive sense of humour and tried to send both her daughters to their rooms. It was only when Kate pointed out that Charlie was actually thirty, and perhaps a bit too old for that sort of punishment, that their mother finally reneged and broke into a stiff, pink-coloured smile.

Not only is the conversation stilted at Rose Cottage, but

the atmosphere is icy, due to Jim and Jennifer's fundamental belief that the cold is good for you and central heating an invention of the working class. The hotter your house, so their theory goes, the lower down the social scale you are. Jim and Jennifer, having once owned the large house in the village and down-sized for their retirement, like to keep their pseudo-aristocratic roots on display by keeping their house the temperature of a cold box. If either one of their daughters complains, they have simply become suburban since leaving home.

Also, while Kate's cooking is a fat gourmet's wet dream, her mother's is their worst nightmare. With all the preparation and seasoning of a road kill, the dinner table at Jennifer's is attended under sufferance with a fistful of Rennies at hand. Influenced heavily by the radically minimal flavouring of the 1950s, infused with her own personal sense of parsimony and the inability to throw anything away, no matter how old, cold or inedible, her cuisine is enough to petrify the taste buds of even the most starving guest.

Her cold cuts pick-and-mix mélange lunch is probably the worst. No amount of Franglais can disguise its hideousness. Served usually on a Wednesday lunchtime, it will happily contain offcuts from Sunday's roast mixed with the dried peas from Monday's supper, plus a couple of carrots from Tuesday and three old, fluffy tomatoes rescued from the back of the pantry. The smorgasbord is usually served with tepid boiled potatoes and dollops of Heinz salad cream and tastes entirely of old fridge.

So to say that Charlie is excited about coming home as she draws into her parent's short tarmaced drive after her forty-five minute journey is a bit of an exaggeration. She parks up Kate's four-by-four – complete with a brace of baby seats as recommended by *Watchdog* – behind her father's old

Mercedes shooting brake and hears her mother's voice call before she has even taken her bag out of the car.

'Hi, darling, over here!' Jennifer's clear diction travels well in the autumn air. Charlie turns round and, looking left and right, is unable to see her mother anywhere. 'I'm over here in the garden,' shouts her mother. 'I'm pulling leeks for lunch.' Charlie looks in the direction of the garden and through a gap in the leylandii hedge can see her mother smiling and waving a green suede gardening glove, a fecund trug in the crook of her arm. Dressed in a navy Guernsey jumper pulled hard over her round hips and a pair of bright red 'fun' cords, Jennifer is obviously already dressed for lunch, save for her short, black plastic gardening boots. Her grey-blonde hair has been blow-dried smooth and straight and curled immaculately under onto the shoulders using one big roller. She has piled on her usual bright pink lipstick. She smells of White Linen as she leans over and kisses her daughter on the cheek.

'Darling, how lovely to see you,' she says, patting Charlie on the shoulder with a green suede hand. 'Lovely to see you,' she repeats, before taking a step back to look her daughter up and down. 'You're very brown, darling. Have you put on weight?' She smiles. 'You can't afford to do that you know, darling, particularly at your age.' Jennifer's ability to say the wrong thing at the wrong time is as legendary as her cooking.

'Do you know, mother, I haven't,' smiles Charlie, giving her mother a kiss and an affectionate squeeze of the shoulders.

'Are you sure?'

'You look well,' continues Charlie valiantly. 'It's great to be home.'

'It's wonderful to see you too,' nods her mother. 'Come inside, I know your father is looking forward to seeing you.'

Charlie walks into the house, passing a row of mud-covered wellington boots sitting in the hall, to be greeted by two old and overweight black Labradors. Bournville is the mother of

Beetle, but at this late stage in the proceedings it is increasingly difficult to tell them apart. Both gallop half-heartedly towards her, their broad back legs bowing under the weight of too many treats.

'You see, they vaguely remember you,' declares Jim, standing in the doorway to his study smiling at his daughter. 'Jolly clever animals, the two of them.'

'Hello, Pa,' says Charlie, walking over to give her father a kiss. He smells tartly of aftershave and soap.

'Hello, Charlotte,' he says, squeezing her rather too tightly. 'Back from the Dark Continent, so I see.'

'Sure am,' she replies, looking at her father who appears, unlike his wife, to have aged quite dramatically since she last saw him.

He is wearing, bizarrely, what appear to be 'comfortable' backless shoes and loose trousers, a dark green cardigan with brown leather buttons and a dark green checked shirt. His erstwhile thick dark moustache is thinner and almost white at the ends, like he's been drinking milk. And he has a piece of loo paper stuck to his neck, where he obviously cut himself shaving this morning. His frailty is striking. He is no longer nimble on his feet and he lets out a strained sigh as he lowers himself off the step, walking towards his daughter.

'So,' he says, still holding her shoulders and pushing her away from him to examine her more easily. 'You look no different at all, does she, Jennifer? Almost no different at all.'

'Well, give or take a few pounds and the suntan, not really, dear. I'm inclined to agree with you,' says Charlie's mother, shouting above the noise of the running cold tap as she starts to wash the leeks efficiently in the kitchen sink.

'Now,' says Jim, walking slowly towards what he and his wife rather smartly refer to as the drawing room. 'I'm sure you'd like a drink after your long journey.'

'It wasn't that far,' says Charlie. 'But I would love a drink anyway.'

'Still can't understand why you didn't take the London train – so much easier.'

'Kate lent me her car,' says Charlie with a tight smile.

'Mm,' replies Jim. 'Now, what would you like? I have gin, sherry, whisky and I think a little bit of vodka left over from the last time Kate and Alex were down in the summer.'

'I'd love some vodka,' nods Charlie enthusiastically. 'With some tonic – if you have any.'

'I think I might have some of that down here,' says her father, exhaling loudly as he bends slowly down towards the lower cupboard in his mahogany drinks cabinet. One large-jointed, pink, rough-skinned hand tightly grips the side as he searches in the cupboard below. 'Here we go,' he declares, bringing up a dusty bottle. 'Knew we had some somewhere.'

Charlotte stands at the other end of the drawing room warming her backside by the fire. Recently lit, the damp wood is causing it to smoke quite heavily and it is not throwing out much heat. Her parents have predictably not turned on the heating and if she looks carefully when she speaks she can see her own breath.

'God,' she says, rubbing her hands together and moving from one foot to another. 'I think it's warmer outside than in.'

'Possibly,' replies her father. 'This a very difficult house to heat, not like the other place which was properly built. Shoddy workmanship,' he adds, shaking his head.

'Right,' nods Charlie. 'I don't remember the Rectory being much warmer.'

'Oh it was,' replies her father. 'Take it from me. It was a much better constructed house. Anyway, it's only because you've spent all that time abroad that you feel the cold so much.' He picks up the bottle of vodka and turns it on its side to see how much is in there. 'I'm afraid it's gins after this,' he continues, holding the bottle up to the light. 'Not an awful lot in here.'

'I could go out and get some more,' suggests Charlie.

'No need for such extravagance,' says Jim. 'We've got plenty of alcohol to finish off here.' He gets out an old cut glass and slips in two rather melted pieces of ice using a silver spoon from the silver ice bucket. He pours in the remains of the vodka and cuts a thin, almost transparent slice of lemon with a bone-handled knife. He cuts the slice in half, making sure that he places one tranche on a plate for later, and opens the tonic. Warm and barely capable of fizz, it expends its last effervescent gasp as it hits the melting ice. 'There we go, darling,' says her father as he hands over the warm, flat drink. 'Now don't go at that too quickly,' he smiles. 'Cheers,' he says, raising his sherry in a small cut glass. 'Welcome home.'

'Thanks, Pa,' smiles Charlie. 'It's wonderful to be back.'

'Drinking us out of house and home already, I see,' says Jennifer as she hustles into the drawing room, in a pair of pink marigolds and holding two saucers of peanuts. 'Now don't go eating these,' she orders. 'They're for the guests.'

'Family hold back,' jokes her father, taking a sip of his sherry.

'How much of that have you had?' asks Jennifer, bending over a highly polished coffee table to arrange her nuts.

'This is my first,' replies Jim, taken aback at the sharpness of his wife's tone.

'Good,' says Jennifer, standing up and putting her pink marigolds on her hips. She pauses for a second and then, irritated at the lack of argument, returns to kitchen.

'Africa was amazing,' says Charlie, by way of conversational opener. Having decided while listening to the radio in the car that it would be too frustrating to wait for any interest from her father, she forges forth of her own accord.

'Good, I'm glad to hear it,' replies her father with his back to her, slicing the lemon just in case there is a rush when the guests arrive.

'I had some of the most amazing experiences and met some of the most fantastic people. There was this one time when out in Tanzania –'

'Not now, darling, we have an awful lot of people about to turn up for drinks and lunch and I need to concentrate. Could you go and ask your mother if I should slice all this lemon or does she need it for her cooking, and can she remember if the Scotts drink whisky?'

'Right,' says Charlie, sounding hurt.

'I'm sorry, darling,' says Jim, turning round slightly from the drinks cabinet and looking over his shoulder, 'but there will be plenty of time for your little stories later, once we've got this all organised.'

'They're not that bloody little,' mutters Charlie under her breath as she walks past her father on the way into the kitchen.

'What?' asks her father, looking up from his lemon.

'Nothing,' says Charlie, her shoulders already starting to slouch like the teenage daughter she always reverts to within fifteen minutes of arriving home. Walking into the kitchen, she is immediately conscripted by her mother.

'Darling, great,' she says. 'Now that you're here, you can do the leeks.' Handing her daughter a sharp knife she pushes her in the direction of the stainless-steel sink.

'Dad has a couple of questions,' says Charlie.

'Has he?' replies Jennifer. 'Well, he can wait for a second. We are very busy in here . . . Darling,' she suddenly declares with a loud, long, jaded sigh. 'What are you doing?'

'What?' says Charlie, standing by the sink with her jumper

sleeves pulled up, cutting off the mud-packed root-stem of a leek.

'Don't say "what" and leave your mouth open like that, darling, it's very unattractive,' says her mother. 'And what are you doing washing leeks in that expensive jumper? Are you made of money? Or do you always char in cashmere?'

'No . . .'

'Really,' says her mother, rattling behind the kitchen door. 'You can put this monstrous thing on. No one will see you.'

'Oh my God, it's hideous,' says Charlie, agreeing with her mother for the first time that day.

'I know,' says Jennifer, pulling the strap over her daughter's head, and flapping out the straps, before tying them round Charlie's waist. 'It was a present from Alex last Christmas. He thought it was hilarious. I found it so offensive. I have never worn it and it's been hanging on the back of the door ever since. You're the first person to use it,' she smiles. 'There you go,' she adds, tapping her on the shoulder. 'You can get back to the leeks now.'

'Mum, it's hideous,' says Charlie, looking down at the shiny plastic apron to be confronted by an enormous pair of comedy breasts complete with swinging tassels, and black frilly pants with a bona fide lace trim.

'Oh my God,' says Jennifer as her daughter turns round. 'It's infinitely more hideous than I thought.'

'You say Alex bought it?' asks Charlie.

'Yes,' says her mother. 'I have a feeling it was an after-lunch purchase.'

'Yes.'

'Anyway, at least it does the trick. Hurry up, darling,' chivvies Jennifer. 'It's quarter past twelve – they'll be here in a minute. I'm just going to lay the table. You carry on in here.'

Jennifer's kitchen has not changed since she moved in about seven years ago after Jim retired from Lloyd's. He had been an insurance broker for the best part of fifty years commuting to and from London every morning and evening on the train. Deciding to live more frugally, they'd sold the Old Rectory and moved to Rose Cottage, using the interest on the excess sale money to supplement Jim's pension. Instead of wasting money on doing up the kitchen, shipping in new units, replacing the stained red lino floor, Jennifer had insisted it was fine and needed no work whatsoever. As a result it is a gloomy and not very attractive room. The units, such as they are, are covered in a bleached turquoise Formica. The cupboard doors are a sad old blue, but the actual surfaces themselves are covered in a swirling grey pattern that is pretending very hard to be marble. The cooker is electric and would be happier in a student hostel, and the dishwasher can only just about cope with one carefully stacked plate at a time. It is no wonder the food that comes out of the place is so revolting; it is not a room conducive to culinary creativity.

While Charlie cuts and slices the leeks in the freezing cold water, her hands becoming ever more pink and more numb, she can hear her mother clattering away in the next-door room laying the table and sighing out loud. Her father comes in to hand back half the lemon, obviously under orders.

'Jesus Christ,' he swears uncharacteristically. 'What on earth have you got on?' For Jim actually to blaspheme the apron must look truly awful.

'Is it bad?' smiles Charlie, looking at her father who starts to giggle, wrinkling his nose and covering his mouth like a child who has suddenly discovered something quite racy and shocking.

'Go and have a look in the hall mirror,' he winks. 'I haven't seen a sight like that since I assessed a fire in a brothel in Soho back in the early sixties.'

'Really?' smiles Charlie. 'That bad?'

'Go and take a look,' grins her father, indicating towards the hall.

Charlie walks through towards the hall and wonders what on earth Alex was thinking when he bought this ugly thing. For it is indeed ugly, as Charlie confirms when she admires her newly acquired Page Three breasts, strikingly sharp hips and itchy-looking briefs. She is even sporting, for reasons best know to its creator, a long, fat, pearl necklace that curls round the edge of the apron to finish in an unrealistic knot in the cleavage, like some pornographic flapper. Charlie smiles at her reflection. Putting her wet, cold hands on her hips, she shimmies her shoulders and then bends over, buttocks out, curling her little finger around her lower lips striking glamour girl pose.

'Hiya-a-a-h,' she half whispers to her reflection. 'Come and get it, big boy . . .'

She hears a polite little cough from behind and spins round to find the Scott family – mother, father and son – standing in a row by the front door, hands swinging limply by their sides as they stare.

'Oh,' says Charlie.

'Hello,' says Major Scott. 'It was open,' he explains, his little round currant eyes staring over bright pink cheeks that sport red broken veins like an Ordnance Survey map. 'And we've been standing outside for a while . . .'

'The doorbell's broken,' smiles Charlie, her hands moving from her sides to her front and back again, not knowing whether protocol dictates that one should modestly cover comedy breasts or leave them swinging carelessly in the breeze.

'Gosh, right, hello,' says Mrs Scott, turning round to

take off her stiff navy blue tweed coat and reveal a pair of playroom curtains posing as a dress. 'Charlie, isn't it?' she smiles. 'Haven't seen you around here in a while,' she continues, maintaining strict above-the-nipple eye contact. 'Do you remember my son? Dominic?'

'Ah yes, hello, Dominic,' says Charlie, moving from one foot to another like she's standing on hot coals. She doesn't really remember Dominic, but thinks it is polite to pretend. She has a vague recollection of a stuck-up little git who refused to play with Kate and her in the large garden at the Rectory. He walked around with a book, or was it pocket solitaire? She couldn't remember. Either way he insisted he wouldn't play with girls.

'Nice outfit,' says Dominic. 'I'm afraid I don't remember you at all. But apparently we knew each other pre-puberty so to speak.' He smiles, staring at the knotted pearls between her breasts.

'Apparently so,' smiles Charlie. 'All I remember is that you didn't like girls. Is that still the case?'

'Wouldn't you like to know?' laughs Dominic, whipping his short nose back to reveal nostrils packed with tightly cropped nasal hair.

'Ha ha ha,' laughs Charlie. 'Absolutely . . . not,' she whispers, as she turns towards the kitchen. 'Mum, Pa!' she shouts. 'Your guests are here.'

'Oh Lord,' says Jennifer, coming out of the dining room. 'Rosemary, dear,' she says, scurrying over to touch opposite shoulders and brush cheeks with Mrs Scott. 'I'm so sorry I didn't hear you. You've met my daughter?' she adds, standing back and holding her hand out by way of presentation. 'Honestly, Charlotte, go and take that ghastly thing off! Now! Really,' she says, clutching her own bosom. 'The young!'

'But Mum, this is your apron.'

'Just run along and take the monstrous thing off,' whispers

her mother, her eyes round with irritation. 'And tell your father to mix some drinks.'

They all gather in the cold drawing room. They stand in a circle facing each other in front of the smoking fire. Rosemary Scott clutches her gin and bitter lemon, both the Major and Dominic Scott have a beer, Charlie smiles with her warm, flat vodka and tonic and Jim and Jennifer quietly sip their sherry wine.

The Scotts live in the Old Moat House, a large Elizabethan building on the edge of Cranford village, and as fellow large house owners they have been friends ever since any of them can remember. Dominic is their only son, who Rosemary took a long time in conceiving. As a result his talent, humour and good looks are, according to his mother, legendary. Educated at boarding school, he was almost never at home in boring old Surrey. He spent most of his holidays on glamorous locations skiing in Switzerland, windsurfing in the South of France, or just generally bronzing himself in the Caribbean with friends. His parents scrimped and saved and gave him everything, and now he rarely patronises them with his presence, and when he does, he is rather pleased with himself and distinctly spoilt.

'So, Jennifer,' smiles Rosemary. 'Been doing a lot of pruning?'

'Just mainly deadheading roses, actually,' replies Jennifer. 'In the hope that I might get a couple of late bloomers when we have this Indian summer they keep talking about.'

'It's bit a late for that now, isn't it?' says Rosemary. 'What do you think, dear?'

'Think about what?' asks the Major, his small mouth packed with peanuts, making it difficult for him to speak.

'Indian summers? When should we lose all hope that they might appear?' enquires Rosemary.

'Mm,' replies the Major, his hand in the air, chomping

away on his peanuts. 'Mm, mm, mm,' he repeats as he chews, his eyes watering with effort. Everyone stares and waits for him to finish. 'Mm,' he swallows. 'Mm … I'm afraid I don't know.'

'Oh,' says Rosemary, taking a sip of her gin. 'So,' she says, turning to face Charlie, still maintaining diligent above-nipple eye contact just in case. 'Glad to be back?'

'Very much so,' nods Charlie, already halfway down her glass. 'It's a bit different.'

'Bit cold, I expect,' says Rosemary. 'After all that time in . . . where was it?'

'Africa' smiles Charlie.

'That's right,' nods Rosemary. 'Gordon and I were talking about it in the car and I couldn't remember where it was, Asia, Africa or America, but I knew it was somewhere fairly ghastly. Africa, that's right, I remember now. Africa,' she repeats. 'The white man's grave.'

'Actually, that's West Africa. I was in the East, based in Kenya. Although there were certainly a good few people killed over that half of the continent too.'

'I know Kenya really well,' says Dominic.

'Oh yes?' smiles Charlie.

'Went there on holiday once. Stayed in this great place near Mombasa.'

'Great,' nods Charlie, keen to get any sort of conversation going.

'Fabulous,' he says. 'The facilities were great. Hot and cold running drinks. Didn't have to leave the resort once.'

'Great,' nods Charlie again.

'What were you doing out there?' asks the Major.

'I was on holiday,' says Dominic.

'Not you,' says the Major. 'Charlotte,' he smiles, licking his lips.

'Photographic journalist,' replies Charlotte, moving towards her father. 'News and features. Photographing the civil wars, bombings and major disasters in and around southern and East Africa.'

'Very impressive,' says Dominic in a way that implies he doesn't think so. 'Aren't you a right little tomboy Lara Croft?'

'It's just a job,' shrugs Charlie. 'Anyway, what do you do these days?'

'Dominic is between jobs at the moment, aren't you, Dominic?' replies his mother.

'Yeah,' says Dominic, running his hands through his thinning blond hair. 'The company I was working for downsized and I was part of the natural wastage package. Well, I opted for voluntary redundo. Quite frankly, I was bored.'

'Oh that wouldn't do now, would it?' says Charlie. Dominic and his short nose are beginning to get up her own and she is too tired and too bored to stop it from showing.

'No, it wouldn't,' agrees Rosemary, pleased that Charlie understands.

'No, it wouldn't indeed,' smirks Dominic, unfortunately mistaking Charlie's curtness for flirtation. 'Maybe a big grown-up career girl like you could point me in the right direction.'

'I don't think I would be much help,' smiles Charlie through gritted teeth. 'Shall I offer round the nuts?'

'Good idea, darling,' smiles Jennifer. 'I'll just check on my veg.'

Charlie goes round the outside of the circle, offering around the small porcelain Royal Worcester bowls of peanuts while Gordon and Jim discuss the possible new bypass for the village, and Rosemary and Dominic talk about Dominic some more. Fresh from checking her vegetables, Jennifer comes back into the room.

'No need to overdose on those peanuts, darling,' she says to Charlie who was just about to serve herself some. 'Lunch will be ready in a couple of minutes, if you'd like to go through.'

'Take your glasses with you,' adds Jim. 'We've got some wine as it's a special occasion.'

'Oh really,' says Rosemary, rubbing her hands at the prospect of some gossip. 'Special occasion,' she repeats. 'No, no, don't tell,' she says flapping her hands, the mole on her chin joins in. 'You've finally got yourself a man and you're getting married!' She grins at Charlie, throwing her arms round her and wrapping her tightly in the playroom curtains. 'Let me be the first to congratulate you,' she continues without drawing breath. The mole nods. 'I know I'm not speaking out of turn when I say I know your mother is thrilled that you have finally put her mind at rest. The worry, the worry,' she smiles. 'And the rest of us, for that matter. We thought it would never happen.' She collapses on to Charlie with a fitful high-pitched giggle.

'Um, I wasn't meaning that sort of celebration at all,' says Jim rather slowly, standing stock-still, holding stiffly on to his sherry wine. 'The fact that Charlotte is back home after nearly five years was the idea I had in mind . . . Unless, of course, she has something to tell me of which I am blissfully unaware?'

'I'm afraid not,' smiles Charlie, from within the playroom armpit. 'I have nothing to announce in that department at all.'

'Oh . . . my . . . God! I am so-o-o-o sorry,' says Rosemary, immediately extracting herself from the celebratory embrace. Bright pink and in a panic, she is crucified by the embarrassment of her faux pas. 'I am so, so, so sorry. I had no idea. I am so, so, so terribly sorry.'

'It's fine, Mrs Scott, honestly,' says Charlie. 'It's absolutely fine.'

'I am so, so sorry, really, I had no idea. When your father said celebration – all I could think of was a wedding. – Oh dear, oh dear . . . I am so, so . . .'

'Honestly, Rosemary dear, it's fine,' says Jennifer, putting her firm navy woolly arm around her distraught friend's technicolour shoulder. 'You weren't to know the nature of the celebration. It's a mistake anyone could have made.' She ushers everyone through to the dining room with a flick of her undercurled hair.

'But Charlotte?' she says in a small mortified voice.

'Good Lord,' hoots Jennifer. 'Don't worry about Charlotte. She's tough as old boots, aren't you, darling?'

'Oh yes,' smiles Charlotte. 'Tough as old boots, me. It's all water off a duck's back, nothing touches me at all. Hard as nails.'

'See,' says Jennifer triumphantly. 'Now let's have lunch – it's all forgotten.'

They walk through into the dark, cramped dining room with a polished table and high-backed hard chairs that are obviously used to more glamorous surroundings. Under the stern gaze of various grey relatives who hang from the yellow walls, they sit down on the small skiddy cushions that slip around on the shiny waxed chairs, occasionally taking the coccyx with them. Jennifer stands by her large hotplate and serves the lunch.

'Chicken and ham in white sauce with leeks and potatoes,' she announces in a manner that expects a round of applause. 'From the garden,' she adds.

'From the garden?' repeats Rosemary, desperate for any form of conversation to get going. 'I think kitchen gardens are *so* important, don't you, Charlotte,' she says, testing the water.

'Very much so,' agrees Charlotte, feeling rather sorry for the old biddy, who looks on the verge of tears. 'Do you garden?' she asks Dominic pleasantly, holding on to the table as she slips in her chair.

'No,' says Dominic. 'I'm far too busy at weekends out and

about with my girlfriend.' He smiles. 'But I expect you must be rather good, Charlotte. All those hours to fill.'

'I don't normally wake up till quite late at the weekend in Kenya, I'm out too much with mates at the Horseman, or Euro Nite at the Carnivore,' she replies, bristling with confrontation and too much information.

'Still out nightclubbing at your age?' sighs Dominic, shaking his head.

'Not so much nightclubbing – you know, going out to bars . . .'

'Drinking a lot?' asks Dominic.

'No, not really,' says Charlie, sounding ridiculously defensive. 'Anyway, I don't have much free time. I'm away a lot, travelling,' she adds and then immediately regrets it.

'I expect you like it that way,' smiles Dominic, popping one of Jennifer's overcooked potatoes in his mouth. Exploding like cotton wool, it soaks up the vitriol seeping from his mouth for a second.

Rosemary, suddenly feeling all confident again after Charlie's tacit acceptance of her apology, says, 'So what do you do at the weekends in Africa when you're not working? I expect it must be quite lonely, just like it is for single women over here,' she smiles, pity writ large all over her face. 'I've read that Sunday night is the worst. I suppose it's the same whereever you are when you're on your own.'

'Charlotte likes being on her own,' says her father, finally leaping to her defence. 'She's always been like that ever since she was a child. Hasn't she, Jennifer?'

'Not that I particularly remember,' replies Jennifer, trying to fork a piece of brown sleazy chicken that keeps skidding around her plate. 'Do tuck in, everyone, by the way,' she says. 'While it's still warm. Oh good,' she adds. 'Dominic I see you have already started.'

Charlie looks down at her plate and for once is pleased that

116

her mother is such a frightful cook. The ham and chicken in a white sauce is doing its damnedest to look like vomit. The leeks are in a watery pool all of their own making and the potatoes sit on the edge of the plate like the straggling survivors of a nuclear holocaust. Jim, used to such culinary inarticulacy, is filling his belly while he can, and Jennifer is simply refuelling, oblivious to the lack of flavour, texture and pleasure of any kind. Meanwhile, Rosemary is politely eating her vegetables – they are from the garden after all. And the Major and his son are rendered mute as they try and try again to swallow their dry potatoes. The last thing any of these guests deserves, thinks Charlotte as she flicks her food round her plate wishing she had eaten more peanuts, is to enjoy themselves at all.

The conversation trawls on. With Charlotte's lack of partner deemed too sensitive a subject to bring up again, nice, easy, simple things like dogs, health, and the possibility of the pantomime at Christmas take over. Jim finishes off the bottle of Bulgarian red from the village stores and offers to open another. The Major is keen. Rosemary is not. Eventually she is overruled. Dominic and Charlie, as children, are of course not consulted.

As Jim leaves the room, a vile and positively toxic stench seeps out from nowhere. A virulent combination of rotten eggs, old meat and generally fetid material, it is truly revolting. Everyone can smell it, but everyone ignores it and carries on talking with a renewed and purposeful vigour. Rosemary laughs a little loudly at the memory of last year's panto. Jennifer is very keen to find out if there will be another one this year, as last year's was so terribly good. Each person around the table knows that they personally have not farted. Each tries to catch the eye of another, subtly communicating that they are not the perpetrator of such a deed. The only one left is Jim. Surely that is why he was so insistent on leaving the room in the first place? Jim re-enters, open bottle of wine in his left hand. Everyone turns to stare.

'What?' he says, looking taken aback at so much attention. And then it hits him. Mugged by methane, he retches slightly. 'Good Lord,' he says, his eyes watering slightly. 'Is there a dog in this room?'

'A dog?' repeats Jennifer, so pleased it is not her husband. She shoves her head between her scarlet cord trousers and looks under the table. 'Bournville, Beetle, get out of there!' The two flatulent Labradors skulk out from under the table and leave the room at a speedy trot. 'How ghastly,' says Jennifer, finally acknowledging the problem, waving her hand in front of her nose. 'I'm so sorry.'

'Quite all right,' laughs Rosemary, flapping away. 'Ours does it all the time.'

The conversation turns back to dogs, the panto again, for Jim's benefit, and on to everyone else in the village. The rice pudding comes and goes. Everyone has a small amount and covers it in bright pink raspberry jam to make it more edible, and then they move through to the drawing room for coffee and Bendick's Bittermints. These are a rarity in the house. Well, not in the house, exactly, because there is always a box of Bendicks in the present drawer in the kitchen. It is just that they rarely, if ever, get opened. They are passed from house to house, from present drawer to present drawer. Over the years, the same box often returns. Kate and Charlie marked one with a biro once. It came back to them three times in the space of a year, only to disappear off into another social circle for ever. Judging by the flavour and looks of these, thinks Charlie as she eats her third white and stale mint, they must have been doing the rounds since 1986.

Eventually the Scotts leave, claiming they have dogs to walk, although Charlie suspects the loud rumbling of Dominic's stomach has more to do with it. With perfunctory handshakes and thank yous exchanged, the two men are not out of the house quickly enough. But as she leaves, Rosemary gives Charlotte a little cold, clammy kiss on the cheek and whispers, 'Good luck' quietly in her ear. She shakes her hand and, just in case her sadness isn't communicated loudly enough, gives her a little pat on the back of the hand.

This is Charlotte's last straw. The idea of spending the whole evening with her parents, listening to her mother ask her again if she has a man and then going through her list of potential suitors, all of whom are the colour of Weetabix and devoid of a chin, only then to answer questions about why she isn't more like Kate – all settled and happy – makes Charlie want to leave.

She is perfectly polite when she makes her excuses. An unforeseen, awful emergency in London. It is genuinely lovely to see them. She will come down again very soon. But she has to leave to sort this thing out.

She gets into Kate's car, puts the radio on full blast and drives back to London so fast that she gets flashed twice by speed cameras. She arrives at Kate's at seven in the evening. It's a Friday night and the house is empty. It is bizarre, but comes as a bit of a relief. She fixes herself a vodka and tonic and, sitting back in one of the cream sofas, she lights a cigarette and relaxes. She hears the key in the lock and shouts a cheery hello as the front door opens.

'Oh, hello,' comes Alex's voice. 'Who's that?' he says, sounding surprised.

'Charlie,' says Charlie.

'Charlie,' he says, poking his head round the door. 'I thought you were spending the night in Cranford?'

'Yeah,' says Charlie, exhaling her cigarette. 'It was more stiff and fraught than I expected.'

'Mm,' he replies. 'They're not that bad as olds go.'

'Yeah, they did look old.'

'Well, that's because you haven't seen them for a while.'

'Talk about stating the obvious,' says Charlie, leaning forward in her seat, smiling, trying to be pleasant to the tricky Alex as he stands in his suit with a sports bag over his shoulder. 'Where have you been?' she asks. He looks flushed.

'Oh . . .' He pauses, putting down his bag. 'Squash,' he says.

'Again!' Charlie laughs. 'Did you win?'

'Of course,' replies Alex, executing a rapid pelvic-thrust movement in the doorway like an overexcited terrier. 'Gave them a good seeing to,' he smiles. 'I'm off to take a shower.'

'Oh, right,' says Charlie, looking puzzled.

Alex disappears off, leaving his bag in the doorway. Weird squash gesture, thinks Charlie, as she stares at the bag. People play air-squash when they talk about squash, just as they play air-guitar when they talk about their favourite bands. The thrust was odd. And why is he in his suit? Why didn't he shower at the club? And if he didn't shower at the club, how come he is dressed already? Curiosity finally gets the better of her and, hauling herself off the sofa, she walks over and opens up the bag. Her blood runs cold. Inside are Alex's squash clothes – washed, ironed and bone dry.

5

Charlie says nothing to her sister about her husband's fabulous ability to play a full clammy game of squash in his business suit. She knows she needs more proof if she is going to confront Kate. She knows she needs concrete evidence before she can go any further. After all she could be wrong. She could be putting two and two together and making five. There could very easily be a nice simple explanation for what happened on Friday night. He didn't, for a start, look guilty, sheepish or anything like he had been busted at all. When he showered and came back downstairs he was good-humoured and pleasant, and made Charlie a couple of drinks before settling down to watch telly, waiting for Kate and the children to get home.

Maybe he'd borrowed someone else's kit? Maybe she'd misunderstood him? Perhaps he has two sets of stuff, one lot he keeps at the gym? Either way, nice, crisp, clean gym kit is no reason to break up a happy home.

A happy home, she smiles, sitting on the sofa four days later pretending to read a magazine. What is a happy home? Something that children conjure up in their own heads playing in their Wendy house at the bottom of the garden, serving tea to their teddies, waiting for their fictitious knights in shining armour to come home. But is Kate's house just a little make-believe Wendy house of happiness in her mind because Charlie cannot understand it at all? A little domestic kingdom made of cards, with its two children and very own goddess wafting around making edible treats for its truculent, unfaithful king?

Maybe Kate likes it this way? Maybe she knows her husband is having an affair but turns a blind eye? Like some old-fashioned domestic arrangement? Maybe it is the only way she can keep him? Maybe she has thought about confrontation and decided against it? Keeping a silent and sunny disposition is the only way she can save her little Wendy house from collapsing in front of her eyes.

Or maybe, thinks Charlotte, this is the way the world works. Men are allowed their little dalliances, their flirtations, their affairs, and then they come home and everything carries on as normal, as if nothing has happened. What would she know? As everyone keeps pointing out, she doesn't have a relationship to speak of, and hasn't had one for quite a while. She has never lived with anyone for any length of time and has never been properly proposed to on bended knee with a ring. The only man she ever really loved is dead and she won't speak about that to anyone, because it is far too painful. So what does she know? The lonely old career girl who is as hard as nails? She sighs out loud.

'What?' asks Kate, who has come into the room unnoticed.

'What, what?' asks Charlie, looking puzzled.

'Why are you sighing?'

'I'm always sighing,' she replies. 'It's an irritating byproduct of my thinking.'

'Well don't.'

'What, think? Or sigh?'

'Think, of course,' smiles her sister. 'Are you nervous?'

'Nervous about what?'

'Your award, silly,' Kate smiles again. 'I wish I was coming with you. I can't believe you gave what's-her-name *my* ticket.'

'I'm sorry about that,' says Charlie, 'but her need is greater than yours. You're . . . married and she's got men to bed,' she continues. 'Any men.'

'Happily married, don't you mean?'

'Yeah, that too,' says Charlie. 'Alice doesn't have anyone and has taken a desperate, some might say tragic, fancy to Andrew Edwards – the man I'm in competition with, I might add –'

'You see,' says Kate, pointing with a short, shaped nail. 'If you were taking me like you said you would, I would have been loyalty personified.'

'I know, I'm sorry,' says Charlie. 'I really am. Alice did have a ticket, but for some reason best known to itself, it was taken away from her. She has got to go, it's her job – you know, photography.'

'It was my big night out,' says Kate, her bottom lip sticking out like one of her children.

'Okay, if Alice marries the Andrew bloke, will you forgive me?' asks Charlie, her hands in the air admitting defeat.

'Might do,' says Kate, looking at her watch. 'Shouldn't you be getting ready now? Isn't Alice coming to collect you at six-thirty?'

'Yes,' says Charlie. 'And it's only a quarter past five.'

'What do you mean, "only"?' says Kate, her eyes round with urgency.

'It doesn't take me over an hour to get ready.'

'Yes it does,' insists Kate. 'If you're doing it properly. Just how many awards are you planning on getting nominated for in your life?' she asks.

'A few more,' says Charlie.

'But this is your first?'

'Yes.'

'So we are going to do it properly.'

'We?' repeats Charlie.

'Yes,' says her sister. 'Follow me, I'm running you a bath.'

Charlie follows her sister upstairs and into her bathroom. Although aurally familiar with Alex's daily shower routine, it is the first time that she has been back in the bathroom since the meet-and-greet tour. It is a beautiful room, she thinks, looking at the rows and rows of bottles and tubs, of creams and lotions and big glass jars of cotton wool balls, buds and luxuriant puffs. It appears less intimidating and chichi than it did when Charlotte arrived just over a week ago. Kate runs her fingers along the row of Jo Malone essential oils and bathtime treats. Choosing a delicious-smelling 'rose', she pours some drops into the running bath. The room fills with steam and the smell of a country garden in full summer flourish.

'Oh God, smell that,' says Kate, half closing her eyes. 'I don't know a man on earth who can resist that.'

'Or a woman,' says Charlie. 'It's gorgeous.'

'Get in,' says her sister. 'We haven't got long.'

Charlie strips. She throws her jeans, jumper and T-shirt into a pile in the middle of the floor. She stands braless, in a pair of not-so-white cotton pants she must have had for at least five years. Compared with the white-tiled bathroom, she looks a dark golden brown. Slim and toned, she has a pretty round bosom and the sort of backside Hollywood women hand over their platinum cards for.

'Those pants are horrid,' says her sister, looking Charlie up and down. Coming from the same long, lean gene pool, Kate is used to girls looking good in their underwear. But she is certainly not used to underwear of such poor quality.

'They are quite sorry, aren't they?' smiles Charlie. 'That's months of hand-washing on assignment for you,' she adds, looking down at her grey knickers.

'Actually, I would go so far as to say they're revolting.'

'That's mean.'

'But true,' shrugs Kate. 'Get them off and I'm throwing them away. How many more have you got like that upstairs?'

'I'm not saying. I'm rather fond of them,' says Charlie, slipping off her grey pants and stepping into the hot glass bath. 'Hey,' she says, sitting down. 'This bath isn't glass, it's perspex.'

'I know, glass would be far too cold, you arse,' comes Kate's voice from the other room.

'Talking of which,' says Charlie, twisting over the edge, 'can you see my arse through this thing?'

'Only your thighs,' says Kate, holding up a La Perla cream silk thong for her sister's admiration and approval.

'How about if I do this?' asks Charlie, inhaling and holding her nose before she ducks under the water and twists to one side, flattening her bare buttocks against the side. 'What does that look like?' she asks, resurfacing, smiling broadly, rose-scented bubbles stuck to her blonde hair. Kate is laughing as she slides slowly down the tiled wall next to the basin, the La Perla thong still in her hand. 'Does it look good?' asks Charlie keenly, really quite excited about the possibilities of the transparent bath. 'Could you see everything, or should I do it again?'

'Once is quite enough,' laughs Kate. 'God,' she says, smiling broadly, 'I'd forgotten what a fool you are.'

'This is great,' says Charlie, relaxing back.

'Do you want this?' asks Kate, waving the thong.

'What for?'

'To wear to the awards.'

'Do you think so? It doesn't look very comfortable.'

'Take it from me, it is.'

'Whatever you say,' smiles Charlie. 'I have no idea what I'm doing.'

'Have you shaved your legs, by the way?' asks Kate, sitting on the floor.

'But my tan will come off,' insists Charlie, poking her head over the top of the bath.

'Don't worry, I've got some cream for that,' sighs Kate. 'God, where have you been?'

'Africa,' burbles Charlie from under the water.

'No need to be a smart-arse.'

'Did you say arse?'

'No, no, no,' screams Kate, flapping the thong as she leaves the room. 'Hurry up,' she yells from the safety of her bedroom.

'Okay,' replies Charlie. 'I'll do my legs and wash my hair. Promise I won't be long.'

All smooth, clean and depilated, Charlie sits at her sister's dressing table in her white thong and her cream silk dressing gown, while Kate blow-dries her hair. Charlie did make an attempt with the hairdryer but only succeeded in creating a bird's nest at the back of her own head, so Kate insisted on taking over and, being salon-savvy, is making rather a good job of it. Straightening out the kinks and curls she is coming up with her own version of 'show biz' hair.

'Okay, okay,' says Kate, really rather enjoying herself as she steps between Charlie and the mirror. 'You aren't allowed to look until I've done your make-up as well.'

'But I look crap in make-up,' protests Charlie, trying to push her sister out the way of the mirror. 'Like a pre-op transvestite.'

'That's only because you put it on like a child,' replies Kate, grabbing hold of her elder sister's chin and applying lipstick.

'I hate lipstick,' mumbles Charlie.

'Will you shut up,' says Kate, almost nose to nose with her sister.

'Sorry,' says Charlie. 'Do you know you can be quite frightening when you want to be?'

'Shut up,' replies Kate. 'I'm concentrating.'

'Sorry.'

Kate gets out all her blushers and powders and brushes and curlers and things. Pretending to be a glamorous make-up artist on a swish shoot, she gets to work on her sister. Highlighting here, shading there, glossing and lining, forgetting her two boys and husband, she is enjoying being a bit girly and having some female company in the house.

'Right,' she says, her mouth full of brushes as she turns her sister's face left and right in the light. 'There you are. A vast improvement, even if I say so myself.' She steps out from in front of the mirror for her makeover reveal. 'Tadah!' she says, her hands out, fingers splayed. 'What do you think?'

'My God,' says Charlie, leaning towards the mirror to take a closer look. 'I don't recognise myself at all.'

'Is that good or bad?' asks Kate.

'Good,' says Charlie, sounding slightly unsure. 'Really good. Hello,' she says to herself in the mirror. 'My name's Charlie. I am a nominee. For the David Lawrence Award.'

Both girls laugh.

'Hurry up and get changed,' says Kate. 'I want to see the full makeover result.'

Charlie rushes upstairs and takes out the black starlet's dress she bought with Alice the week before. Slipping it over her hips with a quick wiggle, she pulls it on and does the zip up at the side. Standing in her white bedroom with the sky blue ceiling she stares at herself in the full-length mirror. The image looking back at her is transformed, to say the least. The fitted black strapless dress is ruched all the way down her slim body and flares slightly like a fishtail at the end. Higher at the front than it is at the back, the effect is very Marilyn Monroe. Her tanned skin is glossy and shines with some shimmer effect stuff that Kate has sprinkled all over her chest. Her hair is as smooth as satin and swinging straight and blonde at her shoulders. If only Jack had seen her like this, she smiles. Always in jeans and T-shirts, poor bloke, she laughs, she can't ever have been that alluring. Walking barefoot down the stairs, she sees Kate waiting for her at the bottom.

'Wow,' she says, clapping her hands with joy and excitement. 'Have you got a bra on under that to keep it up?'

''Course,' says Charlie, flicking a piece of elastane.

'You look gorgeous, Charlie, really, you look gorgeous,' she says, standing back like a plump-breasted matron to admire her own handiwork. 'Boys!' She shouts up the stairs to where Peta is entertaining her children. 'Come and see how lovely Auntie Charlie looks before she goes out.'

Two little blond heads of hair appear at the doorway to Peta's flatlet and crane round. Dressed in their matching navy brushed-cotton pyjamas, they look pink and box-fresh.

'Gosh,' says Alfie, looking remarkably snot-free. 'You look lovely.'

'Just like a princess,' says Ben. 'Are you going to a ball?'

'A party,' says Charlie.

'Oh,' says Ben, sounding disappointed. 'Princesses always go to balls.'

'It's almost a ball,' says Kate.

'Yes,' agrees Charlie quickly. 'Very, very nearly.'

'Mm,' replies Ben, obviously not convinced by these adult lies.

'Anyway,' smiles Kate. 'See you in a minute. I'll come up and say goodnight when Auntie Charlie has gone.'

The boys disappear and Charlie pads downstairs.

'What are you wearing on your feet?' asks Kate all of a sudden.

'I hadn't actually thought. My sequin flip-flops?'

'Oh God, you're rubbish,' says Kate walking back into her bedroom. 'Borrow these,' she says, picking out a pair of black Guccis with transparent heels.

'I won't be able to walk in them,' protests Charlie.

'Tough, you're wearing them,' says Kate as the doorbell goes. 'Put them on and I'll answer that,' she says, going downstairs towards the door.

Kate and Alice kiss and exchange pleasant compliments on the threshold, while Charlie slowly negotiates the stairs.

'Bloody hell,' says Alice as she sees Charlie. 'I came here to pick up Charlie Adams. I don't believe we've met?'

'Shut up,' says Charlie, pinking with embarrassment.

'You look great,' says Alice.

'So do you,' replies Charlie, taking in Alice's short black minidress with lace-up bodice and knee-boots. 'Very racy.'

'Tits and legs,' nods Alice. 'Gets them every time. Shall we go? The minicab is waiting.'

By the time Charlie and Alice arrive downstairs in the ballroom at the Dorchester Hotel for the Photographer of the Year awards, the room is already quite full. They walk past a line of waitresses and, relieving them of a flute of champagne each, make their way into the main room. Each national newspaper seems to have a table, as well as various supplements and specialist magazines.

Charlie sips and nods her way through the room in the general direction of a gang of picture editors, who are almost unrecognisable trussed up in their rented black-tie ensembles.

'Hi,' she mouths to someone as she links arms with Alice. 'Who the hell is that?' she says out of the corner of the mouth.

'No idea,' waves Alice. 'But be careful,' she adds. 'Some of these people have a degree in lip-reading.'

'Where the hell is our table?' asks Charlie.

'I have absolutely no idea,' replies Alice, coming to a stop in a gap between golden catering chairs. 'I suppose you must be near the front,' says Alice. 'Being a nominee.'

'Right,' says Charlie as they turn to face the stage. 'Was there a plan thing on the way in?'

'Probably,' says Alice.

'Hey, Charlie,' comes a familiar voice from close to the front of the room. 'You're over here, you sexy thing.'

Charlie shields her eyes from the glare of the stage light and crouches under the beam to see who is shouting her name. She recognises the voice – the South African twang, the lilting up at the end of the sentence give him away – but she can't see where it's coming from.

'Art,' she shouts, waving blindly. 'Where the hell are you?'

'Here,' comes his voice. 'Right in front of the stage.'

'Oh my God!' Charlie positively squeals with excitement and, running, throws herself into his strong arms. He smells of warm spices and Africa. 'Oh my God, what are you doing here? Why are you here? Why didn't you call me? Where are you staying? Where are you sitting?' Her questions come one after the other without waiting for his replies.

'Sit down,' he smiles. 'I'm next to you.' He raises his eyebrows. 'Well, at least I am now,' he adds, putting his name down next to hers. 'Do you want some of this rather poor-looking wine?'

Art looks stunning in his black tie. Charlie has never seen him in anything other than his baggy khaki shorts or trousers, and a filthy T-shirt nowhere near passing the doorstep challenge. Tanned and handsome in a crisp white shirt and a badly tied bow tie, his mass of dark curls makes him look like a reckless matinee idol awaiting a mission. Clean-shaven and smiling, his large brown eyes shine with a naughty glint.

'You look beautiful,' he says, putting his hands on Charlie's hips and pushing her away from him slightly so he can take in the full picture. 'I don't think I have ever seen you look quite so –' he licks his lips and chooses his word carefully – 'sexy.'

'You look really quite foxy yourself,' she smiles, blushing slightly at the uncustomary attention, yet hugging him tightly again all the same.

'Um, who is your friend?' asks Alice, clearing her throat, bored by the lack of attention and intrigued by the obvious bond between them.

'Oh, I'm sorry,' says Charlie, quickly. 'This is the divine Art.'

'Ah,' nods Alice, looking him up and down, checking him over like a trader at a horse fair.

'My partner in crime, and my very best mate,' grins Charlie, totally overexcited.

'Well, that's a very good introduction for such a handsome man,' says Alice, giving him one of her largest red-rimmed smiles and a flick of her mahogany hair.

'Thanks very much,' nods Art, bowing slightly as he clicks his heels. 'Art MacDonald at your service.'

'And polite to boot,' smiles Alice. 'I think the evening has just taken a turn for the better.'

'It has indeed,' grins Charlie, grabbing hold of Art's hand. 'I can't believe you're here and you didn't tell me.'

'I wanted to surprise you.' He winks.

'You did?'

'Oh, yeah,' he says, rubbing his hands together. 'The look you had on your face just then was priceless and worth every mile of my BA flight.'

'How long have you known that you were coming?' she asks.

'A couple of days before you left.'

'A couple of days before I left!' she says indignantly. 'You shit.' She slaps him across his broad chest. 'And you didn't tell me?'

'I'm very good at keeping secrets, especially when they concern me,' he smiles.

'So how long are you staying?' she asks.

'About a week, maybe ten days,' he replies.

'Where?'

'A lovely new hotel near Portobello.'

'Why didn't you say?' she asks, slapping him again. 'You could've come and stayed with my sister.'

'What, with you, her, her husband and two small children? Take it from me, no house is that big,' he grins.

'And a nanny,' adds Alice, lighting a cigarette and trying to join in the conversation.

'And a nanny,' he repeats.

'Fair enough,' Charlie agrees. 'This is the nicest man in the world,' she says to Alice. 'And the best person to be with in a war-torn crisis. He's just so goddamn resourceful! I mean, if there is booze for barter in any armpit town anywhere in the world, this man will find it. He also carries equipment when you're too knackered to do it any more.'

'Actually, it's only your equipment I carry,' he corrects. 'Don't try and flog me as some carthorse.'

'And,' she continues, standing back admiringly, 'he is amazing, generous, funny, kind. And the most brilliantly talented photographer who has won loads of awards.'

'Nominated this year, are you?' asks Alice through her eyelashes.

'Not this year,' says Art, pulling back his golden chair. 'This year is pure pleasure.'

'He won best newcomer four years back, didn't you Art?' says Charlie, showing off for her friend.

'That was a long time ago,' says Art. 'Now, who wants some of this wine?'

Charlie sits down next to Art, and Alice sits the other side of her. Art pours out the glasses of wine and lights both their cigarettes. Meanwhile, the room behind them fills with all the freaks and uniques who inhabit the weird and wonderful world of photography.

First are the powerful picture editors, plump on expense-account lunches. They are accompanied by their pushy, nubile, sidekick assistants, whose poker faces control access to their bosses. Then there are the daredevil war veterans who stride fearlessly around the place, downing the free drink, feeling fab and sharp and witty on lines of cocaine. Quieter and slightly harder to find are the romantic, Bohemian, National Geographic types who are more at home in the Hindu Kush than they are in social situations. Thrilled at being able to spend an evening chatting in their mother tongue, they start out garrulous enough and usually end the soirée collapsed in a chair, high on alcohol and company. And finally, scattered to the four corners of the room, are the feral wildlife guys, who, dressed up in their cord finery, having put a comb through their beards, sit quietly observing the feeding frenzy, nursing a solitary beer.

'Ladies and gentlemen,' shouts a fat, florid man in a frilly blue shirt. 'Will you please take your places. Dinner will be served in five minutes.'

The noise level doubles as everyone worries where everyone else is sitting.

'I'd better move over to my seat,' smiles Alice as she wafts over in her lace-up minidress to the other side of the table, hidden by the huge bowl of pink lilies and undergrowth that are passing for an interesting centrepiece. 'Good luck,' she says, leaning over and blowing a kiss across the table.

'Have fun over there,' replies Charlie, cupping the side of her mouth to exaggerate the distance between them. 'Who have you got?' she motions as she watches Alice leaning over to check on the two empty places either side of her. She gives a massive thumbs-up.

'Andrew Edwards,' she mouths.

'No!' grins Charlie returning the thumbs-up sign. 'Fantastic,' she yells, cupping her mouth again. 'Alice has got Andrew Edwards,' she whispers into Art's ear. 'She's very excited.'

'I thought you didn't like him,' says Art.

'Well, everyone says he's awful.'

'Haven't you met him?' asks Art, sounding surprised.

'No,' says Charlie.

'But you're always so rude about him.'

'I know,' says Charlie. 'That's reputations for you.'

'There he is,' says Art, indicating with his breadstick. 'The man himself.'

'God,' says Charlie.

'I know,' nods Art. 'Handsome, isn't he?'

'Well, yes,' agrees Charlie. 'He's gorgeous.'

'Don't think he gets all those girls into bed on charm alone,' laughs Art. 'All right mate?' nods Art in Andrew's direction.

'Art!' comes a fabulous smile across the table. Andrew stops pulling out his golden catering chair and comes immediately over. Alice and Charlie look at each other through the lilies in surprise. 'Art!' he says again, his arm outstretched ready to shake hands. 'God, how are you? How are you? How wonderful to see you. What a wonderful surprise.' Art gets out of his seat and the two men embrace, slapping each other butchly on the back, touching cheeks. 'Jesus,' continues Andrew. 'I honestly can't remember the last time we saw each other.'

'A couple of years ago now, I think,' says Art. 'In some shit-hole refugee camp on the Somali border.'

'Oh God,' says Andrew. 'Fuck, I remember that place. Hell on fucking earth.'

'Yeah,' nods Art.

'Crazy days,' he says, slapping Art's arm. 'Crazy days, hey,' he smiles. He pauses for a second. 'Hey, mate,' he adds, his voice quietening and softening at the same time. 'Um, I'm sorry to hear about Jack,' he says, his eyes closing. 'He was a lovely, lovely bloke. And a brilliantly talented young man.'

'Thanks,' says Art, squeezing Andrew's arm. 'Thanks, mate. Oh,' he says, turning round. 'Have you met Charlie?'

'Charlie?' smiles Andrew, staring straight down Charlie's cleavage. 'I don't believe I've had the pleasure,' he says, making as if to bend down and kiss her.

'Charlie Adams,' says Charlie getting smartly up out of her seat to shake hands.

'*The* Charlie Adams?' he says.

'Um, yes?'

'Well, you are just as lovely as everyone says you are,' he says, his dark blue eyes flashing at her.

'Thank you,' she says, suddenly finding herself running her hands through her blonde hair. 'Um, I believe you and I are head-to-head tonight, so to speak,' she smiles.

'I believe we are,' he smiles back, raising his eyebrows in amusement. His thick dark hair shines in the bright stage light. 'I've seen your work,' he adds. His voice is accentless, rootless, English and totally international. 'It's really very good.'

'I loved yours on Chechnya,' she enthuses, clasping her hands together.

'Thank you,' he nods. 'May the best man, or woman, win.' He turns to go back to his place. 'See you later, mate,' he says to Art.

'Yeah, right,' nods Art.

'Lovely to meet you,' smiles Charlie.

'And you,' grins Andrew with a nod of his square male jaw.

'Well, you've changed your tune,' whispers Art out of the side of his mouth as he raises a glass to the opposite side of the table.

'I am a sucker for good looks,' says Charlie, trying to recover her composure. 'Why do you think I love you so much?'

'You're a two-faced cow,' says Art, turning to kiss her on the cheek. 'Fancy flirting with Cheesy Edwards. You're pathetic.'

'Isn't it ghastly?' laughs Charlie, hugging him back. 'But if you think I'm bad, watch a professional in action.'

They both turn to watch Alice. No sooner does Andrew sit down and re-introduce himself than she is out of the starter gates. She flicks her hair left and right, she licks her lips, she bats her eyelashes and pushes her laced-up, underwired bosom so close to his face that at one point he is in danger of licking her cleavage. Alice laughs with such force and abandon, Andrew must be telling simply the funniest stories and jokes. The man is besieged with foreplay and sexual innuendo and seems to take the whole thing in his stride. Occasionally, Charlie catches him looking at her through the lilies and gives him a smile, but his attention is entirely taken up with Alice.

A fleet of waiters arrives bearing a salmon and spinach roulade starter, and it is only then that Charlie realises quite how nervous she is. Unable to eat anything, she leans over and asks Art for some more drink.

'Careful,' he says. 'You might have to give a speech.'

'I have a feeling it's not very likely,' smiles Charlie. 'Anyway I'm far too nervous to do anything but smoke and drink.'

Charlie shifts in her seat. She keeps feeling like she needs to go to the loo, her chest is tight and her conversation is distracted. Totally ignoring the junior picture editor to her left, she claims a bottle of white wine as her own and drinks most of it herself, while attempting to chat and laugh with Art, reminiscing about old times.

'Do you know Andrew Edwards well?' she asks, having run through the gossip from the past ten days.

'Charlie!' he complains.

'What?' she replies. 'I'm only asking.'

'Not all that well,' says Art, his long dark eyelashes catching the bright light. 'I've been on about five or six stories with him, spent a couple of weeks with him in Haiti once, but that was a while ago.'

'God, I love you men,' says Charlie rolling her eyes. 'What do you mean you don't know him that well? In my book, we'd be the best of friends. Two weeks in Haiti, five or six stories together, that's bosom buddies.'

'Yeah, well,' shrugs Art. 'He's not much of a man's man.'

'You don't like him!' accuses Charlie with a delighted smile on her face.

'I never said that.'

'The man who likes everyone. The man who never has a bad word to say about anyone – finally dislikes someone,' she grins, wagging her finger.

'Actually, if you'd listened, Charlie, I didn't say that,' replies Art, shifting in his seat.

'You did,' she says.

'I didn't,' he says firmly. 'Anyway, can we drop it? I came here to see you,' he says squeezing her hand. 'I have flown halfway across the world to have an evening out with you, not to talk about Andrew Edwards.'

'Of course,' smiles Charlie, squeezing his hand back and hunching her shoulders. 'I agree with you. Look at him, smug bastard,' she laughs. 'He doesn't even look nervous, all smooth and chatting up Alice, and I'm sitting here, chain-smoking and drinking like my life depended on it.' She picks up her glass and chinks Art's. 'Here's to drinking and chain-smoking.'

'And winning.' He smiles.

'Yeah, that too, I suppose,' she adds, taking another sip.

The waiters return to remove the roulade and replace it with chicken breasts stuffed with porcini mushrooms, with potato croquettes and a selection of baby vegetables.

'Mm,' says Art, tucking in. 'This is great.'

'Mm,' replies Charlie. 'It's like chewing a trainer.'

'That's only because you're nervous,' says Art, patting her knee.

'I know,' replies Charlie, pushing her food around on her plate. 'I wish they'd hurry up.' She pours herself some more wine.

'Careful,' warns Art.

'I'm just dulling the pain of inevitable defeat,' she says. 'But not terribly successfully,' she adds by way of observation. 'I'm not managing to get at all drunk, at all quickly enough.'

'That'll be the adrenaline,' says Art, dabbing his wide smile with his napkin. 'It's when it goes that you'll have a problem,' he grins, tapping the side of his nose. 'I should know. I ended up with my head in a plate of cheese after I lost an award in South Africa a few years back.'

'I remember that,' laughs Charlie. 'Wasn't that for the Mutilados story with Jack?'

'Yeah,' says Art, raising his eyebrows quickly and looking straight down at his food.

'Yeah,' smiles Charlie. A cold breeze blows briefly between them. Charlie rubs her bare shoulders with the palms of her hands. 'Oh well, by the time I've drunk a bottle of wine, I won't care,' shrugs Charlie. 'Oh look,' she taps Art's arm, regaining his attention, indicating towards the stage. 'Here goes.'

'Ladies and gentlemen,' announces the florid man in the frilly shirt. 'I would like to welcome you to the Photographer of the Year awards and would ask you to welcome on stage your host for the evening, Adam Slaine!'

'Who?' says Art, clapping away.

'No idea,' replies Charlie, doing the same, as a slim dapper man in a black tie and two-tone silk morning suit, shot black and dark blue, comes on stage.

'Ladies and gents,' he says. 'I'm Adam Slaine and I'd like to say what a great pleasure it is to welcome you all here on this prestigious evening, in this prestigious hotel, for these prestigious awards, and what a great pleasure it is for me to be standing behind a desk for once!' He slaps the top of the podium. There are a few knowing laughs around the room. Art and Charlie look at each other and shrug. 'Thank you, thank you,' says Mr Slaine, acknowledging his own humour. 'Anyway, as you all know, photography is an art form . . .'

Charlie sits back, head lowered, and smokes another cigarette, lighting one from another in her anxious, heightened state. Art has his back to her. Turned towards the stage, he is smiling, engaged in the ceremony, admiring the work of the first nominees currently displayed on the big screen. Through the pink lily centrepiece Charlie suddenly feels the dark blue eyes of Andrew Edwards staring at her. She can feel them on her face, her shoulders, her breasts. She looks up and catches him. But instead of turning away, he carries on. He doesn't smile. He doesn't acknowledge her. He just stares. It's deep and penetrating. It is embarrassing and deeply erotic at the same time. Charlie feels her cheeks flush and her stomach tighten. Alcohol, adrenalin and desire course through her veins. It is a heady cocktail. She turns away. Shifting in her seat, she leans towards Art, touching his arm as she does so. Andrew Edwards is extremely unsettling. Art turns round and takes hold of her hand.

'Not long now,' he whispers, his dark curls tumbling forwards as he leans in. 'I know you can do it. I know you can. I have faith in you. You're the best framer in the business.

No one crops and frames like you do.' Charlie smiles and Art kisses the back of her hand.

Some drunken man with a lank, dank hairline that recedes almost to the back of his head is standing behind the podium weeping, thanking his mother, his agent, his art teacher, his girlfriend, everyone at the agency and Kodak film. He can't believe that he was nominated for 'best foreign story brackets not news and current affairs' let alone won it.

'Thanks very much,' says Adam Slaine, approaching the podium as he applauds in the air like a game show host, indicating for the overemotional winner to leave the stage. 'Right, next up is the best foreign story brackets current affairs, as opposed to the next award, which is best foreign story brackets news.' A murmur of amusement goes round the room. 'So the nominees for the best foreign story brackets current affairs, otherwise known as the David Lawrence Award, are Andrew Edwards for Chechnya – The Forgotten War. Amy Mo for The Aral Sea – The Human Cost. Charlotte Adams for Mozambique – After the Deluge. And finally, Trevor Jackson and Human Traffic – The Kidnap Wars of South America.'

Charlie is smiling. Her table is bathed in light. She can't see. Her hearing is strange and slurred. She is vaguely aware that photographs of devastation are being applauded. There are numerous little taps on her back and shoulders and mutters of 'Good luck' in her ear. 'And the winner is . . .' Some pretty girl from a daytime soap is slinking on stage in something tight and sexy, swinging the sturdy silver camera statuette by her side. 'And the winner is –' she smiles, all lips and gloss, leaning so close to the microphone that her sibilants pop – 'Andrew Edwards for Chich-en-iyah – the Forgotten War, yeah-hey,' she enthuses before launching a hand into the air and applauding. She leans forward, trying to look through the bright lights out into the crowd.

The auditorium applauds back in agreement, whistles and

shouts of approval echo around the high ceiling. Andrew Edwards is obviously a popular win. Charlie sits in her seat, biting the inside of her mouth as she claps and smiles, trying to look brave. She feels the occasional pat on her back, this time out of commiseration rather than encouragement. Her eyes are stinging, she feels hot, she digs her fingernails deep into the palms of both her hands. Leaning forward, she presses her thumb hard between her eyebrows. She read once that it stops you crying. But it doesn't seem to do the trick. She looks up to see the handsome Andrew Edwards saunter onto the stage and collect his award. He cups the buttocks of the slinky soap star, whose back arches and lips part with compliancy as he kisses her on both cheeks.

It is not until she sees him up there, on the stage, the silver camera statuette in his hands, that Charlie realises how much she actually wanted to win the David Lawrence Award. She has been pretending all day, all week even, that it doesn't matter, that she doesn't really care, that she isn't feeling emotional about it all. And she knows now that she was lying, as she sits there willing herself not to cry, trying to look chic and relaxed about losing. It's always the way with her. She always pretends the things she really cares about don't matter at all. It's self-preservation, a survival technique. She told someone they mattered once and they went away and never came back. She is sure as hell never going to make that mistake again.

'You okay?' comes Art's gentle voice as he puts a large hand on her shoulder.

'Yup,' lies Charlie, inhaling suddenly like she has hiccups.

'Never mind,' he says. 'I think you're a genius. And anyway, that man can't light to save his life. Look at that shot,' he points to the stage. 'It's shit.' He squeezes her shoulder. 'There's always next year.'

'Yeah, yeah,' she smiles. 'Next year . . .'

'Um, first of all I'd like to say thank you for this award,' says Andrew Edwards, holding his statuette aloft. 'It's a great honour to receive the David Lawrence especially considering the long list of wonderful photographers who have won it before me. I would also like to add that I was up against some fantastic and stiff competition with Mo and Jackson, and I would like to thank them for their contribution, but I would particularly like to single out Charlie Adams and her great work in Mozambique. Thank you for that,' he says, looking down from the stage. Charlie looks up, stunned. 'It's been a great year for me this year. I have been to some amazing, beautiful and truly desolate places. Let's hope it's a great one for everyone else next year. And let's all strive to make the world of newspapers and magazines a more aesthetic place.' With that, he holds the award up in the air again, shakes it, kisses it and walks off stage.

'Now that is the behaviour of an arsehole,' says Art, filling up Charlie's glass and his own. '"Great" this, "great" that . . . "Make the world a more aesthetic place", indeed. Who does he think he is, bloody Picasso? The man can't take a photo. And all that stuff about singling you out. What the hell was that about? The patronising git. He's just rubbing it in.'

Charlie is lost for words. She doesn't know what to make of Andrew's little speech. Should she be flattered? Should she be offended? She has no idea which emotion to feel.

'Do you think he was being rude?' she asks, sounding puzzled.

'Of course!' says Art. 'Well, at least *I* think so.'

Alice appears, squatting on the back of her high-heeled boots at Charlie's feet, her breasts balancing on her knees as she tugs at her skirt trying not to show her thong. She looks remarkably uncomfortable.

'Are you okay?' she says, rubbing Charlie's thigh.

'Yeah, yeah, I'm fine. Just a little deflated, really,' says

Charlie, feeling like a cord of tension has been cut above her head. She feels less sharp and less excited and more drunk than she did before the award was announced. 'I am a bit disappointed,' she adds. 'And I can't really work out that speech, either.'

'Oh my G-o-o-o-d,' says Alice, rocking on her heels. 'That was amazing.' She squats with her mouth wide open.

'It was?'

'Fuck, yes,' says Alice, her eyes round with shock. 'He's in love with you. It's that simple.'

'You talk such rubbish,' dismisses Charlie. 'Anyway, Art thinks I should be offended. That he was being patronising.'

'He does?' says Alice. 'You do?' she adds, leaning forward across Charlie's knees. 'I thought it was dead romantic.'

'No,' says Art, sounding irritated. 'I think he was definitely being rude. Anyway, let's not talk about him . . .'

'But that's all *he's* been doing,' interrupts Alice, flicking her burgundy bob.

'What?' says Charlie.

'That's all he's been doing,' repeats Alice, her head moving from side to side. 'You know, talking about you.'

'Who?' says Charlie.

'Andrew Edwards.'

'What?'

'Talking about *you*!' says Alice, pointing at Charlie. 'You have no idea how boring it is sometimes, being your friend.' She rolls her eyes. 'I mean, there I was, hot to trot, laying it out on a platter for him, giving him the old double hair flick and pout routine, and he's not interested. He even reintroduced himself, having not remembered me from the last time we met. I had constructed a whole future life together, named our children, even watched them win a cup on sport's day and he couldn't even remember my name. Anyway, it's hopeless. He fancies you.'

143

'No he doesn't,' says Charlie, tickled, but suspicious of Alice's enthusiasm.

'He does!' she insists, holding on to the table for support. 'All he's done is ask questions about you.'

'Really?' asks Charlie, smiling. 'Like what?'

'Who are you going out with? Are Art and you an item . . . all that type of stuff.'

'And what did you say?' asks Charlie.

'Oh God, that you and Art are brother and sister and you haven't had a shag in so long you probably don't remember how to do it,' she laughs.

'Shouldn't you get back to your seat?' suggests Art. 'Some people are trying to concentrate on the awards here.'

'You didn't!' says Charlie, covering her mouth.

'Might have done,' laughs Alice as she weaves her way back to the other side of the table.

'Your friend is a troublemaker,' says Art, taking a swig of his wine.

'No she isn't,' says Charlie. 'Honestly, Art, what has got in to you tonight? That's two people you don't like in one evening – it must be a record.'

Art doesn't respond but turns his back firmly on Charlie, pretending to be very involved in the rest of the awards ceremony. Charlie sits and smokes, staring at the empty seat next to Alice. A procession of bearded photographers walk on stage and collect various awards from best wildlife shot brackets with a hide, to best wildlife shot brackets without a hide. There is best underwater shot, won by a man with a shiny scalp and remarkably little hair. There's best news photo won yet again by the man from the *Independent*. And best fashion photo is won by a young man in a pair of very tight leather trousers that ride so high up his backside that he walks like he's sitting on barbed wire. And still Andrew Edwards doesn't return to his seat. Alice is remarkably unfazed and flaunts her underwired magic at the young man to her left, who flowers and flourishes with her attention. Art pretends to be fascinated by the awards, while Charlie continues to polish off her bottle of cheap Chardonnay that smells like baby sick.

What sort of game is Andrew Edwards playing? she thinks, sitting there with her glass of wine in hand. To pique her interest like that, to flirt with her – if Alice is right – in front of hundreds of people and then, just when she's interested, to disappear. How very odd, she muses, staring at his seat. The longer she waits, however, the less intriguing and the more irritating the man becomes. The more the ceremony drags on, the more personally she takes his absence. Art is right, she concludes, the man is a shit. A handsome shit, but a shit all the same.

After another half an hour of toing and froing and applause, Adam Slaine finally packs up his podium and the nominees and their guests are released from their tables and allowed to wander, networking, flirting and abusing each other at will.

'Come on then, Art,' says Charlie, determinedly rising to her slightly unsteadly feet, giving him a kiss on the side of his neck as she does so. 'Let's go and have some fun, do some networking and things.'

'After you, darling,' says Art, springing to his feet at her touch, linking his arm quickly through hers. 'You and me together,' he announces with his familiar lilt. 'Come on, let's see what damage we can do.'

'Quite right too,' says Charlie, leaning on him rather heavily.

'Where shall we go?' asks Art.

'I have no idea,' replies Charlie. 'You're the bloke, you lead for a change. Anyway, I can barely walk in these bloody shoes.'

'Chri-ist,' he grins, putting his arm around her shoulder as he looks down. 'I've never seen you in anything like that. God, Jack would have loved those, he was a sucker for heels.'

'God,' smiles Charlie as Art's removes his arm. 'I thought just the same thing earlier today.'

'Yeah, well,' smiles Art, sighing out loud. 'Lean on me,' he grins. 'And let's go and congratulate the *Independent* on their marvellous win again in the hope that they publish our Africa stuff a bit larger next time.'

'That's the best idea I've heard all night,' says Charlie, brightening up enormously.

'Are you okay about the award thing?' asks Art quickly just before they set off.

'Bugger them all if they can't recognise superior talent,' says Charlie.

'Yeah, right,' says Art, giving her arm a squeeze. 'Let's go and choke ourselves up the arse of the picture editor of the *Independent*.'

'I warn you,' smiles Charlie, 'I'll be fighting you for space up there.'

'I would expect nothing less.'

They march off arm in arm over to the *Independent* table and join the queue of acolytes trying to secure themselves contracts or positions or any form of name or contact to call later next week for a lunch, a drink, a coffee, a chat.

'Yeah, yeah, yeah,' says a young man with long hair and a Bohemian jacket. He has one runny nostril and the other frosted like a margarita glass. 'But the thing is . . . the thing is . . . the thing is,' he repeats over and over, trying to interrupt the conversation, 'the thing is there are heroes and heroes,' he says. 'I mean, heroism in our sort of field is two a penny, but the real heroes, the real heroes in my book, are the paedophiles. The real heroes are the paedophiles who don't sleep with children.' The whole table falls silent and stares at him. 'Don't you think, Mike, don't you think?' he repeats, tapping another man on the shoulder. 'The paedophiles who don't sleep with children are amazing?'

Charlie stares open-mouthed and Art starts to snigger.

'Jesus Christ,' she says, moving away from the queue. 'Who is that nutter?'

'I don't know,' laughs Art. 'What the fuck was he saying? All I know is that he's been for one power-piss too many tonight. I have never heard such rubbish in my life.'

'Amazing,' she laughs.

'Excuse me, excuse me, can I borrow your handsome date?' interrupts Alice, swaying drunkenly in her boots.

'What for?' says Charlie, clasping Art's hand. 'Haven't you found one of your own?'

'Mine's gone and got talking to some people who have a studio in the same studios as him. They're talking tea- and coffee-making facilities and I can't bear it,' moans Alice. 'There's a dance floor over there, and they're playing great music. I only want Art for one dance. Please, please, pretty please . . .'

'I don't dance,' says Art.

'Now you and I both know that's a lie,' grins Charlie. 'Art is one of the sexiest dancers I've ever seen.'

'I'm not,' he protests.

'You know you are,' smiles Charlie. 'I've seen you on the beach shaking that delicious backside of yours too many times for you to lie. You've been known to pull on the strength of your pelvic thrust alone.'

'Please,' says Alice. 'I don't often beg.'

'But . . .' he says. 'Oh, all right,' he agrees. 'But only one dance. Back in five,' he adds.

Charlie waves them off. Standing near the *Independent* table, she wonders whether to join the queue or get herself another drink, or work the room in the vain hope that some of the hard-core war boys from Africa have made it here after all.

'On your own?' asks an unmistakable international voice.

'Um . . .' says Charlie, turning round, trying to think of something witty to say, 'Yes.' She smiles.

'Drink?' he asks, handing over a glass of champagne.

'Please,' she replies. It's already in her hand. 'Where have you been the whole evening?' she asks, immediately regretting her lack of cool.

'Oh?' he replies, his dark eyebrows raised in amusement. 'Giving interviews, newspaper and radio, plus a couple of TV spots.'

'Oh, right,' says Charlie.

'Not just me,' he says. 'All the, um . . . winners.'

'Oh, right,' says Charlie, staring at him.

'I meant what I said on the stage, by the way,' he says, looking directly into her eyes.

'You did?' says Charlie, looking down at the floor.

'I did,' he smiles. 'I think you are a wonderful photographer, a truly wonderful photographer. Extremely talented. It's a rare and beautiful quality.'

'Thank you,' she smiles.

'Do you want to come and sit somewhere a bit quieter,' he says, taking hold of her hand. 'I think you and I have a lot in common.'

Charlie doesn't really know why she follows him. She is supposed to be waiting until Art comes back from his dance. That is their tacit agreement. But instead Andrew leads her off into a dark corner at the opposite end of the room. This is the man she was furious with only ten minutes before and now she is following him across the room. And it is not as if she doesn't know his history. She has counselled enough broken-hearted females to know that Andrew Edwards is dangerous. But there is something so beguiling about him, something so deliciously hypnotic about his voice, those dark blue eyes and the way he takes control, that he is impossible to resist.

6

Charlie wakes up with a four-lane bypass in her head. The mixture of cheap wine, champagne and too many cigarettes plus an emotional fall-out with a best friend is enough to make even the hardest of heads feel truly rotten the next morning. Slowly opening her eyes and stretching, she realises two things at almost exactly the same time. First that she is in totally unfamiliar surroundings, and second that she is nearly naked – wearing a man's pyjama top and her sister's thong. Sitting bolt upright in bed, she immediately regrets her decision to act so quickly as her brain takes a whole two seconds to follow, crashing into her forehead with considerable force.

'Oh God,' she moans, holding her head in the palm of her right hand. 'Where the hell am I?' Falling back against two fat pillows in crisp, clean-smelling ironed white linen cases, Charlie lies there and admires the view. She is horizontal in a deluxe bed in a deluxe apartment, the like of which she has never seen, let alone been in, before. 'Jesus,' she says as she flattens the thick white linen duvet cover down either side of her legs for a better view. 'Wow.'

Before her is an open-plan loft conversion with wide-plank oak floorboards and exposed brick walls. Down in the far corner at the opposite end of the enormous room is a stainless-steel kitchen. Taking up half of one wall of the loft, it has a steel cooker with individual units made up of butcher's blocks and steel-fronted cabinets on wheels, inside which Charlie can see a collection of copper pans and lots of different-coloured glass. Over the other side of the room is a long grey sofa with a long wooden Indian table in front of it, around which are two leather club chairs and a designer chaise longue made of black and white cowhide. Behind the cowhide chaise are two steel french windows that look out on to a roof terrace that appears to be home to a giant cactus and a silver trough of bamboo. On the other side of the room from the bed there is a curved half-wall over which Charlie can see the top of a large silver showerhead, while either side of the huge, high, linen-drenched bed, are fitted wardrobes.

The decoration of the flat is minimal to say the least. Apart from some fifties-looking fans and an old boiled-sweet dispenser made of chrome, there is nothing but photographs. Large framed black and whites of figures, naked girls, ethnic children and a landscape on the walls. Plus clusters of smaller framed photographs on various surfaces all over the flat. The style and the work are familiar. This must be Andrew Edwards' apartment, concludes Charlie lying half naked in Andrew Edwards' bed. But where is Andrew Edwards? And more importantly, why is she here? And did she have sex with him?

She whips her legs up suddenly under her chin and covers her mouth with her hand. Did she have sex with Andrew Edwards? What sort of hideous question is that? Never in her life has Charlie had sex and not been able to remember it. She has read it about it happening in books, and seen it in films, but has never really believed that it could possibly happen. Now she is in the same situation. And of all the people for it to happen with. The most notorious heartbreaker and sleep-around tart in the business.

But she doesn't feel like she's had sex. Then again she is certainly not in the clothes she arrived in. So he undressed her. She winces. It is a given, then, that he has seen her almost naked.

'Oh Lord,' she exhales. A cold reality sweat coupled with

alcohol guilt and general shame begin to creep and crawl all over her. She feels sick, itchy and is shaking. Waves of panic grab her gut as she holds on to the duvet and pulls it towards her.

The other half of the bed has definitely been slept in. She can see where his head has been, and can smell a trace of his citrus aftershave. His smart black-tie suit is hanging up on one of the door handles to the cupboards, his tie wrapped around the hanger, his white shirt on the back of a chair. But where are her clothes? Charlie sits up in her navy blue cotton pyjama top with white piping and scans the room for anything that might belong to her. She finds her handbag on the Indian coffee table and visibly relaxes. At least she can get out of here, she thinks.

Pulling back the duvet, she swings her legs over the side of the bed and suddenly sees a Polaroid of herself on the bedside table. She recoils slightly in shock, not entirely sure what she feels about men taking photographs of her while she is asleep.

'Weird,' she says out loud, picking it up to take a closer look. Fast asleep, with the morning light coming across her face, her blonde hair lying in curls across the pillow, it is a good shot, she thinks, shrugging. Turning it over, she finds a yellow Post-it note on the back. 'Good morning, sleepy head,' it says. 'Had to rush out. Back in a bit with breakfast. Make yourself at home – Andy X.'

Andy kiss? What does that mean, she thinks, getting out of the bed and walking over to the kitchen area, contemplating a pot of coffee. Andy kiss? Andy kiss? He doesn't strike her as an 'Andy'. Andys are sweet, cosy people. Old dark blue eyes, Andrew Edwards, is the sort of man who has women for breakfast. Often. And here Charlie is, joining the long, long list of previous occupants of the large bed, with linen sheets.

She flicks on the chrome kettle and kicks herself for being such a fool. She doesn't really know what came over her last night. She was drunk and overemotional. That she knows

155

for sure. She lost the award and her own head by the looks of things. Flirting with Andrew Edwards? It's pathetic. She and her girlfriends in Kenya have laughed about this sort of situation hundreds of times. Silly women who run after serial shaggers like Edwards. How can anyone fancy a bloke who has been around that much? It's tragic. It's a cliché. Charlie is surely bigger and better than to fall in love with someone like Andrew Edwards. Thinking you can change someone, thinking that you are the special one who can stop their womanising ways is the saddest, most doormat thing that Charlie has ever heard of.

She sighs out loud as she walks back across the high-ceilinged loft, trying to work out where he might have put her clothes. Opening the first set of fitted cupboards, she is greeted by a neat and immaculate display of clothing worthy of a shop. One end of the cupboard is full of white shirts, about thirty of them, all on hangers, all covered with plastic wrappers straight from the dry-cleaners. Some are from the Gap, others are from Helmut Lang, but most of them seem to be the same $15\frac{1}{2}$-inch collar shirt with bone buttons from Paul Smith. The other end of the cupboard is for all things black. Black Paul Smith T-shirts; there are eight of them. Black Helmut Lang shirts; there are five of them. Plus black Smedley jumpers, and a couple of cashmere V-necks all wrapped in transparent plastic. The drawers below are more or less the same. Piled high with black Calvin Klein pants that have all been ironed into four, like handkerchiefs.

'Some people think I'm anally retentive, I can't think why,' says Andrew, standing in the middle of the apartment watching Charlie riffle through his clothes.

'Oh Christ, um, hello,' she smiles weakly, tugging at the pyjama top, willing it to grow longer. 'Um, I was looking for my clothes.'

'Right,' he smiles. 'There's a dressing gown in the bathroom if you want to borrow it,' he adds. 'Your clothes are hanging up in there too.'

'Oh, right, good, thanks,' she smiles.

'Do you want some breakfast?' he asks, raising the two plastic bags he is carrying.

'Um,' replies Charlie, not knowing whether to stay or run away as fast as she can.

'Toasted bagels, smoked salmon and cream cheese,' he says.

'Um . . .'

'Go on,' he smiles. 'I can't eat them all on my own.'

'OK, then,' says Charlie, walking slowly round the half-wall to be confronted by her dress hanging up on a wooden hanger, her sister's Gucci heels underneath, with her strapless bra placed carefully over the top.

'All there, isn't it?' he asks from the other side of the apartment.

'Um, yes, thank you,' she replies.

The evidence of her lack of control is both embarrassing and shocking in equal measure. Charlie checks her face in the mirror, finding it hard to look herself in the eye. Bearing in mind how rotten, terrible and embarrassed she feels, she has seen herself looking worse. Her eyeliner has only pandaed slightly on her left eye but the right one is fine. Her old lipstick has managed to stain her lips, making them darker than usual but at least it has not smeared all over her face. The only thing, apart from her dignity, that she really has to worry about is her breath. Scanning the basin, she comes across some whitening toothpaste and, squeezing a small amount of it onto her finger, she smears it across her front teeth and then rinses her mouth under the tap. Hanging on a stainless steel hook just next to the basin is a dark grey cashmere dressing gown with a navy blue silk collar and belt. It is well worn and smells of citrus and Andrew. Charlie puts it on and draws it closer to her skin, luxuriating in its feel.

'It's lovely, isn't it?' smiles Andrew as he sees Charlie come round the corner in his dressing gown.

'God, yes,' replies Charlie. 'Where did you get it?'

'Someone bought it for me a long time ago in Italy,' he replies nonchalantly.

'A girlfriend?' Charlie asks and then immediately regrets it. For not only does she already know the response, she is angry with herself for asking and appearing to care about the reply.

'Yes it was,' he answers. 'How cooked do you like your bagels?' he asks without pausing as he bends down to check on the grill.

'However they come,' she says.

'Nice . . . and . . . easy, just how I like it,' he says, pulling out the grill and turning over the bagels. 'Oh Christ,' he says, turning towards her. 'Charlie, I am sorry, I didn't mean it like that. I wasn't suggesting . . .'

'Don't be silly,' she says. 'I didn't take it like that at all.'

She smiles at him standing in his glamorous kitchen. Dressed in a black V-neck from his extensive collection, Andrew has a fish slice in one hand and a fork in the other. He is wearing jeans and a pair of beaten-up old deck shoes with no socks. Close up, in the mid-morning light, he is more obviously attractive than he was the night before. His eyes are the same dark blue, but his hair is not as dark she thought. Brown and thick it has stripes of blond and copper running through it, bleached by the sun. His skin is also gently bronzed with the remnants of a tan from some foreign assignment or other. His nose is straight, his jaw is square, and his lips curl before he smiles. No one could say that Andrew Edwards is not a good-looking man.

'Right,' he says smiling, evidently relieved that she is not offended. 'I'm sorry I wasn't here this morning,' he explains. 'I had to do a Radio Five live interview.'

'Oh,' says Charlie, pleased that she had not asked that question at least. 'Not another winner's perk?'

'Um, yes,' he says, rather embarrassed. 'Nine-thirty this morning.'

'Well, thank God I lost the award,' she exclaims. 'I would never have made that in a million years. I was rather drunk last night,' she ventures with a weak smile, trying to work out the exact extent of her humiliation and the bounds of her contrition.

'You weren't that drunk,' he lies diplomatically. 'Just upset. Your friend Art . . .'

'Oh God, Art,' replies Charlie, the whole of last night returning in a series of vivid and virulent flashbacks. The row at the party. The hysterical cab ride back to Andrew's place. The rambling nonsense she spouted while sitting on his grey felt sofa, drinking Spanish brandy. Her brows furrow as she relives the whole glorious night in bright Technicolor. 'Um, did we?' She clears her throat and looks at Andrew, imploring him not to have to spell out her obvious question.

'Did we have sex?' he asks, politely taking up the baton as he looks up from the hot bagel he is spreading with a thick layer of cool cream cheese. 'Contrary to popular opinion, I am not in the habit of bedding weeping women who are slightly the worse for wear,' he says in a tone that is more matter of fact than terse. 'So your answer is . . . No, we didn't have sex.'

'Oh,' says Charlie, feeling a bizarre mixture of relief and disappointment that the man who has had half of London didn't want her. 'It's just that . . .' She tugs at the blue pyjama top.

'I took your kit off,' he smiles. 'You'd passed out on my sofa in what looked like rather an expensive dress, so I thought . . .' He smiles, laying out the pink salmon on the white cheese. 'Nice arse,' he adds, licking his fingers as he hands her a bagel on a plate.

'Thanks,' she says, trying to look him in his bold blue eyes. 'Good bagel.'

'Cheers,' he says. 'One of my fortés –' he adds, before

sinking his teeth into the bun '—breakfast,' he mumbles, wandering over towards his steel french windows and opening them wide to let in the morning air.

Standing bathed in sunshine admiring his view, Andrew Edwards looks just as impressive from behind. Long legs, broad shoulders, tight buttocks. Charlotte stares at him rather wishing she had had sex with him last night. She shivers.

'Are you cold?' he asks, turning round.

'Um, no, not really,' she replies.

'Are you sure?' he asks, lowering his lashes as he moves slowly towards her, putting down his plate.

'Um,' she says.

'Because there is something I can do to help with that,' he says.

His voice is low and quiet, teasing slightly as he stands above her blocking out the sun. Charlotte sits on her bar stool as Andrew slowly undoes the silk dressing-gown cord. 'Feeling warmer yet?' he whispers, licking his lips. The cashmere slides fall away to reveal her sitting there in his blue pyjama top and her white La Perla thong. Leaning forward, he runs his fingers up her legs. 'Warmer?' he whispers again. Slipping his hand under her top, he cups her tight bosom and kisses her, gently touching his lips against hers at first while he runs his hand fleetingly over her breasts. 'Warmer?' he mumbles. He moves closer and closer, forcing her thighs apart with his knees, squeezing her breasts harder and harder, teasing her mouth and lips apart with his tongue. Charlie arches her back and moans, opening her legs wider. Andrew inhales, running his tongue across her jawline and down her neck, finishing with his forehead between her breasts. He suddenly pulls away.

'I don't think this is a good idea,' he says.

'Why?' asks Charlie, her lips swollen, her cheeks flushed. She can see his erection in his jeans. 'I think it's an excellent idea,' she says, running her hands through her hair, exhaling. 'Why did you stop?' She tries to put her arms back around his neck and pull him towards her. He twists away.

'I just don't think this is a good idea,' he says, shaking his head as if trying to come to his senses and moving away.

'How can something be a good idea one minute and not the next?' she asks.

'I'm sorry,' he says. 'I just got carried away . . . seeing you there in my clothes, you looked, well . . . Anyway,' he smiles, 'you should go.'

'Go?' she repeats, puzzled.

'Yeah, go.' He nods.

'But we were just having breakfast.'

'I know, I know, I'm sorry,' he says, 'but I've got things to do and you should go and sort things out with Art.'

'With Art?' says Charlie, angry as well as confused.

'Yeah,' says Andrew, his back turned to her as he waves away her question with a movement of his hand.

'What has Art got to do with any of this? You and me?' she says, standing up from her stool and pulling the dressing gown around her.

'I just think you should go,' he says. His voice is cold, quite unlike the one that wanted to warm her up less than a minute before.

'Right,' says Charlie, stomping back towards the curved bath area in search of her evening dress.

'Hang on a sec,' says Andrew. Charlie turns round, hoping he has realised his mistake. 'Do you want to borrow some clothes . . . you know, to leave in?'

Charlie stands there as Andrew looks through his wardrobe, finding a pair of tracksuit bottoms and a black round-neck jumper for her to wear. 'There you go,' he smiles. 'And don't worry,' he adds. 'You can keep them.'

'Burn them, more like,' mutters Charlie as she stands in the shower area getting dressed. Her humiliation is total, she thinks, feeding her legs into his large sweatpants. What has she done? Why doesn't he want her? A wave of hideous self-loathing engulfs her as she slips on his itchy citrus-smelling jumper. Not only did she embarrass herself last night, making a fool of herself in public in front of future employers, but now she has practically begged a man to have sex with her. It's a total wipe-out, she sighs, looking at Kate's stratospheric heels staring at her from the floor. She picks up her dress, her strapless bra and the Gucci sandals and walks out barefoot into the apartment.

'Um, here,' says Andrew, offering her a pair of quilted, rubber-soled airline flip-flops. 'First class,' he says. 'Virgin.' He smiles. 'Well you can't go home in those.' He indicates towards the sandals. 'Don't forget this,' he adds, putting her handbag next to her on the floor as she slips the flip-flops on. 'Do you want me to call you a cab?'

'No thank you,' says Charlie, attempting to look defiant. 'I think I can look after myself. If I've got out of Mogadishu, I think I might manage to leave a flat in fucking . . . Islington,' she says, looking out of the window for a point of reference.

'Clerkenwell,' he corrects.

'Whatever,' she replies, bending down to pick up her stuff. 'See you around,' he says, moving to kiss her goodbye on the cheek like they have just met for a drink.

'I don't think so, do you?' she says, avoiding his attempt at civil niceties on the way to the door. 'Enjoy your breakfast,' she smiles. 'Try not to choke on it.'

It is only when she gets the other side of his front door and halfway down his cold, concrete, utilitarian staircase that Charlie collapses into a heap and starts to cry. She doesn't sob or cry out. Hot tears of indignation merely crawl slowly down her cheeks. That had to be one of the worst nights of her life, she thinks, sitting in the unforgiving stairwell, squatting on the floor. The place smells of cat piss. She exhales. People did warn her about Andrew Edwards. Why didn't she listen? Even Art doesn't like him, and Art likes everyone. Art, she smiles. Art. She sinks lower into the corner. She should really try and find him. He'll be nice to her at least.

It takes her ten minutes to find a hangover recovery kit. A newspaper, a packet of ten Camel Lights, a diet coke, a cab and a plastic carrier bag to hide her telltale dirty-stop-out wardrobe. Sitting on the black leather seat with the heater on full blast and half a can of coke in her stomach, Charlie is beginning to feel a whole lot better. Who needs arses like Andrew Edwards? Charlie flicks through the pages of the *Evening Standard*. Because that's exactly what Andrew Edwards is . . . an arse. Treating her like that. What was he thinking? She turns the page to find his pretty face staring right back at her. The newspaper is reporting on all the awards at last night's do. Yet they have used his blue-eyed mug shot to illustrate the story. 'Andrew Edwards,' it says, 'a popular winner.'

'That depends on who you talk to,' mutters Charlie, folding up the newspaper and flicking it across to the other side of the cab. 'Twat,' she says, looking out of the window. 'I think it's just a bit further along here,' she says, sliding back the glass driver window.

'Right you are, then,' responds the cabbie, his brakes squealing as he pulls up outside a modern-looking hotel on Westbourne Road.

Inside the minimalist lobby, the designer-clad receptionist directs her to Arthur MacDonald's room. She finds it at the end of a corridor, with a 'Do Not Disturb' sign still swinging from the handle and a pile of newspapers in a bag outside on the floor. It is obvious that Art is still fast asleep. Charlie knocks on the door and waits. There is no reply. She knocks again.

'Okay, okay, okay, hold on, hold on,' comes the muffled reply.

Art opens the door. Tall, toned and tanned, dressed only in a pair of white cotton shorts, he stands holding on to the door, trying to focus. His eyes are puffy, his hair is in a semi-dreadlocked state, and he smells of stale sweat and old alcohol.

'Oh,' he says. 'It's you . . . You'd better come in, I suppose.'

'That's not very friendly,' says Charlie, trying to be breezy.

'I'm not in a very friendly mood,' says Art, walking in an uncoordinated manner before flopping back down on to the low bed. 'I've got a hangover, I feel like shit, I've just woken up and I'm really pissed off with you . . .'

'I know, and I'm sorry,' says Charlie, following Art into his room. 'Jesus,' she says, waving her hand in front of her face. 'What have you been doing in here?'

'Oh, I don't know,' says Art, his dark curls on the pillow, his well-cut stomach turned towards the ceiling, his arms and legs splayed out like a starfish.

His rather swish room is in a very unswish state. The air is old, the windows remain unopened and there is a trail of clothes all over the floor, from the door to the bed. Starting with his dinner jacket crumpled over the back of a chair at the entrance to the room, Charlie can see the route he took to disrobe. His trousers lie in a pool of cloth the other side of the chair, followed by his tie, his shirt and one sock after the other ending up by the bed. The bed itself appears to be covered in a sprinkling of dry-roasted peanuts. In a drunken attempt at a late-night snack, Art must have burst open a packet of peanuts, exploding the contents all over his duvet. There is a small collection of drained minibar bottles by the bed. And, of course, his bagful of camera equipment filed in the corner by the door.

'So,' says Charlie, 'what time did you get home last night?' Her tone is jolly and enthusiastic, trying to break Art's morose mood.

'I left soon after you left with that twat,' he mutters, staring at the ceiling. 'I came home and obviously made very good friends with the minibar, although I don't really have any great memory of that.'

'Were you pissed, then? Last night?' she asks.

'Absolutely wankered,' he replies, as if it were an admirable state to be in.

'Oh, right,' she smiles, hoping that the amount of alcohol he consumed might go some way to explaining Art's behaviour. But Charlie has been drunk with Art on many an occasion and in some truly terrifying circumstances, and he has never behaved badly, or boorishly, or aggressively in any way before. So why would he now?

'But I still meant what I said last night,' he says, sounding sharp.

'What exactly did you say last night?' asks Charlie. 'I can't quite remember.'

'That's fortunate for you,' says Art, propping himself up in bed. 'I'm going to order some coffee, do you want one?'

It is the first friendly move Art has made since Charlie arrived, so she jumps at it.

'Don't you move,' she says. 'Let me organise it.' She gets out of her leather armchair and walks over to a telephone on a small round coffee table and, pressing the room-service button, orders a pot of coffee and some croissants. 'That'll make us both feel a lot better,' she says.

'It'll take more than a pot of coffee and some croissants to make me feel a lot better,' says Art.

'Hangover that bad?' she asks.

'No,' says Art, sounding childish.

'Look, Art,' says Charlie, trying to sound unconfrontational. 'What is it exactly that I've done?'

'I don't really want to talk about it,' he says.

'But that's all you wanted to do last night,' she mutters.

'If you want to hang out with cheesy twats like Andrew Edwards, then it's your business,' he says.

'Well, actually, it is,' says Charlie. Defending somebody who has just made her feel so small, so insignificant and so unhappy seems bizarre. But Art's behaviour is just as strange, and has put her on her back foot. 'Anyway, what has the man ever done to you?'

'Oh, never mind,' sighs Art, picking peanuts out of his bed and flicking them across the room. 'You don't know the half of it.'

'Try me,' she says.

'No, never mind,' he says, peeling back the duvet and sitting up. 'I'm going to have a shower. Will you answer the door when room service comes?'

'Friends?' asks Charlie.

'Always friends,' replies Art with a weak smile as he slopes off to the bathroom.

Charlie turns the television on and, confronted by a hair makeover challenge show, flicks through to CNN. Relaxing back in the armchair, dressed in her itchy citrus-smelling jumper, she half listens to the broadcast, letting the rolling news roll over her head. She can hear Art in the shower. He has left the door open, and the bedroom is filling with steam as he puffs and splashes around. There is a knock on the door and room service arrives with breakfast for two laid out on a small table that is wheeled into the room by a pale-looking man in a grey Chinese suit.

'Breakfast for two,' he says in an Eastern European accent. Charlie smiles and signs for her second meal of the day.

'That's better,' says Art, coming out of the shower, one white towel tied round his taut brown waist, another drying his dark curly hair. 'I feel much more like a human being,' he smiles.

'You smell a hell of a lot better,' says Charlie.

'Did I stink?' he grins.

'Ugh,' says Charlie, holding her nose.

'That's what comes of mixing Malibu with Martini,' he replies.

'Yuk,' says Charlie. 'Did you?'

'Apparently so,' he shrugs, picking up two small bottles and rattling them at Charlie.

'God you must have been pissed. You hate sweet drinks,' she says.

'Yup,' says Art, walking over to the wheelie table. 'Will you be mother?'

'Nothing I'd like more,' smiles Charlie, picking up the pot and pouring. 'So,' she says, trying the conversational approach. 'What are you going to do in London while you're here?'

'I haven't really thought out a proper itinerary,' he says, rubbing his hair dry. 'All I'd planned on was to hook up with you and see what happens sort of thing.'

'That's so you,' laughs Charlie.

'What?' he smiles, pulling up a chair and sitting down opposite, watching her hands as she pours. Still wearing one towel around his waist, he stops rubbing his hair and pulls the other smaller white towel around his shoulders like a poncho.

'Taking it all how it comes.'

'Well, I have a few meetings,' he says.

'Like what?'

'I don't know,' he says, picking up a croissant. 'I'm lying,' he grins. 'I haven't rung anyone yet.'

'How long are you staying?'

'I told you last night,' he says. 'A week, maybe ten days.'

'Right,' she says. 'What else are you going to do?'

'Oh, I don't know. I thought I might meet up with a couple of other Africa bods, there's some drinks thing later this week in the Bush. Don't you love that?' he chuckles. 'The Bush . . . The outback?'

'I think we're the only people who find that amusing,' she replies. 'Most people think it refers to female genitalia.'

'Oh,' he shrugs. 'Weird. What day is it today, anyway?'

'Wednesday.'

'Oh right,' he smiles. 'We could always just go out to lunch round here and do some shopping. There are some really good photographic bookshops.'

'What? Right after breakfast?'

'Well, it's a thought.'

'Um.'

'Do you have anything planned?' he asks.

'Not really,' she replies. 'I suppose if I had won last night I might be in great demand today.'

'Yeah, probably,' he smiles, running his hands through his hair. 'But you're here for a break, really.'

'I need a bit of time out,' she agrees.

'All the misery gets to you after a while . . .'

'Tell me about it,' says Charlie.

'Do you remember that French reporter in Rwanda?'

'Xavier or something?'

'Yeah, that's him . . . well, he shot himself last week in his hotel room in Nairobi.'

'Christ, really?'

'Yeah . . .'

'That's horrible.'

'I know. Apparently there was quite a mess. So,' he smiles, 'if you think you need a break you should bloody take one. No one looks after you, Charlie, so I'm telling you.' He is smiling and wagging his finger.

'Yeah,' she agrees.

'Can you pass the butter?' he asks.

'Yeah, sure,' she smiles, standing up and leaning over. 'There you go.'

Art says nothing. He simply stares. 'What are you wearing?' he asks very quietly, his face turning white.

'Um . . .' says Charlie.

'What are you wearing?' he repeats, but more slowly this time as his addled brain starts to work. 'Are you wearing his clothes?' His question is polite and to the point.

'Whose clothes?'

'You know damned well whose clothes I'm referring to,' says Art, standing up.

'Whose clothes?' she says again.

'Let me spell it out for you,' says Art, two pink patches appearing on his cheeks. 'Andrew Edwards' clothes. Does that jumper and –' he looks over the top of the table, feigning surprise – 'Oh! And do those grey trousers belong to Andrew Edwards?'

'Um, yes,' replies Charlie in a quiet voice.

'How could you?' asks Art, sitting back down at the table, sounding wounded and defeated. 'How could you after all I said last night?'

'But you didn't say anything really last night.' Charlie protests, defending herself.

'The man's a total tosser,' continues Art. 'And you ignored all I said and you went home and you slept with him . . . I can't believe it.' Art is becoming increasingly irate. He lifts his head and shakes it from side to side in anger and disbelief. 'Oh Charlie, Charlie, Charlie,' he says. 'Of all the people to sleep with . . .'

'I didn't sleep with him,' she says slowly.

'Oh, don't lie!' Art's voice is high and patronising. 'You've got his clothes on, you're wearing his shoes, and look!' he points, 'the dress you wore last night is in a grotty little plastic bag. Don't tell me you went home, slept on your own then popped by Andrew's shag pad this morning for a quick change, because I won't believe you.'

'I didn't sleep with him,' she says.

'Oh shut up,' says Art, taking his towel off his shoulders and hurling it on to the bed. 'Good, was he?' he asks. The sarcasm

169

in his voice makes him spit. 'Really good, was he?' He pauses. His mouth contorts. 'Better than my dead mate?'

'Now that is totally unfair,' says Charlie, her hands limp by her side with shock that Art can play such a low card. 'I don't have to stand around and listen to this shit.'

'No, you don't, actually,' says Art, his eyes flooding with emotion as he looks at the floor. 'In fact I would quite like you to leave.'

'Don't worry, mate, I'm going,' she says, hurriedly picking up her plastic bag for the second time that morning. She walks towards the door and turns around defiantly. 'I didn't sleep with the man,' she says quietly. 'I didn't sleep with him,' she repeats.

'You'll forgive me if I don't believe you.' Art is gently shaking his head, pointing towards the door. Charlie goes out into the corridor. 'Did you ask him what happened in Haiti?' asks Art quietly.

'No.'

'Well, ask him,' says Art with a wounded smile. 'And then see how much you like your lover-boy,' he adds before firmly shutting the door.

Charlie stands at the other side of the hotel room door, astonished by Art's behaviour. What has got into him? she thinks. What is wrong with him? He has never used Jack in an argument with her before. He even shocked himself. He is supposed to be her best friend. They have been through so much together. They always confided in each other. Even when she fell out with Jack. Especially when she fell out with Jack. Art was the one who always took her drinking when they'd had a row. Art was the one she called when she was in tears. So why was he being so unpleasant now? She knocks on the door.

'Art?'

'Go away,' comes Art's muffled voice.

'Art,' she says through the door. 'I think we need to talk.'

'Go away.'

'Really we do.'

'Leave me alone.'

'I promise I didn't sleep with him,' she says finally, hoping to appease him.

'I don't care . . . Leave me alone. What part of that don't you understand?'

'I'll call you later?'

'Whatever.'

Realising it is probably better to leave Art to wallow in his self-pity, hangover and unforgivable comments, Charlie takes a cab back to the sanctuary of her sister's house.

'Good God, what happened to you?' asks Kate as Charlie walks into the kitchen hoping to pour herself a cup of coffee that she might actually get to finish this morning.

'It's a long story,' says Charlie, putting down her plastic bag by the side of the steel-topped kitchen table and turning on the kettle. Sitting down, she sighs. 'In fact I've had quite a morning.'

'So?' interrupts her sister.

'So?'

'Did you win?'

'No.'

'Oh . . . Oh,' says Kate, sounding put out. 'Oh dear. Bad luck,' she says, smiling.

'Yeah, well.'

'Oh dear,' she smiles tightly. 'That's a bit of an error.'

'Why?'

'I told a few of my friends that you'd won.'

'Oh dear.'

'Yes, well,' says Kate efficiently. 'Maybe they won't remember.'

'Yes,' nods Charlie. 'They won't know. None of them read newspapers anyway.'

'That's true,' says Kate, staring at her sister deep in thought. 'God,' announces Kate. 'Have I had a morning!' she continues, rolling her eyes and curling her smooth hair round her moisturised fingers. 'The organic food delivery people have failed to turn up for the second week in a row. I mean, what is the point of ordering all your stuff on-line so that they can deliver it for you if you have to wait in all morning for it to turn up? Tell me, where is the convenience in that? That's two whole mornings in two weeks I've been trapped in the house, unable to go out because of them. I've been on the phone to them all morning and they promised they're on their way. But honestly, really.'

'Why? What did you want to do?' asks Charlie, holding her head slightly, wishing the world would slow down as she throws some coffee granules into a mug. 'I'm here now, you can go out and I'll stay in and wait for it all if you want.'

'I don't have anything particular I want to do,' explains Kate. 'But that's not the point. I might have had something I wanted to do – you know, something important.'

'Oh, right,' says Charlie. 'Um, do you want some coffee?'

'Do you know, yes, I would, I haven't sat down all day,' says Kate, shifting in her seat. 'Anyway,' she asks, pulling her boots up a rung on her chair, hunching up, all smiling, tense and keen. 'Where have you been *all* night? When I checked your room this morning, I couldn't believe it – all undisturbed and unslept in . . . Amazing! Who was it? Who is he? Are those his clothes? They look okay . . .' she leans over to check the label of the black jumper and nods her approval, 'and if you tell me you have not found Mr Right after all the effort I've been to,' she shakes her head, 'I will be furious, to say the least.'

'Well . . .'

'What's his name? Do I know him? Come on, come on, we've all been waiting ages for this moment.' She sighs.

'It isn't what you think.'

'Oh,' says Kate, taking a sip of her coffee, trying not to sound bored. 'What is it then?'

Charlie leans forward and, picking up a pen, doodles all over her newspaper as she tells Kate the story. She starts with the awards, tells her all about the flirtatious conversation she had with Andrew, the way he complimented her on her work, the row with Art and her leaving. She describes his apartment, the breakfast, the kiss and the way he asked her to go and all that happened when she went to visit Art.

'God,' exhales Kate when Charlie has finished and both their coffees have long since gone cold and greasy. 'You've had quite a morning,' she says.

'Yeah,' says Charlie, smiling, enjoying being in her sister's company and feeling a whole lot better now that she has told someone the story. 'So what do you think is the reason behind all this?'

'Oh, I don't know,' shrugs Kate. 'Maybe Andrew's gay.'

'What?' says Charlie, laughing at her sister's explanation.

'His flat sounds very gay,' says Kate, optimistic about her analysis. 'His clothes look gay.' She's laughing. 'Stranger things have happened.'

'Have you listened to a word I've said?' asks Charlie.

'I promise I have,' replies Kate, her hands in the air, surrendering.

'Andrew Edwards is one of the most red-blooded males I have ever come across.'

'So?' says Kate.

'He has had more lovers than you, me and half of West London put together.'

'So?' says Kate.

'He's got two children.'

'Now that's just a cover,' nods Kate, laughing at the ludicrousness of her own argument.

'He's got two children,' laughs Charlie, continuing her case. 'One lives in the Lebanon and the other lives in Haiti . . .' She stops laughing.

'What? What?' says Kate. 'Don't tell me I'm right. Don't tell me I was right all along. You see, you see . . . I knew it.'

'No, hang on a sec,' says Charlie, getting slowly out of her seat. 'Do you mind if I use your phone?'

'Sure,' says Kate. 'You look serious.'

Charlie picks up the walkabout telephone and dials Alice's number.

'Alice Fraser Associates,' says Gavin with pen-pushing efficiency.

'Gavin?'

'Yes.'

'Hi, it's Charlie.'

'Charlie,' he says, moving into scold mode. 'You are a naughty, naughty girl.'

'Why?'

'My boss is in such a terrible state because of what you did to her last night, she can hardly say her own name.'

'No!' exclaims Charlie, smiling.

'Yup,' confirms Gavin.

'Can I have a word with her?'

'It's Charlie, can she have a word with you?' asks Gavin across the office. There is a mumbled reply. 'Only if you are very, very kind.'

'I promise,' smiles Charlie.

'Hello,' says Alice in a voice that Charlie barely recognises, like whisky and cigarettes churning in a barrel of gravel. It sounds as if Alice has undergone a botched tracheotomy since last night.

'You sound terrible,' says Charlie. 'Does it hurt?'

'Only when I try and shout, and then my head joins in as well,' she says.

'I need to speak to you,' says Charlie. 'About Andrew Edwards.'

'Oh, right,' says Alice, breaking into a whisper. 'Don't worry about him,' says Alice, muffling the telephone slightly and lowering her voice to a point where it is almost inaudible. 'I scored someone else last night.'

'You did!' Charlie squeals despite herself.

'What?' says Kate.

'Tell you later,' says Charlie, covering the telephone. 'That's great,' she says to Alice.

'Mm,' agrees Alice. 'I can't really talk right now.' She adds brusquely for the benefit of someone else, 'I'm trying to run an agency.'

'Yeah, yeah, I've heard that before,' laughs Charlie.

'No, I'm serious,' says Alice. 'Someone from Sony has just arrived.'

'Oh, right.'

'Can we meet later? Drinks in Soho? At the Century Club on Shaftesbury Avenue?'

'I'll find it,' says Charlie. 'Seven?'

'Done.'

Charlie puts the phone down and smiles at her sister. 'Do you want to come?' she asks. 'Out with me and Alice for a few drinks? We're going to a place called Century. It might be fun . . .'

'Oh, I know that place,' says Kate, sounding pleased with herself. 'My best friend Claire's a founder member – she's always talking about it. She's there all the time. She meets lots of her celebrity pals there after her launch parties and things. It's quite glamorous. I think it's open quite late.'

'Come, then. Call Claire and bring her with you.'

'She's not around tonight, I've already spoken to her,'

replies Kate. 'She's got a dinner with someone very important in town, or at least that's what she said. You'll probably see her in Century later.'

'Well, you should come,' repeats Charlie.

'It's sweet of you,' says Kate, 'but I've given Peta the night off. She wants to see that new film with Russell Crowe and Alex is off playing squash and having dinner with someone from work, so it's my turn to babysit.'

'Can't you get someone in?' asks Charlie. 'Aren't there agencies for that sort of thing?'

'Oh no,' says Kate, horrified. 'I couldn't leave them with someone they haven't met.'

'What, socially?' says Charlie.

'You know what I mean.'

'How about someone you've used before?' she suggests.

'I've never left them with other people,' says Kate. 'If you have children of your own . . .'

'Fine,' says Charlie, wanting to avoid another argument. She has had enough of those for one day. 'As you wish,' she adds. 'Anyway, doesn't Alex play far too much squash?'

'He really enjoys it,' says Kate with a tight smile. 'And anyway, anything to keep him fit,' she adds. 'He's got to watch his cholesterol.'

Charlie spends ten minutes walking up and down Shaftesbury Avenue trying to find Alice's club. It is obviously so damned discreet that you need a special glamour radar to find it. On the point of giving up, she asks two rather handsome boys in chic black coats for directions. They lead her to a low-key wooden entrance next door to a pasta chain and guide her up the steep stone stairs, introducing her to the pleasant women on the door. Alice is in the second-floor bar, they tell her, just up the stairs. All white and limestone with dark wooden furniture and leather armchairs, Century is quite unlike all the other members' clubs that Charlie has ever been invited to. Devoid of dusty, fusty sofas and flatulent alcoholics florid and incoherent with red wine, the atmosphere is laid-back and businesslike at the same time, peppered with pinches of opulent laughter and elegant networking. There is a huge floral fan arrangement like a displaying peacock on the bar and an attractive Frenchman mixing cocktails behind.

Alice is already ensconced in the far corner and dressed in something black and bat-winged, waving at Charlie to come over. She has a pink drink in one hand and a cigarette in the other.

'I strongly recommend the Cosmopolitans in here,' she says, speaking as a connoisseur. 'They are some of the best in town, and they come by the half pint,' she smiles, raising a large half-drained cocktail glass.

'I thought you weren't feeling too good?' asks Charlie, sitting down in a ginger armchair and slowly sinking as her knees edge towards her chin.

'I'm not, or should I say, wasn't,' grins Alice. 'The only way to deal with bastard hangovers like this,' she announces, 'is to drink through them.'

'I'd better have one of those and play serious catch-up,' says Charlie, getting out of the armchair and making her way to the bar.

'Get a couple of bowls of chips and mayonnaise as well,' demands Alice. Drinks and chips on their way, Charlie settles down to pick what is left of Alice's brains. Recounting the proceedings of the night before and this morning, she leans forward in her armchair awaiting Alice's response.

'Well, your guess is as good as mine,' she says uselessly.

'Oh come on, Alice,' says Charlie. 'I thought you were the authority on the man.'

'I am, I am,' says Alice, disliking her authority being questioned on any subject.

'Okay, tell me what you know about Haiti, then,' says Charlie.

'Oh Lord,' puffs Alice, taking a large swig of her cocktail. 'I don't know that much, except – and this is all gossip mind –' she says, pointing her finger in the air. 'Andrew had an affair with some local girl and got her pregnant. A five- or six-year-old boy, or about that age, and that's all I really know.'

'Is that it?' asks Charlie. 'I knew that already. Surely you must know something else?'

'Um,' says Alice, dragging on her cigarette, trying to think very hard indeed. 'The girl was apparently rather glamorous, beautiful,' she embellishes. 'Some politician's daughter who translated for lots of members of the press. Ask Art, he probably knows her.'

'How do you know that?' asks Charlie.

'They were all out there at the same time, weren't they?' says Alice, flicking her ash.

'Yeah, but . . .'

'Well then, he must know,' says Alice, inhaling some more cocktail. 'You're like a bloody pack of hyenas. Travelling around together from story to story, hellhole to hellhole.'

'When was this?'

'Oh, I don't know,' says Alice, lounging back in her chair and immediately regretting it. 'I'm useless at that sort of thing,' she adds, sitting up. 'Some sort of armed conflict in Haiti . . . with the Yanks?'

'God, I remember that,' says Charlie, eating three chips at once. 'I had a mate Deborah who went there in the mid-nineties to do that story for American TV. It was a bit before my time. Clinton sent in troops.' She stares off into the ether. 'Of course, they would have all been together,' she mutters to herself. 'It was a big story.'

'Yeah, well then,' says Alice, finishing her drink. 'Shall we have another round?'

'Good idea,' says Charlie. 'I want to hear all about you and what you got up to with – what's his name?'

'Patrick,' says Alice, perking up at the attention and coming out with a long languid, dramatically sexually sated sigh.

'Oh God,' moans Charlie. 'Was he really that good?' Alice smiles. 'I don't know if my sad unfulfilled life can cope with all your gymnastics,' continues Charlie. 'I definitely need another drink before I hear your blow-by-blow, thrust-by-thrust account.'

Drink follows drink and story follows story as Alice shares every single salacious, unnecessary detail about her date last night. From party to penetration, Charlie hears about Patrick's ability to charm with his tongue both and in and out of bed. She hears how, after Art stormed off in his terrible mood, Alice lured Patrick away from his in-depth conversation about tea- and coffee-making facilities and how Alice persuaded him to go late-night drinking.

'After that, quite frankly he was putty in my hands,' she smiles. 'It was all back to mine for some serious fun and games.'

'And he was good?'

'Oh my God yes,' says Alice, throwing her head back in remembered ecstasy. 'He was wonderful.'

'You are a bad woman,' says Charlie.

'I know,' smiles Alice.

'So will you see him again?' Charlie asks.

'Might do,' says Alice, flicking her ash. 'It depends how I feel.'

'Has he called?' asks Charlie.

'Called?' says Alice, sounding surprised. 'Don't be ridiculous,' she smiles. 'I haven't given him my number.'

'Oh,' says Charlie. 'Am I that old-fashioned?'

'Yup,' says Alice. 'You're about as with it as a ra-ra skirt.'

'Are they no longer in fashion?' says Charlie, feigning

surprise. 'Now you tell me . . .' She laughs. 'I've got to go to the loo,' she says, standing up, swaying slightly as she walks. 'Back in a sec,' she says. 'Do you know where it is?'

'Over there,' says Alice, pointing towards the stairs.

Wandering across the second floor, Charlie teeters gently down the stairs and, following the directions of the barman, finds herself behind a screen at the back of the room next to the gents and a disabled loo. The disabled loo is engaged. She waits. She leans against the wall and thinks about anything other than running water. Moving uncomfortably from one foot to the other, she gives the disabled door another little knock. There is no reply.

Five minutes later, she decides the cubicle must be empty and, leaning against the door, she gives it a bit of a kick. It swings open to reveal a couple, a woman astride a seated man, in the full, sweaty, panting throes of sex. Her expensive skirt is hitched up around her waist, her tights and lace pants are in a complex knot on the floor, and her jumper and bra are pushed up under her chin. She flicks her blonde head of highlights from side to side, grinds her rippling bare buttocks and makes highly appreciative sounds. She doesn't appear to notice Charlie in the doorway. The man is also blissfully ignorant. Trousers round his ankles, in a suit and tie, sitting on the toilet, were it not for the enthusiastic female bouncing up and down on his groin, he could have been doing something entirely different.

'I am so-o-o sorry,' giggles Charlie, falling against the door frame. The couple stop. They both turn their puce, sweaty faces towards the light and stare. 'Jesus Christ,' says Charlie, holding on to the door handle. 'Alex! Claire! What the fuck are you doing?'

Alex's mouth opens slowly in shock. Botox prevents Claire from looking surprised.

7

Charlie doesn't hang around to listen to their duplicitous explanations. Leaving them still sitting in their petrified state like a couple of cheap Kama Sutra statues, she sprints up the stairs. Shouting something garbled and frantic in the general direction of Alice who seems to comprehend that something is up, she is straight out of the door and on to Shaftesbury Avenue. Tearing up and down the street, her eyes frantically scanning the traffic for an accommodating orange light, she is determined to get to her sister's house before Alex. Driven on by powerful surges of adrenaline and sibling protectiveness, Charlie dodges traffic like an immortal in a computer game, hurling herself in front of cars, running down the centre of the road, her arms in the air, waving at random vehicles.

Two, if not three, cabbies actively avoid her. One switches off his vacancy light as soon as she approaches, another locks his doors, while one carriage simply drives on by, possibly unaware that she is shouting and waving at him. Eventually, as she approaches Eros and the milling hordes at Piccadilly Circus, she starts to calm down. Walking past the pavement artists who paint their subjects like Hollywood pin-ups, Charlie realises that she is crying. It must be the shock of the whole situation, she thinks, as she weaves her way through the slow, doughy throng of tourists tucking into their flip-top polystyrene boxes of fast food. Although she has suspected Alex's infidelity all along, somehow seeing it made flesh, gyrating mounds of sweaty pink flesh, has hurt her much more than she ever thought possible. She has never really liked Alex. What little she knows of him does not appeal that much. He has always come across as a pedantic cold fish who has never paid her much attention. She has tolerated him because of her sister. His competitiveness, his middle-aged manner and ability to patronise at thirty paces have been bearable only because he supposedly loves her sister and she loves him. But she never really expected him to be capable of such a betrayal. And with his wife's best friend of all people. What an unattractive couple they make. Adulterer and traitor wrapped around each other like a couple of copulating octopuses on Ecstasy.

She has to get home before him. Her adrenaline is pumping, her heart firing on all four cylinders. Eventually, as she turns the corner into Regent Street, she finds an empty taxi in the queue at the lights. Tugging at the door, she collapses back into its black leather interior and sighs with relief before immediately sitting forward, desperate to impart a sense of urgency.

'It's really important that we get there as quickly as we can,' she says, having announced the address.

'Yeah, yeah,' replies the jaded cab driver, pretending he is interested.

'No, honestly,' insists Charlie. 'I know you get this all the time from people who are late for their trains or meetings or lunches –' she is babbling – 'but this really is an emergency. I have to get home before my sister's husband . . .'

Charlie pulls back the partition and, squatting on the floor, recounts her terrible discovery directly into the cab driver's ear, which is so stuffed with hair it looks as if a nest of spiders have set up home. The more the cab driver hears, the faster he goes. Charlie ceases to become a passenger and takes on the role of co-pilot, leaning over his shoulder, her chin on the partition; she offers a litany of both helpful and unhelpful suggestions.

'Left here,' she shouts. 'And then right!'

He weaves through the traffic, jumping red lights and cutting up colleagues, eventually depositing her on her sister's doorstep. Leaping out of the back of the car, she searches through her handbag for her purse.

'No, no,' insists the driver. 'Get yourself in there.'

'Oh my God, thank you,' grins Charlie.

'Good luck,' he replies as she sprints up the path.

'Thanks,' she says, waving, before pulling herself up short in front of the door.

Taking a deep breath, she tries to compose herself before ringing the bell. As she stands with her head lowered sorting her thoughts, the front door swings wide open. Bathed in the soft light of the round paper Conran chandelier, dressed in an elegant pair of purple silk pyjamas and grey felt Boden slippers, is Kate. Her face is cold, her eyes are hollow and she is barring the way.

'Oh my God, Kate,' starts Charlie, shaking her head, her voice all high-pitched with emotion. 'I don't know how to say this, so I'll say it straight out . . .' Charlie makes as if to walk into the house but Kate still bars the way. 'Move out of the way,' suggests Charlie, not really understanding the situation, 'I can't get in.'

'That's the whole point,' says Kate. Her voice is as hard as the grip she has on the front-door frame.

'What?' says Charlie. 'I don't understand . . . Let me in, I have something I want to tell you.'

'Whatever it is, I don't want to hear it,' says Kate. 'In fact, I have no desire to talk to you at all.'

'What are you saying?' asks Charlie, taking a step away from the door in her confusion. 'How do you know what I want to say to you?'

'It'll be something along the lines of my husband is sleeping with my best friend and you have just discovered them

183

together.' She executes a pert little smile. 'Accurate enough for you?'

'But . . .' Charlie's arms fall limp by her sides. 'How . . . ? I'm so sorry . . .'

'And quite frankly I don't believe a word of it.'

'What?' says Charlie. 'I don't understand. I'm telling the truth. What are you saying?'

'He said you would say that.'

'Who?'

'Alex, of course,' says Kate, standing back from the door frame to reveal Alex leaning against the hall wall.

'But how . . . ?' she asks. Alex just smiles and smugly throws his car keys in the air, catching them in his confident left hand.

'But, Kate,' says Charlie, spurred on by the man's arrogance. 'I don't know what he has told you, but they were having sex when I saw them. I caught them red-handed. At it. Plain as bloody day . . .'

'I don't believe you, I don't believe you, I don't believe you,' Kate parrots over and over again, covering her ears and closing her eyes, hearing and seeing no evil.

'*But I saw them fucking!*' shouts Charlie.

Now it is Charlie who sounds hysterical. It is Charlie who sounds unhinged and Charlie who is totally out of control.

'I promise you, I found them doing it in the disabled toilets at Century,' she says quietly, hoping that mention of the precise location might bring her sister to her senses.

'Oh honestly, Charlie,' sighs Kate. She sounds patronising. 'Of course they weren't, don't be insane. Really,' she adds, in an almost concerned tone. 'I know that you've found it difficult to settle in since you've come back from being away. But mucking up my marriage because of your petty jealousy is, I would have thought, beyond even you. Ever since you've come back from Africa you've found my domestic bliss difficult to accept. You want what I've got. You want the children that I have, the husband that I have. You want my life, my marriage, because it is so happy and real – while yours is sad and superficial. And I'm not falling for it.'

'Your happy and real marriage!' pronounces Charlie, shocked by her sister's reaction. 'Don't make me laugh.' She snorts. 'Your happy marriage is about as real and happy a version of domestic bliss as a fucking Wendy house down the bottom of some kid's garden. Don't make me howl with laughter. Happy and real? It's pathetic. You wouldn't know happy and real if it came and vomited all over your soft furnishings.'

'I couldn't really believe it when Alex said on the telephone that you had reacted like this . . .'

'He called you?' asks Charlie, fumbling for some sort of explanation.

'Oh yes,' says Kate. 'As soon as you had jumped to your ridiculous conclusions and rushed out of the club like some nutcase. He warned me you would rush home with all your lurid little allegations. And I didn't really believe him. But look at you! He's right. You're mad . . . and actually, do you know, for the sake of me, Alex and the children, I would like you to leave,' she adds, opening the front door and depositing Charlie's hastily packed rucksack and shiny silver camera case on the doorstep. 'Honesty, I think you need help. It's sad, very sad. I'd hate for you to go through the whole of your life this embittered and this unhappy.'

'Not quite as sad as being stupid and naïve,' says Charlie, bending down to pick up her bags. She starts to laugh. It is a slow, odd and obviously forced chuckle, born from anger not amusement. 'So what has he told you happened, then?' she asks, raising an eyebrow, throwing her rucksack on her back and picking up the case.

'The truth,' says Kate, her hair swinging with defiance.

'What sort of truth?' asks Charlie.

'The whole truth,' smiles Alex, coming out of the shadows.

'I'm not asking you,' says Charlie.

'The simple truth. That Claire was upset and in tears in the Century bar. That she had had some sort of row with Tim. And that Alex had taken her somewhere quiet for a talk where she could stop making a fool of herself and calm down.'

'Oh right,' says Charlie. 'He was dishing out a bit of comfort, was he?'

'Yes,' insists Kate. 'He was.'

'How very modern and sensitive of him,' suggests Charlie.

'Yes,' says Kate.

'So all he was doing was comforting a distraught friend of yours?' says Charlie.

'Yes,' says Kate.

'So, in fact, he was doing you a favour?'

'Exactly,' says Kate.

'Well, that all sounds totally acceptable to me too,' says Charlie, turning round to leave, feeling defeated. 'Except you should ask yourself one question. What on earth was your husband doing with your best friend in Century in the first place? Wasn't he supposed to be out playing squash? Helping his cholesterol? Oh well,' shrugs Charlie, as she walks down the path, carrying her rucksack over her shoulder. 'Sex, squash, I suppose it's all exercise . . . I'll be on my mobile if you need me.'

Charlie turns and starts to walk up the path, fully expecting her younger sister to shout after her. To run after her. To tell her that she, Charlie, is right. That it has all been some dreadful misunderstanding. That they should all calm down, come back inside and have a drink to discuss it all in a rational and cool manner. But instead Kate says nothing. Charlie walks slowly, narrowing her stride, giving her sister ample opportunity to change her mind. It is not until she hears the click of the front door as it closes shut that she understands Kate is for real. Charlie stops outside a house two doors down and contemplates turning back, knocking on the front door, pleading with her sister to listen, if not to her then to reason at least. But it is obvious that Kate will not listen to reason. Or, thinks Charlie as she stands there, she just can't afford to.

Charlie stares at the long dank pavement stretching away ahead of her, wondering where she should go. The glow of the street lamps reflects orbs of orange on the drizzle-drenched stones like a string of false urban sunsets. A businessman, briefcase and umbrella in hand, trips towards her, his shoes tip-tapping on the pavement with their expensive leather soles. The shouts of fumbling drunken youths carry up from the main street and a car alarm goes off in the next-door road. Heaving her heavy bag higher on her back and clutching her living in her right hand, Charlie walks towards the Uxbridge Road and really starts to hate this country. The longer she stays here, the less it feels like home. Home is supposed to be a state of mind, she thinks. There are times when she has felt totally at home in places she has never been to before. Laughing on the beach in Lamu having drunk too many Old Pals. Talking around a campfire out in the bush. Gossiping to Art until four in the morning. But somehow she had always thought of Britain and London as her real home. The place where she belonged. The place where she would eventually return. The place where she always saw herself living when she grew up. The place that she always said she came from. Now, as she stands on the street wondering where to go with her rucksack on her back, she realises that this is no longer her home. She is lost. She no longer knows the rules; she is an outsider who doesn't fit in. But then, she muses, unlike all those professional Londoners before her who couldn't bear being parted from the smells of the city, the sounds of the streets and the chimes of Bow Bells, she is the woman who went away for nearly five years and all she ever missed, apart from her family, was Marmite and smoky bacon crisps.

Reaching the end of the street, Charlie throws her heavy bags on the ground and stares up the road looking for a cab. It is late and wet and the cabs are few and far between. Charlie feels exhausted and deflated and miserable waiting on the corner, her badly packed life lying limply at her feet. Eventually, after a seemingly endless twenty minutes, an unlit cab takes pity on her pleading arm and pulls up outside the 24-hour convenience store.

'Where to?' asks the driver as she throws her bag in the back and clambers in behind.

'Westbourne Grove,' she says, after a moment's hesitation. There really is nowhere else for her to go. Alice will undoubtedly be drinking, dancing or randomly fellating. Oh my God, Alice. Charlie reaches into her bag for her mobile phone. Of all the people to abandon at short notice in a bar, Alice is the sort of person who would be least offended, thinks Charlie, rummaging deep into the dust and chewing-gum depths of her bag. She will understand that there has been an emergency. She will be relaxed about being unceremoniously dumped halfway through a story and a girls' night out. Charlie dials the number.

'Wotcha!' comes the reply, followed by an irritating comedy pause that fools no one. 'Fooled you,' the reply continues. 'I'm probably otherwise engaged. Leave a message after the tone . . .'

'Alice,' says Charlie. 'I am so sorry about leaving you in the middle of the evening, but something came up. Something big. I can't explain now. But I will do tomorrow. I'm sorry. Hope you're okay. I'm okay, so don't worry. Speak tomorrow. Oh, it's Charlie by the way . . . bye.'

'Where do you want on Westbourne Grove?' asks the driver, deftly sliding the glass back with his left hand.

'Oh, that smart hotel place,' says Charlie.

He doesn't reply. He pulls back the partition and turns up the Radio Five late-night phone-in show on the state of the NHS.

'. . . my father died . . .' declares a female voice. Charlie sighs and stares out the window. '. . . and quite frankly it wasn't good enough . . .', '. . . I blame . . .'

The pretty girl on reception is pleasant but firm. No amount of pleading and begging from Charlie is going to get her into Arthur MacDonald's room without him being there.

'Not that you're going to rob the place,' she smiles, quietly valuing her job, 'but it is hotel policy not to let guests into rooms without residents being there.'

'But please, it's supposed to be a surprise,' lies Charlie. Quite used to getting herself into places where she is not supposed to be, she has a list of Pavlovian excuses that she uses. 'I've flown all the way from Kenya to see him. It would be wonderful if he found me asleep in his bed.' Charlie is so overtired and exhausted she feels like she has been stopping juggernauts with her bare hands, and all she wants to do is sleep, curl up between the crisp, expensive sheets of a hotel bed and fall asleep. She is prepared to try any tactic. 'We're planning on getting married,' she declares. But the coiffed receptionist keeps to her corporate guns with her manicured smile, eventually offering Charlie the large grey felt Italian designer sofa to recline on while she waits for her 'fiancé' to return.

It is gone eleven by the time Art weaves his way into reception and finds Charlie curled up on her rucksack in one corner of the designer sofa. He is slightly overinsistent as he shakes her shoulder. She wakes with a start, her face criss-crossed with scarlet creases and an attractive rucksack motif. On seeing Art with his gentle brown eyes and scruffy dark hair leaning over her, she bursts into tears. The relief of seeing a friendly albeit slightly alcoholically overrelaxed face that has slid slightly off its cheekbone moorings is too much for her.

'Oh, Art,' she says, throwing her arms around him like a child. 'My God I'm glad I found you. I have had the most terrible time. I'm so glad you're here. Thank God you're here. I had nowhere to turn. I don't know what I'd do without you. My sister . . .'

It looks like Art has no idea what to do either. He stands with his arms hanging limply by his sides while she cries and sobs, sniffling down the right side of his neck. It is less than twenty-four hours since their row. The first real fight that Art and Charlie have ever had. And the man has come back after an evening of drowning his sorrows to find her at the scene of the crime, in a total state, asking for his help. None of it would make any sense to anyone. He and Charlie were supposed to be on non-speaking terms, or at least giving each other a frosty shoulder or two. It all appears to be a bit of mystery to him, especially as he has had quite a few pints.

Undeterred by his bemused response, Charlie carries on hugging him and pulling him towards her. So he hugs her tightly right back, muttering odd, loud 'shushes' that make him sound much more drunk than he actually is. Tucked in his armpit, Charlie notices that he smells strongly of pub, cigarettes and beer. 'It's all okay now,' he assures her as he picks up her rucksack in one hand, putting his arm over her shoulder. 'I'm looking after you now,' he announces, clearly enjoying his role of hunter/gatherer/protector/man. 'It's all okay.' Ushering her in the direction of the lift, he presses the 'call' button with his arm still around her. He waits until they are inside before he asks what has actually happened.

'She threw me out,' says Charlie in her high-pitched, put-upon voice that immediately reverses the puberty process.

'Threw you out of where?' asks Art, his anaesthetised face furrowing slowly.

'Her house,' Charlie whispers with indignation. Her bottom lip is puffed out with injustice and her fists are clenched. 'I can't really understand,' she says, her vision clouding again with tears. 'I was trying to be her friend.'

Art's face is concertinaed with confusion. Charlie is not releasing information in a coherent and useful manner and he is saying 'There, there' repeatedly. Like most wise people confronted with a situation they don't quite understand, Art avoids words like 'the bitch' just in case it is not appropriate to the proceedings or might come back to haunt him at a later date. He says, 'There, there,' some more and walks with his arm around her until they get to his room.

Once inside he dumps the rucksack and the camera case in the corner of the now immaculate, fully valeted bedroom. In his absence, the place has been cleaned and tidied almost to the point of redecoration. The towels have been replaced, the curtains drawn, the organic slice of chocolate laid out and the carpet swept, fluffed and plumped to the standard of a virgin make-up cleansing pad. Charlie doesn't notice as she walks slowly over to the large double bed with crisp sheets and, perching on the corner, sits motionless, staring at the curtains in disbelief. Art cracks open the thankfully restocked minibar and silently starts to make vodkas and tonics.

'I was really only trying to help,' says Charlie suddenly, her head spinning round to stare at Art. 'You understand, don't you?'

'Um,' says Art. 'If I am being honest, Charlie, I don't really know what you're talking about, or what you have done to upset your sister . . .'

'What I have done to upset her?' she retorts, her eyes widening. 'No, no, you've got it wrong, you don't understand.'

Mechanically she takes the glass of vodka and tonic out of his hand. 'She's the one who's upset me.'

'Oh,' says Art, perching next to her on the bed, leaning over and looking concerned. 'Are you okay?'

'Not really.'

'You can talk to me,' says Art. 'You can always talk to me.'

'I do always talk to you,' smiles Charlie, chinking his glass.

They both sit sipping their drinks, staring at the blank television screen in a comfortable silence. Charlie is deep in thought, running the whole argument over and over in her head. Occasionally she exhales or inhales sharply, wincing and flinching at bons mots missed and points unscored. Her hurt is slowly commuting to anger, her wounds bleeding less raw as emotion cedes to logic. Art just drinks his drink, patiently waiting for her to talk.

'Do you know what?' asks Charlie, turning to face him, her knee brushing against his. 'I think she's in denial about the whole thing.'

'What thing?' asks Art, trying to understand the situation.

'That her husband is having an affair,' she says, rubbing an eye with the back of her hand.

'Oh right,' says Art. 'That's what the argument's about then.'

'Of course it is,' says Charlie. 'I caught her husband at it, and she doesn't believe me.'

'Did you?' exclaims Art, sounding surprised and slightly shocked.

'Yes,' says Charlie, sounding sad. 'It was one of the most depressing things I have ever seen.'

'Oh,' says Art, any iota of gossipy relish leaving his voice. 'It was?'

'Well, she's my sister and I would rather die than have anything upset her.'

'Of course,' says Art.

'Anyway,' she says, suddenly shaking her head as if trying to dislodge something unpleasant. 'How are you?' she asks, smiling through the effort of her subject change.

Her eyes might be swollen from crying, her mouth plump and her cheeks pink, but Charlie is still attractive. It is unusual to see her looking so vulnerable. Funny and sometimes overbearingly feisty, Charlie is the sort of girl who is always in control. Of all the members of the Kenyan hack-pack that both she and Art mix with, Charlie is always one of the first on a story. News-obsessed, always watching the wires, hanging out at the press centre in Koinange Street, she has a sixth sense for a breaking story. Over cigarettes and Tusker beers, she has spent hours debating the next 'place to be'. Southern Sudan, Rwanda, Zaire, Charlie and her cameras are on the first bi-plane out there. First with the facts and the wherewithal to get there, she has, ever since Art has known her, kept the show firmly on the road. Except when Jack died, of course, but then neither of them can remember much about that period.

'I'm fine,' he smiles back. His face is soft and relaxed and glows golden-bronze in the low light. 'If a little pissed.' He giggles.

'Oh?' says Charlie, a small smile crawling across her lips.

'I'm afraid so,' he says, shrugging his shoulders.

'I'm sorry about earlier today,' she says, lowering her gaze. 'I hate it when we fight.'

'We don't, usually.'

'I know. Anyway . . . I'm sorry.'

'No harm done,' says Art, giving her shoulder a gentle squeeze. 'Except for my liver, of course. Anyway,' he adds, patting her knee as he gets up from the bed, 'it's me who should be apologising. I feel very guilty. I'm the one who caused the scene.'

'Yeah, well, never mind,' replies Charlie. The emotional roller-coaster of her day, the sobbing in Andrew's foul concrete stairwell, the fighting with her best friend and now with her sister, all on a hangover and very little food, have taken their toll. She flops back on the crisp, clean-smelling bed and inhales. 'Mmm. God,' she says, 'what a shit twenty-four hours.'

'Yeah,' says Art, only really knowing the half of it and deeming that half bad enough. 'Listen,' he says, taking a fortifying sip from his second glass of vodka and tonic. 'You're very welcome to stay here,' he smiles, looking straight at the fluffed carpet, avoiding any awkward eye contact. 'You know – if you don't want to go back there. If it's all too difficult . . . I'll sleep on the sofa, just in case.'

'Just in case what?' says Charlie, enjoying feeling horizontal as the alcohol seeps through her bloodstream, warming up her tired legs.

'Just in case you feel uncomfortable,' he mutters quickly, bobbing the ice in his glass with his finger.

'Oh,' says Charlie. 'Why would the idea of the two us sharing a bed be uncomfortable? We're mates . . .'

'Oh, right,' says Art, his head still lowered. 'I think it would be better if . . . anyway.'

'Mmm, whatever,' mumbles Charlie. She is passed-out, past caring and about to become dead to the world. She flicks her yellow trainers off with her toes and, closing her eyes, starts to unbutton the navy blue Helmut Lang trousers that Kate made her buy.

'I think I might just . . .' says Art, moving next door to the bathroom. He busies himself, brushing his teeth and washing and moisturising his face. It is an unfamiliar and convoluted routine. By the time he comes back into the room, he finds

Charlie's clothes in a pile on the floor and her lying flat on her back under the covers, her white bra straps peeking out over her shoulders, her blonde hair all over the pillow. She is breathing deeply, making the occasional crackling sound at the back of her nose, promising the possibility that she might suddenly break into a full-blown snore.

But she doesn't. And Art should know, because he hardly sleeps all night. Too tall for the modern sofa, he twists and turns on its unaccommodating length, desperate for a position that might induce sleep. Charlie's regular breathing does little to hypnotise him. His belly of beer is uncomfortable, his neck is being asked to perform tricks that are beyond even the most flexible of pre-teen Russian gymnasts.

'Did you sleep well?' asks Charlie in the morning as she stretches out languidly in her soft sheets.

'Great,' says Art, not quite daring to move his neck. 'You know me, sleep anywhere. How about you? Are you okay?'

'Mmm,' says Charlie. 'Very good.'

'Good,' he smiles. 'Just so long as you're happy. You are feeling better aren't you?'

'A little,' she says.

'That's great,' says Art, rubbing his hands together. 'I'm pleased.'

They order breakfast and it arrives promptly enough, wheeled by the same Eastern European waiter in the grey Chinese uniform.

'So what shall we do today?' asks Charlie, her fingers threaded around a cup of coffee.

'Hadn't you better sort out your problem with your sister?' suggests Art. 'I always used to find with Jack it was better if you clasped the bullock by its proverbials the day after rather than let it fester.'

'But you and Jack didn't argue.'

'Oh, we did,' he nods, forcing a whole triangle of decrusted toast into his mouth. 'These eggs are very yellow,' he says suddenly, looking at the slithers of road kill on his square white plate, or 'dead, dead crispy bacon' as they were advertised on the room-service menu.

'They're from Italy,' says Charlie, distracted by the morning sun flirting with Art's curls.

'Fucking hell,' he says. 'Are they really?'

'Well that's what it says on the menu,' she continues, waving the piece of card that boasts 'sustainable forest' origins.

'Isn't that a waste of money?' shrugs Art, loading his fork with his jet-set ingredients. 'Eggs from Italy, bacon from Copenhagen, butter from France, tomatoes grown in Spain. Doesn't anyone grow anything here any more?'

'Doesn't sound like it,' agrees Charlie, reaching over and snapping off the end of his globetrotting pork.

'Anyway,' says Art. 'Don't change the subject.'

'I didn't.'

'Oh,' he smiles. 'Well, you're avoiding the issue.'

'I am?'

'Yes.'

'Okay, I am,' she agrees, picking up the diminutive silver salt cellar and proceeding to empty its contents into a neat pyramid.

'I think you should apologise.'

'But I haven't done anything wrong,' she says, still pouring.

'That isn't really the point,' he says. 'It's famously always much easier to apologise when you haven't done anything wrong than if you have. That way you get to guilt-trip the person into saying they might have made a mistake.'

'Oh,' says Charlie. 'Do you really think so?'

'Works all the time.'

'Since when did you get so wise?' she smiles.

'Oh, I don't know, sometime between the bed and this table,' he smiles right back.

'So what did you and Jack ever row about,' she asks, looking up through her lashes as she plays with the salt.

'Oh, half-witted things mainly,' says Art. 'Like any close couple.'

'We don't row about half-witted things.'

'I know, but you're not my partner,' he replies, pulling a toast triangle in half and putting some in his mouth. 'We used to argue about mad things like who would have the window seat on the plane. We always both wanted it because we had always stayed up the night before packing and drinking and smoking. And all either of us wanted to do was go to sleep.'

'God,' sniffs Charlie. 'I remember the two of you always being hungover at airports.'

'Yeah,' smiles Art. 'We argued about you, once.'

'No!' says Charlie, leaning across the table with her mouth wide open. 'When? Why?'

'Oh, you know,' says Art, leaning back in his seat.

'Don't be a tease,' complains Charlie. 'It's not fair.'

'Well,' says Art, getting out of his chair. 'Needless to say, it was a long time and ago and Jack won . . .'

Standing opposite her, separated from her by a wheelie table, Art looks handsome as hell. Charlie has always known Art is good-looking. The way girls look at him. The way he fails to notice. He has always had a very attractive quality about him. Many's the time she has listened and nodded along to girls drunkenly confiding in her late at night in nightclubs all over Nairobi. She and Art laughed about it sometimes. How girls always tried to befriend Charlie to get to Art.

Even when she first met both him and Jack, she remembers how handsome she thought he was. But since she has loved – and lost – Jack, Art has become her best friend. The only one who really and truly understands. The only other person to love Jack as much as she did. He is her confidant. Her strong shoulder to cry on during the bad times. Her pal to get rip-roaringly drunk with at the end of a long hot day out in the field. The person whose advice she listens to. The only other photographer whose eye she trusts. The things they have seen together. The lessons they have learnt together. The hell they have seen. The time he pulled her to the ground during a gun battle in Somalia. She says he saved her life. He always tells her to stop being so damned melodramatic.

But now, looking at him chatting away with his curly straight-out-of-bed hair, something is different. Maybe it is because he is out of Africa that Charlie can suddenly see him for the man he is. Or maybe because it is the first time that she has actually drawn breath and opened her eyes. But his golden-brown arms encased in a large, overwashed white T-shirt make it difficult for her to concentrate entirely on what he is saying. There is a beguiling light in his eyes and a charming energy emanating from him that she has not noticed before. Maybe, she concludes, as he stretches his arms towards the ceiling, unconsciously flashing his taut brown stomach, she is not as observant a person as she once thought.

'. . . anyway, back to the matter in hand. Making the first move is always the best policy,' he announces with a laid-back smile.

'It is?' she asks.

'Oh yeah,' he replies, his southern hemisphere roots making his voice go up at the end. 'You know . . . where rows are concerned.'

'Oh right, rows,' says Charlie, her voice flattening.

'What did you think I was talking about?' he asks.

'Rows of course,' says Charlie, sounding unreasonably snappy.

'Right,' he says. 'Good.'

'Yes, good,' repeats Charlie.

'So are you going to?'

'What?'

'Call her?'

'Yes, of course,' says Charlie, suddenly flustered as the hotel room appears to shrink in size.

'Off you go then.'

'Yes, off I go then,' she smiles, hurrying over to the telephone. She would not normally make this call to her sister, but Art's persuasion and her increasing lack of comfort in the diminishing bedroom make her compliant and overly efficient.

The telephone rings. Art smiles. Charlie nods and smiles. She is on the point of giving up when Peta finally answers the phone.

'Hello,' huffs a heavy-breathing, big-breasted voice that has obviously jogged, fecund appendages in tow, from the garden or the top of the house.

'Oh, hello,' says Charlie. 'It's Charlie.'

'Right, hello,' says Peta. 'Phew, sorry,' she continues. 'It's very busy here.' A loud wailing like the sound of cats fighting follows her into the room. 'Boys, boys, be quiet,' she insists. They don't appear to be listening.

'Um, is my sister there?' starts Charlie, feeling suddenly rather sick.

'No, no,' says Peta. 'She is at the gym.'

'The gym?' says Charlie, her voice shooting up the scale in shock. 'The gym? She's gone to the gym?'

'Yes, yes,' says Petra.

'When?'

'Oh, quite a short while ago,' says Peta, matter of fact.

'Which one?' asks Art, joining in.

'Which one?' repeats Charlie.

'Total Tone.'

'Right,' says Charlie, sounding unsure.

'It's quite new,' says Peta. 'Near Portobello Road.'

'When will she be back?' asks Charlie.

'I am not certainly sure,' replies Peta as the background screaming threatens to break the sound barrier. 'I'm afraid I have to go . . . bye,' she says. 'Alfie! Ben!' she yells in demonic tones as the line goes dead.

'Oh well,' says Charlie with a shrug as she puts the phone down. 'She's at the gym. So I suppose I'll have to sort it out tomorrow.'

'Really, Charlie,' says Art. 'I'm disappointed in you.'

'Why?' she replies, sounding defensive.

'Your sister's marriage is on the verge of collapse . . .'

'And she is squat-thrusting in some gym,' replies Charlie, throwing her arms in the air.

'Doesn't that make you think she might be having some sort of crisis?'

'No, just that she's more concerned with the state of her cellulite than her bloody marriage,' she determines.

'I don't think you really believe that,' says Art with a wide smile.

'Yes, well . . .'

'Well nothing,' says Art, rather enjoying his new moral authority. 'I think you should go over there.'

'There's no need to sound like a superhero.'

'I'm not, I'm just speaking the truth.' Art smiles again.

'All right, I'll bloody go and find her.'

'Great,' says Art, clapping his hands together like some American motivational speaker.

'Yes, well,' says Charlie, sitting back down on the bed.

'Well? What are you waiting for?'

'Oh, I don't . . .'

'Off you go – now!'

'Will you come with me?'

'What?' says Art, half smiling, looking like he's interested. 'No,' he says. 'I really think it's something you should do on your own.'

Walking alone along Portobello Road, as instructed by a niftily dressed woman with a nippy Land Rover pushchair on the corner, Charlie comes across the converted red-brick Victorian school building that now houses the gym. Round the corner from an AIDS hospice, the irony of the terminally fit running on the spot near the terminally ill is not lost on her. Wandering into the echoing atrium, the smell of vegetarian lasagne just fails to beckon her into the airy cafeteria facilities. Instead she stands in a towel queue behind a fat man in shiny relaxing trousers with a back so hairy his aerated workout shirt fails to make contact with his spine. The assistant with a tight American smile swipes his card, hands him two white towels and wishes him a good 'session', then proceeds to walk to the other end of the meet-and-greet counter. Charlie follows.

'Um, excuse me,' she says.

'Yes,' says the short, brown-haired person of indeterminate sex.

'I'm looking for my sister,' smiles Charlie, sensing by the previous wiping-swiping routine she has just witnessed that this is not one of those wander-around-at-will places.

'Right?' says the brown-haired assistant, whose name-tagged breast/chest sports the unhelpful name 'Al'.

'It's a bit of an emergency and I need to find her.'

'What sort of emergency?' says Al, looking concerned and businesslike at the same time, while obviously trying to remember the protocol for emergencies apropos members.

'I need to speak to her,' says Charlie.

'Oh,' says Al, gossiping and/or chatting obviously not rating highly enough on the training flow chart. 'Are you a member yourself?' asks Al, in the sort of sibilant heavy voice associated with profound professionalism.

'No,' says Charlie with uncharacteristic honesty.

'Well I'm afraid I can't help you, then,' says Al, patting some crisp and chafe-inducing towels. 'You will have to wait in the café facility until the member has finished.'

'Could you just tell me if she's here or not?' smiles Charlie, trying flirtation. 'You know, so I don't hang around and wait for no reason.' Al looks unmoved. Charlie tries another tack. 'It's only a quick contract thing . . .'

'A contract, you say?' says Al in a manner that implies that business, work and progress must come before anything else, even possibly (although this is an idea not openly shared in Total Tone) before exercise itself. 'I'll check for you.'

Al walks down to the other end of the meet-and-greet counter with a brisk swish of nylon-on-nylon thighs. The turned back and the movement away from the counter reveal a white bra strap just below the shoulder blades and a pair of pink trainers. Al's a girl, thinks Charlie, moving from flirtation to girl-bonding in a flicker of a smile.

'What's your sister's name?' asks Al, clicking away.

'Kate . . . Kate Murray,' says Charlie, leaning on the counter.

'Right,' says Al. 'She's here. She arrived at 10.47 a.m. and so she's in "Bums and Tums for Young Mums".'

'Right,' says Charlie, trying to get to grips with the idea. 'How long is that?'

'Bums and Tums for Young Mums is an hour and fifteen minutes long – fifteen minutes less than normal Bums and Tums. So if you want to wait in the café facility she'll be along in about twenty-five minutes.'

'Fine,' says Charlie. 'Are you sure she's in that class?'

'Oh yes,' nods Al, pursing her lips at such a sugges-tion. 'The only other things we have on at the moment are Yogalates – a mixture of yoga and pilates – but that,' she adds, 'is a maternity class. She isn't pregnant is she?'

'Er, not as far as I know.'

'. . . and Power Punch, which is an advanced boxercise class which no one turned up for this morning.'

'Oh,' says Charlie. 'And she's not likely just to be in the gym area?'

'Not unless she's invisible,' laughs Al, revealing a cluttered lower jaw worthy of Highgate Cemetery. 'I've just been on towel duty through the gym and there are only a couple of men there who I told off for wearing singlets.'

'Right,' smiles Charlie. 'Not very busy then?'

'Well, it's near the end the year,' she states. Charlie looks confused. 'You know, you're packed in January with the New Year-New Me crowd. Then you get your Spring Slimmers, summer is the Fast Track Bikini Pack, come September/October no one really minds that much. There's a bit of an upturn come November for those on the Party Frock Plan, but otherwise the only steady stream are the pregnant ladies.' She smiles and nods towards the swing doors covered in sensational works of art donated by the on-site crèche. 'Here come the Yogalates class.'

Flipping through the double doors in various stages of flush, exhaustion and expectancy come a group of about eight to ten women. The first is a nubile twenty-something, her hair in jaunty bunches, with bangles all the way up her arms and her bump on show like a pop star. She rushes straight past, rattling around in her camel-coloured bowling bag, looking for her ringing mobile phone. Following a lot less elegantly behind is a thirty- or possibly forty-something woman in an enormous hide-all, cover-all T-shirt that announces 'Frankie Says Relax' in large black letters. Listing from one leg to another, her plump pink face positively sloshes with water retention as she huffs and puffs her way to the nearest table in the café facility. Next out are what look like two best friends who are going through the pregnancy experience together, perhaps a touch competitively. Dressed in tasteful Calvin Klein stretch grey short-sleeved tops and the same linen drawstring trousers and the same glossy striped blonde hair, they are comparing manicures and bra-cup sizes.

'Do you know?' says one to the other. 'The woman in Rigby and Peller announced I was a G-cup.'

'No-o-o, ama-a-a-zing,' says the other, flapping her hand at her friend. 'What were you doing in Rigby and Peller in the first place?'

'Oh God,' says the other, like her friend must be the last person in the world to know this. 'You've got to have nice underwear if you're pregnant!'

'I know that,' says her friend, rolling her eyes like her pal is beyond stupid. 'Rigby and Peller is very last millennium. Everyone goes to Agent Provocateur these days.'

'Only if they want no support whatsoever,' lies her friend, flicking her hair like she's just stepped out of the salon. 'Do you want some lunch?'

'Lovely,' says her pal. 'Great idea.'

Charlie sits on her own pretending to read a newspaper that is attached to an eccentrically long piece of wood. She half-heartedly turns the pages, contemplates a double skinny latte from the orange-coloured, tantastic girl behind the glass counter and eavesdrops on the best friends' conversation.

'So you're having yours at the Portland, aren't you?' says Blonde.

'Oh yes,' replies Blonder, sucking up some juice from a box with a straw.

'Yes, well,' Blonde says, leaving doubt and social faux pas hanging in the air as she plays with her organic skin-free chicken salad from the bar.

'What?' says Blonder. 'I've been booked with the Portland

since the beginning. Everyone goes there. Posh, Zoë Ball . . .'

'Mmm,' says Blonde. 'Well, I'm at Queen Charlotte's, so, you know, if anything goes wrong – it's all there,' she smiles, leaning back and stroking her rotund stomach.

'What's going to go wrong?' says Blonder. 'I've my C-section booked. Simple.'

'Ahh,' says Blonde. 'I've been reading about that . . .'

Just as Blonde is about to launch into an unresearched debate about the pros and cons of caesareans, the 'Bums and Tums for Young Mums' class is released into the atrium; the place becomes a cocktail party.

'Belinda,' shouts Blonde. 'Over here!'

'Laura! Hi,' yells Blonder with a little wave. 'Come and have some lunch.'

'Suzie, Christ, hi, we must stop meeting like this,' giggles Blonde.

They all laugh hilariously.

Soon everyone's pulling up chairs, comparing figures and talking about having a great, fun, girls' lunch of salad, mineral water and possibly a bread roll for those who are eating for two. In amongst the milling and bonding group of fragrant ladies, Charlie spots Kate. She is holding back from the rest of the young mums and she doesn't look good. Her face is white, her eyes are hollow and her smile is more fixed than anything the service industry has thrown at Charlie since she arrived.

'Kate?' says Charlie, standing up from behind her silver-topped café facility table. Kate looks around in the vague direction of the sound of her name, but fails to see anyone. 'Kate,' repeats Charlie. 'Over here.' Kate looks again. Her expressionless face trawls the crowd for something or someone recognisable. 'Kate?' her sister repeats. Kate finally catches her sister's eye but remains rooted to the spot. She does not react. But, as Charlie notices with huge relief, neither does she turn and walk away. 'Kate, Kate,' says Charlie, walking around the silver-topped table towards her. 'I'm so sorry about last night. I really am.'

'It doesn't matter,' says Kate, in the quietest and smallest of voices. 'It doesn't matter. Nothing really matters any more.'

Charlie puts her arm around her sister's stiff shoulders. She remains inert, staring ahead. 'I'm so sorry,' she repeats.

'Don't be nice,' says Kate flatly. 'I'll only cry.'

'You're allowed to cry if you want to,' insists Charlie.

'No, I mean really cry,' says Kate, turning to face her sister, the weakest of smiles trying to curl her lips.

'You can do it here if you want to.'

'Did you hear what I said?' asks Kate slowly.

'Do you want to go somewhere else?' asks Charlie.

'Yup,' is about all Kate manages.

Charlie puts her arm around her sister and walks her slowly like a sick patient towards the door. Blonde and Blonder are holding court with the rest of the Young Mums' Bums and Tums group.

'. . . there are some people whose figures just snap back into shape again after the birth and there are others who just have to work and work at it . . .'

'There are a few people who let everything just fall apart . . .'

'Mmm, did they really try at all? I mean, if you look at Madonna . . .'

The two sisters wander slowly up the street until they come to an impersonal imported coffee chain where the seats are hard, the service swift and no one is supposed to hang around very long. Perched on high stools, their faces are pointing out through the smeared plate-glass window at the Portobello Road beyond. It's raining again. Not anything too powerful or penetrating but just enough to make the sky grey and everyone miserable. Straight outside the window is a woman selling flowers. With a long nose and hennaed hair, she is huddled under green and white striped awning, her arms crossed against the cold. In front of her stand buckets and buckets of flowers, round pools of intense colour, some clashing, some blending, some bleeding into one another so that, through the wet window, they look like a well-used artist's palette.

'I've always rather liked this part of town,' sighs Kate, her cheeks resting in the palms of her hands as she waits for her skinny latte with maple syrup to cool down. 'Alex was always rude about it, saying it was full of pretentious people. As if Shepherd's Bush is much better. Full of bankers and wankers, all they talk about down there is when The Cross sale is on, that someone saw Nigella Lawson in the cheese queue at Lidgates, and what time they want to meet at the Bush Bar and Grill.'

'I'm afraid I don't really know what any of that means,' says Charlie, taking a sip of her coffee, burning her tongue in the process. 'Anyway, ouch,' she says. 'About last night . . .'

'Don't,' says her sister, leaning forward some more, her hands covering her eyes, her fingertips massaging her forehead.

'But . . .'

'No, don't, honestly, you were right,' she says, letting her hands flop forwards as she sits back in her high chair. 'You were absolutely right,' she repeats, her fingers tapping on the Formica, her eyes turning scarlet. 'Claire rang all apologetic not long after you left, and she started to say sorry and explain and say it hadn't been going on long . . .' She smiles as she gazes at the smears in the glass. 'Stupid wankers hadn't even managed to get their stories right. She'd presumed he'd told me as there really was no way out, after such an eyewitness report, and he'd thought that if he carried on denying it I would eventually believe him, which of course I did.' She laughs. It makes a dry hollow hiccup sound. 'So you were right . . .'

'It's not really about me being right. Are *you* all right?' asks Charlie. The more she sits next to her sister the more concerned she is. Kate is being distant, and although she looks upset she seems to be strangely unmoved. Maybe she is still in a state of shock, wonders Charlie. Or maybe something else? Maybe she is angry with Alex? Or perhaps it is all directed towards the messenger?

'Of course I'm not all right,' says Kate. The sarcasm in her voice is so loud and heavy that it flattens and dulls all conversation in its wake. Their corner of the coffee franchise outlet goes quiet. 'My husband is sleeping with my best friend and my sister is the one who tells me . . .'

'I'm so sorry,' interrupts Charlie. 'But you know I was just saying what I saw. I didn't know what else to do.'

'Well,' says Kate, turning to face her, pink stripes of anger and emotion glowing on her cheeks. 'You could have ignored it.'

'Ignored it?' asks Charlie, not quite sure that she had heard correctly.

'Yes,' says Kate. 'You could very easily have ignored it . . .'

'What?' says Charlie, suddenly aware that she is dealing with a situation that she knows nothing about.

'Don't you think I didn't suspect what was going on? Don't you think that I didn't have my doubts? But we were getting on with it. Don't you think that I was turning a blind eye for a reason? To keep my family together . . . To make sure my children had a father and we all had a decent roof over our heads, and now . . . you've ruined it.'

'*I've* ruined it?' says Charlie, slapping her hand down on the wood-effect sideboard. 'What do you think your husband has gone and done?'

'You don't know what I'm talking about,' says Kate. 'You just don't understand. With your selfish agenda. Your superior views about our shallow lives. Who's to say that you know any better? We were happy until you came along. And now it hurts like hell.'

'I'm sorry,' says Charlie, not really understanding why she is apologising.

'Sorry doesn't really work for this,' says Kate, taking a sip of her coffee.

'I don't really understand . . .'

'You see, that's it,' she smiles. 'You simply don't understand, and what you don't understand you shouldn't meddle with. It will only blow up in your face.'

'But . . .'

'But nothing,' smiles Kate again. 'Alex has moved out. As of this morning the children have no father, and I am at home with Peta on my own. That's quite a swift week's work even for someone of your talents,' she adds, standing up and smoothing down her grey-flannel Bums and Tums for Young Mums trousers. 'I mean, look at you!' says Kate. 'What have you done with your life that makes it so much better than mine?'

'What?' asks Charlie, her palms sweating, her heart racing.

'You're thirty-five years old and you don't have anything,' snorts Kate.

'What? What do you mean?' says Charlie

'You rent your house. You have no children and you don't have a husband or boyfriend to speak of. It's pathetic. Do you think anyone is that interested in your stories? Do you think anyone cares about where you've been and what you've seen?' She laughs. 'Do you know?' she adds, turning towards the door. 'People aren't impressed by your career, your big Germaine Greer feminist thing. They feel sorry for you . . . they feel sorry for you because you're not married. You don't have anyone in your sad little selfish, empty, me-me life. Why did you have to come back and meddle? Did you think you were doing us all a favour? Exposing my marriage? Telling the truth, as you see it? Am I just another one of your crusading stories?' Kate stands up. Her face flashes with anger. Her hands are defiantly on her hips. 'My husband may well be sleeping with my best friend, but at least I've got one. Or did have one until you came along!'

8

As Kate strides off down Portobello Road, passing the damp, lunchtime queue of vegetarians outside the Natural Grain Store, Charlie reluctantly thinks that maybe, somewhere in her unreasonable and unpleasant argument, her sister might have a point. She does rent a room in Sophia's house in Nairobi. She doesn't have a husband, or a boyfriend. And what is so wonderful about rushing around from war zone to war zone, ostentatiously having a career? In fact, what is so fabulous about 'having it all'? If this is what having it all means. What is so liberating about paying your own way all the time? Being strong and brave and feisty is exhausting, she thinks, sitting back down on her hard stool and stirring her cooling coffee. All those magazines she read, all those films she watched, all those feminist ideals she imbibed – was the joke on her all along? In the end, what is terribly wrong with having a heavily interior-designed house, two-point-zero children, a nanny and a cupboard full of happy food products? Even if one's husband is not entirely honest about his extra-curricular hobbies?

She sits and stares at the passers-by, bent against the drizzle as they weave their way about their busy business. It isn't that Charlie particularly wants a boyfriend, or a husband, or a man. It's that since Jack died, she hasn't been able to bear the idea of anyone else. The grieving process has been much longer and harder than she ever thought possible. She has thrown herself into her work and the thought of a new man just hasn't occured to her. She has become one of those terribly busy women who is always rushed off her feet, always on her way somewhere. She hasn't even had the time to think about, let alone feel, jealousy when the jiffy bags showing Kate's progress through life have arrived in the various poste restante addresses around Africa. Or at least perhaps that's how she has planned it. If you are too busy to think, then you don't have to. Kate was just being Kate and doing her own thing. But now that she has arrived back in London, Charlie realises that it wasn't Kate just being Kate. It was Kate being like everyone else and Charlie is the one left behind. The world has taken a left-turn while Charlie is still marching ahead, all feisty and female, having it all while everyone else is watching her dinosaur moves with a little bit of pity in their eyes.

'Oh God,' she says quietly to herself, picking the blue bits out of her muffin and bursting them with her back teeth. Slumped forward on the counter, her nose pressed against the window, she sits making morose breath circles against the plate glass as she thinks. What should she do? Who should she be? How did she end up like this? Just as she contemplates apologising to Kate again for something they both know she hasn't done, there is a gentle tap on the window. Charlie leans back, trying to pull the world into focus. It's Art. His forehead against the window, he is waving. His dark curls are damp with the rain but his smile is wide and warm. Charlie waves slowly back.

'I take it it didn't go too well,' he says, sitting down next to her, sighing loudly as he dumps his bag of photography books at his feet.

'Not desperately well, no,' smiles Charlie.

'Not that big on apologies then, your sister?' he asks, breaking off some blueberry-free muffin and popping it into his mouth.

'Apparently not,' smiles Charlie, feeling relieved that Art came along when he did.

'Oh well,' he shrugs. 'At least you tried.'

'Yeah,' replies Charlie.

'Yeah,' says Art, rubbing her shoulders. 'She'll come round,' he adds optimistically. 'She has to.' He grins. 'You're related. Honestly, don't worry too much. It's her problem, really. It's got nothing to do with you. It's Kate who really has to sort it out.'

'Yes, well it just feels an awful lot like my problem at the moment,' says Charlie, picking at her muffin, trying to find another piece of blueberry in the sponge. 'My big fat problem.'

'Come here,' he says, his arms outstretched like Jesus. His hug is strong and male. His large damp blue woollen jumper smells comfortingly like a wet dog. 'What are we going to do with you?' he asks.

'I don't know,' she replies. 'I have no idea what to do with myself half the time.'

'That doesn't sound like you,' he says, smoothing a loose strand of blonde hair behind her ear. 'You're normally so positive and full of energy.'

'Am I?'

'Oh God, yeah,' he says his voice rising. 'The number of times I've sat around your kitchen table in Karen or at the Horseman after too many Dana cocktails talking about the hideousness of the human race and you've been positive and optimistic, insisting that people are fundamentally good, it's just circumstance that makes them wicked. I've lost count. Honestly . . .'

'It's coming back here,' says Charlie. 'I had no idea how weird it would be. How much the world had moved on and that I'm still stuck somewhere in the last millennium.'

'It's your family,' he says, brushing her cheek with the back of his hand. 'They're bringing you down with their complicated relationships.'

'Do you know my mother even tried to fix me up with

someone called Dominic?' says Charlie, her mouth curling into a smile.

'No,' says Art, sitting back in his seat, running his hands through his hair. 'What was he like?'

'Oh, horrible,' says Charlie with a smile. 'Really rather horrible.'

'That's a shame,' he says.

'I know,' laughs Charlie. 'They think I'm desperate. D'you know they sort of implied that I should cut my losses and go for second-best. Like my time has run out and I should grab the closest man I can.'

'That would be me then,' says Art, grabbing hold of her arm and making a joky growling noise.

'Yeah,' laughs Charlie, reclaiming her arm. 'And you're Jack's best friend . . .'

'Er, yes,' smiles Art, putting both his hands back on his lap and sitting up straight. 'I was certainly that.' He smiles, slapping the top of his own thighs. 'Jack's best friend.'

'God,' sighs Charlie, rubbing her forehead and blinking. 'We did have a laugh, you, me and Jack . . .'

'We certainly did,' agrees Art, his voice sounding a little clipped. 'The three of us . . . lots of fun.'

'Do you remember,' says Charlie, suddenly turning to face him, a large smile on her face, 'when we were on the night train together from Nairobi to Mombasa and you and Jack had been drinking that home-made moonshine stuff?'

'Yup, I remember, and you dared him to take all his clothes off and run the length of the carriage, I remember,' says Art in a flat voice as he gets out of his seat and searches around on the floor for his bag of books. 'Listen,' he says, clenching his fist enthusiastically. 'I bet I know you well enough to get you out of this depression,' he says, lightly tapping her thigh.

'Okay, then, what?' she replies, with all the enthusiasm of a teenager being docked their pocket money.

'Well, if being here makes you feel odd and a bit like a tourist,' he grins, warming to his own idea, 'then you should behave like one.'

'What do you mean?' she asks, not one hundred per cent sure that she is going to enjoy the hilariousness of the idea. Irony can only be stretched so far before it ceases to be ironic and simply becomes unpleasant.

'Okay, perhaps not tourist stuff then,' he says, sensing her lack of interest. 'But something different, something comforting. Trust me,' he smiles, tapping the side of his nose. 'I'm a photographer.'

Ten minutes later, after dumping his shopping, Charlie and Art are on the top of a double-decker bus. Sitting at the front, they both grip on to the bar in front of them pretending to be on a fairground ride. Next to them, on the opposite pew, are two schoolgirls looking distinctly less excited by the journey up West. Linked together by two sets of earphones plugged into the same minidisc, like some latter-day chain-gang, they masticate their chewing-gum in time to the music that screams into their ears. The one closest to Charlie has dark brown shoulder-length hair with two thick yellow strips at the front like swipes from a highlighter pen. She has a bolt through her eyebrow and a collection of ever-smaller curtain rings in a crescent formation hanging from her ear. The other girl, whose shiny white cheek is leaving foundation tracks all over the window, is between hairstyles. Her bleached white hair turns from orange to brown towards the parting, while the ends strain to stay bunched in fluffy elastic bands for the full Lolita effect.

'Shouldn't they be at school?' whispers Charlie into Art's ear, nodding over her right shoulder.

'Don't ask me,' says Art. 'I'm not from round these parts,' he winks. 'Would you like me to go and ask them?'

'No-o,' hushes Charlie, fully aware that Art might actually

carry out his threat and that the hip, hard, sour girls might not find his naïve out-of-town act at all amusing.

'No, no,' he says, half getting out his seat. 'I insist. The only way you learn about a people and their culture is by mixing with them.'

'Sit down,' says Charlie, pulling at his trousers. 'Stop it,' she says. 'You're embarrassing me . . .'

'That's fantastic,' says Art, starting to laugh. Hot pink circles of mortification have sprung up on Charlie's cheeks. 'I can't believe you're embarrassed. You of all people . . .'

'Well I am,' admits Charlie, slightly sheepish. 'So sit down and stop it.' She slaps the top of his leg. 'Shush,' she adds.

They sit in silence. Art has his back twisted against the side of the bus and is turned towards Charlie. The rain finally ceases and the last drops slither down the window like silverfish as the sun breaks through. The light catches the end of Charlie's eyelashes as she blinks, looking straight ahead. Art sits and stares intently at her profile, apparently lost in thought.

'What?' says Charlie, turning to catch him.

'What?' says Art, defensively.

'You just made a very strange moaning noise.'

'Did I?'

'Yes,' she says, shaking her head. 'Very odd.'

'Maybe I'm hungry or something.'

'It didn't sound like that.'

'Oh. Look!' he says. 'Quick, here's our stop.' He points out of the window.

The two of them herd down the stairs and out into Charing Cross Road. They splash through the puddles past *Les Misérables* and on into Soho.

'Where are we going?' asks Charlie, shouting after him.

'Just follow me,' grins Art, the weak sunshine gilding his cheek.

They turn up a side street and stop suddenly outside an open door and a flight of bleached red lino-covered stairs that lead into a basement.

'What is this place?' asks Charlie as they clatter down the stairs, lured on by the smell of garlic and disinfectant.

There is a queue at the bottom. Four people lean in a line against the yellow wall opposite a large cork noticeboard that is covered in adverts for flat rentals and handwritten notes about bicycles and fridges that need shifting. At the front are two handsome Italian men in black roundnecks, jeans and neat leather belts. Both have smooth hair, smooth accents and are smoking and talking and laughing at the same time. Next to the Italians is a diminutive Japanese girl in a retro punk outfit. Perched precariously upon a pair of knee-high platform boots, in a pair of orange and white striped barber-shop tights, a tartan miniskirt and a cobweb jumper, she stares transfixed at the wall, quietly waiting her turn. Behind her, and in front of Art, is a tall, lanky man whose wax-white skin makes him look like he has recently been exhumed. Dressed in an army surplus trench coat, he is nose-deep in an art magazine. He has a roll-up stuck to his bottom lip and one eye closed, guarding against faglash.

'This is one of my most favourite places,' whispers Art, resting his chin for a moment on Charlie's shoulder.

'Really?' says Charlie, both surprised and intrigued. 'Why?' she asks, as the level of banter in the main dining room reaches raucous.

'It's just great fun and the food is fantastic,' smiles Art as he pokes his head around the corner to see how much longer they might have to wait for a table. 'Oh hi, Maria,' he says, nodding in the vague direction of the dining room. There is the most almighty scream, which bounces off the steamed-up walls like a thunderclap. 'Oh God,' says Art, out of the corner of his mouth. 'Here comes trouble.'

And Art is right. For Maria comes tumbling up the dining room and around the corner with the velocity of a bull in full charge. Short, dark and fat with a vast soft sofa of a cleavage, her bare arms are in the air and her bingo wings flap like two large pink blancmanges. As accurate as an Exocet, she hurls herself at Art, encasing him in her folds.

'Arrtor, Arrtor, Arrtor, where have you be-e-e-en?' she squeals, pushing him away from her for a better viewing and then pulling him straight back to her bosom with enough speed and strength to give the man whiplash. 'Two years, three years . . . really, you have been away for so, so long, I was beginning to think you must have died in one of your wars.' Grabbing hold of his arm with a firm, dimpled hand, she leads him straight to the front of the queue, shouting, 'Franco, Franco, look who is the bloody fuck here!' at the top of her voice.

Franco, an old man the size of a schoolboy, comes out from behind a split bamboo-fronted bar, repeatedly wiping his hands on his large, white, tomato-stained apron.

'Arrtor!' he exclaims, his hands shaking enthusiastically as he holds them out. 'I can't believe it. Finally you return. Finally you come back to see us, after all this time. My God, Gino,' he shouts at a rather handsome, neat, short young man dressed in a white shirt and black trousers standing behind the bamboo bar. 'Bring us some wine!'

The commotion is total. The restaurant is turned upside down. The general conversational level dips, then goes through a period of total silence before returning to full volume. Within a couple of minutes a group of four at the corner table are ushered out, following swift payment. The paper cloth is replaced, along with a carafe of red wine, a brown plastic basket of bread and a bundle of knives and forks wrapped in paper towels like sausage rolls.

'Okay, okay, okay,' fusses Maria. 'Now you two sit down here,' she says, smoothing the paper tablecloth over with her plump hands. 'Sit down here,' she repeats. She smiles at Charlie. The orange bleached hairs of her moustache flash in the purple-blue glare of the strip light. 'So you are Arrtor's girlfriend,' she says in a manner that is more of a statement than a question.

'Oh, um, no,' shrugs Charlie, so embarrassed by the last five minutes of emotional outpouring that not only is she pink-faced and hot, she is actually sweating.

'Oh,' replies Maria, sounding mildly put out that Art would bring anyone less special than a girlfriend to her restaurant. 'Shame,' she adds, pinching Charlie's cheek between her porky fingers. 'You are rather pretty. Arrtor, she is rather pretty.'

'Very pretty,' agrees Art, apology writ large all over his face. 'Very pretty indeed.'

'Right,' says Maria, folding and losing her arms underneath her ample chest. 'What are we missing? What are we missing?' she asks, inspecting the table. 'Breadsticks, breadsticks . . . the bloody breadsticks . . .'

She turns and launches herself through the swing doors into the kitchen, shouting loudly in a southern Italian dialect that makes the words, although not the meaning, impossible to understand.

'I'm so sorry,' says Art, pulling apart a slice of ciabatta bread and dipping it into an ashtray of olive oil. 'I haven't been here for a long time . . .'

'That's obvious,' smiles Charlie, taking the other half of his bread and dipping it too.

'I know,' he grins. 'I used to come here nearly every day when I was a student.'

'I didn't know you were a student in London?'

'It was a long time ago,' he says.

'But I've never heard you talk about it.'

'You never asked.'

'What did you study?'

'English at King's.'

'But Jack was the words and you were the pictures.'

'Yeah,' he laughs, pouring them both a glass of red wine. 'That's what we always said.'

'Well I'm amazed,' she says, taking a sip from her glass. 'Arthur MacDonald. You become more intriguing by the day.'

'So, indeed, do you,' he says, raising his glass.

'Do I?'

'Oh yes,' he smiles.

'Cheers,' she says, clinking his glass.

'Okay, okay,' interrupts Maria, her large bosom breaking up the conversation before she does. 'Right, two pasta dishes, meat or no meat,' she says, slapping down a packet of breadsticks. She pulls a short pencil out from behind her ear with one hand, while fishing around in her flowery, frilly pinny pocket for a pad with the other. 'Four starters – salami, bruschetta, insalata and broad beans ... like the Romans eat,' she says, turning to smile at Charlie. 'Have you been to Italy?'

'Yes,' nods Charlie.

'Good,' replies Maria. 'That's good, Arrtor, she has been to Italy,' she says in a manner that suggests Charlie's local knowledge makes up for her lack of amorous status. 'Right,' she says. 'Mr MacDonald, what d'you want?' Art makes as if to open his mouth. 'No, no, no.' She shakes her head. 'Let me, let me ...' Her porky palm is raised. 'Salami and meat.'

'Yes, absolutely, of course, you're right.' Art smiles. 'Ab-so-lute-ly r-ight.'

'Like you have every time you come here ...'

'Like I have every time.'

'And for you,' she says, closing her eyes at Charlie like some culinary clairvoyant. 'For you . . . salad and no meat.'

'Yes,' says Charlie with laughing good grace. 'How clever of you.'

'I always know what everyone wants,' she announces before walking back into the kitchen.

'Yes, yes,' smiles Art. He leans forward. 'Is that what you wanted at all?'

'Um, honestly?' asks Charlie.

'Honestly,' he winks.

'I quite fancied the bruschetta.' She laughs.

'I know, I know,' he nods. 'She does it every time. I have never been allowed to eat the vegetarian pasta since I've been coming here . . . which is now over ten years.' He takes another sip of wine. 'But you can see why I love it, though, can't you?'

'Oh, of course,' says Charlie.

'The food is amazing,' declares Art again. 'You won't find anything like it in London.'

'I'm very flattered you brought me here,' she smiles.

'I'm pleased you like it,' he says, raising his glass for her to chink his again.

One of those well-hidden London treasures, Il Pane is known only to those impecunious enough not to mind paper napkins, erratic service, diminutive choice and sharing tables with whomsoever walks in before, or after, you. Although the food itself is sensational and quite often exceeds the quality of the swankier trattorias in their area, anyone with a friend to flex or cash in the bank would quite frankly not be seen dead in there.

'I used to dream about this place when lying in the bush or in some godawful hellhole,' smiles Art. 'I don't know, there's something about these sweaty faded posters, the plastic chairs and Maria's bolognese that's rather comforting, especially when you're scared out of your mind.'

'That's a feeling I understand,' nods Charlie. 'It's very cosy here.'

'That's why it's always full, I suppose,' says Art.

And today is no exception. It is packed with the usual array of unusual people. There's a hessian-wearing hippy with hair like hemp eating two bowls of pasta. There is a trio of Goths eating plates of cold meat. The Japanese neo-punk and the man in a trench coat are now sitting opposite each other.

'Do you know?' muses Art. 'What I love best is that when everything else keeps changing, there are some places that stay the same.'

Charlie smiles. She is charmed. She sits back into her seat, sliding her legs forward. For almost the first time since she came back she feels relaxed and happy. Art has let her into his secret world. She sips more of her red wine and chomps on her breadstick like a chipmunk.

'So what's next?' she asks. Leaning forward to rest her elbows on the table, a curl of her blonde hair falls across her cheek.

'Oh, I don't know,' says Art, smiling. 'Back to Africa, a beachhouse and then who knows?' he says, spinning his fork in a circle on the paper tablecloth.

'No, I didn't mean next . . . next,' smiles Charlie. 'I mean this afternoon, you fool.'

'Oh, right,' says Art. Suddenly sitting up straight, he pauses and stares back at her. 'Um,' he says, his eyes shining slightly. He shifts in his seat and runs his hands quickly through his hair as if trying to think of something else. 'We could go to the National Portrait Gallery?'

'Mmm,' says Charlie, her mouth full of breadstick. 'That would be great. I haven't been there in about ten years,' she

laughs. 'But then again I could say that about most museums.'
She grins.

The lines around her eyes smile like the sun's rays. The
wine has made her lips glossy and plump and a darker and
deeper red. The warm steamy atmosphere of the restaurant
has brought a gentle rose tint to her cheeks.

'But we all do that, don't we?' she continues. Taking all
the dough out of the ciabatta, she dunks only the crust
in the oil.

'What?' he asks, staring at her but appearing not to be able
to follow her conversation.

'Well, going to museums in foreign countries, but never in
our own town,' she laughs. Art says nothing. 'I remember
when I did live here, I never went to the theatre or anything.
Only when my parents used to come up would Kate and I do
anything cultural at all. People always say that they could never
be an expat because they would miss the culture of London
or the UK too much. And it's bollocks. They never went to
the theatre, so why should they care so much about it now?
Anyway, as far as I can work out, the only people who do
go to the theatre apart from single women and gay men are
expats and tourists.' She laughs. 'Am I boring you?' she asks,
suddenly aware that Art has not reacted to her speech at all,
save for a curious smile that plays with his lips.

'Oh no, not at all,' he says quickly. 'What were you saying?'

'You see, I am boring you,' she says, throwing her arms in
the air in a manner that is both playful and slightly serious.
Charlie knows that her conversation is not exactly riveting,
but Art is supposed to be a friend, and surely the definition
of a friend is someone who listens to your stories and laughs
at your jokes and then allows you to repeat them again while
they react with similar enthusiasm. But Art is not playing
the game like he's supposed to, and she is beginning to
feel self-conscious.

'So,' says Maria, her thrusting bust all of a quiver as she carries over the starters. 'Salami for you, Arrtor, and salad for you, Arrtor's friend.' Such is her serving speed that the plates leave her hand about an inch above the table. She swishes back a couple of seconds later with a carafe of water and a chair for herself. 'So,' she repeats sitting herself down, corkscrewing her buttocks into position, her large upper arms flapping with all the movement. Her arrival is trumpeted by an acrid aroma of old sweat and mothballs. 'So, Arrtor,' she says, squeezing his knee under the table with her firm, fat hand. 'Where have you bloody been? What have you bloody been doing?'

'Oh well, this and that,' says Art, breathing through his mouth and away from her armpits. For someone who works in the service industry, Maria has remarkably little knowledge of personal hygiene.

'Don't you bloody say "this and that" to bloody me,' she says, giving him a painful yet supposedly jaunty shoulder shove. 'It's Maria you have here, not your bloody mother.'

'Yes,' smiles Art. 'Well, if you really want to know, I've been in Zaire following some warlord and his tribe of rampaging lunatic followers as they try and take over some villages in the north . . .'

Art goes on to explain some of his more hairy experiences in a jovial manner. While he turns frightening situations into good anecdotes, Maria nods and laughs, occasionally saying 'yes' or 'si', depending what she has said the time before.

'Good,' she says, clapping her hands together across her chest. 'I have a story for you,' she announces. 'It is so bloody interesting. I can't believe it hasn't been on television stations and cable stations all over the world already.'

'Right,' says Art.

'It is amazing, it's quite a bloody amazing and I will give it to you as a world exclusive,' she continues, selling her story better than the hardest of hard-nosed hacks.

'Yes,' says Art.

'Well, an uncle of mine . . .' And Maria is off telling a story that involves cousins and aunts and a very complicated conspiracy theory that is linked to '. . . none other than Nixon and Lady Di – God rest her soul.' Throughout the quite frankly insane story, Charlie notices, Art nods his head in sweet and kind agreement. He smiles in the right places, and inhales when he should, and exhales with relief when it's all over. Maria's fingers, meanwhile, gesticulate like a rope of pork sausages swinging in the breeze. The more she leans forward the deeper the dimple just above her elbow becomes. By the time Lady Di is involved, the crevice is deep enough to inspire pot-holing trips and something to do with the Duke of Edinburgh award scheme.

'So what do you bloody say to that?' Maria asks, leaning back in her chair with evident satisfaction.

'It sounds unbelievable,' says Art.

'You?' asks Maria, turning to Charlie.

'Truly unbelievable,' says Charlie.

'I know, I know, I know,' says Maria, leaning on the table and heaving herself up from her chair. 'Un-bloody-believable.' She nods, smoothing down her floral, frilly pinny. 'That's what I say to . . . Gino,' she shouts suddenly. 'Why haven't you cleared these bloody plates?'

Gino whips out from behind the split bamboo-fronted bar to clear the dishes just as his father comes through the swing doors with two plates of steaming hot pasta held aloft. He places them in front of Art and Charlie with rather greater elegance than his wife, turning the large white bowls round so that the small blue mark that vaguely resembles a royal crest faces the top.

'*Buon apetito*,' he says with a small nod before returning to the kitchen.

'This really does look delicious,' says Charlie, leaning over her shiny green pasta parcels of spinach and ricotta and breathing in the smell of garlic, olive oil and parsley. Gino arrives with a pepper mill the size of Canary Wharf and grinds it all over both her and Art's food. 'I always think those huge mills must be inversely proportional to the size of the vendor's penis,' whispers Charlie as Gino walks back to bar.

'Do you think?' smiles Art.

'Oh yeah,' nods Charlie, taking a large sip of her wine. 'You know, like with cars. Fast car, small cock – it stands to reason.'

'What if you don't have a car?' asks Art.

'Enormous,' she announces. 'You must have an enormous penis.'

'Well, that's nice to know,' he says, sitting back in his plastic chair.

'But you have got a car,' says Charlie.

'Not here I haven't,' he smiles.

'Interesting,' she says, placing her finger on her lips. 'Does that make you better endowed whenever you leave Kenya?'

'That's for you to find out,' he winks, pouring himself some more wine.

'Right,' she says back, draining her glass and offering it over for him to refill. She laughs weakly.

Did she hear that correctly? Did Art just flirt with her? She feels a shot of adrenalin course through her veins. Everything suddenly seems sharper and brighter and a lot more acute. She feels hot. She runs her hands through her hair and sits watching his long brown fingers wrapped around the neck of the glass carafe pouring the red wine.

'There you are,' he says, handing back the glass.

'Thanks,' she says, careful not to touch his fingers, fearful that she is mistaken.

'Yours looks great,' she adds, nodding her head firmly at his bowl of bolognese to avoid any form of double entendre.

'So does yours,' he says, launching his fork into the middle of his plate and spinning.

'Mmm,' says Charlie, popping two green ravioli parcels into her mouth and letting the delicious warm ricotta and spinach combination slither down the back of her throat. 'Wow,' she says, swallowing. 'That is amazing. I don't think I have ever eaten anything like that in this country before.'

'Mmm, mmm, mmm,' nods Art, his mouth full in firm agreement. 'It's all handmade,' he says eventually, between mouthfuls. 'The food has got to be good here,' he says, taking another large sip of wine. 'Look at the size of the woman who makes it.'

'Do you think she samples her own produce?' she asks, starting to giggle, curling the ends of her hair around her right index finger.

'Wouldn't you?' whispers Art, leaning in.

Charlie licks off any last remains of olive oil from around her mouth with her tongue. Her lips glisten.

'I'd be enormous,' she whispers back, leaning over, glancing out of the corner of her eye. 'Really enormous.'

'How really enormous?'

'Really, really enormous.'

'Now there's an image to conjure,' smiles Art, leaning back in his chair, his eyes closed. 'An enormous you . . .'

His smile is wide, his teeth are white in comparison to his brown face and his curled eyelashes spring like spiders from his lids.

'I'm rather enjoying the idea,' he announces.

'Oh stop it,' says Charlie, picking up a paper napkin and screwing it into a ball before throwing it at him.

'Stop what?' he asks, catching the napkin in the palm of his right hand.

'You know,' she says coyly.

'Well, not really, no,' he says, leaning on both his elbows, staring at her.

'You two seem to be having a nice time,' interrupts Maria, taking away Art's half-consumed bowl of pasta before he can protest. 'Finished?' she asks Charlie.

'Um, yes,' says Charlie, pushing her bowl into the centre of the table. She had been gut-gnawingly hungry before they sat down. It was the combination of blueberries, too much coffee and the smell of vegetarian lasagne at the gym that had set her off. But since all her exchanges with Art that have just culminated in some jaunty throwing, she has rather lost her appetite. The only thing that really tickles her fancy is another glass of red wine and at least half a packet of cigarettes.

'Would you like another carafe of red?' asks Maria, waving the empty carafe at arm's length, like she is checking the contents of a catheter bag.

'Oh, yes please,' says Charlie immediately, thinking there is nothing she would like more than to while away the afternoon in Art's company. 'But only if you fancy it, of course,' she adds hastily, rather regretting the keenness of her wine-loosened tongue.

'No, no, whatever you want,' says Art, waving his index fingers in front of him like windscreen wipers.

'No, you . . .'

'You . . .'

'Oh God,' says Charlie, wishing for once in her life that someone else might actually take the lead and organise things.

'Do you know what, Maria?' says Art suddenly. 'I think we'd like one more glass of house red each and the bill . . .'

'What?' says Maria, sounding shocked. 'No coffee? But you always have coffee here, and maybe some grappa as a welcome-back present?'

'I'd love to,' smiles Art. 'But you can't be a creature of

habit for ever, particularly if you're under seventy,' he laughs. 'Anyway, Charlie and I have plans.'

'Oh yes,' replies Maria, raising a painted half-moon eyebrow and greasy lid. 'You have plans . . . do you?'

'Yes,' nods Charlie. 'We have museums to see.'

'Right . . . museums,' she nods, turning with a rustle of her floral pinny.

'That told her,' says Charlie.

'D'you think?' he says, his curled head moving from side to side. 'I just wanted her to go away. You know . . .' He pauses. 'Do you think I've offended her?'

'I should imagine that it takes more than a polite carafe refusal to put Maria's nose out of joint.'

Sure enough, five minutes later Maria is back, nose still straight and bingo wings flapping in the breeze. Nestled in her yard of cleavage is a tray with two large glasses of red wine, and two stout shots glasses like thimbles glowing with luminous limoncello.

'I don't bloody care what you say,' she says. 'Here . . . you have your two glasses of red wine . . . and two little somethings from Franco and me.' She grins. Her smile contains more shiny gold than a rapper's bathroom.

'Thank you very much, Maria,' nods Art, once more defeated.

'Yes, thank you very much,' says Charlie.

The sun is still shining when they eventually trip up the faded red plastic staircase and out into the street. Charlie inhales deeply the crisp autumn air, and exhales the smoke from the pit of her lungs.

'That feels good,' she says, smiling at Art.

'Oh yes,' he says, stretching slightly in the sun, unconsciously linking arms.

Arm in arm, they stroll up the street back towards *Les Misérables*, joking about how Art ostentatiously paid for the lunch with the full force of a twenty-pound note, and then spent the next five minutes trying to extricate himself from Maria's hirsute and fecund embrace.

'And then,' laughs Charlie, turning to prod in the chest. 'And then Franco comes over and hugs and kisses you . . . you should have seen your face, squashed between his hands,' she declares.

'Oh God, I know,' says Art, wrinkling his nose.

'Art,' says Charlie. 'I know you're a bush boy, but you should probably get in touch with your feminine side a bit more than that.'

'Why?' says Art.

'Because it's good for you.'

'Why?' says Art, smiling. 'Why is it good for me?'

'Because it is,' says Charlie, realising that there is no real argument to her argument.

'But I like kissing *girls*,' Art announces loudly. A middle-aged couple in his-and-hers macintoshes both stare at him like he might need help. 'I like kissing girls,' he says quietly into Charlotte's ear.

'Right,' she laughs, a sudden rush of eroticism shooting through her.

She flicks her hair again, not really knowing where to put herself or what to do with herself. Art has never really behaved like this before. Is he teasing her? she wonders, her arm laced through his as they walk down past Stringfellow's and on towards Trafalgar Square. Or does he just feel sorry for her after what she has been through in the last couple of days, and is using his immense charm to make her feel better? Whatever he is doing, she shrugs, it's working – because she is feeling wonderful. Intoxicated. And in the company of a handsome, charming and charismatic man, what better and more blissful way is there of spending an afternoon?

'Are you enjoying yourself?' he smiles.

'Oh God, yes,' she smiles back.

'Good,' he says, squeezing her hand tightly. 'That makes me happy. I'm glad I've managed to cheer you up.'

'Cheered me up,' she repeats. 'Yes, you've, um, certainly done that.'

They walk down towards the National Portrait Gallery in silence. Charlie continues to hold Art's hand, but it becomes increasingly hot and heavy and uncomfortable. Eventually she coughs and he removes it as they turn towards the gallery steps. They both slow down. Charlie doesn't want to break the moment. She doesn't want the distraction of something else intruding into their increasingly intimate world.

'Um,' says Art.

'What?' says Charlie, hoping that he might have changed his mind.

'Do you, um, really fancy it?' asks Art

'Fancy what?'

'You know . . . going in?' says Art.

'Well . . .'

'I know it's a fairly weak-willed thing to do and it smacks of terrible laziness, but quite frankly . . .'

'Yeah, I agree,' agrees Charlie.

'I mean, it's a nice afternoon, and I'm enjoying your company too much to want to go and stare at dull old men with chins like testicles.'

'No, no, fine,' says Charlie. 'If that's how you feel.'

'Great,' he says. 'So it's decided.'

'Yes.'

'Good,' he says, taking her hand. 'Let's go and feed some vermin in Trafalgar Square.'

'What?' says Charlie, finding herself swept along by Art's enthusiasm as he weaves his way through a coach-load of tourists who have just been deposited guideless and directionless outside the gallery. 'What are we doing now?' she shouts as she follows along behind him, dragged along by her hand.

'We're going to feed the pigeons,' he declares, like it is the finest idea in the world.

Art strides through the traffic and on towards the bronze lions and the fountains. Finding an old man in a tweed coat covered in birds, Art parts with a pound and is immediately given a brown paper bag full of hard, old breadcrumbs.

'Great,' he says, scooping out a handful of crumbs and pouring them into Charlie's outstretched palm. 'I've always wanted to do this.'

'What do you do?' asks Charlie.

'Like that,' says Art, nodding over at the group of French schoolchildren who are standing in clusters of three and four, their hands above their heads, their eyes closed against flapping wings as a flock of pigeons fight each other for palm space and bits of bread.

'Do you want to go first?' suggests Charlie.

'Oh go on, then,' says Art, grabbing a handful of crumbs and standing with his eyes closed and palm stretched above his head. Within seconds his hand is invaded by a couple of sharp-eyed birds. It doesn't take long before the remainder of the flock follow suit. 'Oh my God!' laughs Art, his shoulders hunched. 'I can feel them pecking my hand. Oh my God!' he repeats. 'It's so ticklish. It tickles, it tickles, it tickles.' He laughs, his curls bounce around his screwed-up face. 'Hurry up,' he says. 'Hurry up.' He finally shakes the last few crumbs off his hand on to the paving. They are immediately leapt upon by birds not audacious enough to eat off a human hand. 'That was fantastic,' grins Art, his eyes now open. 'A weird experience . . . It's your turn,' he says, nodding at her fistful of crumbs.

'I'm not sure I want to,' says Charlie. 'It doesn't look that much fun.'

'Oh go on,' urges Art. Charlie looks unconvinced. 'You'll love it.'

'All right then,' she smiles. 'I'll give it a go.' Charlie thrusts her fist in the air, her eyes closed, her faced scrunched. She laughs and squeals and giggles. The dimples dance on her cheeks and the sun plays on her golden hair. 'Oh my Go-o-d!' she wails, her feet stamping up and down on the spot like a terrified toddler. 'It does really tickle, really, really tickle . . .'

'Hold it right there,' shouts Art, bending down slightly, encircling her with his elegant fingers. 'That would make such a good photo.'

'Leave me alone,' she squeals. 'And stop framing me, you bastard, I can't believe you made me do this. I can't believe I trusted you . . .'

'That's what I love about you,' laughs Art. 'Your delicious trusting nature.'

'You bastard!' she laughs. 'You lied, you lied . . . It's horrible, the claws, the pecking, I can't take the pecking,' she says, throwing her hands in the air and letting all the crumbs tumble on to the pavement. 'Yuk,' she says rubbing her hands together. 'That was really very unpleasant.'

'You should have seen your face,' laughs Art, walking towards her. 'It was a picture . . . an absolute picture.' He leans forward and, taking hold of her shoulders, kisses her on the cheek. 'A very . . . pretty . . . picture,' he says, half closing his eyes as his cheek brushes hers.

'Yes, well,' says Charlie, her stomach tight and her breath shortened by his hold.

'It's a bit cold,' says Art suddenly. 'I think we should go back to the hotel.'

The journey back to the hotel is entirely different from the relaxed and flirtatious bus ride out. Sitting in the back of the cab, the atmosphere is tense. Charlie shifts uncomfortably in the back seat. She stares out of the window. Her mouth is dry and her heart is quick. She repeatedly curls a lock of hair around her finger as she plays out erotic sexual fantasy after erotic sexual manoeuvre over and over in her head. He is taking her clothes off. He is kissing her face. He is cupping her breasts. She doesn't dare engage Art in conversation for fear of not being able to finish her sentence, or be responsible for her actions. Art, however, is talkative and continuously trying to get her attention.

The traffic slows along Westbourne Grove. The red traffic lights seem endless. And the double-parked white vans keep on multiplying. Charlie stares determinedly out of the window, her cheeks flushed by her own imagination. Eventually the cab pulls up outside the hotel and Charlie is inside the lift before she has a chance to think. The lift doors shut and they are left alone together. Neither of them says anything. Charlie stands staring at her own warped reflection in the silver doors. She squeezes her hands into her fists and digs her nails into the palms of her hands.

The lift finally grinds to a halt and a microwave sound announces its arrival on the second floor. Charlie follows Art along the corridor, the half carafe of wine plus lemon grappa chaser only going some of the way towards taking the edge off her anxiety. Art opens the door and Charlie follows him in. He turns to face her.

'So?' he says, lightly touching her shoulder with the tips of his fingers. His head is bent, avoiding eye contact.

'So,' replies Charlie as, with uncharacteristic forwardness, she tentatively places her hands either side of his hips.

It seems as if years of frustration and emotion are released in him. He runs his brown hands over Charlie's shoulders, around her waist and pulls her towards him. He lets out a gentle moan as his lips finally touch hers. His embrace is soft and teasing at first, and becomes more powerful and urgent. Charlie's passionate response surprises even herself. She feels entirely comfortable in his arms. The smell of his skin and his breath, the feel of his soft lips against hers, make her want more and more of him. She can feel his erection against her thighs as he pushes her towards the wall. Charlie runs her hands over his hard buttocks as his body weight throws her up against the wall. She smacks the back of her head, but doesn't seem to notice or care. She wants Art and she wants him now. He is kissing her face. His hands are on her bosom, making her nipples hard. She is hot. She bites her bottom lip as she runs her fingernails down his bare back underneath his jumper and baggy T-shirt. Art moans and arches his back, pushing himself harder up against her thigh. Charlie pushes him back so she can get at his belt. She tugs away at the leather, pulling and weaving it through the buckle, while Art slips off his jumper and T-shirt and starts on Charlie's coat and shirt.

In less than a minute they are both naked. Their clothes at their feet, they are still standing just inside the door. Art kisses her lips, teasing her slightly. He then kisses the side of her neck. He cups both her breasts, running his thumbs gently over her nipples. He starts to run his tongue down her collarbone towards her breasts. Charlie is too turned-on to move. She stands still, her mouth open, her eyes closed. What is this man doing to her? Still teasing her nipples with his thumbs, he lowers himself down towards her toned flat stomach, circling her navel with his tongue.

Art then suddenly kneels on the floor. His hands run over her hips. The anticipation is such that Charlie thinks she might orgasm even before Art's tongue reaches the top of her thighs. He starts just above the knee and works his way slowly up, his hands gripping her buttocks as he does so. Charlie can't cope any more.

'Oh God,' she whispers under her breath. 'Oh God. Oh God. Oh God.' Art's face is right between her thighs. He pulls her hard towards him, his fingers digging deep into her buttocks, and she comes. She throws her head back against the wall. 'Oh . . . my . . . God!' She says before exhaling and sliding down the wall. 'Oh my God!'

They make love immediately afterwards on the floor by the bed, and then again on the bed itself. Charlie is in bliss. The beautiful Art, the man who has always been her friend, her ally, her calm in the storm is now her lover too. Could things be any better?

'You are wonderful,' says Art, running his hand through her blonde curls as they rest on his chest.

'Mmm?' says Charlie from her delicious pillow.

'You're wonderful,' he repeats. 'Do you have any idea quite how wonderful you are?'

'Mmm,' she mumbles, half asleep. 'So are you.'

Art lies there staring at the black ceiling, listening to Charlie breathe deeply on his shoulder. He slips out from underneath Charlie's sleepy head and makes his way to the bathroom for a glass of water. He checks his watch. It is only ten-thirty. He can't sleep. He walks back into the bedroom and sits down in the chair. Her bronzed naked body glows gold with the light from the street. He sits and watches Charlie as she sleeps, a blissful smile shining in his eyes.

Charlie's mobile phone bleeps with a message received. It glows green in the dark on the bedside table. Art stares at it for a second. He hesitates. He picks up it and, releasing the lock, he reads the message.

'Loved last night – We should talk – Love Andrew Edwards.'

9

Charlie sleeps late. The combination of smooth sheets, thick curtains and total happiness means she doesn't begin to stir until about eleven. Stretching like a contented cat in the sun, she rolls over to find a cold, empty pillow next to hers. Art must be in the bathroom, she thinks, moving back to her toastier side of the bed, listening for the sound of the shower. But all she can hear is silence. A silence that is gently disturbed by the long-distant knocking of housekeeping somewhere down the corridor.

Charlie sits up in bed. For some reason she senses that something is wrong. Some primeval fear stirs within her. Where is Art? She looks around the room for evidence of life – a half-eaten breakfast, a wet towel on the floor, a tepid dressing gown flung over the back of a chair. But there is nothing.

She gets out of bed. Naked, holding her own breasts, feeling vulnerable and suddenly cold, she scrambles around on the floor, picking up her frantically discarded clothes. She puts on her pants and a shirt, and stands by the bed, static with thought and fear, not really knowing what to do. Where are his clothes? Last night they were left in a pile intertwined with hers and now they are nowhere to be seen.

Charlie walks into the bathroom and runs the tap, preparing to brush her teeth. Picking up her toothbrush and squeezing out the paste, she suddenly drops them both into the basin. All Art's stuff has gone. His toothbrush has gone. His wash bag has gone. She turns and looks into the bath. His shampoos have gone. The man has gone. She rushes back into the bedroom and stands stock-still by the bed. His suitcase has gone. His cameras have gone. Slowly the situation becomes clear – the cold bed, the lack of clothes, the empty bathroom. He packed up and left in the middle of the night and she knew nothing about it.

Charlie sits back down on the bed in shock. Why would he have done this? Where has he gone? She starts to shake. Her stomach is tight, her legs are shivering; she wraps her arms around herself. What did she do wrong? What did she say? Did she upset him? Was she really that bad in bed? She runs through what happened the night before, scene by scene. It was beautiful. It was romantic. It was love. The last memory she has is of him muttering something about how wonderful she was as she drifted off to sleep.

She stands up and starts frantically searching for a note. He must have left a note. Surely he has left a note? She leafs through the writing paper on the desk. She looks through her pile of clothes. Maybe it slipped on to the floor? She crawls around on her hands and knees, looking under the bed, through the bed linen that has slid on to the floor. And still she finds nothing. If she were to put a note somewhere, where would she put it? she thinks, flicking through the pads of paper on the bedside table, picking up her mobile phone.

'Of course!' she says out loud to herself. She should call reception. Everyone leaves messages at reception. She sits down on the bed and presses zero.

'Hello, reception,' says reception.

'Hello, it's Charlotte Adams, from Arthur MacDonald's room. I was just wondering if he has left a message for me,' says Charlie, trying to sound as relaxed as possible.

'Arthur MacDonald?' repeats reception.

'Yes, yes that's the one,' says Charlie.

'Oh,' says reception, clicking away at a keyboard. 'That's strange.'

'What?'

'Arthur MacDonald?' says reception, again.

'Yes?'

'He checked out last night.'

'Are you sure?' Charlie tries to quell the terrible feeling of panic.

'Oh yes, quite sure,' says reception. 'He checked out at about 10.53 p.m.'

'Last night?'

'Yes, last night. He paid the entire bill, madam, if you're worried about that,' continues reception helpfully. 'Although whatever you've consumed from the minibar this morning and anything that you've ordered on room service will have to be paid for separately.'

'Yes, yes, whatever,' says Charlie. 'Um . . . did he leave a note, or say where he was going or anything like that?'

'One minute,' says reception, putting Charlie on hold and into some sort of ambient relaxing-music hell. Her hand is sweating as she clutches the receiver too tightly. 'Hello?'

'Yes, hello,' says Charlie.

'I'm afraid not.'

'What, nothing?'

'Yes, nothing.'

'Oh . . .'

'Can I help you with anything else?' asks reception.

'I don't think so,' says Charlie. 'But thank you,' she adds, putting the phone slowly down.

Sitting on the bed, Charlie brings her bare legs up underneath her chin. She is too shocked to cry. Too stunned to do anything at all. She sits and stares straight ahead, her forehead frowned in thought, her body rocking backwards and forwards slightly on the edge of the bed. None of this makes sense. How can someone make love to you, tell you that you are wonderful and then disappear in the middle of the night without saying why? It's not as if it was a one-night stand, thinks Charlie. They had been building up to it for months, years even. She loved his friend. Maybe it's guilt? Defiling his friend's memory? The idea of going where he shouldn't? Or perhaps it is the emotion of it all that was too much for him? Maybe he thought they might have to have a proper relationship and he isn't ready for that? Perhaps he just wanted to fuck, and now that he has he is no longer interested? It has happened before. Men do it all the time. Spin all sorts of lines, say all sorts of shit, just to get into a girl's knickers, and once they have they couldn't give a toss and they're off. But Art isn't like that, Charlie insists. Or at least she has never seen that side of him before. But then again, she has never slept with him before.

The telephone rings. Charlie answers it before it manages a second bell.

'Art,' she says frantically, her legs curling under her in anticipation.

'Um, no, I'm afraid not. This is reception,' says reception.

'Oh.'

'We were just wondering . . .' She clears her throat in an attempt to sound more tactful. 'Would you be staying another night, because it's check out at twelve o'clock?'

'Twelve o'clock?' says Charlie weakly.

'Yes . . . um, midday.'

'Oh,' says Charlie again. 'What time is it now?' she asks, looking around for the clock on her mobile phone.

'It's ten to twelve.'

'Okay,' says Charlie coming to a decision. 'No, don't worry, I shall be checking out,' she says. The idea of hanging around at the scene of the crime is not appealing in the slightest.

Whatever Art's problems are, she is not going to solve them sitting here in her underwear, waiting for him to call.

Being asked to leave stirs Charlie into action. She showers, dresses and packs in a matter of minutes. With everything folded neatly and efficiently, tidied away in her bags, she looks round the room for the last time, checking she hasn't left anything behind. She spots her mobile phone on the bedside table. Dropping her bags she walks over to pick it up. The key guard is unlocked and there is an opened message on the screen. She scrolls down. 'Loved last night – We should talk – Love Andrew Edwards.'

Charlie drops her phone. Both her hands swiftly cover her mouth. Andrew Edwards? What was he doing contacting her? How did he get her number? What is he doing? She stands and stares at the telephone on the carpeted floor. Then it dawns on her. The message, the unlocked telephone. Art saw this message and left. He flew off the handle. He had unlocked her telephone, read her message, thought that she'd lied about the night of the awards, and left in the middle of the night without giving her a chance to explain. She picks up the telephone and scrolls through to check the time the message arrived. 10:32. Art read the message, left the room and checked out in twenty minutes flat. Charlie shakes her head in disbelief. Why didn't he wait for her to explain? Was it too much to ask for him to have woken her up, confronted her and given her the right of reply? He must have been really hurt, his judgement clouded by an angry mist. What is his problem with Andrew Edwards?

Charlie checks out with as much dignity as she can muster, but the sympathetic smiles from everyone on the front desk are testimony to how convincing she was a couple of nights previously as the enthusiastic fiancé just flown in from Africa.

'Hope you enjoyed your stay,' says the svelte, smooth

blonde behind the desk with a weak smile. 'Would you like anyone to order you a cab,' she adds, as Charlie picks up her heavy rucksack and camera case, making for the door.

'Don't worry,' says Charlie, sounding ostentatiously brave. 'I'll be fine,' she adds, looking anything but.

She walks out into the weak autumn sunshine. The air is cold and the sharp breeze cuts through her cotton trousers. She turns and walks aimlessly along the street past the glamorous boutiques boasting capsule wardrobes that could double as postman's uniforms. She crosses over at the traffic lights where their taxi dallied just a bit too long the night before. A smell of fig wafts out of the doors of the scented candle and lipstick shop.

The walk is making her feel better. The monotonous practicality of it all and the heavy bag make her feel like she is paying some sort of penance. But quite what for she doesn't yet know. Eventually she comes across a coffee bar and, dropping her heavy bags at her feet, she orders a half-pint paper cup of something milky and sits on a stool staring at the hardware store opposite. There is something going on here, she thinks, resting her chin in the palm of her right hand. Something odd and strange. People don't react like that to messages. They don't run away. They wake people up and ask them to explain themselves. Unless there is some other part of the situation that Charlie doesn't understand. With typical reporter's instinct, she is determined to find out.

She picks her phone out of her handbag and, taking a fortifying sip of her coffee, she scrolls through her messages. Finding Andrew Edwards' number, she calls him. The telephone hardly rings.

'Hello?' comes the brusque reply of someone obviously waiting for an important call.

'Hello . . . Andrew?' says Charlie.

'Hello,' he says again, automatically warming to a female voice.

'Hello, it's Charlotte,' says Charlie.

'Charlotte?' says Andrew, audibly flicking through a Rolodex of past conquests, working out how much purr to put into his voice.

'Charlotte Adams,' says Charlie, rather more tight-lipped than she intended.

'Oh right,' he enthuses, paying more attention. 'Charlotte Adams, Charlie, how the hell are you?'

'You texted me,' she says, more as a statement than a question.

'Yes, yes, I did,' he replies. 'I just felt a bit terrible about the way you left the other day. It was awful. I felt awful. The whole thing was awful. I just, well . . . you know, wanted to say sorry. To find out how you are . . . to see if you're okay. Find out how you are . . .' he repeats and then pauses. 'I do so hate starting off on the wrong foot with . . .'

'With people who work in the same industry?' says Charlotte sarcastically. For one moment then, for a split second, she was being sucked in. But the 'wrong foot' line makes her realise that she is dealing with a real operator. A man so smooth and oleaginous that he has left a trail of broken-hearted women around the world like an oversexed slug.

'Yes . . . no . . . small world,' he says, sounding confused. 'No, no, I was worried about you leaving that suddenly and, you know, everything . . .'

'Well, I'm fine,' lies Charlie.

'Oh, good,' he says, sounding genuine. 'I am pleased.'

'Good,' she says, not knowing what to say next. 'Working hard?' she asks, like she cares.

'Um, yes,' he replies, slightly surprised. 'Got lots of commissions since . . .'

'Since you won,' adds Charlie helpfully.

'Um, yes . . .'

'Listen,' she says, abruptly. 'I wonder if we could meet?'

'Right,' says Andrew, trying to stifle the automatic flirt in his voice.

'Today?'

'Well, I'm a little busy . . .'

'I'm not going to weep on your shoulder and ask you to marry me,' says Charlie. Her voice is hard and clipped and serious.

'Oh,' says Andrew in a manner that implies there is little reason to meet otherwise.

'It's important,' insists Charlie.

'OK, lunch,' he sighs. 'In an hour.'

Fired on by a new determination, Charlie takes a cab into the middle of Soho and calls Alice to inform her somewhat bemused friend that she is on the way over. Alice takes her arrival firmly in her stride and then regales Charlie with all the details of her positively pornographic conquest of an up-and-coming actor she picked up last night. Punctuated by her constant dragging on a cigarette, plus the occasional pause for flicking and a loud litany of 'fucks' as Alice spills her Diet Coke all over her new iMac, Charlie gathers that last night was a success. She picked him up at a shoot and they'd reached first base before cocktails. Alice is thrilled, if feeling a little ropey.

As Charlie walks into the scruffy, matt black office, with framed fashion front shots all over the walls. Gavin is waiting for her with a mug of black coffee. Dressed in a pair of jeans with a large silver belt, some cowboy boots and an open-necked black shirt, he looks like every YMCA fantasy.

'Here,' he says, handing over a pink mug that says 'I am a princess' all over it. 'We thought that you might be having a bit of a crisis,' he shrugs, dabbing the end of his nose with a tissue.

'Thanks,' says Charlie. 'It isn't going that well, I have to say,' she adds, putting down her bags. 'Are you all right?'

'Oh God, ignore him,' says Alice, rolling her eyes in total boredom. 'He has a terrible bout of cocktail flu,' she says. 'Serves him right for spending his evening sniffing toilet seats.'

'Sorry?' says Charlie.

'I had a bit of a late one,' smiles Gavin sheepishly. 'Rooting and tooting all at the same time. She's just jealous that it wasn't her, or at least one of her friends, so she can get a blow-by-blow account of what I'm like in bed.'

'Oh pur-leese,' says Alice, flicking her ash into one of her dying pot plants. 'I've already had you test-driven, and quite frankly you were, by all accounts, shite . . .' Gavin doesn't respond. He simply flicks his boss a V-sign and walks back over to his desk. 'Right,' says Alice. 'Where were we? Ah . . .' she announces . . . 'You.'

'Yes, me,' says Charlie, sitting down on a slippery-smooth black leather chair that is designed to intimidate. 'I'm sorry about the other day.'

'Oh don't be so ridiculous,' says Alice, waving the apology away like an irritating gnat. 'Honestly, poor you,' she says. 'I heard a bit on the grapevine. What happened?'

'Well, I found them there, shagging in the disabled loos.'

'What? Your sister's husband and the best friend?'

'Yeah, and in the end, Kate asked me to leave and then the husband left soon after . . .'

'Oh dear,' says Alice, scooping ash off her desk and throwing it into the bin. 'That sounds messy.'

'Yeah, it is,' sighs Charlie.

'So,' says Alice, sounding really quite serious, wrapping her red lips around another cigarette and taking a big fat drag. 'What can I do?'

'Can I stay?' asks Charlie, thinking it much better to come

straight out with her request than flannel around. Alice is not the flannelling type.

'Um,' says Alice, scratching the back of her neck, weighing up the inevitable loss of horizontal activity that having someone to stay will incur versus a friend in need. 'I only have a sofa,' she replies.

'I don't mind,' says Charlie. 'I've slept propped up against trees before.'

'Then fine,' says Alice. 'Of course you can. How long for?'

'Literally a couple of days,' says Charlie. 'I have a couple of things to sort out with my sister and I've got lunch with Andrew Edwards and then . . .'

'Christ!' screams Alice, clapping her hands with joy, flicking more ash all over the desk. 'It took you long enough to tell me,' she squeals. 'Gavin,' she says across the room. 'Hold all my calls.'

'There aren't any,' he says smugly, dabbing his nose.

'Hold them anyway,' says Alice. 'Tell me everything. Tell me everything.'

'There's nothing really to tell,' lies Charlie, quite wanting to get to the bottom of the Andrew/Art axis herself before anyone else throws in their two pound coins' worth.

'Oh,' says Alice with an irritated ash flick. 'Have it your way . . . but I won't let you get away with that tonight,' she adds, the idea of a flatmate suddenly becoming a whole lot more appealing. 'Tonight it's a bottle of wine each and no holes barred.'

'Absolutely,' says Charlie.

'Good,' says Alice.

'Do you mind if I put my stuff here,' asks Charlie, 'while I have lunch?'

'No, please,' flaps Alice with her hands. 'There's nothing else going on here, except . . .' she raises her voice . . . 'a rather gay attempt at fighting a hangover.'

'Piss off,' says Gavin, not even bothering to raise his head out of *Heat* magazine. 'One day you'll bore yourself to death.'

Charlie leaves her bags propped up against the wall below on arty crotch shot of a girl seemingly unaware that her legs are wide open, and walks up the street to the Groucho Club.

Andrew had hummed and haaed on the telephone suggesting various bijou places in Hoxton off secret streets and culs-de-sac that Charlie had never even heard of. Eventually they had settled on his club. Charlie has never been to the cosy confines of this media stronghold before. She has friends who talk of nothing else. How drunk they were there. How they'd spoken to so and so there. How they hadn't got home until *really* early in the morning. So although Charlie is nervous of Andrew, she is secretly quite thrilled about lunching somewhere so glamorous.

The rush of adrenalin she feels as she walks through the revolving doors is enough to make her unsteady on her feet.

'Andrew Edwards,' she says to the women behind the reception bar.

'He's at the bar,' she announces, looking Charlie up and down.

'I'm Charlotte Adams,' says Charlie.

'I know,' replies the woman. 'He's signed you in already.'

Walking through the double glass doors to the left of reception, Charlie sees him already sitting at the long dark bar. His back turned, his muscled shoulders are unmistakable even from a distance. He is engaging the waitress in conversation. Her eyes are shining, her cheeks are flushed and she giggles with all the attention. Andrew is shifting around on his stool, his hands gesticulating as he tells some wildly hilarious story. Or at least it seems that way, judging by the girl's outlandish reaction. Her mouth open, her hands splayed, her ponytail is spinning with delight as Charlie approaches.

'Hello,' says Charlie, clearing her throat.

'Charlie, says Andrew, immediately getting off his stool. He throws his arms around her like they have been bestest friends for years. Pulling her to his taut-toned chest encased in a black Helmut Lang shirt, he smells of his expensive citrus aftershave. 'How have you been?' he asks in his international drawl, like they haven't seen each other in years.

'I'm fine,' says Charlie curtly, feeling rather annoyed at the expansive nature of his welcome. They have only met once; he'd led her on and then rejected her in the final furlong. It was hardly the basis of great friendship or even a relationship. But then again, that is probably how a man like Andrew Edwards does make friends, she thinks. His rootless past and his baseless present can hardly be good foundations for anything other than passing flirtations, endless acquaintances and the odd matey ex-shag. 'I'm fine,' she repeats.

Still the girl with the ponytail hangs around. Resting her breasts on the bar, her gaze doesn't leave his dark blue eyes, her smile remains fixed to her rather pretty face.

'Would you like a drink?' she asks Andrew.

'Charlie?' he says immediately, turning towards her and placing his hand in the small of her back.

'Um,' says Charlie. Uncomfortable with his familiarity, she moves to sit on a stool.

'Well, I'm going to have a Bloody Mary made with rum not vodka as it's *so* much better,' he says. 'It's a habit I picked up in New York back in the early nineties,' he continues. The barmaid seems very interested.

'Right,' says Charlie. 'I'll have the same.'

'It'll change your life,' smiles Andrew. 'You'll never do vodka again.'

'I doubt that,' says Charlie. 'I'm always willing to give anything a try, once.'

'It's the adventuress in you,' he grins. His straight teeth

shine in his curled mouth. The man exudes charm when he wants to.

'Yes, right,' nods Charlie with an amused smile.

The barmaid takes this as her cue to leave. Having felt the full wattage of Andrew's flirtation before Charlie arrived, she is clearly feeling cold and exposed now that its beam is being directed elsewhere.

'Could you send our drinks over there,' says Andrew, indicating towards the large leather sofa by the door. Moving out from behind the stool, he picks up a bowl of crisps and pops one in his mouth, letting it melt on his tongue. Charlie follows. Shifting a pile of well-thumbed newspapers from the middle of the sofa they both sit down, sinking back into the leather. 'So,' says Andrew, leaning over and touching her knee. 'What's so important?' he asks, furrowing his handsome brow. 'What can I do for you?'

'It's not really what you can do for me,' says Charlie, moving her knee as she suddenly, for the first time that morning, begins to question the sanity of this meeting. 'I just want some information from you.'

'Information?' he says.

'Yes,' she replies.

'Oh,' he says. 'I just rather wanted to apologise for the other morning . . .'

'I'm not really that worried about that,' says Charlie, putting a crisp in her mouth and hoping that she sounds rather cool.

'You're not?' says Andrew. Shifting to attention on his leather cushion, he pulls his jeans out of his crotch in shock.

'No, not really,' says Charlie.

'But I want to tell you my reasons,' says Andrew, sounding slightly offended. It is so unlike him to turn down any form of sexual opportunity, he appears quite put out that the very attractive girl in question is not even curious as to his motives.

'Bloody Marys,' says the barmaid, placing the two tall glasses on the small round table in front of them before mincing back with a full supermodel swagger to behind the bar.

'Mmm, you're right,' says Charlie, sucking on her long black straw. 'The rum is delicious.'

'Yes, well,' says Andrew. 'I'm not often wrong . . .' He removes his straw from the glass and takes a large swig. 'But about the other night . . .' he continues undeterred.

'No, really,' says Charlie. 'It doesn't matter. You didn't fancy me, I got the wrong idea. It's simple . . .'

'No, no,' says Andrew, sitting on the edge of the sofa facing her. 'That's simply not the case.'

'It's not?' asks Charlie, slightly surprised.

'No,' says Andrew, putting his glass down in earnest emphasis. 'It's . . .'

'Actually,' says Charlie, putting her hand in the air. 'I don't really mind what it was. I've actually come here to talk about Art.'

'Art,' says Andrew, not sounding at all surprised.

'Yes, Art,' says Charlie, staring at his undeniably handsome face for any reaction whatsoever. And she is not disappointed. His dark blue eyes flicker, his brow creases slightly and his mouth narrows.

'I was wondering when his name might come up,' says Andrew, his right leg bouncing up and down, his face lowered. 'Where is he?'

'I have no idea,' she says, worried. 'Do you?'

'No, I'm afraid not,' he says. 'Why do you think I would know?'

'I don't know,' says Charlie, leaning forward. 'But there's something going on between you two that I can't get to the bottom of. There's something strange that I don't quite understand. So when he ran off this morning I thought you might know where he is, or at least what the problem is. Maybe I'm wrong,' she shrugs. 'But my journalistic sixth sense says that I'm right.'

'He ran off this morning?' he says, his brow now deeply furrowed.

'Yes,' says Charlie, wondering suddenly why she is trusting this man.

'Why?'

'Oh God,' she says, breathing deeply as she makes the decision to carry on. 'He read the text message you sent me, and disappeared off.'

'Oh,' says Andrew. 'I'm sorry.'

'Yes . . .'

'But I sent that last night,' he says.

'I know, but he read it while I was asleep and when I woke he was gone.'

'Oh I see,' nods Andrew. He rolls his eyes and runs his hands through his thick brown hair. 'Oh dear . . .'

'Yeah,' says Charlie. 'Oh dear . . .'

'I promise you I have no idea where he might be,' he announces, both his hands in the air.

'I didn't really think you would know exactly where he was, but I thought you might have an idea,' she says.

'Nope, I'm afraid not,' he shrugs.

'Well, could you explain his behaviour?' says Charlie, determined not to let this bone drop.

'How do you mean?'

'No one reacts like that to a text message – or at least most people would wake someone up and allow them the possibility of an explanation, if not have the good manners to ask for their point of view. But he didn't.'

'Yes, well . . .'

'So I'd quite like to know what's going on between you two,' she says. 'Art is normally a nice guy. He is sweet and

251

funny and charming. But when you're around he becomes something very different . . .'

'Yes . . .'

'So I would like to know why.' Charlie sits up and tries to get firm eye contact with those navy eyes. Andrew is looking everywhere but back at her. He starts picking non-existent fluff off his immaculate jeans.

'Yeah,' he says finally. 'It's a very long story.'

'Do I look like I'm moving?'

'No,' he says shifting. 'But I think we should go and have some lunch.' He motions towards the back of the room, past the piano lined up against the bottom of some ornate stairs and beyond. 'I'd feel much better doing this over a bottle of wine,' he smiles, looking up through his lashes.

'OK, if you think so,' says Charlie, smiling ruefully to herself, thinking this man could charm himself out of a firing squad. 'I'll follow you,' she says, standing up. 'But you're not getting out of this . . .'

'I'd rather gathered that,' says Andrew, draining his glass. 'You're worse than any Chechen freedom fighter I've ever had to deal with.'

Charlie follows Andrew's toned, denim-clad buttocks past the piano and into an airless greenish-coloured room with a pale floor and a banquette perimeter. To her right as she walks past sit two young men, their whites faces puffed in toxic shock, nursing hangovers from the night before. Both dressed in tight black tops, their voices are nasal and their attitude unfriendly. Next to the two boys is a large woman *d'un certain age* with a hefty cleavage and brown frizzy hair in need of Clairol. Smoking a long thin brown cigarette, on her second bowl of crisps, she turns her expectant face towards the glass door every time it swings open.

In the greenish dining room things are decidedly more jolly. Over in the far corner a glossy-looking couple are drinking flutes of champagne, furiously smoking cigarettes and laughing loudly at each other's jokes. Towards the middle of the room is a group of six suits knocking back bottles of fizzy water, leafing through sheets of paper, comparing power paunches and executive cufflinks. Up the right hand side of the room there are three sets of girls lunching. The first, closest to the entrance, are chic and tapered and hardly draw breath. The other two are slightly less beguiling. They look stiff and gauche like they are either old friends with nothing left to say, or a power couple where one woman is distinctly more powerful than the other.

Charlie and Andrew are shown to their table in a quiet corner at the end of the line of lunching ladies. The conversation in the row palls as Andrew walks by, although he doesn't appear to notice. He must be used to a dearth of female conversation wherever he goes. Sitting down facing the room so he can keep an eye on the departures and arrivals, Andrew orders a bottle of house red, a bottle of fizzy water and a burger without looking at the menu. Charlie orders the Niçoise with dolphin-friendly tuna, or at least that's what the waitress claims. She lights a cigarette and draws it in.

'So,' she says as the waitress arrives with a bottle. 'I'm all ears.'

'Right,' says Andrew, pouring them both a large glass of red wine. 'It's quite a long story . . .'

'Yes?' she encourages.

'It all happened in Haiti,' he says, looking down and starting to fiddle with his napkin. 'About six years ago, when we were all younger, more impetuous and less wise. Art and I were out there on a story together. Well actually, Art had been out there a couple of months before me. He'd been doing some big magazine piece with Jack and they were quite well bedded down, if you see what I mean?'

'No, not really,' she replies.

'It was before you knew them, actually,' nods Andrew, taking another large sip of his dark red wine. 'Anyway, Art had been out there for a bit, doing some background research for this and that, firing off a couple of voodoo stories with the usual beheading chicken shots – that sort of thing – waiting or half hoping for the big story with Clinton and the troops to break. But in the meantime he had fixed himself up with this girl Pascale. She was his translator. Art's French isn't very good – actually, I think it's non-existent,' he laughs. 'So she followed him everywhere. They were quite an item,' he smiles. 'She was tall, brown, with loads of long hair, great tits and her father was a government official and her mother was an ex-beauty queen. Her English was more or less perfect and what she mispronounced was so cute, you couldn't help but fall in love with her. Which Art did. He was madly in love with her. They could hardly keep their hands off each other. When I first hooked up with Jack, we spent an evening together drinking rum in Port-au-Prince, and all Jack did was complain about his mate's obsession with Pascale. Anyway . . .' Andrew pauses and sighs. 'It all got a little complicated.'

'Right,' says Charlie, lighting up another cigarette and taking a sip of wine. 'You mean *you* got a little complicated.'

'Well, kind of,' he says, his face suddenly looking quite sad. 'It wasn't entirely my fault.'

'Right,' says Charlie.

'Oh look, here's our food,' smiles Andrew, looking across the restaurant.

'Don't try and change the subject,' says Charlie.

'I'm not,' he replies. 'It's just that I'm starving,' he announces as the waitress puts down his burger. 'Now that,' he says pointing with his slim brown finger, 'that looks delicious.' The waitress giggles. Andrew runs his hands through his hair. 'Yours doesn't look too bad either,' he says to Charlie.

'You were saying,' she says.

'Well, yes, I was saying,' he says, mechanically coating a chip in tomato sauce. 'Well, it was all going fine. There was a gang of us, all hanging out together, staying in the same hotel, drinking in the same bar, you know, the usual sort of stuff.' Charlie nods. She has been there so many times – the tall tales, the tall drinks, the traumas, the tears, and the people who go out one morning and don't make it back. She nods again, knowing exactly what he is talking about. 'Anyway, we all decided to hire this speed boat to go deep-sea fishing. It was a Sunday. Nothing was happening, it was quiet. I think there were some diplomatic manoeuvres going on. Anyway, we all went out on this boat, Jack, Art, me, some English bloke called Julian, an American girl, and a couple of other people, plus Pascale. In fact, if I remember correctly, she organised the whole thing. Anyway,' he pauses, staring at Charlie with his navy eyes, 'things got a bit out of hand. We all got drunk and smoked up a bit, and the boys decided that enough was enough. We were all so bored with Art going on and on about Pascale that Julian and this guy Adam bet me I couldn't seduce her – or fuck her for fifty bucks was exactly how it was put.'

'What?' says Charlie, leaning in towards the table.

'I know,' nods Andrew, letting his head fall into the palm of his right hand. 'To this day I don't really know why we did it, or more to the point why I did it. It's not as if Art was unpopular, he and Jack were such a great couple of lads together . . .' He pauses and takes a sip of his red wine. He raises his eyebrows and stares at Charlie, although he doesn't appear to be able to see her. 'I think perhaps maybe we were all a little jealous of him. We'd been together for a while. We were all far away from home. It sends you mad. Anyway,' he says, sitting up straight and scratching the back of his head. 'So . . . So I flirted all day, we were all drinking rum. She wore a yellow bikini – I remember it very well.'

'It sounds wonderful,' says Charlie, loading on sarcasm with her French dressing. 'Where was Art during all of this?'

'That's the thing,' says Andrew. 'He was there, at the back of the boat, reeling in fish, all brown and handsome and showing off his angling prowess and blissfully unaware of what was going on.'

'Meanwhile?' says Charlie, raising her eyebrows.

'Meanwhile,' he sighs, 'it was a case of I've started so I'll finish,' he says, dipping another chip, staring at the table as he chews it. 'To be honest, none of us expected it to work, but that night she came back to the hotel with me.' He looks up, catching Charlie's eye. 'I think we remained locked in my room for about three days. I missed the story, of course. I broke Art's heart. He hammered on the bedroom door threatening to kill me when he found out what we'd done. He said he'd never forgive me and to this day I don't think he has.' He smiles ruefully. 'Anyway, then I was called away at short notice to the Middle East to do some Intifada story . . .' He sighs. 'I didn't find out until nearly a year later that she'd been a virgin, I'd got her pregnant and she'd had my baby.'

'Oh my God,' says Charlie.

'I know,' says Andrew, shaking his head. 'I'm a total wanker, aren't I? Not only did I shit on a friend for fifty bucks, but I totally fucked up a young girl's life . . . And all because we'd had too much rum, and too much dope, on a boat, in the sun. It would be pathetic if it weren't so awful . . .'

'I'm afraid you don't come out of the story terribly well,' says Charlie with a weak smile, attempting to lighten his mood.

'I've been back to Haiti to try and see her,' he continues, 'but her father had me detained at the airport and since then I've never seen her . . . or my son.' He picks up his glass of wine and takes a large sip. 'But I have learnt from my mistake,' he says, leaning in.

'Of course you have,' smiles Charlie tightly. 'You've turned over a new leaf and kept your pants firmly on.'

'But this is what I'm trying to tell you,' says Andrew sounding quite agitated.

'What?'

'I have changed.'

'Yeah, right,' she laughs. 'You're radically different.'

'I am,' he insists. 'With you and Art, for instance. Art loves you pure and simple. I realised that as soon as I saw you at the awards ceremony. I thought you were gorgeous myself. That's why I flirted so hard and took you home. But when I finally had you in my kitchen, I just couldn't go through with it. Art is one of the nicest, most decent men I have ever met, and I broke his heart once and I thought I could never do it to him again. That's why I couldn't . . . you know, don't you see?' Andrew's new-found morality sits uncomfortably on his shoulders. He finishes his glass of wine, his chin high in the air as the last drops trickle down the back of his throat. 'Anyway,' he sniffs. 'So now you know.'

'So now I know,' nods Charlie. Her back is stiff. Her shoulders are rigid as she looks at the table, mechanically tweaking a lettuce leaf with her fork.

She is stunned. How did she not notice what possibly the least sensitive man in the world found so glaringly obvious? Why did she not see that Art was in love with her? Or at least he was until last night. How blind is she? How insensitive and thick-skinned can someone be? It's been obvious all along. When Art was uncharacteristically sharp about Andrew Edwards as he turned up at the ceremony. His drunken tirade. He even yelled 'Ask him about Haiti' as she and Andrew left together. That's why he was angry when he thought they might have slept together. And that finally explains why he ran off.

'History repeating itself,' mutters Charlie, staring into her plate.

'Yes,' says Andrew jabbing his finger repeatedly. 'That's exactly it. History repeating itself.' He pours himself some more wine. 'But it's not going to. You've got to find him,' he says excitedly, his smooth, tanned cheeks flushing pink with alcohol and excitement. He leans forward, his elbows on the table. 'Fight for what you want. Don't let history repeat itself.' He sighs again, playing with a chip. 'You do love him, don't you?'

'I think so,' says Charlie.

'Well, that's good,' says Andrew, smiling 'That's half the battle, admitting that to yourself. I never can,' he says, sounding wistful. 'I find it far too difficult, probably never will. To be honest, I'm not the long-haul type of guy. When the going gets tough, I get going.'

'But you will hang around one day,' says Charlie, her eyes briefly smiling.

'Yeah, well,' says Andrew. 'Possibly. But don't hold your breath.'

'No, honestly,' she says, finding herself nurturing the one man who has put her own happiness in jeopardy. But sitting there opposite her, his large blue eyes filled with self-pity and sadness, his cheeks rosy with emotion, Charlie finds it hard not to feel sorry for this Greek god in a crisis. Maybe it is the wine that's making him so open. Or the mistakes he has made. The opportunity he missed, the child he has never seen. Either way, it is quite extraordinary how quickly his cool demeanour crumbles. 'You'll be fine,' she reassures, giving his hand a squeeze.

'Of course I will,' he says, a weak smile on his handsome face. 'I'm always fine.' He taps the table with determined hands. 'Right,' he says. 'Would you like another glass of wine?'

'D'you know?' says Charlie. 'That would be lovely.'

She and Andrew sit, relaxed, at the table for another hour. He tells her about his extraordinary childhood travelling all over the world – his early years in New York, his adolescence in communist Prague and his glamorous finale on the slopes of the Swiss Alps. Charlie listens and smiles. She finds him much less arrogant, much sweeter than anyone has ever given him credit for in the past. But then maybe that's because she doesn't find him pant-droppingly attractive any more. The tension has disappeared. The quasi-cheesy veneer has dissipated. What had made her flirt and preen before has vanished before her very eyes. And as a result Andrew is very much more entertaining.

'So how's work?' he asks.

'Oh God,' moans Charlie. 'What with Art and my sister I've done nothing about anything since I've been over here.'

'Well I hear nothing but nice things about you wherever I go,' he says encouragingly.

'Yeah, right,' she laughs.

'No, seriously,' he insists. 'Anyway, what's wrong with your sister?'

Andrew sits quietly and listens while Charlie talks him through the whole Kate–Alex debacle. She describes their domestic bliss, their two children, the big-breasted nanny and the penetrative sex in the disabled toilet facilities.

'On the first floor?' he asks.

'Yeah,' nods Charlie. 'That's the place.'

'I've had sex there,' says Andrew nonchalantly.

'Oh my God,' she squeals, her hands over her mouth. 'Have you? Have you really? You are terrible.'

'I know,' he says, raising his eyebrows, his spirits mounting with his remembered conquest. 'So was she.'

'Tut, tut,' says Charlie.

'But anyway, that's not the point,' he says. 'You should make it up with your sister,' he says. 'Really you should. Family is important,' he says. 'Take it from someone who doesn't really have one. Don't lose what you have.' Andrew sounds like a daytime TV show host and he knows it. 'I know that sounds crass but it's true. Honestly,' he smiles. 'And on that pearl,' his blue eyes flash, 'let's get the bill.'

In the end, after some squabbling, Andrew pays, repeating that it's the least he can do. As they walk back past the row of ladies lunching, only the two languid friends are still eating. They are not actually eating, of course. Girls that thin and that glamorous never consume more than a few leaves at lunch and perhaps a scallop. But they are on their third bottle of mineral water and second shared packet of cigarettes. They giggle like overexcited schoolgirls as Andrew walks past.

Through the revolving door and outside in the street, Andrew puts his arms around Charlotte's waist and kisses her goodbye.

'Thank you for a lovely lunch,' he says as his lips touch one cheek and then cross over her nose to the other. 'I don't ever get to have real conversations with women.'

'I really enjoyed that,' says Charlie, giving his shoulders a squeeze. 'It was lovely to have a proper conversation with you and find out exactly what happened. Oh, and for the record,' she smiles, 'I would never have slept with you in your kitchen anyway.'

'Really?' says Andrew.

'Yes, really,' says Charlie.

'Are you sure about that?'

'Perfectly,' she smiles.

'Well, somehow I doubt that very much,' he smiles, and turns to walk down the street. 'But sadly we shall never know.'

'Bye,' says Charlie. Andrew carries on walking. With his back to her he throws up his right arm and waves. Charlie is left standing on her own in the street, a smile on her lips as she contemplates walking back to Alice's office. Art is in love with her. That's all she can think. Art, she smiles. Where is he? She has got to find him and tell him she feels the same way. She needs to tell him that Andrew Edwards is one ghost that won't be haunting him any more. She turns in the direction of Alice's office. She doesn't quite know what she will say. So much of what Andrew said over lunch seems too private to share, lounging and laughing, knocking back vodka shots on a girlfriend's sofa. She will have to tell her something, she realises, walking up the road, but not all the details and not all the emotion. Alice will be furious, Charlie smiles, but she'll live. Turning left off Dean Street, into Alice's road, Charlotte's mobile telephone rings in her coat pocket. Pulling it out, she looks at the number. It glows 'Kate hme.'

10

The conversation is stilted, stiff and rather protracted. Kate, to the accompaniment of screams and wails and attention-demanding slaps from her children, doesn't so much as apologise but, by making the first move, opens the door to the possibility of a rapprochement. And Charlie grabs at it enthusiastically. In fact, she rolls over like a grateful Labrador keen to ingratiate herself with all around. She repeats 'sorry' and 'I know, you're right' over and over again, as if she is repeating a peace mantra. Walking into Alice's office, her ear glued to the receiver, she nods and agrees for a solid ten minutes before finally saying, 'Yes, yes, great, absolutely' and hanging up the phone.

'Jesus Christ,' says Alice, loosening her black jumper from around her neck with incredulity. 'I hope that was a job.'

'What?' says Charlie, distracted and slightly disorientated by her arrival in Alice's office.

'All that grovelling and kowtowing, I hope it was worth it?'

'Oh, it was,' says Charlie, vaguely looking around for her rucksack.

'Are you all right?' asks Alice, her red shiny lips pouting with concern.

'I've just had rather a lot of news to cope with today, and now my sister wants to see me,' says Charlie, running her hands through her blonde hair.

'Isn't that a good thing?'

'Yes, of course it is,' agrees Charlie. 'But it's also quite tricky.' She sits down in the slippery leather chair and lights a cigarette. 'It's odd,' she says as she exhales.

'What do you mean?'

'Oh, it's a sibling thing. It's all a bit strange,' she smiles. 'It's just that I'm the oldest and have always, you know, called the shots. Everything we did, I did first. Kate looked up to me, and I could tell her things she didn't know. I always had an attentive audience. But now things are different. You know, she has her own life and she no longer needs my approval. It's odd. Not that I bullied her, at all – although,' Charlie smiles again, 'I'm sure she'd say that I did. But it's a very weird feeling now. I suppose she's grown up.' She laughs a short laugh. 'She's the grown-up and I'm the child,' she shrugs. 'The tables have turned and she's the one doing the turning. I'm welcome back into her life, just so long as I abide by her rules. It's all about compromise.'

'Life's all about compromise,' says Alice, flicking the bottom of her cigarette with her red fingernail. 'Tell me something I don't know.'

'Well, I don't think I've ever done it before,' says Charlie.

'Oh dear,' laughs Alice, smiling broadly at her friend.

'Yes, well,' smiles Charlie.

'So I presume you no longer need my sofa then,' says Alice, blowing smoke out of the corner of her mouth. Having warmed to the idea of a flatmate she suddenly feels a bit disappointed.

'I suppose not,' says Charlie. 'She's asked me to come back and stay with her. Do you think I should go and face the music?'

'We could have a glass of wine first?' suggests Alice hopefully.

'No thanks,' says Charlie, suddenly standing up and clenching her fists with determination. 'I think I should go. Wish me luck.'

'You don't need it,' says Alice, stubbing out her cigarette and putting her arms around her. 'But I'll wish you it anyway.'

Standing on her sister's doorstep, her bags at her feet, Charlie is rather wishing that she had gone for the glass of wine. She takes a deep breath, smooths down her hair as if she were going for a job interview, and rings the bell. The sound of chaos detonates from behind the backlit door. Charlie hears muffled orders being issued and eventually the door swings open to reveal Alex. Sporting a pair of dark Boden moleskin trousers and a purple shirt, he looks pleasantly conservative as he holds open the door.

'Hello, Charlotte,' he says. 'Would you like a hand with your bag?'

'Um, wow, no thank you,' says Charlie. She is so surprised to see him that she blushes a deep scarlet right to the edges of her ears. Bending over to fiddle around with her luggage, she buys herself some time to compose herself. 'Isn't it a bit early for you?' she asks, trying to explain away her embarrassment.

'I would normally be at work,' he grants. 'But I've taken a few days off.'

'You have?'

'Yes, he has,' says Kate, swanning in behind her husband, putting her arm around his waist. Dressed in a pair of grey flared flannel trousers and a white cotton shirt, Kate is *très* Californian relaxed, and attempts to exude confidence. 'Isn't that sweet of him?' she asks her sister in the tone of voice that makes agreement compulsory.

'Yes,' says Charlie. 'Very sweet indeed.'

'You're in the white room, same as before . . .' says Kate.

'Same as before,' repeats Charlie. 'I know the drill,' she

265

says, walking slowly upstairs past the faux Matisse. 'I'll be down in a sec.'

Ten minutes later they are all sitting in the kitchen around the stainless steel-topped table. Alfie and Ben are sucking on some well-adjusted pasta made with happy tomatoes and politically correct olive oil. Their short forks skid and slide around the plate along with their food. Alfie's slither of green snot, which slips in and out of his right nostril as he breathes, seems to have been inherited by his younger brother. They sit and sniff and stare at Charlie like she's the devil incarnate. Occasionally one or the other demands 'juice' of some sort which Peta delivers with Dutch efficiency. Meanwhile Kate and Alex drink vodka and tonics with limes. The conversational flow is such that the ice in their drinks makes more noise than they do.

'So,' says Kate pleasantly, trying to make pleasant conversation with her sister. 'Where have you been staying?'

'Oh, in this hotel in Portobello,' says Charlie trying to be as natural and uncomplicated as possible.

'Very po-wsh,' says Kate, taking a large swig of vodka. 'Bet that set you back,' she adds, raising her eyebrows.

'Actually, Art paid,' replies Charlie, irritation at her sister's reaction getting the better of her.

'Art?' says Kate. 'I thought you two weren't getting on.'

'We weren't, we aren't . . . it's all very complicated,' Charlie fails to explain. 'He hasn't called here, by any chance?' she asks, with a weak expectant smile. It's not beyond the realms of possibility. Her nails dig so deep into the palms of her hands that her knuckles turn white.

'No? Why would he?' asks Alex, his elbow sliding across the steel-topped table as he slouches forward and stares at her.

'Oh, no reason,' says Charlotte, smiling through her disappointment.

She is damned if she is going to unburden her soul with that two-timing tosser in the room. Her sister may well have been able to forgive him for his crimes and misdemeanours, but Charlie saw the whole thing. She had a bowlside seat, as it were. And she will never forget Claire's thrusting buttocks, his grabbing hands and his ghastly office trousers around his ankles for as long as she lives. The fact that they continue to play happy families is something she is going to take a bit of time getting used to.

'Oh,' says Alex, sitting up and draining his glass. 'I do hope you haven't fallen out,' he smiles. 'I just thought that, what with you having gone out with his mate, you would be best of friends.'

'We are,' says Charlie defensively.

'Lost your mobile number then, has he?' asks Alex, getting off his stool and stretching languidly. 'Oh God,' he yawns. 'It's hard work not working,' he announces. 'I think I'll have a shower before I go out.'

'Go out?' asks Charlie, sounding too pleased.

'Yes,' says Kate, sitting neatly in her stool. 'I've sent him out for the night. He's going round to watch football at Sam and Emma's. I thought we needed a girls' night in together and Alex, of course, agreed.'

'Absolutely,' says Alex, walking past and ruffling Kate's expensively blow-dried hair. She smiles. 'Whatever you want, darling. Whatever you want.'

'Juice,' says Ben again with a slithery sniff, shoving his plastic beaker in front of his father's face.

'Peta,' says Alex, turning towards the au pair who is up to her elbows in Ecover bubbles washing up the pans and knives in the sink. 'Would you mind?' he smiles, 'I've got to get ready to go out.'

'No, sure,' she smiles, battling with the fridge in her rubber gloves. 'Alfie, would you like some juice too?' she says in a special singsong voice reserved for the under-fives.

'No,' he replies, hammering the ends of his knife and fork down on the steel-topped table. 'No, no, no,' he slams, punctuating each pronouncement with a bang. 'I want milk.'

'OK,' says Peta. 'Milk for you and organic apple for your little brother.'

'Bye, kids,' says Alex with a little wave from the door. 'See you in the morning.'

'Say bye to Daddy,' insists Kate with a caring, sharing grin directed at the children.

'Bye,' says Alfie. His younger brother doesn't bother. He is much more interested in pouring his apple juice into attractive little circles on the table.

As soon as Alex walks out of the kitchen, the tension dissipates. Kate's shoulders drop to below her ears. Peta's washing-up becomes less frantic and the children seem to take renewed interested in their supper.

'It's a bit tense, isn't it?' says Kate out of the corner of her mouth.

'Sorry?' says Charlie, taken by surprise at her sister's sudden candid confession.

'Well,' she says, raising her eyebrows. 'We're all trying very hard. But it's all a bit difficult round here, isn't it?'

'Well, yes,' smiles Charlie.

'It'll get better, it'll get better,' she says.

'Of course it will,' agrees Charlie with a breezy faux optimism.

'Shall we go next door?' says Kate quickly, her eyes glowing red, looking as though she might cry.

'Great idea,' says Charlie swiftly. 'You go. I'll take your drink.'

Kate rushes out of the kitchen and into the sitting room. When Charlie arrives, she is smiling bravely, already perched on the sofa next to the his-and-hers black and white portraits in black polonecks. She looks smaller and younger. Her feet are tucked up under her. She is withdrawn and pensive.

'Are you OK?' asks Charlie, collapsing next to her on the cream sofa, handing over her drink.

'I'm fine,' she insists. Her voice is quiet and childlike, exhausted from the fight. 'It's just that it's a bit of a strain.'

'I'm sure it is,' says Charlie, rubbing her sister's knee. 'It must be a terrible strain. Worse than that, it must be miserable.'

'It's not really what I thought married life would be like,' says Kate.

'I know,' says Charlie.

'He wasn't supposed to sleep with my best friend,' she says, pulling a cushion on to her stomach and kneading it like bread.

'I know.'

'I mean, what did I do wrong?' Her eyes are spherical. The whites have turned scarlet, the veins engorged with blood. Dry strings of white saliva join the corners of her mouth.

'Nothing,' smiles Charlie. 'Absolutely nothing. It's all his fault and hers and it's nothing to do with you.'

'Well,' she says, patting the cushion, determined not to cry. 'We're still together,' she says optimistically with a strained smile. 'Whatever that means. We've talked and talked and shouted and screamed. He's promised to never stray again, and I've promised to be less boring.'

'Is that what he wants?'

'Apparently.'

'What, more fun?'

'Yes, he says I spent too much time with the kids and not enough time with him.'

'Wow,' says Charlie, her jaw falling open. 'I'm amazed. I'm amazed you stand for that.'

'Yeah,' she shrugs. 'Well, we've analysed it until we're blue in the face and that's what we've come up with.'

'Well,' says Charlie, not knowing what else to say. The two girls sit in silence, each with their own misery.

'Are you all right?' says Kate suddenly.

'Not really,' says Charlie. 'I've had a shit day.'

Charlie lights up a cigarette and Kate automatically reaches over and takes one. Getting up off the sofa, Kate wanders around her pistachio sitting room looking for the old Conran ashtray, furred by overwashing. As Charlie talks her sister through the last couple of days, she does not stint on detail. She takes her through everything, moment by moment, right down to the explosive orgasm against the wall. The mutually frank and confessional conversation causes the spiky tension between them to disappear.

'He did what?' asks Kate, spanking the cushion now between her legs with her right hand.

'He walked out.'

'Un-bloody-believable!' she announces, flicking her cigarette into the mounting ash in the ashtray. The second glass of vodka and tonic that the sisters consume more than lubricates the conversation. Kate's cheeks are slightly flushed and Charlie's eyes glisten, the combination of stress, strain and alcohol performing its own special alchemy. 'Does he have no respect at all?' she says. 'The man had his head between your thighs,' she continues with an impressed squeal. 'The least he can do is wake you up and ask for an explanation.'

'I know!' laughs Charlie, slapping her own cushion and flicking her cigarette. 'And Andrew says that Art's in love with me.'

'Really?' says Kate, draining her glass and sitting up. 'What, he actually said "Art's in love with you"?'

'Yup,' says Charlie, nodding vigorously.

'Fuck me,' says Kate, standing up. 'Do you want another

drink?' she asks, halfway towards the door, already knowing the answer. 'Hold that thought,' she says, her hand in
the air.

'What, shagging you?'

'No,' she says with a little laugh. 'The "love" thing . . .
That's so exciting. I'll be back. Don't you dare move.'

Kate returns with a huge bowl of hand-cut crisps bathed
in rock salt and two more vodkas of New York nightclub
strength.

'So he thinks Art's in love with you,' she says without
missing a beat as she puts down the tray and springs back into
the warm corner of the sofa. Her sister's love life is proving
to be a deliciously welcome distraction from her own. 'And
what did you say back?'

'Nothing, I don't think,' replies Charlie.

'Oh God,' says Kate. 'I remember that wonderful feeling of
being in love,' she sighs. 'That first moment where you think
you can't breathe, you can't eat, all you can think about is
them. Oh God, that's blissful,' she smiles, looking at the Posh
and Becks shots on the table. 'God . . . it was so long ago.'

Charlie smiles. 'Yes,' she says.

'So, do you love him?' asks Kate, suddenly looking rather
serious.

'I haven't ever really dared think about it before,' says
Charlie. 'But out of Africa, here in London, I'm beginning
to think that I really do.'

'What, really really?'

'Yes . . . really,' Charlie smiles, her eyes brightening at the
idea of her own emotional confession. 'I really do love him.'

'Aren't you worried about the Jack thing?' asks Kate, her
eyebrows raised, her head cocked to one side.

'About them being best friends?'

'Yes,' she nods.

'It's one of those awful things. You know, I loved Jack. I'll always love Jack. He was my best friend. He was Art's best friend. But life has to go on, doesn't it? I can't sit in the past like a dark room with the windows closed with no fresh air for the rest of my life, can I? You know, I miss him every day. And every day it does get a little less. I have to keep going,' she smiles. 'You know, elbows out, chin up, eyes focus, keep the show on the road . . .'

'I think so,' agrees Kate, clenching her fist and giving the surrounding air a supportive punch. 'And I bet that's why Art's taken so long to come anywhere near you as well.'

'Do you think so?'

'Oh yes, absolutely,' she nods knowledgeably. 'So what are you going to do about it?' says Kate overexcitedly, both her hands slapping the cushion at the same time. 'The man travelled halfway across the world to come and claim you. He's serious . . .'

'He is, isn't he?' says Charlie, her mouth curling into a smile.

'Oh yeah,' nods Kate, sounding like she knows everything there is to know about relationships. 'He means business . . . Come to that, what the hell are you doing here?'

'I don't know what to do,' admits Charlie, shifting down to her end of the sofa. 'I've drawn a blank. I asked Andrew where he thought Art might be and he had no idea.'

'What are you asking the competition for?' sighs Kate as if Charlie has just come up with the most appalling and ridiculous idea in the world.

'I don't know,' says Charlie. 'He doesn't really have any friends in this country.'

'Have you tried any of your mates in Kenya?'

'D'you think?'

'Well, where would you go to lick your wounds?'

'Um . . .'

'OK, where would he go?'

'Oh well,' she smiles wistfully. 'That's easy now that I think about.'

'Yes?'

'He'd go back to Nairobi.'

'You see!'

'I can't imagine him hanging around here for long,' she says.

'Well, there you go,' says Kate, clapping her hands with joy. 'Problem solved.'

'D'you think?'

'It's easy,' says Kate. 'Ring him up. Tell him he made a mistake . . .'

'Do you think it's as easy as that?'

'I don't know,' says Kate, biting the inside of her mouth. 'But you have to start somewhere. Alex and I are nowhere near being back on track. But after two days of crying, screaming and swearing and shouting, you have to agree on something. You know,' she says, starting to pick at the piping on her cream cushion with heavy tasselled corners – she is talking more to herself than to her elder sister – 'you know, if you have two children together and you've built a home at quite a lot of expense, you can't just let it all slip through your fingers just because one person's made a mistake. And if someone truly says that they're sorry, you have to forgive them, don't you?' she asks. Looking up, her eyes are large and questioning. 'Don't you?'

'I don't know,' says Charlie, taking a fistful of crisps. 'I can only imagine your situation. Actually, I can't even begin to imagine your situation. The days where I could advise you on things and have answers to your questions are long gone. You and I went our separate ways long ago. The sacrifices we've made and the goals we're after are entirely different.'

'Oh don't say that,' smiles Kate. 'You're still my big sister.'

'Not any more,' says Charlie. 'I think you're probably bigger than me.'

'I bloody hope not,' laughs Kate. 'Especially after all the effort I put in doing Ashtanga yoga and Bums and Tums for Young Mums.'

'How can you do a class called that?' asks Charlie, taking a swig of her vodka.

'Fuck knows,' smiles Kate. 'I think I've become immune. Honestly, when you have children I think you join a whole new human race. Before birth you can actively not be a part of society. You know you can sleep late, never get dressed, watch endless amounts of television, go to Paris on a whim. You don't care about anything that doesn't directly affect you. Have children and you never have a lie-in ever again. You develop a Pampers' brain and suddenly the machinations of the local government authority appear deeply interesting. You become fascinated by local schools, catchment areas, and suddenly things like how often your rubbish is collected a week takes on an importance all of its own . . .'

'Christ,' says Charlie.

'I know,' nods Kate. 'And you think I'm joking. D'you know what?' she announces. 'The one thing that this whole affair business has taught me is that I'm going to start doing things for myself again. I used to have a life,' she says, taking another large swig of her vodka. 'I used to be rather swish and glamorous with my job in advertising. I had friends, a social life and very occasionally I had witty conversation.' She taps the side of her nose. 'Only very occasionally, mind,' she grins. 'These days, however, all I ever seem to talk about is children, limestone floors and exactly how organic my olive oil is.' She sighs and her shoulders slope. 'How did I end up here?'

'It's not so bad,' says Charlie trying to sound optimistic. 'You could be a sad old spinster like me. The sort of person who everyone talks about rather quietly, with a load of earnest nodding, plus some sensitive silences. They say things like, "Have you heard about poor Charlotte? Thirty-five and still not married. Really, still? She's bruised fruit these days, you know. Shop-soiled. She's far too difficult and set in her ways for anyone to cope with her now. Isn't it sad? Poor Charlotte. She's the woman who thought she could have it all and has ended up with nothing. She's very keen on her career, though. But we all know it's because she doesn't have anyone or anything else. Ahh. Poor Charlotte. She should really take the first man who comes along, who shows her any sign of any interest, and be done with it.""

'They don't say that,' says Kate, now totally red-faced from overtoxification.

'Perhaps not to my face,' agrees Charlie.

'No, no . . . not to your face,' nods Kate.

'But certainly behind my back,' laughs Charlie.

'Oh most certainly,' agrees Kate, 'But quite frankly, fuck it,' she announces dramatically. 'We'll show them.'

'D'you think?' asks Charlie.

'I've had it. I've really fucking had it. I absolutely flatly refuse to be Sad Old Kate and Poor Old Charlotte any more.'

'What?' says Charlie, surprised at her sister's alcohol-fuelled defiance.

'Oh yeah,' says Kate. 'We'll bloody show them. Let them look and learn,' she says, raising her glass to chink with her sister. 'Cheers.'

'Yeah, right,' says Charlie enthusiastically. 'Cheers.'

They both lean forwards from their respective ends of the sofa and touch tumblers. Kate's smart blow-dry is now look-ing definitely unsmart and Charlie's poorly applied eyeliner has melted down her face. They are both red-cheeked and watery-eyed. They look at each other and smile. Kate is the first to move closer. Charlie follows. They hug each other, squeezing each other's shoulders like their lives depend on it.

'God, it's nice to have you back,' says Kate, pulling away. 'It's nice to be back,' smiles Charlie.

Sibling rebonding completed, the two sisters collapse back into their respective corners and with a new bottle of chilled Pinot Grigio plus a packet of cigarettes proceed to dissect the last four to five years.

Charlie leans against the arm of the sofa, slowly covering it in ash and smiles. This is how she had envisaged her first night back with her sister when she'd initially knocked on her front door all tired and full of airline food. They were supposed to sit down, crack open a bottle of something strong and talk about Love, Life, Men and Why do they always get in the way? They were supposed to dissect the Wedding, Work, and her sister's Sex Life. And eventually end up talking about Underwear and Kate's racy fantasies concerning Russell Crowe.

'D'you know what?' says Kate, her finger floating about in the air like this is a sudden and inspired aperçu. 'I just want to be taken roughly from behind by Russ,' she announces with a broad grin of imagined pleasure. 'Preferably over some bins . . . over some bins . . . out the back of a restaurant.'

'I can't believe you just said that,' says Charlie, worryingly on her third attempt at lighting the wrong end of a cigarette. 'That's filthy,' she says, barely capable of saying the word.

'I know!' squeals Kate, flopping back into the fat sofa. 'To tell you the truth,' she adds, trying to focus on her sister whose body rather annoyingly keeps dividing and rejoining and dividing again. 'I'd quite like him to tug at my hair like this –' she demonstrates by grabbing the back of her own head – 'you know, as he does it and possibly, I could finish up with a bit of wall chaffing across the cheek . . . what d'you think?'

'I think it sounds as if you've thought about this far too much,' laughs Charlie.

'Well . . .' Kate's finger is pointing everywhere. 'You've got to think of something when you're forced to watch Alex's bloody *Gladiator* DVD for the fifteenth time,' she grins.

Kate and Charlie go to bed before Alex has got anywhere near putting his keys in the door. Their alcohol intake is enough to sozzle Oliver Reed. Charlie lies with her arms and legs akimbo like a star, looking up at the painted variety on her ceiling, willing the universe to stop turning, while Kate curls up in the middle of the bed, utterly incapable of movement. So when Alex comes home an hour later, he stands not a chance of moving his wife anywhere, no matter how much hell he unleashes.

But Kate is the first down next morning. Peta has Saturday mornings off and Kate and Alex normally take turns each week to do children's breakfast or be allowed to sleep in. This weekend it is Kate's turn, as it seems to have been for the last couple of weeks. But somehow this morning she doesn't seem to mind. She feels as if she has turned a corner as she wanders into kitchen wearing her lilac silk pyjamas with her two children in tow. Her sister is back. They are still the best of friends and she, Kate, is going to change her life, get it back on track and do the things that she wants to do. She turns on the yellow leather Roberts radio just below the window by the sink. The one thing the errant ways of her husband have taught her is that she is a fool for relying on him solely for her happiness in the first place. Wafting around switching on the kettle, throwing some bread in the toaster to the soporific tones of Radio 4 as she does most Saturday mornings, she walks over and suddenly changes station. Something poptastic sings though the static and Kate starts to dance. Swinging her hips gently at first around the steel-topped table, she starts tentatively to sing along. It's a long time since she has disco-danced on her own.

'Da-la-la,' she says clicking her fingers, assiduously avoiding her reflection in the window for fear that embarrassment might stop her in her tracks. 'La-la . . .' she carries on, circling her hips like she's a sex goddess, pelvic-thrusting her way towards the fridge.

'Mummy?' asks Alfie, looking puzzled. He has already placed himself in the correct position to receive a boiled egg and soldiers to the accompaniment of John Peel. And this, quite frankly, is not in the programme. 'Mummy?' he asks again. 'What are you doing?'

'It looks as though Mummy is having fun,' says Charlie, standing in the doorway, all brown legs and arms in a short tight T-shirt and white knickers.

The sisters smile.

'Do you know, Alfie darling, Aunt Charlie is right,' announces Kate, speaking loudly above the disco beat. 'Mummy is having fun, great fun.' She executes a spin with a whoop and adds 'shoulder shimmy' by way of explanation to her sister.

Despite their sweaty faces, thick heads and furred tongues, the atmosphere around the kitchen table could not be more relaxed. After all the talking and the sharing and the laughing from the night before, neither of them seems to mind their state of undress and the dearth of showering and flossing that has gone on before their appearance at table. In fact, they both appear perversely delighted by their mutual shoddiness.

'You look attractive,' opines Kate sarcastically as her sister perches in her pants at the end of the table, her bare feet filed on the next-door chair.

'Well you're hardly bloody all manicure and fannicure

yourself,' replies Charlie. 'And anyway, where's the pot of black coffee you promised me?'

'When did I promise you that?' asks Kate, putting eggs in boiling water.

'Last night, before you went to bed.'

'Oh God,' she dismisses. 'Don't expect me to remember that,' says Kate, dancing over to turn the kettle on for the third time.

'You were full of promises you couldn't keep last night,' smiles Charlie. 'Honestly,' she continues. 'Your mother,' she says to Alfie. 'She's absolutely terrible.'

'No, she's not,' he replies crossly, collecting fistfuls of butter in his right hand and squeezing it though his fingers like fat yellow snakes.

'Crikey,' says Charlie looking down. 'I do hope that's organic.'

'Of course it is,' says Kate brusquely, handing out slices of toast to her two boys.

'Thank the Lord for that,' says Charlie, her voice heavy with sarcasm. 'Otherwise we would all be in terrible trouble.'

'Yes, well,' says Kate, buttering Ben's toast before looking up to catch her sister's smiling eyes. 'Oh stop,' she says, putting her knife down. 'Stop it with your teasing and get back to Africa.'

'Talking of which,' says Charlie, suddenly quite serious. 'Can I make some calls? Art should be there by now.'

'Of course,' replies Kate. 'Go and lie in the sitting room and I'll bring you a cup of coffee when it's ready.'

After almost an hour of telephoning and holding and waiting to be put through, it looks as though J.R. Hartley had more luck tracking down his fly-fishing book than Charlie is going to have finding Art. Her first ports of call are Sophia, her boho-aristo flatmate, and a collection of their mutual friends in the Karen district of Nairobi. Sophia and her new, rather temporary, man, Dom, have just come back from a week's safari and haven't heard anything when Charlie calls. They are both very excited to hear her news.

'I can't believe you didn't win that bloody award,' pronounces Sophia between puffs of her roll-up. 'But I always knew you and Art would get it together. You know . . .' Her voice is languid, and although she is speaking faultless English she could be from almost anywhere it the world. 'You know,' she says again, 'neither of you were really kidding anyone with your "we're just great friends" routine.'

'Really?' asks Charlie, already on her third cigarette of the morning.

'Oh yeah,' asserts Sophia, warming to her subject. 'It's a soul thing. You guys are always together and will always be together. You've been through so much. And anyway, I've never heard two people chat together so long about so much rubbish in my life – photos, framing, lighting, all that sort of stuff. No one ever gets a word in edgeways. You're made for each other. Everyone knows it, apart from you two, apparently.'

'Right,' says Charlie, sounding faintly surprised at the apparent general knowledge about her relationship with Art.

'Anyway,' says Sophia, yawning into the receiver. 'Art's definitely not around here. I mean, I know I've just got in and everything, but I am the centre of the bush telegraph as you know, so I would know. Have you tried Kenya Coast?'

Charlie sits there leafing through her address book, looking at telephone numbers written in green pen, red pen, eyeliner, with their codes missing, trying to work out where on earth Art might have gone. The friends down in Mombasa are useless. They've been to an all-night party that started in a hotel and finished in someone's beach house just south of Mombasa – and they've not heard a thing. Dex mutters something about

Art going up north whenever he's miserable and that maybe he's checked into the Peponi Hotel.

'You know, it was the last place that he and Jack were happy,' says Dex, sniffing slightly. 'You know, really happy.'

'Yeah well, maybe,' says Charlie.

'Look, sorry,' says Dex. 'I haven't been to bed yet . . . maybe I'm being a bit emotional.'

Peponi is Charlie's last hope. But she knows it's futile even as she rings and waits, flicking ash into a saucer on her stomach. The singsong-voiced receptionist is helpful and has even heard of Art, or actually even met him, although she's not quite sure. The curly hair and handsome smile sticks in her memory. But he is definitely not in the hotel. Nor is he around Shella. He would have been in and had an Old Pal cocktail if he had been.

'No one,' she says, trying to be helpful, 'would come here and not have an Old Pal,' she assures, 'no matter how miserable they were.'

She is right, of course, thinks Charlie, putting down the telephone. If she knew Art at all he would be propping up the bar, drowning his sorrows, working out who was available to take a dhow out fishing. She lies back and stares at the ceiling. She has run out of options. She can't believe it. Where has he gone? Freelance boys like him can run off anywhere. How will she ever find him? Large tears begin to fall out of the corners of her eyes and run down the sides of her face. The thought of not seeing him again fills her with panic. Art has always been around. In her darkest days, he was always there. So why should things change? But they have changed. It's all changed and Charlie doesn't know, for the first time in years, what to do any more.

Lying on the sofa in her T-shirt and pants, she starts to shiver. It's cold in Kate sitting room. She sits up and, tucking her feet up underneath her, she starts to rock backwards and forwards, staring at her collection of butts in the astray. The full horror of his abandonment hits her like a bucket of ice-cold water and she really starts to cry. It finally dawns on her how awful it is to realise that you actually love someone just at the point when they choose to disappear. Fat tears of self-pity that only moments ago started to trickle down her cheeks give way to a deluge of emotion. 'Art, where are you? Art, where are you? Art, where are you?' she mutters over and over again, between big gasping breaths. A searing pain burns in her chest. 'Where are you?' she shouts, picking up her address book, she hurls it across the room, knocking the Posh and Becks shot of Alex and Kate with a shattering sound on to the wooden floor. 'Fat fucking piece of useless shit you are,' she shouts at the address book.

Kate rushes into the room, still in her pyjamas, her cheeks pink from dancing with her children.

'Are you OK?' she asks Charlie, ignoring the fact that her smart studio photograph is on the floor.

'No, not really,' says Charlie. Her eyelashes are stuck together like stiff spiders. The whites of her eyes are scarlet and she has more snot pouring out of her nose than Alfie and Ben put together.

'You'll find him,' she says, not knowing if she is speaking the truth or simply lying gently to make things better.

'Do you really think so?' asks Charlie, wiping her nose on the shoulder of her T-shirt.

'Of course I do,' lies Kate. 'It can't be that hard. The world isn't that big a place.'

'I really hope so,' says Charlie, between giant breaths. 'Because I don't think that I can live without him.'

'In which case you have to find him,' suggests Kate, sounding calm and matter of fact. 'It's as simple as that.'

'I do have to find him,' says Charlie, starting to rock again. 'I really do have to find him.'

Kate puts her arms around her sister and lets her mutter and cry on her shoulder. She strokes her hair and kisses her forehead and waits for her to calm down.

'I think I'll run you a bath,' she suggests. 'That'll make you feel a whole lot better.'

It actually takes over a month before Charlie begins to feel in any way better at all. Try as hard as she can, she doesn't manage to track Art down. He has somehow managed to disappear off the face of the earth. She speaks to his rather elderly mother in South Africa who is delightful and charming on the telephone, but has almost as little idea as Charlie. She says she thinks he might be in South America but that really is as much as she knows. She appears quite relaxed about the whole thing. She says her son is wont to disappear off for months at a time researching some story or other, and actually she finds it quite hard to keep up. He apparently sends postcards, but they always take months to arrive. Art will turn up, she assures, he always does. Charlie supposes her laissez-faire attitude is born out of years of fretting to the point of exhaustion. The woman has probably had enough trauma in her life without fretting over what she must perceive as a lover's tiff with a woman who, if she remembers correctly, used to go out with her son's best friend.

The picture-desk editors are equally helpful. Art apparently has a *Sunday Times* commission to do a Gaucho story in Argentina, following a Welsh settlers' trail. The *Telegraph* have said they might be interested in something about the pink river dolphins in Columbia. But other than those lacklustre clues no one really knows where he is, or when he'll be back. He calls in occasionally to keep them up to speed. But no one has a number for him. And no one seems unduly worried. Art is a foreign news 'fireman', dispatched at a moment's notice to some of the shittiest places on the planet. The man can look after himself, they say in butch tones. He is always off on his own, they add. He spends most of his time in Africa.

Charlie wants to say that she has spent most of her time in Africa with him. She wants to explain that on most of the stories he has done, she has been there too. But there doesn't seem any point.

Kate has asked her to stay for 'a while'. Neither of the sisters knows how long that means exactly. But Kate insists that Charlie is not really in any state to go back to Africa on her own. And Charlie for once in her life doesn't have the energy to argue. The great thing about having a maternal sister, she has realised, is that they are great in a crisis.

So Charlie moves semi-permanently into the bedroom with the sky-blue ceiling and, dusting down her Leica M6, her Nikkon F3 and her Nikkon DI, starts to accept the photographic off-cuts from the home picture desks' tables. She does the Education Secretary opening a new school for the *Independent*. She snaps fat women who've lost weight, eating cucumber, for the *Daily Mail*. She spends a whole day with former Crack addicts for the *Guardian* and does a whole series on people who left their real jobs to open 'really great' boutiques for the *Evening Standard*.

Africa without Art, she tells Kate, doesn't appeal any more. The idea of hanging out in their old haunts, smoking the same Sportsmen cigarettes, sitting in the same planter chairs, watching the sunset on the same balcony – by herself, without his curls and his smile sitting next to her – is something she cannot bear to do.

Instead, she tries to make the best of it here. But she continues to lose weight, along with her tan, and refuses, with a strained smile, her sister's brave attempts at setting her up with some eligible men.

Charlie slips into as much of a routine as a freelance photographic existence can take. She waits around in Shepherd's

Bush in the morning for a call from any of Fleet Street's finest picture desks to send her on a job. She spends her days working and her evenings as the odd number at 'couples' dinners. She arrives on her own and leaves on her own – the only difference being that the bottle of wine she brought with her sits in her stomach on the way home. She continues to elicit special sympathetic stares when her single status is discussed. She still calls *The Sunday Times* and *Telegraph* foreign desks, vainly hoping for news of Art. And with increasing regularity, she goes out and gets riotously drunk with Alice, coming back to Kate's disapproving looks at the breakfast table in the morning.

But Kate's new confidence is such that she thinks she can conquer all. Her return to work, albeit only three days a week, has heralded the return of her humour and naughtiness, but has done nothing to diminish her insistence on the domestic idyll. She maintains that if she and Alex can work through their problems and come out the other side with their marriage intact, then surely there is hope for everyone? She has her sister firmly under her wing, and if Art is not on the scene, then she is going to follow a 'keeping her eyes peeled' policy of pimping her elder sister whatever Charlie says.

'So,' she announces to Charlie one Friday morning as she stands doing her lipstick in the reflective surface of the kettle while waiting for it to boil. 'You're here for supper and I'm fixing you up.'

'Honestly,' says Charlie, dressed in a jumper and jeans, half-heartedly crunching the corner of her toast, half-heartedly waiting for the *Daily Mail* to ring her up for a story. 'There really is no need. I'm in love with Art,' she says. 'It's just that he is somewhere in South America avoiding my calls. And I will not give up. Until he tells me to my face that he's not interested.'

'Mmm, yes, well,' says Kate, smoothing off the edges to her lipstick with a neat, clipped-tipped finger. 'It's a long way to go just to avoid talking to you.'

'There's always Australia.'

'That's as may be,' says Kate, smoothing down her slim-fitting black skirt and doing up the buttons on her jacket. She is looking radiant. 'But that doesn't mean you have to take yourself off the market entirely. You know, limited shelf-life and all that.'

'I've never really thought of myself as an unpopular yoghurt about to turn. But thank you for the image, it should really help me get through the day,' says Charlie.

'I didn't mean it like that,' says Kate, trying to be pleasant. She pours herself a cup of coffee, takes a sip, burns her lips and puts the cup down again.

'I know you didn't,' smiles Charlie. 'It's just that it's two months now since Art left. People are beginning to talk about where they are for Christmas, and . . .'

'You can always stay here, you know that,' says Kate.

'Thanks,' smiles Charlie. 'But you know, I mean, I can't stay upstairs for ever, much as I've got used to it. I just don't know what . . .'

'You could always go to Mum's,' says Kate, starting to laugh.

'I'd rather kill myself.'

'Not before tonight,' says Kate, rushing out of the door. 'It's an eight o'clock start, so don't be late.' She kisses her sister on the cheek, shouts something to Peta, who is upstairs with the children, and marches out the door.

That evening Charlie does indeed arrive late for her sister's dinner. She's been sitting outside a pop star's house all afternoon in the hope of a misery shot to accompany the article on her divorce that is running in tomorrow's paper. She has spent most of the afternoon sitting, smoking cigarettes and drinking tea in a four-by-four with an amusing bloke from the *Mirror*, who's been cracking jokes and telling who's had what lifted, and tweaked, and tucked. But it is disheartening stuff. Somehow Charlie has always justified her taking photographs of poor, sick children in poor, sick countries, as being a means to an end. She creates an awareness of something, and those who can do something about it, do. But snapping a divorcing pop star and hoping for tears, or at least an upset-in-sunglasses shot, is not something she finds easy to justify.

She arrives back at Kate's cold, tired and a little depressed. Alex and Kate are in the sitting room serving an apple martini cocktail that Kate has read about in a magazine. Sam and Emma are sitting opposite each other. They tensely occupy their ends of their sofas, staring at Sam's mobile phone.

'Are you sure it's working,' says Emma, her horsy features unfortunately highlighted by her new, practical, short hair-do.

'Yes,' sighs Sam, picking up the telephone and staring at the screen. 'We're on a full signal here.'

'Really?' asks Emma, her short chin straining forwards.

'Look if you want to,' he replies. 'But you should really learn to trust me,' he mutters, irritated.

'Don't start,' she says, raising her hand and dropping her head. 'I'm extremely tired.'

'Charlie,' says Kate, handing her an apple cocktail. 'You remember Sam and Emma, don't you?'

'Um,' says Charlie.

'They've just had a baby,' says Kate, trying to be help-ful. 'Eve?'

'Oh right,' says Charlie, nodding away with a tight smile.

'It's the hair,' says Emma, running her hands through her crop. 'It had to go . . . I never had time to wash it properly,' she adds. 'No one recognises me.'

'Yeah, hi,' says Sam, getting off the sofa holding his mobile phone. 'I remember . . .'

'There's no need to hold the phone all the time,' snaps Emma.

'You bloody have it then,' he says, petulantly throwing it across to the other sofa.

'Sam,' hisses Emma, turning swiftly both to pick up the telephone and to check it is working. 'Sorry,' she smiles pleasantly. 'It's the first night that we've left her with the new nanny.'

'Who?' says Charlie.

'Eve,' she smiles.

'Oh right,' replies Charlie, taking a sip of her apple martini.

'Anyway,' says Kate, trying to keep the show on the road. 'Charlie, this is Jim.' She says his name like she's just pulled a marvellous new beauty product out of her handbag.

'Hello Jim,' says Charlie.

'Hi,' he replies. He shakes his shoulder-length blond hair as he speaks. His leather trousers squeak when he shakes her hand.

'Good.' Kate smiles like her work is done. 'OK, supper I think,' she announces, clapping her hands.

Through into the kitchen and Kate's relaxed supper looks rather relaxed. The table is laid with the bare minimum of equipment – knives, forks, side plates and one glass each. The napkins are paper and there is a large baguette in the middle of the table that no one has got round to cutting up. Kate retires to the kitchen for a second and returns with side plates of chicken-liver pâté, which she hands round.

'Just tear yourself off some bread,' she says as she sits down.

'Mmm, this looks good,' says Emma, leaning over to sniff her plate. 'Did you make it yourself?'

'Um,' smiles Kate, wondering whether to lie or not. 'It's Selfridge's food hall,' she admits. 'I work these days, you see.'

'Of course,' nods Emma. 'What's that like?'

'It's a bloody nightmare,' says Alex, draining his martini glass. 'All we get to eat these days is Selfridge's food hall stuff, the occasional reheated Marks and Spencer thing and that's it.' He sounds like he is joking but deep down it is obvious he is not. 'I mean, I bet this baguette isn't even organic.'

'Yes . . . well,' says Kate, pouring herself a large glass of white wine. 'I've got other things to think about now.'

'Nothing wrong with a few chemicals,' jokes Charlie. 'You've got to die of something. The idea of you living for ever is just plain scary.'

'Ha ha,' says Alex. 'And what are you? A scientist?'

'No,' says Kate. 'She's a photographer. Aren't you, Charlie?'

'Yes,' she nods.

'Jim's a photographer, aren't you, Jim?'

'I am indeed,' he beams, running his hands through his luxuriant hair.

'Jim did the photos of us in the sitting room,' continues Kate.

'Oh, nice,' nods Charlie.

'Don't you remember?' she says. 'I bet you two have loads of friends in common.'

'Well,' nods Charlie. 'Probably,' she smiles, not wanting to sound rude.

'I'm in portraits, fashion, that sort of thing,' he says, sounding very pleased with himself. 'You know, mainly for the glossies.'

'Right,' says Charlie, buttering and pâté-ing her bread.

'You?' he says.

'Oh, I've worked mainly out of Africa, wars and things.'

'Oh,' he says, tearing at his bread, sounding deeply bored. 'Do you know Art MacDonald? He does all that shit.'

Charlie drops her food. She forgets to breathe. Her face flushes pink. 'Art,' she repeats his name. 'Oh my God, Art . . . how do you know him?'

'I don't really,' he says, not understanding the enormity of this woman's reaction. 'I met him in Brazil. We were in the same hotel in Rio. I was doing this big bikini shoot for *Elle* magazine and he'd just come back from this trip around the whole of South America, and, you know . . . we saw each others' photo bags in the lobby and got talking. Nice guy,' he sniffs.

'When was this?' asks Charlie, hardly daring to hope.

'A week ago, something like that . . .'

'A week ago,' Charlie whispers as she sits back in her chair, totally dazed. 'Was he . . . well?'

'Well?' He chuckles. 'He was bloody brown if that's what you're asking. Quite fit-looking, though. He's obviously been carrying his equipment himself,' he snorts. 'But we had a bloody good night together before he left.'

'Left?'

'Yeah,' says Jim, not really that interested. 'This is great food, by the way, Kate, Selfridge's or not.'

'So he's left Brazil?'

'Yeah,' replies Jim. 'So you know him, then? Art?'

'Yes,' says Charlie.

'They've known each other for years,' says Kate, joining in.

'Do you know where he is now?' asks Charlie.

'Now?' repeats Jim, blowing out his cheeks as he thinks. 'Well, he should be here.'

'Here?' repeats Charlie, her body now entirely rigid as she stares at him, her mouth open. 'What, here? In London?' Her heart is racing as her hopes soar. 'Right . . . here?'

'Yeah, he's flying through. He's been here a while. He had a four-or five-day stopover. I wasn't really listening, to be honest. I think he said that he was staying somewhere in Portobello, but he may well not be here.'

'Oh my God, I'm sorry,' she says to her sister as she stands straight up, making the knives and forks leap off the table. Her face is contorted. She looks in terrible pain. She doesn't know whether to laugh or cry or both. Joy and fear are seeping from every pore. 'I've got to go. I've got to go. I've got to find out. Oh my God . . .' Her hands are clasped together in a tight ball.

She hears her sister shout something hopeful and positive as she runs straight out of the house, snatching her bag from the hall. It is not until she reaches the end of the road at a full sprint that she realises that it is a cold, wet, night with a wind bracing enough to chap cheeks and she has left her coat in the hall. Amazingly she finds a cab within minutes and directs it to the hotel on Westbourne Grove. She is not even sure that he is staying there. There are plenty of hotels around Portobello but Charlie has to start somewhere, hope somewhere, and she doesn't have any other ideas.

Sitting in the back, her hair lank and damp and sticking to her head, she wills the driver to go faster and faster and the traffic to disappear. Art has got to be still there. He has to be. He has to. Her fists are clenched by her side. Please God, let him have stayed five nights or more. Her whole body is taut with total concentration. Her mouth is dry. She hardly dares breathe. Come on, come on, come on – she rocks her head back and forth, hoping to increase the taxi's speed. She picks the route through the traffic, sighing loudly when he turns a different way. Eventually he pulls up outside the hotel, and throwing a twenty-pound note through the window she doesn't wait for the change before she runs in through the door.

'Hello,' she says as she arrives, palms first, feet last at Reception. 'Um, sorry . . .' she huffs and puffs.

'Yes?' says the manicured girl at the desk.

'I was just . . .' Charlie smiles as she tries to catch her breath . . . 'I was just wondering if you had an Arthur MacDonald staying here?'

'One moment, please,' says the girl, her buttock-skimming hair swishing behind her as she looks down and clicks on her computer screen. 'MacDonald . . . Arthur, did you say?'

'Yes?' says Charlie, leaning over the counter straining to read the green writing on the screen.

'He's checked out,' she says, scowling at her screen just to make sure.

'He's checked out,' says Charlie, her head falling forward as she collapses on to the counter. 'He's checked out? When did he check out?' she asks, her voice feeble. Her eyes are clouding with tears, she is totally emotionally drained. All this wait. All this time. And she has missed him.

'Oh,' says the receptionist, looking down again. 'Um, oh,' she says again. 'That's confusing . . .'

'What?' says Charlie, grasping at the slimmest and shortest of straws.

'How odd,' she says. 'He hasn't paid yet, which means he's in the process of checking out.'

Just as Charlie is trying to digest the complexity of this news, the lift sounds behind her. She spins round. There he is. Art. Tall and strong and tanned, he is holding a suitcase in each hand. Dressed in jeans and a pair of well-scuffed desert boots, a white T-shirt and a long leather coat, his dark curls bleached brown by the sun, he looks more handsome than Charlie remembers. She wants to cry out, shout his name. Ask where he has been? Why he didn't wake her? That he has got it all wrong. That she loves him. That she has always loved him. But she can't. He appears distracted, like he is thinking about something and doesn't see her. She wants to run towards him. Throw herself at him. Kiss him all over. Instead she stands rooted to the spot, unable to move, just capable of watching his graceful walk to the counter.

'Oh, there he is!' announces the receptionist to the whole of the lobby, pointing Art out with a neat, French-polished finger. 'There he is, over there. That's him. Hello! Excuse me . . . Mr MacDonald! Coo-ey,' she shouts, slightly forgetting herself. 'Um, Mr MacDonald, excuse me.'

'There he is,' whispers Charlie.

Art turns round and stands stock-still like a cornered criminal. Charlie stands her ground and smiles, searching his face for some sort of reaction. Has he forgiven her? Does he love her? Please let him love her. Art does nothing. He stands. He stares, almost like he can't see her. Almost like he doesn't dare see her at all. Slowly he puts down his bags. He looks up. A broad, beautiful smile breaks across his brown, luminous face. He walks slowly towards her, his arms outstretched.

'I've found you,' says Charlie, her voice weak, her arms hanging limply by her side.

'You've found me,' he says, pulling her towards him, holding her close against his chest, inhaling the soft smell of her skin.

'Please don't leave me again,' says Charlie, turning her face up to kiss him.

He smiles before bending down to kiss her right back.